All these cowboys want is...a date?

Date with a COWBOY

Three sensational novels from Diana Palmer, Joan Hohl and Mary Lynn Baxter

Special treats for February.
Want a date with a gorgeous man?
Look no further!

Date with a
COWBOY

DIANA
PALMER

JOAN
HOHL

MARY LYNN
BAXTER

MILLS
BOON

Mills & Boon, an imprint of Harlequin (UK) Limited, Eton House, 18-24 Paradise Road, Richmond, Surrey TW9 1SR

DATE WITH A COWBOY
© Harlequin Enterprises II B.V./S.à.r.l 2013

Iron Cowboy © Diana Palmer 2008
In the Arms of the Rancher © Joan Hohl 2009
At the Texan's Pleasure © Mary Lynn Baxter 2006

ISBN: 978 0 263 90280 8

009-0213

Harlequin (UK) policy is to use papers that are natural, renewable and recyclable products and made from wood grown in sustainable forests. The logging and manufacturing processes conform to the legal environmental regulations of the country of origin.

Printed and bound in Spain
by Blackprint CPI, Barcelona

IRON COWBOY

DIANA PALMER

Diana Palmer has a gift for telling the most sensual tales with charm and humor. With over forty million copies of her books in print, Diana Palmer is one of North America's most beloved authors and considered one of the top ten romance authors in the USA. Diana's hobbies include gardening, archaeology, anthropology, iguanas, astronomy and music. She has been married to James Kyle for over twenty-five years, and they have one son.

To Ann Painter in Massachusetts with love

One

It was a lovely spring day, the sort of day that makes gentle, green, budding trees and white blossoms look like a spring fantasy has been painted. Sara Dobbs stared out the book-store's side window wistfully, wishing she could get to the tiny flower bed full of jonquils and buttercups to pick a bouquet for the counter. The flowers were blooming on the street that ran beside the Jacobsville Book Nook, where she worked as assistant manager to Dee Harrison, the owner.

Dee was middle-aged, a small, thin, witty woman who made friends wherever she went. She'd been looking for someone to help her manage the store, and Sara had just lost her bookkeeping position at the small print shop that was going out of business. It was a match made in heaven. Sara spent a good portion of her meager salary on books. She loved to read. Living with her grandfather, a retired college professor, had predisposed her to education. She'd had plenty of time to read when she was with her parents, in one of the most dangerous places on earth.

Sara's father, with her maternal grandfather's assistance, had talked her mother into the overseas work. Her father had died violently. Her mother changed, lost her faith, turned to alcohol. She brought Sara to Jacobsville and moved in with her father. She then launched herself into one scandal after another, using her behavior to punish her father without caring about the cost to her only child. Sara and Grandad had suffered for her blatant immorality. It wasn't until Sara had come home in tears, with bruises all over her, that her mother faced the consequences of what she'd done. The children of one of her mother's lovers had caught her alone in the gym and beaten her bloody. Their father had divorced their mother, who was now facing eviction from their home and the loss of every penny they had; their father had spent it on jewels for Sara's mother.

That had led to worse tragedy. Her mother stopped drinking and seemed to reform. She even went back to church. She seemed very happy, until Sara found her one morning, a few days later…

The sound of a vehicle pulling up in the parking lot just in front of the bookstore stopped her painful reveries. At least, she thought, she had a good job and made enough to keep a roof over her head.

Her grandfather's little two-bedroom house outside of town had been left to Sara, along with a small savings account. But there was a mortgage on the house.

She missed the old man. Despite his age, he was young in mind and heart, and adventurous. It was lonely without him, especially since she had no other living family. She had no siblings, no aunts or uncles, or even cousins that she knew about. She had nobody.

The ringing of the electronic bell over the door caught her attention. A tall, grim-looking man came into the small bookstore. He glowered at Sara. He was dressed in an expensive-looking three-piece gray suit and wore hand-tooled black boots and a creamy Stetson. Under the hat was straight, thick, conventionally cut black hair. He had the sort of physique that usually was only seen in motion pictures. But he was no movie star. He looked like a businessman. She glanced out the door and saw a big, black pickup truck with a white horse in a white circle on the truck's door. She knew about the White Horse Ranch outside town. This newcomer, Jared Cameron, had bought it from its previous owner, lock, stock, manager and resident cowboys. Someone said he'd been in town several months earlier for a funeral of some sort, but nobody knew who he was related to that had died. So many old people had out-of-town relatives these days, even in Jacobsville, Texas, a town of less than two thousand inhabitants.

Standing outside next to the driver's side of the black pickup was a tall, husky man with wavy black hair in a ponytail and an olive complexion, wearing a dark suit and sunglasses. He looked like a professional wrestler. He was probably a sort of bodyguard. Maybe his employer had enemies. She wondered why.

The man in the gray suit was glaring at the magazine counter with both hands deep in his pockets, muttering to himself.

Sara wondered what he was looking for. He hadn't asked for assistance, or even looked her way. But the muttering was getting darker by the minute. She couldn't afford to turn away a potential customer. No small town business was that secure.

"May I help you?" she asked with a smile.

He gave her a cold look from pale green eyes in a tanned

face that seemed to be all hard lines and angles. His eyes narrowed on her short, straight blond hair, moved over her wide forehead, down over her own green eyes and straight nose and high cheekbones, to her pretty mouth and rounded chin. He made a sound, as if she didn't live up to his specifications. She didn't dare make a comment, but she was really tempted to tell him that if he was shopping for pretty women, a designer boutique in a big city would be a better place to look than a small bookstore.

"You don't carry financial magazines." He made it sound like a hanging offense.

"Nobody around here reads them much," she defended.

His eyes narrowed. "I read them."

She did occasionally have to bite her tongue to save her job. This looked like one of those times. "I'm very sorry. We could order them for you, if you like."

"Forget it. I can subscribe." He glanced toward the mystery paperbacks and scowled again. "I hate paperbacks. Why don't you carry hardcover novels?"

Her tongue was stinging. She cleared her throat. "Well, most of our clientele are working people and they can't afford them."

Both thick black eyebrows arched. "I don't buy paperbacks."

"We can special order any sort of hardcover you want," she said. The smile was wavering, and she was trying hard not to offend him.

He glanced toward the counter at the computer. "Do you have Internet access?"

"Of course." He must think he'd landed in Borneo. She frowned. They probably even had computers in the jungles these days. He seemed to consider Jacobsville, Texas, a holdover from the last century.

"I like mystery novels," he said. "Biographies. I like first-person adventure novels and anything factual on the North African campaign of World War II."

Her heart jumped at the subject he'd mentioned. She cleared her throat. "Would you like all of them at once, then?"

One eyebrow went up. "The customer is always right," he said shortly, as if he thought she was making fun of him.

"Of course he is," she agreed. Her teeth hurt from being clenched in that smile.

"Get me a sheet of paper and a pen. I'll make you a list."

She wouldn't kick him, she wouldn't kick him, she wouldn't kick him... She found paper and pencil and handed them to him, still smiling.

He made a list while she answered a phone call. She hung up, and he handed her the list.

She frowned as she read it.

"Now what's wrong?" he asked impatiently.

"I don't read Sanskrit," she began.

He muttered something, took the list back and made minor modifications before handing it back. "It's the twenty-first century. Nobody handwrites anything," he said defensively. "I've got two computers and a PDA and an MP3 player." He gave her a curious look. "Do you know what an MP3 player is?" he asked, just to irritate her.

She reached in her jeans pocket, produced a small iPod Shuffle and earphones. The look that accompanied the action could kill.

"How soon can you get those books here?" he asked.

She could, at least, make out most of the titles with his so-called handwriting corrections. "We order on Mondays," she said. "You'll have as many of these as are in stock at the distributors by next Thursday or Friday."

"The mail doesn't come by horse anymore," he began.

She took a deep breath. "If you don't like small towns,

maybe you could go back to wherever you came from. If you can get there by conventional means, that is," with an edge to the smile that accompanied the words.

The insinuation wasn't lost on him. "I'm not the devil."

"Are you sure?" she queried, all wide-eyed.

One eye narrowed. "I'd like these books delivered. I'm usually too busy to make a special trip into town."

"You could send your bodyguard."

He glanced out the door at the big man who was leaning back against the driver's door of the pickup with his arms folded. "Tony the Dancer doesn't run errands."

Her eyes widened more. "Tony the Dancer? Are you in the mob?"

"No, I'm not in the mob!" he growled. "Tony's last name is Danzetta. Tony the Dancer. Get it?"

"Well, he looks like a hit man to me," she returned.

"Known a few of them, have you?" he asked sarcastically.

"If I did, you'd be double-checking your locks tonight," she said under her breath.

"Can you deliver the books?"

"Yes, but it will cost you ten dollars. Gas is expensive."

"What do you drive?" he asked. "A Greyhound bus?"

"I have a VW, thank you very much, but your place is six miles out of town."

"You can tell me the amount when you call to say the books are here. I'll have my accountant cut the check. You can pick it up when you deliver the books."

"All right."

"I'd better give you the number. It's unlisted."

She turned over the sheet of paper with his list of titles on it and copied down the number he gave her.

"I'd also like to get two financial magazines," he added, naming them.

"I'll see if our distributor carries them. He might not."

"Serves me right for moving to Outer Cowpasture," he muttered aloud.

"Well, excuse us for not having malls on every street!" she shot back.

He glowered. "You're the rudest clerk I've seen yet."

"Get your bodyguard to loan you his shades and you won't have to see me at all."

He pursed his lips. "You might get yourself a book on manners."

She smiled sarcastically. "I'll see if I can find one on ogres for you."

His pale eyes swept over her with calculation. "Just the ones I listed, if you please. I'll expect to hear from you late next week."

"Yes, sir."

He cocked his head. "Your boss must have been pretty desperate to leave you in charge of his sole means of support."

"It's a she, not a he. And my boss likes me very much."

"Good thing someone does, I guess." He turned to leave, pausing at the door. "You're wearing two different shades of hose under those slacks, and your earrings don't match."

She had problems with symmetry. Most people knew her background and were kind enough not to mention her lapses. "I'm no slave to popular fashion," she informed him with mock hauteur.

"Yes. I noticed."

He left before she came up with a suitable reply. Lucky for him there wasn't anything expendable that she could have thrown after him.

Dee Harrison rolled in the aisles laughing when she heard Sara's biting description of their new customer.

"It wasn't funny," Sara protested. "He called Jacobsville 'Outer Cowpasture,'" she grumbled.

"Obviously the man has no taste." Dee grinned. "But he did want us to order a lot of books for him, so your sacrifice wasn't in vain, dear."

"But I have to deliver the books to him," she wailed. "He's probably got people-eating dogs and machine guns out there. You should have seen the guy driving him! He looked like a hit man!"

"He's probably just eccentric," Dee said calmingly. "Like old man Dorsey."

She gave her employer a narrow glance. "Old man Dorsey lets his German shepherd sit at the table and eat with him. This guy would probably eat the dog!"

Dee just smiled. A new customer was just what she needed, especially one with expensive tastes in reading. "If he orders a lot of books, you might get a raise," Dee ventured.

Sara just shook her head. Dee didn't understand the situation. If Sara had to be around that particular customer very often, she'd probably end up doing time for assault and battery.

She went home to her small house. Morris met her at the door. He was an old, battle-scarred yellow tabby cat. Part of his tail was missing, and he had slits in his ears from fights. He'd been a stray who came crying to Sara's back door in a thunderstorm. She'd let him in. That had been eight years ago. Her grandfather had commented that he looked like trouble. Sara defended him.

She never agreed with her grandfather, even after she had to replace a chair and a throw rug that Morris had ripped to shreds. She bought the old cat a scratching post and herself a water pistol. Morris hated water. When he did something he wasn't supposed to, she let him have it. Over the years, he'd calmed down and stopped clawing furniture. Now, he just ate and sprawled in the sun. Occasionally he sat in Sara's lap while she watched her small color television. But he wasn't a cuddling cat, and you couldn't pick him up. He bit.

She stroked him while they watched the latest episode of her favorite forensic show. "I guess it's just as well that we're not overrun with visitors, Morris," she mused softly. "You're definitely an antisocial personality." She pursed her lips as she looked down at him. "I know a guy you'd like," she added on a chuckle. "I must attract animals and people with bad attitudes."

The end of the next week came all too soon. Dee had placed Jared Cameron's order on Monday. Sara was hoping the ogre's order wouldn't come in, allowing her a reprieve to work on her social skills. But all the books in the order arrived like clockwork on Friday.

She phoned the number Jared Cameron had given her.

"Cameron ranch," came a gruff reply.

"Mr. Cameron?" she asked hesitantly, because this didn't sound like the man who'd come into the store earlier.

"He's not here," a gravelly deep voice replied.

She pictured the face that would have gone with that voice, and figured it must be the hit man. "Mr....Danzetta?"

There was a shocked pause. "Yeah. How'd you know?"

"I read minds," she lied.

"No kidding?" He sounded as if he actually believed her.

"Mr. Cameron ordered a lot of books…"

"Yeah, he said they were due today. He said for you to bring them out tomorrow about ten. He'll be here."

Tomorrow was Saturday, and she didn't work Saturdays. "Couldn't I leave them with you, and he can send us the check?"

"Tomorrow at ten, he said. He'll be here."

There was no arguing with stone walls. She sighed. "Okay. I'll see him tomorrow."

"Good."

The line went dead. The voice had a decidedly Southern accent. Not a Texas accent. A Georgia one, if she were guessing. She had an ear for accents. Her grandfather had taught students from all over the country and around the world at the Jacobsville Community College, and he often brought them home. Sara had learned a lot about other places.

She put the phone down belatedly. If the bodyguard was part of the mob, it must be the Southern branch. She chuckled. But now she didn't know what to do. Should she call him tomorrow before she started out, to let him know how much he owed? Surely his bookkeeper didn't work weekends.

"You look unsettled," Dee remarked as she started for the front door. "What's wrong?"

"I have to take the ogre's order out to him tomorrow morning."

"On your day off." Dee smiled. "You can have a half day next Wednesday to make up for it. I'll come in at noon and work until closing time."

"You will?" Sara asked, beaming.

"I know how you look forward to your drawing time," Dee replied. "I just know you're going to sell that children's book you're working on. Call Lisa Parks and tell her you'll come next Wednesday to draw her new puppies instead of tomorrow. They'll make a gorgeous page in your story," she added.

Sara grinned. "They're the cutest puppies I've ever seen. Their father was one of the puppies Tom Walker's dog Moose fathered, and their mother is Cy Parks's collie, Bob."

"Bob is a girl dog?" Dee exclaimed.

"Yes. The puppies look like both their parents. Tom asked for one of them. He lost Moose just last month," she added sadly. "They have another dog a little younger than Moose, but Tom loved that old dog. He had him cremated and put in an urn. He's still grieving, though. Lisa e-mailed a picture of the puppies to Tom and said he could have one. He and his oldest daughter went over to pick it out. They'll be ready to go to new homes in a week or so. They're just precious at this age. I'm going to draw them in a big Easter basket."

"You could sell drawings," Dee said.

"I guess so. But I'd never make a living at it," she replied, smiling. "I want to sell books."

"I think you're going to be selling your own books pretty soon," Dee told her. "You have a wonderful talent."

Sara beamed. "Thanks. It's the only thing I inherited from my father. He loved the work he did, but he could draw beautiful portraits." She grimaced. "It was hard, losing him like that."

"Wars are terrible," Dee agreed. "But at least you had your grandfather. He was your biggest fan. He was always bragging about you, to anybody who'd listen."

"I still get letters from Grandad's former students," Sara said. "He taught military history. I guess he had every book ever written on World War II. Especially the campaign in North Africa." She frowned. "Funny, that's what the ogre likes to read about."

"Maybe the ogre is like that lion who got a thorn in his paw, and when the mouse pulled it out, they were friends for life."

Sara glowered at her boss. "No mouse in his right mind would go near that man," she said.

"Except you," came the amused reply.

"Well, I don't have a choice. What do we do about the check?" she asked Dee. "Do I call him before I go over there, or…"

Dee picked up the slip of paper with his phone number on it. "I'll call him in the morning. You can put the books in a bag and take them home with you tonight. That way you won't have to come in to town."

"You're sweet, Dee."

The older woman smiled. "So are you." She checked her watch. "I've got to pick Mama up at the beauty parlor and take her home, then I'm going to do paperwork. You know my cell phone number. Call me if you need me."

"I won't, but thanks all the same."

Dee looked uneasy. "You need to have a cell phone, Sara. You can get a prepaid one for next to nothing. I don't like you having to drive home after dark on that dirt road."

"Most of the drug traffickers are in prison now," she reminded her boss.

"That isn't what Cash Grier says," Dee replied. "They locked up the Dominguez woman, and her successor, but there's a man in charge now, and he killed two Mexican policemen at a border crossing, as well as a Border Patrol agent and even a reporter. They say he killed a whole family over near Nuevo Laredo for ratting on him."

"Surely he wouldn't come here," Sara began.

"Drug dealers like it here," Dee returned. "We don't have federal agents—well, except for the DEA agent, Cobb, who works out of Houston and has a ranch here. Our police and sheriff's departments are underfunded and understaffed. That's why that man Lopez tried to set up a distribution network here. They say this new drug lord has property around town that he bought with holding companies, so nobody would know who really owned the land. A farm or ranch way out in the country would be a perfect place to transport drugs to."

"Like they tried once, behind Cy Parks's place and at the old Johnson place."

Dee sighed. "It makes me uneasy, that's all."

"You worry too much," Sara said gently. "Besides, I'm

only a mile out of town and I lock all my doors." She looked at the clock on the wall opposite. "You'd better get moving, or your mother's going to be worried about you!"

Dee chuckled. "I guess so. Well, if you need me…"

"I'll call."

Dee went out with a wave, leaving Sara alone.

Later in the afternoon, Harley Fowler came in, dusty and sweaty and half out of humor. He pushed his hat back over wet hair.

"What in the world happened to you?" Sara exclaimed. "You look like you've been dragged down a dirt road behind a horse!"

He glowered. "I have."

"Ouch," she sympathized.

"I need a book on Spanish slang. Ranch Spanish slang, if you've got one."

"We have every Spanish dictionary ever published, including slang ones. I'll show you."

She pointed out a rack with dozens of paperback dictionaries, including specific books just on verbs.

"Just the thing," Harley murmured, reading titles. "Mr. Parks still has an account, doesn't he?"

"He and Lisa both do."

"Well, you can put these on his tab." He picked out four and handed them to her.

"Would it be safe to ask why you want them?" she mused as she went behind the counter to the cash register.

"Why not?" he sighed. "I thought I was telling Lanita, Juan's wife, that it was hot outside. She blushed, Juan jumped me, and we rolled around in the dirt until I finally convinced him that I was just talking about the weather. We got up and shook hands, and then he told me what I'd actually said to her. I was just sick." He groaned. "I speak a little Spanish, but I learned it in high school, and I've forgotten how *not* to say embarrassing things." He groaned. "Juan and the rest of the workers speak English, but I thought I might get along better with them if I spoke a little Spanish. And this happens!"

She pursed her lips. "If you want to remark on the weather, in Spanish you say 'there is heat,' not 'I am hot.' Especially in front of a woman."

"Thanks, I do know that now," he replied, soothing his jaw. "That Juan hits like a mule kicking."

"So I've heard."

She totaled the books on the cash register and wrote down the tally in a book of accounts that Dee kept. "We'll bill Mr. Parks."

"Thanks." He took the bag with the books. "If Mr. Parks wants to argue about me buying them, I'll tell him to go talk to Juan."

She grinned. "Good idea."

He smiled back, and hesitated, as if he wanted to say something more. Just then, the phone rang, and it was one of her long-winded customers. She shrugged and waved at Harley. He waved back as he left. She wondered later what he'd been about to say.

He was handsome and well-known in the community for being a hardworking cowboy. He'd actually gone on a mission with three of the town's ex-mercenaries to help stop Manuel Lopez's drug-smuggling operation. He'd earned a lot of respect for his part in it. Sara liked him a lot, but he didn't date much. Rumor was that he'd had a real case on a local girl who'd made fun of his interest in her and threw him over. But he didn't look like a man with a broken heart.

Sara knew about broken hearts. She'd been sweet on a boy in the community college she attended to learn accounting. So had Marie, her best friend. The boy had dated both of them, but finally started going steady with Marie. A good loser, Sara had been maid of honor at their wedding. Marie and her new husband had moved to Michigan to be near his parents. Sara still wrote to Marie. She was too kindhearted to hold a grudge. Probably, she realized, the boy had only dated her because she was best friends with Marie. She recalled that he spent most of their time together asking her questions about Marie.

She was old-fashioned. Her grandfather had firm opinions about the morality deprived state of modern society. He and Sara went to church regularly and she began to share his views. She wasn't the sort of girl who got invited to wild parties, because she didn't drink or smoke or do drugs. Everyone knew that her grandfather was good friends with one of Police Chief Cash Grier's older patrol officers, too. Her law enforcement connections made the party crowd cautious. It also got around that Sara didn't "give out" on dates. There were too many girls who had no such hang-ups. So Sara and Morris spent most of their Friday and Saturday nights together with Sara's grandfather, watching movies on television.

She wondered where the ogre had gone, and why Tony the Dancer hadn't gone with him. Maybe he was off on a hot date somewhere. She wondered about the sort of woman who might appeal to a man with his gloomy outlook. But then she remembered that he'd been wearing an expensive suit, and driving a new truck, and he owned one of the bigger ranches in the county. Some women wouldn't mind how gloomy and antisocial he was, as long as he had lots of money to spend on them.

He did look like a cold fish. But maybe he was different around people he liked. He'd made it obvious that he didn't like Sara. The feeling was mutual. She hated having to give up her Saturday to his whim.

She phoned Lisa to tell her that she wouldn't be able to come until the following Wednesday.

"That's okay," Lisa replied. "Cy and I wanted to take the baby to the mall in San Antonio on Saturday, but I was going to stay home and wait for you. There's lots of sales on baby clothes and toys."

Like Lisa needed sales, when her husband owned one of the most productive ranches in Texas, she thought, but she didn't say it. "You're always buying that baby clothes," Sara teased. "He's going to be the best-dressed little boy in town."

"We go overboard, I know," Lisa replied, "but we're so happy to have him. Cy and I took a long time to get over losing our first one."

"I remember," Sara said softly. "But birth defects turn up sometimes in the healthiest families, you know. I read about it in one of the medical books we sell. This little boy is going to grow up and be a rancher, just like his parents."

Lisa laughed softly. "Thanks, Sara," she said gently. "You make me feel better every time I talk to you."

"I'll call you Wednesday, okay? Dee's giving me a half-day, so I'll have the afternoon off."

"That will work out fine," Lisa said.

"Thanks."

"You're very welcome."

Sara hung up. Poor Lisa. Her first husband had been killed not long after their wedding. He'd been an undercover DEA agent, whom one of the drug dealer, Lopez's, men had killed. Cy had taken her under his wing and protected her while she waited for the birth of her child. Harley said the baby she was carrying wasn't her husband's, because he had a vasectomy, but she'd thought she was pregnant. Only weeks after marrying Cy, she really was pregnant. But the baby was born with birth defects that were beyond a physician's ability to cure. He'd died when he was only a week old, leaving two devastated parents to grieve. They hadn't rushed into another pregnancy. But this one had worked out without any health issues at all. Their little boy, Gil, was a toddler, and very active.

Sara wondered if she'd ever get married and have a family, but it wasn't something she dwelled on. She was young and the world would have been wide-open for her, except for her one small secret that she wasn't anxious to share with anyone. Still, she was optimistic about the future. Well, except for the ogre.

She sighed. Every life had to have a few little irritations, she decided. And who knew? The ogre might turn out to be a handsome prince inside.

Two

It was pouring rain when Sara reluctantly crawled out of bed the next morning. She looked out the window and sighed.

"Boy, I'd love to go back under the covers and sleep, Morris," she mused as she fed the old cat.

He rubbed up against her pajama-clad legs and purred.

She yawned as she made a pot of coffee and some buttered toast to go with it. Her grandfather had insisted on a balanced breakfast, but Sara couldn't manage a lot of food early in the morning.

She nibbled toast and watched the rain bounce down over the camellia bush next to the window. She was going to get wet.

She dressed in jeans and a cotton blouse and threw her ancient tan raincoat over her clothes. It was embarrassing to wear such a tacky coat to a rich man's house, but it was all she had. Her salary didn't cover many new things. Mostly she

shopped at thrift stores. The coat had a stained neck and two
or three tears where Sara—never the world's most graceful
woman—had tripped over garden stakes or steps or her own
feet and brushed against nails and a barbed-wire fence. She
looked down and noticed that she was wearing socks that
didn't match. Well, it was something she just had to learn to
live with. The doctor told her she'd cope. She hoped he was
right. She was nineteen, and sometimes she felt fifty when she
tried to force her mind to comprehend matching colors.

Groaning, she checked her watch. It was fifteen to ten, and
it would take her almost all that time to get to the White Horse
Ranch. Well, the ogre would just have to make fun of her. She
didn't have time to unload her sock drawer and find mates.
They were hidden under her jeans, anyway, and maybe he
wouldn't notice.

She stepped right into a hole filled with muddy water
getting to her car. Her sneakers and her socks were immediately soaked. She groaned again as she unlocked the little car
and quickly climbed in. The seats were leather, thank
goodness, and they'd shed water. Her VW was seven years
old, but the mechanics at Turkey Sanders's used car lot kept
it in good repair. Despite his reputation for bad car sales,
Turkey prided himself on his mechanics.

She patted its cracked dash. The VW had been wrecked,
so she got it very cheaply. Probably it would fall apart if she
tried to drive it as far as San Antonio. But she never left the
Jacobsville area, and it was dependable transportation.

It started on the first go, making that lovely race car sound
that made her think of luxury racers as she gunned the engine.
If she closed her eyes and did that, sometimes it sounded just
like a Formula 1 challenge car.

"In my dreams," she laughed to herself. She wouldn't earn
enough in her lifetime to make six months of payments on one

of those fancy sports cars. But it was just as well. The little black VW suited her very well.

She pulled out of her driveway onto the dirt road that led out to the state highway. It had been recently scraped and a little new gravel had been laid down, but it was still slippery in the rain. She gritted her teeth as she felt the car slide around in the wet mud. At least it was flat land, and even if she did go into a ditch, it wouldn't be a deep one. All the same, she didn't look forward to walking for help in that molasses-thick mud. She remembered a long walk in similar red mud, overseas, with the sound of guns echoing... She drew her mind back to the present. Dwelling on the past solved nothing.

By downshifting, not hitting the brakes and going slowly, she managed to get to the paved highway. But she was going to be late getting to the ogre's house. She grimaced. Well, it couldn't be helped. She'd just have to tell him the truth and hope he was understanding about it.

"I specifically said ten o'clock," he shot at her when he opened the front door.

He was wearing jeans and a chambray shirt and working boots—you could tell by the misshapen contours of them that many soakings had caused—and a ratty black Stetson pulled low over his forehead. Even in working garb, he managed to look elegant. He looked like a cowboy, but they could have used him as a model for one made of metal. An iron cowboy.

She had to fight a laugh at the comparison.

"And you're dripping wet all over," he muttered, glaring at her clothes. "What the hell did you do, swim through mud holes on your way here?"

"I stepped in a mud puddle on the way to my car," she began, clutching a plastic bag that held his books.

He looked past her. "I don't know what the hell that thing is, but I wouldn't dignify it by calling it a car."

Her eyes began to glitter. "Here," she said, thrusting the books at him.

"And your manners could use some work," he added bitingly.

"'Cast not your pearls before swine!'" she quoted angrily.

Both eyebrows went up under the hat. "If that raincoat is any indication of your finances, you'd be lucky to be able to toss a cultured pearl at a pig. Which I am not one of," he added firmly.

"My boss said she'd call you…"

"She did." He took a folded check out of his shirt pocket and handed it to her. "Next time I order books, I'll expect you at the stated time. I'm too busy to sit in the house waiting for people to show up."

"The road I live on is six inches thick in wet mud," she began.

"You could have phoned on the way and told me that," he retorted.

"With what, smoke signals?" she asked sourly. "I don't have a cell phone."

"Why am I not surprised?" he asked with pure sarcasm.

"And my finances are none of your business!"

He glanced down. "If they were, I'd quit. No accountant is going to work for a woman who can't afford two matching socks."

"I have another pair just like this one at home!"

He frowned. He leaned closer. "What in the world is *that*?" he asked, indicating her left sleeve.

She looked down. "Aahhhhhh!" she screamed, jumping from one leg to the other. "Get it off, get it off! Aaaahhhh!"

The large man in the house came out onto the porch, frowning. When he followed his employer's pointed finger, he spotted the source of the uproar. "Oh," he said.

He walked forward, caught Sara's arm with a big hand, picked up the yellow hornet on her sleeve, slammed it to the porch and stepped on it with a shoe the size of a shoebox.

"It's just a hornet," Mr. Danzetta said gently.

Sara stared down at the smashed insect and drew in a deep breath. "It's a yellow hornet. I got stung by one of them once, on my neck. It swelled up and I had to be taken to the emergency room. I've been scared of them ever since." She smiled up at him. "Thank you." Odd, she thought, how familiar he looked. But she was almost certain she'd never seen him before. Her condition made it difficult for her to remember the past.

The ogre glared at his employee, who was smiling at Sara and watching her with something like recognition. He noted the glare, cleared his throat and went back into the house.

"Don't start flirting with the hired help," he told her firmly after the front door had closed behind Tony.

"I said thank you! How can you call that flirting?" she asked, aghast.

"I'll call the store when I need a new supply of books," he replied, ignoring her question.

She read quickly herself, but he had eight books there. But he might not be reading them, she thought wickedly. He might be using them for other purposes: as doorstops, maybe.

"You brought the books. I gave you a check. Was there something else?" he asked with a cold smile. "If you're lonely and need companionship, there are services that advertise on television late at night," he added helpfully.

She drew herself up to her full height. "If I were lonely, this is the last place in the world that I'd look for relief!" she informed him.

"Then why are you still here?"

She wouldn't kick him, she wouldn't kick him...

"And don't spin out going down my driveway," he called after her. "That's new gravel!"

She hoped he was watching her the whole way. She dislodged enough gravel to cover a flower bed on her way down the driveway.

It was a long, wet weekend. She knew that nobody around Jacobs County would be complaining about the rain. It was a dry, unusually hot spring. She read in the market bulletins online that ranchers were going to pay high prices for corn. Floods in the Midwest and Great Plains were killing the corn there, and drought was getting it in the South and Southwest. Considering the vast amounts of the grain that were being used as biofuel, and the correspondingly higher prices it was commanding, it looked as if some small ranchers and farmers might go broke because they couldn't afford to feed it to their cattle. Not to mention the expense of running farm machinery, which mostly burned gasoline.

She was glad she wasn't a farmer or rancher. She did feel sorry for the handful of small ranchers around town. One day, she thought, there would be no more family agriculture in the country. Everything would be owned by international corporations, using patented seed and genetically enhanced produce. It was a good thing that some small farmers were holding on to genetically pure seeds, raising organic crops. One day, the agricultural community might be grateful, if there was ever a wholesale dying out of the genetically modified plants.

"Well, you're deep in thought, aren't you?" Dee teased as she walked in the door the following Wednesday, just before noon.

Sara blinked, startled by her boss's appearance. "Sorry," she said, laughing. "I was thinking about corn."

Dee stared at her. "OOOOOkay," she drawled.

"No, I'm not going mad," Sara chuckled. "I read an article in this farm life magazine." She showed it to the older woman. "It's about the high prices corn is going to get this year."

Dee shook her head. "I don't know what the smaller ranchers are going to do," she said. "Gas prices are so high that it's hard to afford enough fuel to run tractors and trucks, and now they'll have to hope the hay crop is good or they'll have to sell off cattle before winter rather than having to feed them stored corn." She sighed. "I expect even the Ballengers will be feeling a pinch, with their feedlot."

"It must be tough, having your livelihood depend on the weather," she remarked.

"Yes, it is. I grew up on a little truck farm north of here," Dee told her. "One year, we had a drought so bad that everything we grew died. Dad had to borrow on the next year's profits to buy seed and fertilizer." She shook her head. "Finally he couldn't deal with the uncertainty anymore. He got a job fixing engines at one of the car dealerships."

"It's so bad, you know—floods in the Midwest and drought here and in the Southeast. Too much water or not enough. They need to build aqueducts like the Romans did and share that water with places that need it."

"Not a bad idea, but who'd pay for it?"

Sara laughed. "I don't guess anybody could. But it was a nice thought."

Dee checked her watch. "You'd better get a move on, before we get swamped with customers and you're late leaving."

"I'll do that. Thanks, Dee."

The older woman smiled. "Good luck with those drawings."

Lisa Parks had blond hair and a sweet smile. She was carrying Gil, her eighteen-month-old toddler, when she came to the door to let Sara in. The baby had brownish colored hair and his eyes were green, like his father's. He was wearing a two-piece sailor suit.

"Doesn't he look cute!" Sara enthused over the little boy, while Lisa beamed.

"Our pride and joy," Lisa murmured, kissing the child on his soft nose. "Come in."

Sara stepped into the cool confines of the house. It had been a bachelor house for years, but Lisa's feminine touches made it into a home.

"Want coffee before you start?" Lisa asked, shifting Gil on her hip while he chanted happy noises.

"After, if you don't mind," came the smiling reply. "I always try to avoid work if it's at all possible."

"Don't we all? I've got the puppies out in the barn." She led the way down the back steps, pausing at the sound of a horse approaching. Gil was still making happy baby sounds, cradled on his mother's hip.

Harley Fowler was just riding into the yard. He spotted Sara with Lisa and smiled hugely. "Hi, Sara."

"Hello, Harley. How's the Spanish coming along?"

He glanced at Lisa, who grinned at him. He shrugged. "Well, I guess I'm learning some. But Juan is a better teacher than any book."

"How's your jaw?" Sara asked with twinkling eyes.

He fingered it. "Much better." He smiled back.

"Uh oh, Mama," Gil said, frowning. "Uh oh." He squirmed.

"Uh oh means somebody needs a diaper change," Lisa laughed. She glanced at Harley and, sensing something, concealed a smile. "Harley, if you've got a minute, would you mind showing Sara the pups while I change Gil? We're working on potty training, but it's early days yet," she added on a laugh.

Harley beamed. "I'd be happy to!" He climbed down

gracefully out of the saddle and held the reins, waiting for Sara. "Are you going to adopt one of the puppies?"

She blinked. "Well, I hadn't thought about that. I have a cat, you know, and he really doesn't like dogs much. I think one tried to eat him when he was younger. He's got scars everywhere and even dogs barking on television upsets him."

He frowned. "But you came to see the puppies…?"

She showed him her drawing pad. "I came to sketch the puppies," she corrected, "for the children's book I'm writing."

"Someday she's going to be famous, and we can all say we knew her back when," Lisa teased. "I'll have coffee ready when you're done, Sara. I made a pound cake, too."

"Thanks," Sara called after her.

Lisa waved as she took the baby back into the house.

Harley tied his horse to the corral fence and walked into the dim confines of the barn with Sara. In a stall filled with fresh hay were five puppies and Bob the Collie. She was nursing the babies. In the stall beside hers was Puppy Dog, Lisa's dog, no longer a puppy. He looked exactly like Tom Walker's dog, Moose.

"A girl dog named Bob," Sara mused.

"Boss said if Johnny Cash could have a boy named 'Sue,' he could have a girl dog named Bob."

"She's so pretty," Sara said. "And the puppies are just precious!"

"Three males, two females," he said. "Tom's got first choice, since they're Moose's grandkids." He shook his head. "He's taking Moose's loss hard. He loved that old dog, even though he was a disaster in the house."

"Moose saved Tom's daughter from a rattler," Sara reminded him. "He was a real hero."

"You want a chair?" he asked.

"This old stool will do fine. Thanks anyway." She pulled

up the rickety stool, opened her pad and took her pencils out of her hip pocket.

"Will it make you nervous if I watch?"

She grinned up at him. "Of course not."

He lolled against the stall wall and folded his arms, concentrating on the way her hand flew over the page, the pencil quickly bringing the puppies to life on the off-white sheet. "You're really good," he said, surprised.

"Only thing I was ever good at in school," she murmured while she drew. She was also noting the pattern of colors on the pups and shading her drawing to match. Then she wrote down the colors, so she wouldn't forget them when she started doing the illustrations for her book in pastels.

"I can fix anything mechanical," he said, "but I can't draw a straight line."

"We all have our talents, Harley," she said. "It wouldn't do for all of us to be good at the same thing."

"No, it wouldn't, I guess."

She sketched some more in a personable silence.

"I wanted to ask you in the bookstore, but we got interrupted," he began. "There's going to be a concert at the high school this Saturday. They're hosting a performance by the San Antonio Symphony Orchestra. I wondered if, well, if you'd like to go. With me," he added.

She looked up, her soft eyes smiling. "Well, yes, I would," she said. "I'd thought about it, because they're doing Debussy, and he's my favorite composer. But I didn't have the nerve to go by myself."

He chuckled, encouraged. "Then it's a date. We could leave earlier and have supper at the Chinese place. If you like Chinese?"

"I love it. Thanks."

"Then I'll pick you up about five on Saturday. Okay?"

She smiled at him. He was really nice. "Okay."

He glanced out of the barn at his horse, which was getting restless. "I'd better get back out to the pasture. We're dipping cattle and the vet's checking them over. I'll see you Saturday."

"Thanks, Harley."

"Thank *you*."

She watched him walk away. He was good-looking, local and pleasant to be around. What a difference from that complaining, bad-tempered rancher who hadn't even sympathized with her when she'd almost drowned delivering his stupid books!

Now why had she thought about Jared Cameron? She forced herself to concentrate on the puppies.

Harley picked her up at five on Saturday in his aged, but clean, red pickup truck. He was wearing a suit, and he looked pretty good. Sara wore a simple black dress with her mother's pearls and scuffed black high-heeled shoes that she hoped wouldn't be noticed. She draped a lacy black mantilla around her shoulders.

"You look very nice," Harley said. "I figure there will be people there in jeans and shorts, but I always feel you should dress up to go to a fancy concert."

"So do I," she agreed. "At least it isn't raining," she added.

"I wish it would," he replied. "That nice shower we got last Saturday is long gone, and the crops are suffering. We're still in drought conditions."

"Don't mention that shower," she muttered. "I was out in it, sliding all over Jeff Bridges Road in my VW, bogged up to my knees in mud, just to deliver Jared Cameron's books!"

He glanced at her. "Why didn't he go to the store and get them himself?"

"He's very busy."

He burst out laughing. "Hell! Everyone's very busy. He could spare thirty minutes to drive into town. God knows, he's got half a dozen cars. That big fella who works for him is something of a mechanic in his spare time. He keeps the fleet on the road."

"What sort of cars?" she asked curiously.

"There's a sixties Rolls-Royce Silver Shadow, a thirties Studebaker and several assorted sports cars, mostly classics. He collects old cars and refurbishes them."

"He arrived at our store in a truck," she said flatly.

"From time to time that big fella wearing fancy suits drives him around."

"Do you know where he came from?"

Harley shook his head. "Somebody said he was from Montana, but I'm not sure. He came here for a funeral about eight months ago. Nobody can remember whose."

"A relative, you think?"

He shrugged. "It was at one of the old country churches. Mount Hebron Baptist, I think."

"That's where I go to church," she said, frowning. "Grandad's buried there. But I don't remember reading about any funeral in the bulletin for out-of-town people."

"It was a private service, they said. Just ashes, not even a coffin."

She pursed her lips and whistled softly. "I wouldn't like to be burned."

"I would," he said, grinning at her. "A true Viking's funeral. Nothing wrong with that. Then they can put you in a nice-looking urn and set you on the mantel above the fireplace. Nice and neat. No upkeep."

She laughed. "Harley, you're terrible!"

"Yes, but I do have saving graces. I can whistle and carry a tune. Oh, and I can gather eggs. Just ask the boss's wife!"

* * *

They had a nice meal at the local Chinese restaurant and then Harley drove them to the high school. There were a lot of people on hand for the rare big city musical talent. Both Ballengers and their wives and teenaged kids, and a few of the Tremaynes and two Hart brothers and their families.

Harley caught Sara's arm gently to help her up onto the sidewalk from the parking lot, and then let his fingers accidentally catch in hers. She didn't object. She'd always liked Harley. It was nice, to have a man find her attractive, even if it was just in a friendly way.

He was smiling down at her when they almost collided with a man in line. The man, nicely dressed in a suit and a wide-brimmed top-of-the-line John B. Stetson cowboy hat, turned his head back toward them and green eyes glared belligerently.

"Sorry, Mr. Cameron," Harley said at once.

Jared Cameron gave them both a speaking glance and turned his attention back to the line, which was rapidly moving inside. When he was out of earshot, Sara muttered, "He ran into us. You didn't have to apologize."

He chuckled. "It isn't the place for a skirmish, you know," he teased.

She grimaced. "Sorry, Harley. I don't like him, that's all. He's too full of himself."

"He's just bought that huge ranch," he reminded her. "He must live on a higher level than most of us. I guess he thinks he's above normal courtesies."

She only nodded. She hadn't liked the antagonism in the tall man's eyes when he'd looked at Harley.

They got their tickets and found seats as far away from Jared Cameron as Sara could possibly manage. Then she lost herself in the beautiful musical landscapes created by the themes of Claude Debussy. Harley seemed to enjoy the concert as much as she did. It was nice to have something in common.

On the way out, they noticed Jared Cameron speaking earnestly with Police Chief Cash Grier, who'd shown up just after the concert began and stood at the back of the room. Sara wondered what they were talking about. But it was none of her business.

It was ten o'clock when Harley dropped her off at her home. She smiled up at him. "Thanks, Harley. I had a really nice time."

"So did I. Want to go to a movie next Friday?"

Her heart jumped pleasantly. He liked her! She beamed. "Yes. I would."

He chuckled. "That's great!"

He hesitated. So did she. Her experience of men was extremely limited. Her upbringing had been strict and unrelenting on the issue of morals. Her past wasn't widely known around Jacobsville, but her reputation was rock-solid. It was why she hadn't dated much. Harley knew that. But it didn't seem to bother him overmuch. After a minute's deliberation, he bent and brushed his mouth briefly, softly over hers. "Good night, Sara."

She smiled. "Good night, Harley."

He jumped back into the truck, waved and took off down the driveway,

She watched the truck disappear into the distance, frowning as she considered that brief kiss. It hadn't touched her. She liked Harley. She'd have loved having a steady boyfriend, just for the novelty of the thing. But she hadn't felt anything when he kissed her. Maybe you just had to work up to those feelings, she told herself as she unlocked her door and went inside. It was early days in their relationship. They had plenty of time to experiment.

* * *

It was the week after the concert before her nemesis placed another order. This time he did it on the telephone, and to Dee, who got to the telephone first early Monday morning.

"What a selection," Dee exclaimed when she hung up. She read down the list, shaking her head. "Greek and Roman writers of the classics, some science fiction, two books on drug interdiction and two on South American politics. Oh, and one on independent contractors. Mercenaries."

"Maybe he's thinking of starting a war," Sara offered. "In some other country, of course." She pursed her lips and her eyes twinkled. "Maybe he's anxious to skip town because he's so fascinated by me!"

Dee looked at her over her glasses. "Excuse me?"

"It's just a theory I'm working on," she said facetiously. "I mean, I'm growing into a femme fatale. Harley Fowler can't resist me. What if my fatal charm has worked its magic on Mr. Cameron and he's running scared? He might feel a need to escape before he gets addicted to me!"

"Sara, do you feel all right?"

Sara just grinned. "I never felt better."

"If you say so. I'll get these ordered." She glanced at Sara. "He wants you to take them out to him on Saturday."

Sara grimaced. "He just likes ruining my weekends."

"He hardly knows you, dear. I'm sure it's not that."

Sara didn't answer her.

On Thursday, Harley phoned with bad news. "I have to fly to Denver on business for the boss, and I'll be gone a week or more," he said miserably. "So we can't go to the movies on Friday."

"That's all right, Harley," she assured him. "There will be a movie left when you get back that we can go see. Honest."

He laughed. "You make everything so easy, Sara."

"You have a safe trip."

"I'll do my best. Take care."

"You, too."

She hung up and wondered idly why Harley had to go out of town just before they went on another date. It was as if fate was working against her. She'd looked forward to it, too. Now all she had to anticipate was delivering books to the ogre. It wasn't a happy thought. Not at all.

Well, she told herself, it could always be worse. She could be dating HIM—the ogre.

Three

Sara took the ogre's books home with her on Friday, just as she had the last time, so that she didn't have to go to town. At least it wasn't pouring rain when she went out to her car early Saturday morning to make the drive to the White Horse Ranch.

This time, he was waiting for her on the porch. He was leaning against one of the posts with his hands in his jean pockets. Like last time, he was wearing working garb. Same disreputable boots and hat, same unpleasant expression. Sara tried not to notice what an incredible physique he had, or how handsome he was. It wouldn't do to let him know how attractive she found him.

He looked pointedly at his watch as she came up the steps. "Five minutes late," he remarked.

Her eyebrows arched. "I am not," she shot back. "My watch says ten, exactly."

"My watch is better than yours," he countered.

"I guess so, if you judge it by the amount of gold on the band instead of the mechanics inside it," she retorted.

"You're testy for a concert goer," he returned. He smiled, and it wasn't sarcastic. "You like Debussy, do you?"

"Yes."

"Who else?"

She was taken aback by the question. "I like Resphigi, Rachmaninoff, Haydn and some modern composers like the late Basil Poledouris and Jerry Goldsmith. I also like James Horner, Danny Elfman, Harry Gregson-Williams and James Newton Howard."

He eyed her curiously. "I thought a country girl like you would prefer fiddles to violins."

"Well, even here in Outer Cowpasture, we know what culture is," she countered.

He chuckled deeply. "I stand corrected. What came in?" he asked, nodding toward the books she was carrying.

She handed the bag to him. He looked over the titles, nodding and pulled a check out of his pocket, handing it to her.

"Is it serious?" he asked abruptly.

She just stared at him. "Is what serious?"

"You and the cowboy at the concert. What's his name, Fowler?"

"Harley Fowler. We're friends."

"Just friends?"

"Listen, I've already been asked that question nine times this week. Just because I go out with a man, it doesn't mean I'm ready to have his children."

Something touched his eyes and made them cold. His faintly friendly air went into eclipse. "Thanks for bringing the books out," he said abruptly. He turned and went in the house without another word, closing the door firmly behind him.

Sara went back to her car, dumbfounded. She couldn't imagine what she'd said to make him turn off like a blown lightbulb.

The next day she went to church and then treated herself to a nice lunch at Barbara's Café in town. The ogre's odd behavior had disturbed her. She couldn't understand what she'd said to put that look on his lean face. She was upset because she didn't understand. She wasn't a woman who went around trying to hurt other people, even when they deserved it.

After lunch, on an impulse she drove back to her church, parked her car and walked out into the cemetery. She wanted to see her grandfather's grave and make sure the silk flowers she'd put there for Father's Day—today—were still in place. Sometimes the wind blew them around. She liked talking to him as well; catching him up on all the latest news around town. It would probably look as if she were crazy if anyone overheard her. But she didn't care. If she wanted to think her grandfather could hear her at his grave, that was nobody else's business.

She paused at his headstone and stooped down to remove a weed that was trying to grow just beside the tombstone. Her grandmother was buried beside him, but Sara had never known her. She'd been a very small child when she died.

She patted the tombstone. "Hello, Grandad," she said softly. "I hope you're in a happy place with Granny. I sure do miss you. Especially in the summer. Remember how much fun we had going fishing together? You caught that big bass the last time, and fell in the river trying to get him reeled in." She laughed softly. "You said he was the tastiest fish you'd ever eaten."

She tugged at another weed. "There's this new guy in town. You'd like him. He loves to read and he owns a big ranch. He's sort of like an ogre, though. Very antisocial. He thinks I look like a bag lady…"

She stopped talking when she realized she wasn't alone in the cemetery. Toward the far corner, a familiar figure was tugging weeds away from a tombstone, patting it with his hand. Talking to it. She hadn't even heard him drive up.

Without thinking of the consequences, she went toward him. Here, among the tombstones, there was no thought of causing trouble. It was a place people came to remember, to honor their dead.

She stopped just behind him and read the tombstone. "Ellen Marist Cameron," it said. She would have been nine years old, today.

He felt her there and turned. His eyes were cold, full of pain, full of hurt.

"Your daughter," she guessed softly.

"Killed in a wreck," he replied tonelessly. "She'd gone to the zoo with a girlfriend and her parents. On the way back, a drunk driver crossed the median and t-boned them on the side my daughter was occupying. She died instantly."

"I'm sorry."

He cocked his head. "Why are you here?"

"I come to talk to my grandad," she confessed, avoiding his eyes. "He died recently of a massive coronary. He was all the family I had left."

He nodded slowly. "She—" he indicated the tombstone "—was all the family I had left. My parents are long dead. My wife died of a drug overdose a week after Ellen was killed." He looked out across the crop of tombstones with blank eyes. "My grandfather used to live here. I thought it was a good place to put her, next to him."

So that was the funeral he'd come here to attend. His child. No wonder he was bitter. "What was she like?" she asked.

He looked down at her curiously. "Most people try to avoid the subject. They know it's painful, so they say nothing."

"It hurts more not to talk about them," she said simply. "I miss my grandfather every day. He was my best friend. He taught history at the local college. We went fishing together on weekends."

"She liked to swim," he said, indicating the tombstone. "She was on a swim team at her elementary school. She was a whiz at computers," he added, laughing softly. "I'd be floundering around trying to find a Web site, and she'd make two keystrokes and bring it up on the screen. She was…a child…of great promise." His voice broke.

Without counting the cost, Sara stepped right up against him and put her arms around him. She held on tight.

She felt the shock run through him. He hesitated, but only for a minute. His own arms slid around her. He held her close while the wind blew around them, through the tall trees that lined the country cemetery. It was like being alone in the world. Tony Danzetta was out of sight watching, of course, even if he couldn't be seen. Jared couldn't be out of his sight, even at a time like this.

He let out a long breath, and some of the tension seemed to drain out of him. "I couldn't talk about her. There's a hole in my life so deep that nothing fills it. She was my world, and while she was growing up, I was working myself to death making money. I never had time to go to those swim meets, or take her places on holidays. I wasn't even there last Christmas, because I was working a deal in South America and I had to fly to Argentina to close it. She was supposed to spend Christmas with me. She had Thanksgiving with her mother." He drew in a ragged breath and his arms involuntarily contracted around Sara's slim figure. "She never complained. She was happy with whatever time I could spare for her. I wish I'd done more. I never thought we'd run out of time. Not this soon."

"Nobody is ever ready for death," Sara said, eyes closed

as she listened to the steady, reassuring heartbeat under her ear. "I knew Grandad was getting old, but I didn't want to see it. So I pretended everything was fine. I lost my parents years ago. Grandad and I were the only family left."

She felt him nodding.

"Did she look like you?" she asked.

"She had my coloring. But she had her mother's hair. She wasn't pretty, but she made people feel good just being around her. She thought she was ugly. I was always trying to explain to her that beauty isn't as important as character and personality."

There was a long, quiet, warm silence.

"Why did you decide to live here?" she asked suddenly.

He hesitated. "It was a business decision," he replied, withdrawing into himself. "I thought new surroundings might help."

She pulled back and his arms fell away from her. She felt oddly chilled. "Does it help?"

He searched her eyes quietly. After a minute, the intensity of the look brought a flaming blush to her cheeks and she looked down abruptly.

He laughed softly at her embarrassment. "You're bashful."

"I am not. It's just hot," she protested, putting a little more distance between them. Her heart was racing and she felt oddly hot. That wouldn't do at all. She didn't dare show weakness to the enemy.

"It wasn't an insult," he said after a minute. "There's nothing wrong with being shy." His eyes narrowed. "Who looks after you, if you get sick? Your boss?"

"Dee's wonderful, but she's not responsible for me. I look out for myself." She glanced at him. "How about you?"

He shrugged. "If it looked like I was dying, Tony the Dancer would probably call somebody if he was around—if he wasn't on holiday or having days off. My lawyer might send a doctor out, if it was serious and somebody called."

"But would they take care of you?" she persisted.

"That's not their job."

She drew in a long breath. "I know you don't like me. But maybe we could look out for each other."

His dark eyebrows lifted. "Be each other's family, in other words."

"No ties," she said at once. "We'd just be there if one of us was sick."

He seemed to be seriously considering it. "I had flu and almost died last winter," he said quietly. "It was just after I lost my daughter. If Tony hadn't come back early from Christmas holidays, I guess I'd have died. It went into pneumonia and I was too sick and weak to get help."

"Something like that happened to me this year," she said. "I got sick and I had this horrible pain in my stomach. I stayed in bed for days until I could get up and go back to work. It was probably just the stomach bug that was going around, but I thought, what if it was something serious? I couldn't even get to the phone."

He nodded. "I've had the same thoughts. Okay. Suppose we do that?"

She smiled. "It's not such a bad idea, is it?"

"Not bad at all."

"I would be more amenable to the plan if you'd stop treating me like a bag lady," she added.

"Stop dressing like one," he suggested.

She glowered up at him. "I am not dressed like a bag lady."

"Your socks never match. Your jeans look like they've been worn by a grizzly bear. Your T-shirts all have pictures or writing on them."

"When you're working, you don't look all that tidy

yourself," she countered, not comfortable with telling him the truth about her odd apparel, "and I wouldn't dare ask what you got on your boots to make them smell so bad."

His eyes began to twinkle. "Want to know? It was," and he gave her the vernacular for it so wickedly that she blushed.

"You're a bad man."

He studied her closely. "If you want to be my family, you have to stop saying unkind things to me. Give a dog a bad name," he said suggestively.

"I'd have to work on that," she replied.

He drew in a long breath as he glanced back at the small grave. "Why did you come out here today?"

She smiled sadly. "Today is Father's Day. I put some new silk flowers on Grandad's grave. Sometimes the wind blows them away. I wanted to make sure they were still there."

"I meant to call one of the local florists and get them to come out and put a fresh bouquet on her grave. But I've had some business problems lately," he added without specifying what they were. "I write myself notes about things like that." He smiled wryly. "Then I misplace the notes."

"I do that all the time," she confessed.

He cocked his head, staring at her. "Why can't you wear things that match?" he asked, noting that she had on mismatched earrings.

She grimaced. It was much too early in their ambiguous relationship to tell him the real reason. She lied instead. "I'm always in a hurry. I just put on whatever comes to hand. Around town, people know I do it and nobody makes fun of me." She hesitated. "That's not quite true. When I came here to live with Grandad, some of the local kids made it hard on me."

"Why?"

"Well, my mother wasn't exactly pure as the driven snow," she confessed. "She had affairs with three or four local men, and broke up marriages. The children of those divorces couldn't get to her, but I was handy."

She said it matter-of-factly, without blame. He scowled. "You should sound bitter, shouldn't you?" he queried.

She smiled up at him. "Giving back what you get sounds good, but these days you can end up in jail for fighting at school. I didn't want to cause Grandad any more pain than Mom already had. You see, he was a college professor, very conservative. What she did embarrassed and humiliated him. One of her lovers was his department head at college. She did it deliberately. She hated Grandad."

His eyes narrowed. "Can I ask why?"

That was another question she didn't feel comfortable answering. Her eyes lowered to his tie. "I'm not really sure," she prevaricated.

He knew she was holding something back. Her body language was blatant. He wondered if she realized it.

Another question presented itself. He frowned. "Just how old are you?"

She looked up, grinning. "I'm not telling."

He pursed his lips, considering. "You haven't lost your illusions about life, yet," he mused, noting the odd flicker of her eyelids when he said it. "I'd say you haven't hit your mid-twenties yet, but you're close."

He'd missed it, but she didn't let on. "You're not bad," she lied.

He stuck his hands in the pockets of his slacks and looked at the sky. "No rain yet. Probably none for another week, the meteorologists say," he remarked. "We need it badly."

"I know. We used to have this old guy, Elmer Randall, who worked at the newspaper office helping to run the presses. He was part Comanche. Every time we had a drought, he'd get into his tribal clothes and go out and do ceremonies outside town."

"Did it work?" he asked with real interest.

She laughed. "One time after he did it, we had a flood. It almost always rained. Nobody could figure it out. He said his grandfather had been a powerful shaman and rode with Quanah Parker." She shrugged. "People believe what they want to, but I thought he might really have a gift. Certainly, nobody told him to stop."

"Whatever works," he agreed. He checked his watch. "I'd better get home. I'm expecting a phone call from Japan."

"Do you speak the language?"

He laughed. "I try to. But the company I'm merging with has plenty of translators."

"I'll bet Japan is an interesting place," she said with dreamy eyes. "I've never been to Asia in my whole life."

He looked surprised. "I thought everybody traveled these days."

"We never had the money," she said simply. "Grandad's idea of international travel was to buy Fodor's Guides to the countries that interested him. He spent his spare cash on books, hundreds of books."

"He taught history, you said. What was his period?"

She hesitated as she looked up at his lean, handsome face. Wouldn't it sound too pat and coincidental to tell him the truth?

He frowned. "Well?"

She grimaced. "World War II," she confessed. "The North African theater of war."

His intake of breath was audible. "You didn't mention that when I ordered books on the subject."

"I thought it would sound odd," she said. "I mean, here you were, a total stranger looking for books on that subject, and my grandfather taught it. It seems like some weird coincidence."

"Yes, but they do happen." He moved restlessly. "Did he have autobiographies?"

"Yes, all sorts of first person accounts on both sides of the battle. His favorite subjects were German Field Marshal Erwin Rommel and General George Patton, but he liked the point of view of the 9th Australian Division, as well as British General Bernard Montgomery's memoirs."

"I asked the high school age son of one of my vice presidents which of the generals he liked to read about when he was studying history. He said they hadn't taught him about any individual officers. He didn't even know who Rommel was."

The allusion to vice presidents went right by her. She smiled sheepishly. She'd only graduated from high school two years before, and he didn't know that. "I didn't, either, from high school courses," she confessed. "But Grandad was good for a two-hour lecture on any subject I mentioned."

He pursed his lips, really interested. "Who was the last commander of the British Eighth Army before Montgomery in North Africa?"

She chuckled. "You don't think I know, do you? It was Auchinleck—Sir Claude. He was a big, redheaded man, and his wife was from America."

His eyebrows arched. "You're good. What was Rommel's wife called?"

"Her name was Lucie, but he called her Lu. They had a son, Manfred, who eventually became Lord Mayor of Stuttgart, Germany." She wiggled her eyebrows at him. "Want to know what sort of anti-tank field artillery Rommel used that confounded the British generals? It was the 88 millimeter anti-aircraft gun. He camouflaged them and then lured the British tanks within firing range. They thought it was some sort of super weapon, but they were just regular antiaircraft weapons. One captured officer told Rommel that it wasn't fair to use them against tanks. But it was war."

"It was." He was looking at her in a totally different way than he had before. "Do you ever loan books?"

She frowned. "Well, I never have before. But I might make an exception for you. Grandad would have loved talking with you about North Africa."

"I would have enjoyed it, too." He glanced again at his watch. "Lord, I'm late!"

"I have to get back home, too." She looked down at the tombstone. "I'm sorry about your daughter."

He sobered. "I'm sorry about your grandfather. Holidays are the worst times, aren't they? I stayed drunk for two days last Christmas. It was my first without her."

"I don't drink," she replied. "But my heart wasn't in celebrating. I spent Christmas day at one of the senior citizen homes, reading to a lady who didn't get any company."

He reached out unexpectedly and touched her hair. "I wouldn't have guessed you had so many soft spots. Sara. Isn't it?"

She nodded, thrilled by the faint caress. "Sara Dobbs."

He smiled tenderly. "I'll be in touch."

She smiled back, her eyes twinkling with emotion. "See you."

He drove off in a fancy red sports car like ones she'd seen on televised auto shows. She smiled as she considered his interest in her because of Grandad's favorite subject. First Harley, now the iron cowboy. She felt better than she had in years.

But she wondered if her ogre would still be interested if he found out how young she was. She'd just keep that to herself, she decided, like her past. There was no need for him to know anything about either subject yet. And by the time there was…well, maybe it wouldn't matter anymore.

* * *

On Thursday, when she got home from work, she sorted out Grandad's books, carefully pairing subject matter with time period, in case Jared Cameron wanted to borrow one. She knew her grandfather wouldn't have minded. He enjoyed teaching students about the amazing contradictions of the North African theater, where what many called a "gentleman's war" was fought. Rommel had actually called a truce during one bloody battle and sent his men to help move Allied wounded off the battlefield.

Patton had entered the campaign too late to face off against Rommel, but he had read Rommel's book about the strategy and tactics of World War I. The general was known for his own lightning strike sort of attack; he said that fewer soldiers were lost when battles were won quickly. Both soldiers led from the front, and both were respected by not only their own men, but by the enemy as well.

Her hands touched a book by a missionary who'd worked in Africa and stilled. This had been one of Grandad's favorite biographies, although it had nothing to do with World War II. The author of the book was a physician. He'd gone to Africa, sanctioned as a missionary, and remained there for many years treating natives. The book had inspired Grandad to missionary work, but he'd chosen to become a college educator instead. He'd regretted his decision later in life and had sold the idea wholesale to his daughter's husband.

Sara put the book aside, shoving it into a bookcase with undue savagery. If only he'd realized what the consequences of his fervor for mission work would be…

She stacked the books she was through sorting and got up. Morris was crying to be fed.

As she moved into the kitchen, she felt suddenly nauseous, and that pain in her stomach came back full force. She managed to get the sack of dry cat food and poured some of it into his bowl. Then she sat down and groaned. She was so sick she could barely move. It hurt to move, anyway.

She rested her forehead on her forearm, draped across the scarred little kitchen table where she and Grandad always had meals. She was sweating. It wasn't that hot in the house. She had a window air conditioner, and it was running full tilt.

These sick spells were getting closer together. Could she be having the same virus week after week? she wondered. Or could it be something else?

Her grandmother had suffered from gallbladder disease. She remembered, barely, the old lady being taken to the hospital when Sara was about four years old to have an operation. Doctors had removed it. She recalled that old Mrs. Franklin had complained of terrible pain in her stomach and feeling nauseous.

But gallbladder problems were in the upper right area of the abdomen. This felt like it was dead-center. Could she possibly have an ulcer?

It would pass, she told herself. She'd just sit very still and not move around and it would go away, like it always did.

But it didn't go away. An hour later, it hurt to walk and nausea washed over her unexpectedly. She barely made it to the bathroom in time to lose her breakfast. The pain was horrible. She'd never felt anything like it. She felt feverish as well. Something was wrong. Something bad.

She crawled to the phone in the living room and pulled it down on the floor with her. She pressed in 911.

When the dispatcher answered, she gave her symptoms and then her name and address. The lady told her to stay on the line while she sent the paramedics out.

Sara leaned back against the wall, so sick she couldn't bear the thought of being moved. The pain was in her side, her right side. It was so bad that even the lightest touch of her fingers caused her to jump.

Morris, sensing that something was wrong, came into the living room and rubbed against her, purring. She petted him, but she couldn't let him get into her lap.

Fortunately she hadn't locked up for the night. She'd managed to reach up and turn on the porch light. When the paramedics knocked, she shouted for them to come in.

One of them was a girl she'd gone to high school with, a brunette with short hair who'd been kind to her when other students hadn't been.

"Hi, Lucy," Sara managed as the woman bent over her with a stethoscope.

"Hi, Sara. Where does it hurt?"

Sara showed her. When Lucy pressed her fingers against it, Sara came up off the floor, groaning.

The three paramedics looked at each other.

Lucy put the thermometer into Sara's ear. "A hundred and two," she remarked. "Any nausea?"

"Yes," Sara groaned.

"Okay, we're taking you in to the hospital. What do you need us to do?"

"Get my purse on the sofa and make sure I've turned off everything and then lock the door with the key that's in this side of the dead bolt," she said weakly.

"Will do. Curt, can you check the appliances and turn off the lights?"

"Sure. What about the cat?"

"He can stay here, he's been fed and he has a litter box. I'll get my boss to run out and feed him tomorrow…" She sat back with a sigh. "My goodness, it stopped hurting," she said, smiling at Lucy. "I may not need to go to the hospital…"

"Get her loaded, stat!" Lucy said at once, and moved away

to speak into the microphone on her shoulder so that Sara couldn't hear. She nodded as the reply came back. When she turned, Sara was on her way into the ambulance, arguing all the way. She wouldn't know until hours later that the cessation of pain had been a signal that her appendix had perforated. If she'd argued successfully to stay home, she'd have been dead by morning.

Four

Four

It was all a blur to Sara. She was surprised that they'd prepped her for surgery and had her sign a consent form only minutes after she arrived at the hospital.

Dr. "Copper" Coltrain, the redheaded local surgeon, was already masked and gowned when they wheeled her in.

"Hi, Dr. Coltrain," Sara said, her voice drowsy from the preop meds. "Are you going to carve me up?"

"Only your appendix, Sara," he replied with a chuckle. "You won't even miss it, I promise."

"But it feels fine now."

"I imagine so. That's a very bad sign. It means it's perforated."

"What's that?" she asked, while a capped, gowned and masked woman beside her put something in a syringe into the drip that led down to the needle in her arm.

"It's something to make you comfortable," came the reply. "Count backward from a hundred for me, will you?"

Sara smiled, sleepy. "Sure. One hundred, ninety-nine, ninety-eight, ninety…"

She came to in the recovery room, dazed and completely confused. She wanted to ask them what they'd done to her, but her lips wouldn't work.

A nurse came in and checked her. "Awake, are we?" she asked pleasantly. "Good!"

"Did Dr. Coltrain take out my appendix?"

"Yes, dear," the nurse replied.

Sara closed her eyes again and went back to sleep.

One of the great unsolved mysteries of small town life is how quickly word gets around if someone local is injured or killed. The process seems to consist largely of word of mouth. Someone who works at the hospital is related to someone who owns a small business, and phone traffic increases exponentially. Soon after the incident, it's an open secret.

Exactly how Jared Cameron found out that Sara's appendix had gone ballistic was never known. But he showed up about the time they'd moved Sara into a semi-private room.

Tony Danzetta came with him and stood quietly outside the hospital room while Jared walked into it. The nurse who was making Sara comfortable and checking her vitals did a double take when she saw him and his companion.

"Don't mind Tony," Jared told her. "He goes everywhere with me."

Sara peered at him past the nurse. "Don't worry about it," she told the nurse in a still-drowsy tone. "He's not the only man who carries protection around with him."

The nurse burst out laughing. So did Jared.

Sara closed her eyes and drifted off again.

* * *

The second time she awoke, it was to find Jared lounging in the chair beside her bed. He was wearing working clothes. He looked really good in denim, she considered through a mixture of drugs and pain. He was very handsome. She didn't realize she'd said it out loud until he raised both eyebrows.

"Sorry," she apologized.

He smiled. "How do you feel?"

"I'm not sure how to put it into words." She looked past him at Tony, still standing patiently outside her room. "I seem to have lost my appendix. Do you suppose you could send Tony the Dancer out to look for it?"

"It's long gone by now. You'll improve. While you're improving, I'm taking you home with me."

She blinked. "That will cause gossip."

"It won't matter to your friends and what your enemies think doesn't matter to you. Or it shouldn't."

"Put that way," she agreed, "I guess you're right."

"You can't stay at your house alone, in this condition."

"What about Morris?"

"Tony the Dancer drove over to your house and fed him on his way here," he said carelessly. "He'll look after your cat until you're able to go home."

She was too groggy to wonder how Tony had gotten inside her house. The EMTs had locked it. She moved and grimaced. "I didn't realize that an appendix could kill you."

"It can if it perforates. Those stomach pains you were having were probably a symptom of chronic appendicitis," he said.

"I guess so. I never thought it might be dangerous. How long have you been here?"

"Since they took you in to surgery," he said surprisingly. "Tony and I went out to supper until you were in recovery, then we sat in the waiting room until they put you in a room."

Her eyelids felt heavy. "It was nice of you to come."

"We're each other's family, remember?" he asked, and he didn't smile. "I take responsibilities seriously."

"Thanks," she said weakly.

"Not necessary. Try to go back to sleep. The more rest you get, the faster you'll heal."

She stared at him a little drowsily. "Will you be here, when I wake up?"

"Yes," he said quietly.

She tried to smile, but she wasn't able to get her lips to move. She fell back into the comfortable softness of sleep.

It hurt to move. She tried to turn over, and it felt as if her stomach was going to come apart. She groaned.

The big man who went around with the ogre came and stood over her. He had large dark eyes, and heavy black eyebrows. His dark, wavy hair was in a ponytail. He had an olive complexion. He was frowning.

"Do you need something for pain?" he asked in a voice like rumbling thunder.

Her eyes managed to focus. He looked foreign. But he had that Georgia drawl. Maybe he was of Italian heritage and raised in the South.

He grinned, showing perfect white teeth. "I'm not Italian. I'm Cherokee."

She hadn't realized that she'd spoken her thoughts aloud. The painkilling drugs seemed to be affecting her in odd ways. "You're Mr. Danzetta," she said. "I thought you were a hit man."

He laughed out loud. "I prevent hits," he replied. "I'm Tony. Nobody calls me Mr. Danzetta." The frown was back. "It hurts, huh?"

"It does," she managed weakly.

He touched the call button. A voice came over it. "May I help you?"

"This young lady could use something for pain," he replied.

"I'll be right there."

Minutes later, a nurse came into the room, smiling. "Dr. Coltrain left orders so that you could have something for pain."

"It feels like my body's been cut in half," Sara confessed.

"This will help you feel better," she said, adding something to the drip that was feeding her fluids. "It will be automatic now."

"Thanks," Sara said, grimacing. "I sure never thought losing a tiny little thing like an appendix would hurt so much."

"You were in bad shape when you came in," she replied. She glanced at Tony the Dancer curiously. "Are you a relative?"

"Who, me? No. I work for Mr. Cameron."

The nurse was confused. "Is he related to Miss Dobbs?"

Tony hesitated. "Sort of."

"No, he's not," Sara murmured, smiling. "But Mr. Cameron doesn't have any family left, and neither do I. So we said we'd take care of each other if one of us got sick."

"The boss said that?" Tony asked, his dark eyebrows arching.

The nurse frowned. "How can you be deaf with ears like that?" she wondered.

Tony glared at her. "I am not deaf."

"I should think not," she agreed, paying deliberate attention to his large ears.

"Listen, I may have big ears, but you've got a big mouth," he shot right back.

The pert little brunette gave him a gimlet stare. "The better to bite you with, my dear," she drawled. "You've been warned."

She wiggled her eyebrows at him before she turned back to Sara. "If you need me, just call. I'm on until midnight."

"Thanks," Sara told her.

She winked, gave the bodyguard a glance and waltzed out of the room.

Tony made a rough sound in his throat. "My ears are not big," he muttered.

Sara wouldn't have dared disagree.

He glowered. "People are supposed to be nice to you in hospitals."

"Only when you're sick," Sara told him, smiling. "Thanks, Tony," she said as the pain began to diminish, just a little.

"No problem."

"Where's Mr. Cameron?"

"He had a phone call to return," he said, and looked worried.

"Do you go everywhere with him?"

"Well, not everywhere," he replied. "He gets antsy if I follow him into the restroom."

"I never knew anybody who had a bodyguard," she told him. She moved drowsily. "In fact, I never knew a bodyguard."

"First time for everything," he said, and he smiled.

She smiled back. He'd looked frightening the first time she saw him, standing beside Jared's truck outside the bookstore. But now he was starting to resemble a big teddy bear. She closed her eyes and went to sleep, but not before she heard a soft, deep chuckle. She'd said it aloud.

Jared walked in with a scowl, pausing to stare at Sara, who was fast asleep. "Did they give her something for pain?" he asked Tony.

The big man nodded. He wasn't smiling now. He looked both intelligent and dangerous. "Is something going on?"

Jared looked toward the door, paused to push it shut and

put his cell phone away. "Max thinks they may have tracked me here."

"That isn't good," Tony replied.

"We expected it," Jared reminded him. "We'll have to be extravigilant is all. I told the foreman to put a man with a rifle at the front gate and keep him there, even if he has to have catered meals." He cursed under his breath. "I hate hiding out," he said harshly. "If they'd let me do what I please, we could have handled this on our own, and more efficiently. They're going to protect me to death!"

"Not here," Tony said slowly. "You know they're doing the best they can. Meanwhile, this is the best place to be."

Jared let out a long breath. "It's the waiting."

Tony nodded. He glanced toward the bed. "What about her?" he asked. "She isn't going to be in the line of fire, is she?"

The other man stuck his hands in his pockets and looked stern. "She hasn't got anybody else."

"Yes, but she has no idea what's going on. She could become a target."

Jared glared at him. "Then you'll just have to call in a marker and get some backup, won't you?"

Tony sighed. "I gave up a hot tub and HD TV to come down here."

The glare got worse. "Don't blame me. I was willing to come alone. Your *boss* decided I needed baby-sitting," Jared said irritably.

"My boss was right," Tony replied. He shrugged. "I guess I can live without the hot tub for a few weeks."

Jared put a hand on his shoulder. "Sure you can. You need to reread Sun Tzu."

"I can quote it verbatim," Tony told him. "This isn't my first job."

Jared chuckled. "No. Of course it's not." He stared back at Sara. "We can't let them hurt her."

"We won't," Tony replied. "I promise."

Jared relaxed a little. But just a little.

Sara woke up and it was dark again. She'd slept for a long time. She looked around curiously. She was alone, but there was a cowboy hat occupying the seat beside her bed. It looked familiar.

The door opened, and Harley Fowler walked in, carrying a foam cup of coffee. "You're awake," he exclaimed, smiling.

"Hi, Harley," she replied, returning the smile. "Nice of you to come check up on me."

"I had tonight free."

"No date?" she asked with mock surprise as he moved his hat and sat down.

He chuckled. "Not tonight."

"No exciting missions, either?" she teased, recalling that he'd helped some of the local mercs shut down a drug dealer two years before.

"Interesting that you should mention that," he replied, his eyes twinkling. "We've had word that the drug cartel has re-organized again and been taken over by a new group. We don't know who they are. But there's some buzz that we may have trouble here before long."

"That's not encouraging," she said.

"I know." He sipped coffee. He looked somber. "Two DEA agents bought it on the border this week. Execution-style. Cobb's fuming. My boss is calling in contacts for a confab." His boss was Cy Parks, one of the small town's retired professional soldiers.

Cobb was Alexander Cobb, a senior Houston DEA agent who lived in Jacobsville with his wife and sister.

"Does anybody know who the new people are?"

He shook his head. "We can't find out anything. We think somebody's gone undercover in the organization, but we can't verify it. It's unsettling to have drug dealers who'll pop a cap on cops. They killed a reporter, too, and a member of the Border Patrol."

She whistled softly. "They're arrogant."

He nodded. "Dangerous," he said. "There's something worse. They're kidnapping rich Americans for ransom, to increase their cash flow reserves. They got an heiress last week. Her people are scrambling to meet the deadline, without knowing for sure if they'll return her even so."

She moved restlessly on the pillow. She was sore, but the pain was better. "Aren't most kidnap victims killed in the first twenty-four hours?"

"I don't know, honestly," he said. "Cash Grier is working with the FBI, trying to get informants who might know something about the heiress."

"Our police chief?" she asked

He grinned. "Like a lot of our local citizens, he's not quite what he seems."

"Oh."

He stretched. "Mr. Parks had me working on our tractor all day. I'm stiff. I guess I'm getting old."

She laughed. "No, you aren't, Harley."

He leaned forward with the cup in both hands. "I heard you had a close call," he said.

"I didn't know I had an appendix until yesterday," she said wistfully. "They brought me in by ambulance."

"What about Morris?"

"Mr. Danzetta fed him for me," she said complacently.

"Cameron's bodyguard?" He looked strange.

"What is it?" she asked curiously.

"One of our cowboys was driving past your house last night and saw lights on inside. He knew you were here, so he called the sheriff's department."

"And?"

"When they got there, the lights were off, the doors were all locked and there was nobody around."

She pursed her lips, wondering.

"Did you give the bodyguard a key?" he persisted.

She hesitated. "Well…"

Before she could speak, the door opened and Jared walked in. He stopped when he saw Harley and his eyes began to glitter.

Harley had great reflexes. He exercised them by getting out of the chair, wishing Sara well, promising to check on her later. He walked out with a nod to Cameron. He passed by Tony, who didn't say a word.

"You had company," Jared said quietly.

She wondered what he was thinking. His face gave little away. "Harley came to tell me about my house."

He frowned. "What about your house?"

"He said one of the Parks cowboys saw lights on inside and knew I wasn't there, so he called the sheriff," she began. "But when the deputy got there, all the lights were out and nobody was anywhere around."

He managed to look innocent. "How odd."

He looked too innocent. She frowned. "I didn't give Mr. Danzetta a key to my house, so how did he get in to feed Morris?"

He sat down in the chair beside the bed, looking thoughtful for a minute. "Tony has some, shall we say, unexpected skills."

"Like breaking and entering?" she probed with a grin.

"This is a conversation we shouldn't have right now," he replied with a quiet smile.

Her eyebrows lifted. "Is he wanted by the law?" she asked, keeping her voice low so that Tony wouldn't overhear her.

"Only in two countries," he said absently. "Or was it three?"

She looked shocked.

He scowled at her. "I'm kidding!"

She relaxed. "Okay," she said. "That's a relief."

Outside the door, a tall, dark-eyed man was chuckling silently.

"I talked to Dr. Coltrain," Jared said. "He told me if you're still improving like this, you can be released Monday."

She grimaced. "I'll miss work." Her eyes widened. "Oh, gosh. Dee! I didn't even phone her…!"

"I did," Jared said lazily. "She's coming to see you tonight."

"Thanks," she told him.

"She already knew, of course," he added ruefully. "It's amazing how gossip gets around here."

"We're a very small town," she reminded him.

"You're a very large family," he contradicted. "I've never lived in a place where people knew so much about each other."

She smiled. "I know. I love it here. I can't imagine living anywhere else."

"Well, you'll be living with me for a few days," he replied, crossing his long legs. "My attorney's coming down Monday, so we'll be chaperoned. Less gossip."

"Does your attorney come to stay?"

"Only when I have legal matters to discuss," he said easily. "I've had the same attorney for two years."

She was picturing a tall lawyer like Blake Kemp. Jared must be very well-to-do if he could get a live-in attorney, she was thinking.

"Don't mention anything about Tony feeding your cat, okay?" he asked abruptly. "I don't want the police asking any embarrassing questions. I need Tony."

"Of course I won't," she agreed, but she couldn't help wondering what all the secrecy was about.

"I can't stay long tonight," he said apologetically. "I'm trying to do business by phone, fax and modem, and it's damned hard."

Her eyes were curious. "Where do you live when you're not here?"

He smiled. "That's need-to-know. You don't."

"Well!" she exclaimed. "What a lot of cloak-and-dagger stuff!"

"You have no idea," he replied absently.

The door opened. Tony came in, flipping his phone shut. "Max needs to talk to you again. It's going to take a while."

"We'll go home." He got up, pausing to smile down at Sara. "Get better. I'll be back in the morning."

"Thanks," she said.

He shrugged. "We're family."

He went out with Tony and closed the door behind him.

Max was not happy to learn that Jared was keeping company with some sick girl in the little hick town.

"You need your head read," she muttered on the phone. "You've got enough problems without adding a penniless, clinging cowgirl to them."

"She's not a cowgirl," he replied. "She sells books."

"An egghead isn't much better," she scoffed. "They want you to come back out here and let them give you around-the-clock security."

"We'll never catch the perpetrators if we hide in a fortress," he said. "And we've had this damned argument before!"

"Somebody's getting testy," she purred. "No pillow talk down there, I guess?"

"What do you want?" he interrupted.

She hesitated. "I wanted to tell you that they've tracked three men as far as San Antonio. We're not sure if they're connected to the other, or not, but they're the right nationality."

"What's their cover?"

"How should I know?" she muttered.

"I pay you to know everything," he countered.

"Oh, all right, I'll ask questions. Honestly, Jared, you're getting to be a grouch. What's this girl doing to you?"

"Nothing," he said tersely. "She's just a friend."

"You're spending a lot of time at the hospital."

"Neither of us has family," he said absently. "We decided we'd look after each other if we got sick."

The pause was heated. "You know I'd take care of you if you got sick! I'd have doctors and nurses all over the place."

Of course she would, he thought. She'd hire people to care for him, but she wouldn't do it herself. Max hated illness.

"I'm tired and I've got a lot of work to do."

"I'm flying down there Monday," she told him. "I'll bring some contracts for you to look over. Need anything from the big city?"

"Nothing at all. I'll talk to you later."

"Okay. Sleep well."

"Sure." He hung up. Max was possessive of him. He hadn't noticed it before, and he didn't like it. She was sleek, elegant, aggressive and intelligent. But she did nothing for him physically. He did have occasional liaisons, but never with Max. He hoped she wasn't going to come down to Texas and upset things. He knew that she wasn't going to like Sara. Not at all.

Monday morning, Sara was on the mend. Dee had come twice, on Friday night and Sunday afternoon, bearing baskets of flowers and magazines for Sara to read. She absolutely forbade her to come back to work until the end of the next week. That made Sara feel a little better. She knew Dee was shorthanded when she wasn't there.

Jared had been back to visit, staying for a few minutes at

a time, with Tony always in the background. She wondered why he needed a full-time bodyguard. He changed the subject every time she asked.

Dr. Coltrain released her after lunch. She was wheeled out to the hospital entrance, where Jared was waiting in the big black pickup truck. He bent and lifted her like a sack of flour, putting her gently into the passenger seat and belting her in.

She didn't expect the sudden rush of breath that escaped her lips when he paused in the act of fastening the seat belt and looked straight into her eyes at point-blank range. She felt the world shift ten degrees. His eyes narrowed and dropped to her blouse.

It didn't take an expert to realize that he saw her heartbeat shaking the fabric and knew that she was attracted to him.

"Well, well," he murmured in a deep, sultry tone. And he smiled.

Five

Jared's green eyes burned into Sara's, probing and testing. They dropped to her full mouth and lingered there until she caught her breath audibly. He only chuckled. It had a vaguely predatory sound.

He went around to his own side of the truck, climbed in, fastened his seat belt and started the engine. He was still smiling when he pulled out of the hospital parking lot.

Sara had liked the White Horse Ranch from her first close-up look at it, the first time she'd delivered Jared's books to him. She admired the sprawling white ranch house with its hanging baskets of flowers and the white wooden fences that surrounded a well-manicured pasture. Jared ran purebred Santa Gertrudis cattle here, not horses. Sara enjoyed watching the calves. Pastures were full of them in spring, just in time for the lush new grass to pop up. Or, at least, that would have been the case if the drought hadn't hit this part of Texas so hard.

"How do you have green grass in a drought?" she asked suddenly.

He smiled. "I sank wells and filled up tanks in every pasture," he replied, using the Texas term for small ponds.

"Not bad," she remarked. "Do those windmills pump it?" she added, nodding toward two of them—one near the barn and another far out on the horizon.

He glanced at her amusedly. "Yes. It may be an old-fashioned idea, but it was good enough for the pioneers who settled this country."

"Your grandfather, was he born here?"

He shook his head. "One of his distant cousins inherited a piece of property and left it to him. He ranched for a while, until his health got bad." His face seemed to harden. "He took a hard fall from a bucking horse and hit his head on a fence. He was never quite right afterward. He put a manager in charge of the ranch and moved up to Houston with his wife. One summer day, he shot my grandmother with a double-barreled shotgun and then turned it on himself."

Her gasp was audible.

He noted her surprise. "My father brought him down here to be buried, although nobody knew how he died. None of the family ever came back here after that," he said. "I guess we all have something in the past that haunts us. I shouldn't have been so blunt about it," he added, when he realized that she was upset. "I forget that you grew up in a small town, sheltered from violence."

Obviously he considered her a lightweight, she mused. But it was too soon for some discussions. "It's all right."

He pulled up in front of the house, cut the engine and went around to pick Sara up in his strong arms and carry her up the three wide steps to the front porch. He grinned at her surprise.

"Coltrain's nurse said to keep you off your feet for another day," he mused, looking down into her wide, soft green eyes.

"So you're becoming public transportation?" she teased, and her smile made her whole face radiant.

It made her look beautiful. He was captivated by the feel of her soft, warm little body in his arms, pressed close to his chest. He loved that smile that reminded him of a warm fire in winter. He liked the surge of excitement that ran through his hard body at the proximity. His eyes narrowed and the smile faded as he held her attention.

"Listen, don't you get any odd ideas," she cautioned with breathless humor. "He didn't do that buttonhole surgery, he split me open at least six inches and sewed me back up with those stitches that you don't have to take out later. We wouldn't want my guts to spill out all over your nice clean floor, now, would we?"

The comment, so unexpected, caused him to burst out laughing.

"Good God!" he chuckled. He bent and brushed his hard mouth over her lips in a whisper of sensation that caused her entire body to clench. It was a rush of sensation so overwhelming that she felt her breath catch in her throat.

His eyebrows arched at her response. He pursed his lips and his green eyes twinkled. "What a reaction," he murmured deeply. "And I barely touched you." The twinkle faded. "Suppose we try that again…?"

She started to give him ten good reasons why he shouldn't, but it was already too late.

His hard mouth crushed down onto her soft lips, parting them in a sensuous, insistent way that took her breath away. Her eyes closed helplessly. Her cold hands slid farther around his neck as his arm contracted and flattened her soft breasts against the wall of his chest. The kiss grew demanding.

"Open your mouth," he bit off against her bruised lips.

She tried to answer that audacious command, but it gave him the opening he was looking for, and he took it. His tongue moved deep into her mouth, accompanied by a groan that sounded agonized.

He felt her shiver in his arms. His mouth roughened for an instant until he realized that she was just out of the hospital, and her side hadn't healed. He lifted his head. His eyes were blazing. His face was set, solemn, his gaze intent on her flushed skin.

"Wh…why?" she faltered, all eyes.

An odd expression crept over his face. "When you smile, the emptiness goes away," he said in a rough whisper.

She didn't know how to answer that. But she didn't have to. The door opened suddenly, revealing a tall, very attractive brunette in a blue business suit with a short skirt that stopped halfway between her knees and her panty line.

The brunette raised an eyebrow at the sight of Jared with Sara in his arms, and she didn't smile. "Didn't you expect me, darling?" she asked Jared in a honey-smooth tone.

Jared was still collecting his senses. "Max, this is Sara Dobbs. Sara, Max Carlton, my attorney."

Sara had never seen an attorney who looked like that. The woman could have posed for a fashion magazine. She was sophisticated, beautiful and world-wise. Sara felt like a small child trying to play with adults.

"I have to get Sara to bed. Where's Tony?"

Max shrugged. "I haven't seen him. We have several contracts to go over."

"We'll get to them later," Jared said, with an edge to his tone.

"Suit yourself, it's only money. I like the house."

The lawyer had yet to say one word to Sara. Jared noticed, and his irritation was obvious.

"Sara, you said?" Max asked, smiling at the woman in his arms. "Is something wrong with your leg?"

"She just had an emergency appendectomy and there's nobody at her house to look after her while she heals," Jared said shortly, turning toward one of the downstairs guest bedrooms.

"I see. Well, I'm sure you'll feel better soon," she told Sara as Jared carried her down the hall.

Jared ignored her. He turned into a pretty blue-themed bedroom with its own private bathroom and eased Sara down on the quilted coverlet.

He leaned over her, his big hands on either side of her head, and looked straight into her eyes. "Max is my lawyer. That's all she's ever been."

"She likes you," Sara replied.

His green eyes narrowed. "She likes my money."

"She's pretty."

He bent and brushed his mouth softly over her lips, smiling as they parted for him now. "So are you," he whispered, standing up straight. "I have to sign some contracts for Max. I'll be back in a few minutes. TV control's on the bedside table," he indicated. "We have pay-per-view. Help yourself. I'll have Mrs. Lewis bring you something to eat in a little while."

"Mrs. Lewis? I thought she worked for the Hart brothers."

"She did, but she had to retire just recently from doing heavy housework. Her arthritis got steadily worse and she had to leave them. But her doctor found a new drug that works. She still can't do heavy work, but she cooks for me three days a week."

She studied him curiously. "What do you do the other four days?"

He grinned. "I eat Italian."

"We don't have an Italian restaurant," she began.

"Tony the Dancer can cook," he told her. "He makes the best lasagna I've ever eaten."

She laughed. "He doesn't look like a cook."

"He doesn't look like a lot of things. Amuse yourself until I get Max out of here. I'll be back soon."

"Okay."

He winked at her and closed the door on his way out.

"Are you out of your mind?" Max raged. "The girl's poor! She's just after your money!"

He slid his hands deep into his pockets and glared back at her. "And you discovered that after exchanging two sentences with her, did you?"

Her lips tautened. "You can't get involved with the locals, Jared. You know that, and you know why."

He cocked his head and stared at her intently. "Why are you here?" he asked abruptly. "I can sign contracts at your office in Oklahoma City if I have to. I can't think of a single good reason for you to be underfoot."

Her eyes avoided his. "You're vulnerable right now. You might get involved with someone you'd walk away from if things were normal."

"I pay you a king's ransom of a retainer to look out for my business interests," he said, emphasizing the business. "You start poking your nose into my private life and I'll replace you with a man. After," he added deliberately, "I send a letter of explanation to the Oklahoma Bar Association."

Her anger was gone at once. She pulled herself together. "You're right, I was out of line."

"What contracts are we discussing, then?"

She seemed oddly disoriented. One hand went to her temple and she frowned. "You know, I can't remember."

"Then why don't you go back to your office and think about it?" he suggested.

She sighed. "Okay. But it's still not good sense to trust people you don't know too far," she added.

He didn't reply.

She went into the living room and picked up her attaché case. She laughed self-consciously. "I really just wanted to see how you were," she confessed.

"I'm fine."

"Take care of yourself."

He didn't answer that statement, either. He just stared at her with dark, brooding eyes until she went toward the front door.

"You'll call, if you need anything?" she asked at the door.

"If I need legal advice," he emphasized, "I will."

She grimaced. The door closed firmly behind her.

Jared stared into space as he wondered how he'd missed that possessiveness in Max. Had it been there all along, or was it just starting? She knew he didn't want involvement. He'd said so. Why had she come? Had she been checking up on him and found out about Sara?

He turned toward his study, still deep in thought. She did have a point, about Sara. He knew almost nothing about her.

Tony the Dancer came in with a bag of groceries. He paused at the open study door.

"I met a stretch limo on my way back," he told Jared. "Was it Max?"

He nodded.

"What was she doing here?" he asked.

"God knows," Jared replied curtly. "Warning me off Sara, I guess."

"I thought it would come to that," Tony mused. "Max

likes to live high, and she doesn't make quite enough to suit her tastes."

"Obviously. Her office had better be paying for that limo," he added. "I'm not picking up the tab."

"You should tell Arthur," the other man advised, naming the elderly accountant who lived in and took care of the accounts.

"I will. You cooking?"

"Unless you want to try again," Tony said warily. "I'm still trying to scrape the scrambled eggs off that iron skillet."

"You didn't say I had to grease it first," he growled.

Tony just shook his head. "How's the kid?" he asked, nodding toward the hall.

"She's a grown woman," Jared countered. "She's fine."

Grown woman? Tony wondered if his employer really thought that innocent in his spare bed was fair game. She put on a good front with Jared, but Tony could see through the camouflage, and he knew things that his boss didn't. He wondered if he should mention what he knew to the other man, but the phone rang and Jared picked up the receiver. Tony thought it must be fate, and he went off into the kitchen to cook.

Sara fussed when Mrs. Lewis had to come all that way to serve her a bowl of soup and a salad.

"I can walk, honestly," she protested gently. "You don't have to wait on me."

Mrs. Lewis just grinned as she slid the tray onto Sara's lap. "It isn't any trouble, dear. Tony will pick this up. I have to get back home. My sister's coming over to visit." She chuckled. "Tony's making supper for you and the boss tonight. He walked in with enough Italian sausage and tomato sauce to float a battleship."

Now Sara remembered that Tony cooked Italian dishes for

his boss. The big man didn't look like anybody's idea of a chef. She said as much to the older woman.

Mrs. Lewis raised an eyebrow. "Mr. Danzetta is in a class of his own as a cook. I can do basic meals, but he has a flair for improvising. He saved me a plate of spaghetti just after I came to work here. It was the best I ever tasted."

"I never thought of a bodyguard as being a cook," Sara commented.

The older woman glanced at the open door and moved a little closer. "He wears an automatic pistol under his jacket," she said softly. "I watched out the kitchen window while he was practicing with it. He stuck pennies in clothespins and strung the clothespins on an old wire that was used for a clothesline years ago. And in a heartbeat," she added, "he'd picked off the pennies without touching the clothespins."

Sara's eyes grew wide. "I'm going to make sure that I never tick him off," she murmured aloud.

"He's pretty handy with martial arts, too," Mrs. Lewis added. "He spars with Mr. Cameron."

She hesitated with the soup halfway to her mouth in a spoon. "Mr. Cameron does martial arts?"

Mrs. Lewis nodded. "Tony said he'd never met a man he couldn't throw until he started working here."

"And here I thought Mr. Cameron hired Tony because he didn't want to get his hands dirty."

"Tony isn't quite what he seems," the older woman said quietly. "And neither is his boss. They're both very secretive. And they know Cy Parks and Eb Scott."

That was interesting, because Cy and Eb were part of a group of professional soldiers who'd fought all over the world. Several of the old group lived either in Jacobs County or in Houston and San Antonio.

"Well, that sounds very mysterious, doesn't it?" Sara

murmured as she sipped the hot liquid. "This is wonderful soup, Mrs. Lewis. I can't make potato soup, but I love to eat it."

The older woman beamed. "I'm glad you like it."

Sara paused, thinking. "Mr. Cameron was in a huddle with Chief Grier at the symphony concert," she recalled. "They looked very solemn."

"Gossip says that a new group is trying to establish a drug smuggling network through here again."

"That might explain the serious faces," Sara replied. "Our police chief has solved a lot of drug cases, and made a lot of enemies to go with them."

"Good for him," Mrs. Lewis responded. "I hope they lock them all up."

Sara grinned. "Me, too." She shifted and groaned, touching her stomach under the floppy blouse she was wearing with jeans. "How can a little thing like an appendix cause so much trouble?" she wondered.

"You're lucky you were able to get to a phone," the older woman said gently. "People have died of appendicitis."

Sara nodded. She looked around the pretty blue room. "Mr. Cameron and I agreed that we'd be each others' families when we got sick, but I never expected to take him up on the offer this soon."

"He's a surprising person, isn't he?" she asked. "He seems so cold and distant when you meet him. But he's not like that at all when you get to know him. You wouldn't believe what he did to Mr. Danzetta…"

"And you can stop right there while you still have work," Jared said from the doorway. He sounded stern, but his eyes were twinkling.

Mrs. Lewis made a face at him. "I was only humanizing you for Sara, so she wouldn't think you were really an ogre…" She stopped and clapped a hand over her mouth and blushed.

"It's all right," Sara assured her between mouthfuls of soup. "I did used to call him an ogre, but he improves on closer acquaintance." She grinned at Jared.

He pursed his lips and looked pointedly at her mouth. She almost dropped her spoon, and he laughed softly.

"Well, if you don't need me for anything else, I'm going home," Mrs. Lewis told him. "Mr. Danzetta's got stuff to make supper."

"I saw the sack full of tomatoes and tomato sauce," Jared replied. "He's planted tomatoes out behind the house in what used to be a kitchen garden. Tomatoes, oregano, chives, sage and about twenty other spices I never heard of."

"He doesn't look like a gardener," Sara commented.

Jared didn't answer her. She didn't need to know about Tony just yet.

"He planted poppies in the flower garden," Mrs. Lewis said with obvious concern.

"He likes flowers," Jared began.

"You don't understand," Mrs. Lewis persisted. "He didn't plant California poppies. He planted the other kind."

He frowned. "What's your point?"

"We're barely inside the city limits," she said, "but the fact is, we are inside them. When they begin to bloom, Chief Grier will send one of his officers out here to pull them up."

Jared didn't mention that he'd like to see anyone do that with Tony watching. "Why?"

"They're opium poppies," Mrs. Lewis emphasized.

He whistled. "I'll bet Tony didn't realize it."

"Better tell him," Mrs. Lewis replied. "Before he gets in trouble with the law."

He was going to say that it was way too late for that, but he didn't dare. "I'll talk to him," he said.

"I'll see you tomorrow, then. Get better, dear," Mrs. Lewis added with a smile for Sara.

"I heal fast," Sara replied, grinning. "Thanks."

Jared went out to make some phone calls and Sara finished her soup and dozed off. When she opened her eyes again, it was getting dark outside. She hadn't thought about night-clothes, but it was obvious now that she'd arrived with only her purse and the clothes she'd had on when they transported her to the hospital. She didn't have anything to sleep in.

There was a wonderful smell of spices drifting down the hall. Seconds later, Tony stuck his head in the door.

"You like spaghetti?" he asked.

"I love it," she replied, smiling.

He smiled back. "I'm just about to take up the pasta," he said. "It fell off the wall when I threw it there, so it's got about two minutes left before it's al dente."

"Al who?" she asked.

He glowered at her. "Al dente," he repeated. "Just right for the teeth. When you throw it at the wall and it sticks, it's just right to..."

"What the hell have you done to my kitchen wall?" came a roar from down the hall.

"I have to check that the pasta's ready!" Tony called to him.

Jared stomped down the hall, glaring at his bodyguard. "You've got streaks all over the damned paint!"

"They wipe off, boss," Tony assured him. "Honest."

"You couldn't just stick a strand of it in your mouth and chew it to see if it's ready?" Jared grumbled.

Tony's eyebrows arched. "Who bit you?" he asked.

Jared's face was like iron. He looked furious. "The bread's burning."

Tony rushed back down the hall without another word.

Jared glared at Sara. "Harley Fowler's in the living room. He stopped by to see about you."

"That's nice of him."

"Nice." His green eyes were glaring. "I don't have time to run a hospital complete with visiting hours," he muttered.

She flushed with embarrassment. She hadn't expected Harley to come looking for her.

Jared backstepped at her expression. She'd just had surgery and he was acting like a jealous boyfriend. He caught himself and tried to relax. It didn't work. Harley was poaching on his preserves. "I'll send him in. Don't encourage him to stay long or drop in unexpectedly again without calling first."

"I won't," she began, but he was already halfway down the hall before she got the words out. She felt terrible. She was imposing on him. She should never have suggested that they take care of each other when they got sick. It was apparent that Jared already regretted agreeing to it.

Harley didn't look much better than Sara did. His lips were compressed and he was carrying his wide-brimmed Western straw hat.

"How're you doing?" he asked.

She sighed. "I'm feeling much better," she said.

"You don't look it. Why don't I phone Lisa and see if you can stay with her and Cy until you're back on your feet?" he suggested.

"I really don't need looking after," she replied. She felt uneasy. "Harley, do you think you could drive me to my house?" she added in a low voice.

He scowled. "You're not well enough to look after yourself, Sara. You won't even be able to lift a gallon of milk until that incision heals."

"I don't drink milk and I want to go home." She pulled herself off the bed, grimacing because it hurt. Jared had her pain capsules, but she'd be damned if she was going to ask him for them. It was clear that he didn't want her here.

She moved to the foot of the bed. She'd forgotten that Jared had carried her down the hall. Walking it was going to be an ordeal, and she didn't dare ask Harley to carry her, although she knew he would if she asked.

Harley's arm shot out and caught her as she began to weave. "Here, you're not able to do this, Sara," he said firmly.

"What the hell are you doing?"

Jared walked right around Harley, picked Sara up and put her back in the bed. "Stay there," he said shortly.

She flushed again. "I will not! I just asked Harley to drive me home."

Jared felt his height decrease. "You're not able to stay by yourself yet."

"I am so," she retorted.

Jared glared at Harley as if the whole thing was his fault.

"You'll take her out of this house over my dead body," Jared told the younger man. He said it very softly, but it was a threat. Harley had seen eyes like that over the barrel of a gun. The hair on the back of his neck stood up.

"I'm in the way here," Sara interrupted, sitting up. She winced and held her incision with her fingertips. "I've got frozen TV dinners and I need to get back and take care of Morris, anyway!"

"I fed the cat today," Tony the Dancer said from the doorway. He was wearing a huge white apron and holding a slotted spoon. He frowned. "Something wrong here?" he queried when he tallied up the taut faces.

"She's trying to escape," Jared muttered.

"Hey, don't you listen to him," Tony said firmly, pointing the spoon at Jared. "It was only the one time I dropped baking soda in the sauce by accident. This sauce is perfect. You don't need to run away on account of my cooking."

"You cook?" Harley exclaimed, looking at the tall, muscular man with the olive complexion and wavy black hair in a ponytail. He looked as dangerous as Jared Cameron. And Harley had reason to know what dangerous men looked like.

Tony glared at him. "Yeah. I cook. What's it to you?"

Harley actually moved back a step. "Nothing at all!"

"Lots of men cook," Tony said belligerently. He glanced back at Sara and frowned. She was near tears and she wouldn't look at Jared. Tony's threatening expression melted into concern. He moved to the side of the bed. "I made you a nice apple strudel for dessert," he coaxed, "with freshly whipped cream."

She bit her lower lip. "You're so nice, Tony," she said, trying to sound normal even as her lower lip quivered.

"Here, hold this." Tony put the spoon in Jared's hand and sat down beside Sara, tugging her gently against him so that he wouldn't hurt her. A hand the size of a ham rested against her back, covering almost half of it comfortably as he drew her head to his broad shoulder. "Now, now, it's all right," he said softly.

She bawled. Jared and Harley glared daggers at the big man, but neither of them said a word.

Harley shifted on his feet. "Sara, I've got to get back home. You call me if you need anything, okay?" he added with a speaking glance at Jared.

"I will," Sara said in a thin, sad voice. "Thanks."

"No problem. See you."

He hated leaving her, but the whole situation was getting out of hand. That big fellow who cooked wasn't going to let Jared Cameron hurt Sara in any way. Harley knew she'd be safe, or he wouldn't have budged.

Jared walked out of the room behind him, totally disgusted, still carrying the spoon.

Six

Tony tugged a tissue from the box on the bedside table and dabbed it against Sara's wet eyes.

"Now you stop that," he said, smiling gently. "The boss has a nasty temper and he doesn't always choose his words before he opens his mouth. But he never would have asked you to come here if he hadn't wanted to."

She looked up at him from swollen red eyes. "He was awful to Harley."

Tony grimaced. "There's stuff going on that you don't know about," he said after a minute. "I can't tell you what it is. But it doesn't help his temper."

She blew her nose. "I'm sorry."

"What for? Everybody cries," he replied. "I bawled like a kid when my sister died."

Her green eyes met his black ones. "Was it very long ago?"

"Ten years," he said. "Our mother was still alive then. We lost our dad when we were just little kids."

"I lost my grandad a little while ago," she replied. "I still miss him. He taught history at our local college."

"I like history," he said. He would have liked to tell her that he'd minored in it during his college years, but it wasn't the time for heart-to-heart talks. The boss was already gunning for him because he'd opened the door and let Harley inside.

"How long have you worked for Jared?" she asked.

"Seems like forever, sometimes," he chuckled. "On and off, for about six years, I suppose," he said.

"You know, he really doesn't look like the sort of man who'd need a bodyguard," she ventured.

"He doesn't, does he?" he agreed. "You feel better now?"

She smiled at him with her eyes still red and swollen. "I'm better. Thanks, Tony."

He stood up, and he was smiling now, too. "You're a lot like her. My sister, I mean. She had a big heart. She loved people. She was always giving." His dark eyes grew haunted, especially when he looked at Sara. "Don't you let him push you into anything," he said out of the blue.

She was shocked, and showed it. "What do you mean?"

His black eyes narrowed. "You know what I mean. He's been around the world. You're just a sprout."

"Yes, but I can take care of myself," she assured him. "Nobody will make me do something I don't want to do."

"That's just what my sister said," he told her, and he looked down at his apron. "I'd better get back in there and rescue my sauce. You need anything?"

She shook her head. "But, thanks."

He grinned. "Goes with the job."

If she could have walked, she'd have gone home. She was hurt by Jared's sarcasm and she felt unwelcome. It was going to be an ordeal to get through the next couple of days. She wished she'd never become friendly with him. One thing was for sure. If she ever got sick or hurt again, she wouldn't turn to him for help.

He walked in a short time later with a plate of spaghetti and homemade garlic bread. He pulled a rolling table to the bed and put the meal, plus a tall glass of milk, on it.

She was rigid with wounded pride. "Thank you," she said stiffly, and in a subdued tone that betrayed, even more than her posture, how hurt she was.

He stood still, his hands in his pockets, and stared at her. "He's a good cook," he said, just to break the silence.

She put the napkin on her lap and sat sideways on the bed so that she could eat comfortably. It put him at an angle so that she didn't have to look right at him.

"All right, I was out of line," he muttered. "But it's courteous to ask me before you invite people here to see you."

"I didn't invite Harley to come," she said, eating spaghetti in tiny little bites.

He frowned. "You didn't?"

She ate another bite of Tony's delicious concoction, and never tasted a thing.

"People who live in small towns think of everyone as family. It would never occur to Harley that he wasn't welcome to visit a sick friend, no matter who she was staying with."

His eyes kindled. "It's still good manners to ask first."

"Yes," she had to agree. "It is. I'm sure he wishes he had. I know I do."

That was right on target. He felt smaller than ever. She could have died. He'd agreed to take her home and nurse her, and now he was laying down rules and regulations as fast as he could. He didn't like Harley Fowler in his home, in Sara's temporary bedroom. It made him angry. He couldn't tell her that, of course.

He noticed suddenly that she was wearing the same clothes she'd worn to the hospital before her surgery.

"Don't you have a gown, or pajamas?" he asked abruptly.

"There really wasn't time to pack a bag when the ambulance got to my house," she reminded him.

"Point taken."

"If Tony could go by my house and get me some night things," she began.

"No." It came out belligerently. He shouldn't have said that. But he didn't like the idea of Tony, who already treated her like family, poking through her underthings.

"I'll go," he said. "Where's your house key?"

"It's in the zippered compartment in my purse." She indicated it, hanging over the closet doorknob. "Can you make sure Morris has enough water while you're there?" she added, hating even to have to ask. "Tony fed him already, he said, but Morris drinks a lot of water."

He retrieved the key. "I'll take care of him."

"Thanks," she said without meeting his eyes.

He gave her one last look and left her. He'd made a stupid mistake. He hoped he'd have time to make it up to her.

Tony was just clearing away supper when Jared stopped in the kitchen doorway. "I'm going over to Sara's house to get her a few things to wear."

Tony's eyebrows arched. "You know where she lives?"

He cursed mentally. Of course he didn't know where she lived; he'd never been to her house.

"And you can't go alone," the big man added solemnly. "They'd love to catch you out alone at night. They have all the equipment we've got, and more." He took off the apron and tossed it aside. "I'm going with you."

"That will leave Sara here alone," Jared argued.

Tony pointed a device down the hall and locks slid into place audibly. "She wouldn't be any safer in Fort Knox with the alarm systems activated," Tony told his boss. "Besides, I've got Clayton out there with night vision and a Glock."

He relaxed a little. "Okay. Let's go."

Tony paused by the closet on the way out and retrieved his .45 in its shoulder holster. He took just seconds to get it in place before he opened the front door and shepherded his boss out to the truck parked in the circular driveway.

Before they got into it, Tony waved his hand and a tall, shadowy figure approached the car, going over it with electronic devices.

"All clear," the newcomer said.

"Nobody gets in or out while we're gone," Tony told him.

"Yes, sir."

Tony climbed in behind the wheel, letting Jared ride shotgun. The shadowy figure moved back into the darkness beside the house and settled in.

While Jared was gone, the phone started ringing off the hook. Sara waited for Tony to answer it, but he didn't. There didn't seem to be an answering machine, either. She didn't know what to do. The stupid instrument wouldn't stop. Finally, in desperation, she picked up the receiver by her bed.

"Cameron residence," she said, trying to sound like a secretary.

"Where's Jared?" came a biting reply.

Sara didn't have to ask who it was. That strident tone was unforgettable. "I don't know," she said. "Sorry," she added quickly.

There was a pause. "It's the little house guest, isn't it?" the horrible woman purred. "Well, don't get too comfortable. Jared wouldn't give you the time of day if you hadn't appealed to his senses, but it won't last. He has women like some men have cars, and he doesn't want anything permanent. He'll dump you the first time you sleep with him."

"I do not sleep with men!" Sara retorted harshly.

"You don't?" She laughed. "That's what his last lover said, too. She gave in just like all the rest. And he dumped her just as fast."

"What do you want?" Sara asked, trying to be polite when she felt like screaming at the woman.

"What we all want, dear," the other woman laughed. "To have Jared for keeps. But that won't happen. If he wasn't so financially secure, he might be less attractive," she added.

"I know very little about Mr. Cameron," Sara said stiffly. "And I don't think you should talk about him that way. You're supposed to be his lawyer."

"His lawyer, his lover, it's all the same," came the bored reply. "Tell him I called."

She hung up.

Sara felt sick at her stomach. Surely the horrible woman wasn't right? Jared didn't seem like a heartless seducer. But what did she really know about him? Next to nothing. Could he be a ladykiller? Sara felt insecure. She was still very young. She hadn't dated very much and she'd never had to extricate herself from a dangerously intimate situation. She knew instinctively that Jared was experienced. She'd given in to his hard kisses at once. What if he really put on the pressure? Could she save herself in time?

The thought worried her.

She was still gnawing on it when Jared opened the door and came into her bedroom with a large laundry hamper.

Her eyebrows arched. "You brought my dirty clothes back with you?" she exclaimed, aghast.

He glowered at her. "Tony's got your clothes. I brought your cat."

Her heart skipped. He had to be kidding! She sat up on the side of the bed and looked down into the basket. There was old Morris, curled up asleep and purring for all he was worth, on one of her old hand-crocheted afghans.

She looked up at Jared curiously.

"He didn't touch his supper last night. He wouldn't eat today, either. Tony thinks he's worried about you. So we brought him home with us." Gently he lifted the battle-scarred old marmalade tomcat out of the basket and placed him on the bed with Sara.

Morris opened one green eye, butted his head against Sara affectionately, and went right back to sleep.

"Tony's bringing the litter box. We can put it in your bathroom," Jared said disgustedly.

She cuddled Morris while he was in the mood. "He didn't try to bite you…? Oh!"

He displayed a hand liberally covered with colorful plastic bandages.

"I'm really sorry," she began.

"I had an old hunting dog I was fond of," he said gruffly. "He died last month at the age of fourteen years." He shrugged. "They're like family."

She managed a tiny smile. "Yes."

He heard Tony coming down the hall. "I hope we got the right things."

Tony came in grinning and put down a suitcase on the chest at the foot of Sara's bed. "Here's your stuff. I'll bring the litter box when I come back. He's nice, your cat."

"Well, of course you'd think he was nice," Jared muttered. "He didn't sink his fangs into you!"

"He's got good taste," Tony defended himself.

"Good taste the devil, he knows that you've eaten cats!" Jared shot back. "He was probably afraid you'd serve him up for lunch if he bit you!"

Tony, noting Sara's expression, scowled. "It was only one cat," he pointed out. "And we were all starving. It was a very old and very tough cat. Nobody liked it," he added, trying to hit the right note.

Sara was all eyes. "Where were you?" she asked, aghast.

"Somewhere in Malaysia," Tony said easily. "Mostly we ate snakes, but sometimes you got no choice, especially when the snakes can outrun you." He noted Sara's expression and stopped while he was ahead. "I'll just go get that litter box."

"You'd never be able to eat a snake he cooked," Jared muttered when Tony was in the hall. "He can't make anything if it doesn't go well with tomato sauce."

"I heard that!" Tony called back. "And snakes go great with tomato sauce!"

Sara smiled despite the rough time Jared had given her. He and Tony were a great act together. But she sensed undercurrents. And she thought both men were wearing masks, figuratively speaking. She wondered what they hid.

She finished her dinner and Jared still hadn't said another word.

"This was very nice," she said when she finished her last sip of milk and was pushing the rolling cart away from the bed. "Thanks." She eased back onto the bed, grimacing as the stitches pulled, and drew old Morris close to her. "He doesn't move much these days," she said as she stroked the purring old tomcat. "I've never been sure how old he is. I don't think I want to know." She looked up at Jared. "I would have told you that he doesn't like being picked up, if I'd known you planned to bring him over here."

"Well, the minute Tony picked him up he started purring."

She hid a smile. "I'll bet animals follow Tony around."

He thought of a few women he and Tony had come across in their travels. "It isn't just animals," he said thoughtfully.

She stroked Morris again. "Your lawyer called."

He hesitated. "Max?"

She nodded.

"What did she want?"

She was weighing honesty against peace on earth. Peace on earth won. "She just wanted to tell you something. She said she'd call back."

He frowned. "Was that all she said?" he asked with visible suspicion. "No comments about your presence here?"

The blush gave her away.

"I thought so," he said. "She's good at what she does, but she bores easily and she likes new experiences. She can't resist setting her cap at every presentable male client who comes along. She's already gone through three husbands and several lovers."

Including you? she wondered, but she didn't dare say it out loud.

He watched her stroking the cat and it reminded him, for some reason, of his grandmother. "My father's mother loved cats," he recalled. "She had six at one time. Then they began to get old and pass on. The last one she had was a yellow tabby, sort of like Morris. When she died, he stopped eating. We tried everything. Nothing worked. He settled down in the sun without moving and died three days later."

"And they say animals don't feel emotion," she murmured absently.

"Everything feels. Even plants."

She looked up, grinning. "Did you see that show where they put plants in little greenhouses..."

"...They yelled and praised one group, ignored another

group and played classical and rock music to two other groups," he continued, his green eyes twinkling.

"And the plants that grew biggest were the ones bombarded with hard rock."

He chuckled. "If I thought that would work on hay, I'd have loudspeakers set up in the fields." He shook his head. 'First we had drought for a year in Oklahoma, now we're having floods. The weather is no friend to the rancher this year, either."

"Our dry fields could sure use some of your floods," she agreed.

The conversation ended. He was tired and half out of humor. She was getting over surgery.

"You need your rest," he said.

"Thanks," she called after him. "For bringing Morris."

"What's a little blood between friends?" he mused, holding up his scratched hand. "Sleep well."

"You, too."

But she didn't sleep well. She had violent dreams, just as she had as a child. There was something about this house, this atmosphere, that reminded her of all she'd lost. Guns shooting. Men yelling. Fires burning. The plane almost crashing. And then her mother's fury at Grandad, her accusations, her sudden bizarre behavior. The anger and rage in her mother never abated. Sara was left with nobody except Grandad to look after her. Her mother had destroyed herself, in the end. It had started out as a grand adventure with a noble purpose. It ended in bloodshed and death.

Sara pulled Morris closer to her in the big bed, wiping angrily at the tears. She hated going to sleep. She wondered if there would ever be a night when she'd sleep until morning and there would be no more bad dreams.

She touched her head where the faint indentation marked

the most tragic part of her young life. It was under her thick blond hair, and it didn't show. But Sara felt it there. It was a constant reminder of how brief life was, and how dangerous. She thought about it when she looked at Tony Danzetta, but she couldn't understand why.

Finally, just before dawn she drifted off again. When she woke, late in the morning, it was to the realization that she was still wearing her jeans and the blouse. She'd been too preoccupied even to change into a nightgown.

She stayed with Jared for two more days. He seemed to be avoiding her. He didn't have breakfast, lunch or dinner at the table. He was always in his study or out with the cowboys on the ranch. Tony assured her that it was his normal routine, but something in the way Tony said it made her uneasy.

The fourth day after her surgery, she packed up Morris and her suitcase and asked Jared to let Tony take her home. She wasn't completely over the surgery, but she was getting around very well. There was some residual soreness, but she was already feeling better.

Jared didn't hesitate when she asked to go. It wounded her that he could let her walk away without a qualm. But, then, he was a financially secure man, from all appearances, and she was a poor woman. They'd agreed only to be each other's support in times of need, not to make the care permanent.

Sara and Morris settled back into their routine, and she went back to work.

"At least you look a little better," Dee commented, noting the dark circles under Sara's eyes. "I'll bet you didn't sleep a lot at Mr. Cameron's place."

"It was sort of awkward," she admitted. "But I saw a lot more of Tony than I did of Mr. Cameron," she added.

"Tony?"

"The big guy."

"Oh," Dee recalled. "The hit man."

Sara chuckled. "He improves on closer acquaintance," she told her boss. "And Morris let Tony pick him up. He bit Mr. Cameron. Several times." It felt good, remembering that.

"I suppose Morris is a pretty good judge of character, then," Dee said with a grin.

"Now, now," Sara chided. "Mr. Cameron took good care of me while I was getting back on my feet."

Dee grimaced. "I could have taken you home with me," she began guiltily.

"Dee, you have four kids and your mother lives with you and your husband," Sara replied gently. "You couldn't possibly take care of one more person. But thank you for offering. I'm just grateful that I still have a job."

"As if I'd fire you for being sick," the older woman scoffed. "Now don't you do any heavy lifting. I'll do that. You just sit there at the counter and ring up purchases."

"I can do that, at least," Sara replied cheerfully.

It was just before closing time when Harley Fowler turned up. Dee had gone to the bank with the day's receipts while Sara waited for her to come back and lock up.

"Hi, Harley," Sara greeted.

He smiled. "You look lots better," he said. He grimaced. "I know I got you in trouble with Cameron by just walking in to see you. I'm really sorry."

She was stunned. "How did you find out about that?"

"Mrs. Lewis is kin to one of our cowboys. She heard Tony talking about it. I never thought Mr. Cameron would mind. I guess I should have asked first."

"He's an outsider, Harley," she said gently. "He doesn't

know how people behave in small towns. Nobody else would have had a problem."

"I sort of wondered…" he began, and then stopped.

"Wondered?" she prompted.

"If Mr. Cameron might be jealous," he said.

She laughed. "Oh, that would be the day," she chuckled. "A big time rancher jealous of a piddly little clerk in a bookstore. He's got this gorgeous attorney, named Max," she added, trying to sound lighthearted. "She's educated and beautiful and crazy about him."

Harley sighed. "It must be nice to have a little money. I wouldn't know." He leaned on the counter with his forearms. "The Parks are having a barbecue at the ranch Saturday. Lisa said you might want to sketch the pups one more time before they're old enough to adopt. She says they're growing like weeds."

"A barbecue?" she echoed, smiling. "I love barbecue."

"I know," he returned, grinning. "Suppose I come and pick you up about eleven Saturday morning? I know you're still sore and all. I can drive you home whenever you need to go."

"I'd love to go, Harley," she said with genuine affection.

He smiled. She wasn't beautiful, but he liked being with her. "That's a date, then."

"Will there be dancing?" she asked.

"Oh, yes. They hired a Mariachi band to play. I understand there's going to be a major competition between the Caldwells and Cash Grier and his wife. A tango."

"Wow," Sara breathed. "Matt and Leslie were our champions hands down until Cash Grier got out on the dance floor with Christabel Gaines—I mean, Christabel Dunn, but that was before she married Judd. Can Tippy Grier do a tango?"

"Apparently. It's going to be a night to remember." He hesitated. "Your adopted family's invited, too."

"Mr. Cameron?" she asked warily.

"Yes, and the hit man, too."

"Tony is not a hit man," she said, laughing when she realized that it was her own description of him that was making the rounds in town. "I shouldn't have said that."

"He does sort of remind me of a hit man," he replied dryly. "He's big and slow-looking, though. He can't be that good a bodyguard."

Sara had doubts about how slow-moving Tony was. She had the distinct impression that he was quick as lightning and sly like a fox, hiding his light under a barrel. But she didn't say so.

"Saturday at eleven," he repeated.

"Yes." She grinned at him as he waved and went out the door.

Sara pictured the band and Jared Cameron. She wondered if he'd ask her to dance. She wondered if he could dance. It was thrilling to consider.

Harley came for her exactly at eleven. She was wearing a full skirt with a simple white cotton peasant blouse and silver jewelry. She looked like a pixie.

He was in jeans and a clean plaid cotton shirt, Western cut, with polished black boots and a cowboy hat to match.

"You look nice, Sara," he told her. "Are you feeling okay?"

She nodded. "The stitches catch a little when I walk too fast, but I feel fine."

"Can you climb up by yourself?" he added when they reached his pickup truck. It had a running board, but it was higher than a car.

"Sure, I can," she said. She held on to the inside handle over the door facing, put one foot on the running board and pulled herself up and into the passenger seat. It hurt a little, but she didn't let that show. "Piece of cake," she told him, smiling while she fastened her seat belt.

He grinned back. "Then we're off!"

* * *

Cy Parks's ranch was huge, even by Texas standards. The yard was full of tent pavilions complete with oilcloth-covered long tables and benches for people to sit on. The cowboys had barbecued a steer and their wives had prepared huge tubs of baked beans and coleslaw, and there were baking sheets full of homemade rolls and fresh butter. For dessert, there was everything from cakes to pies to soft-serve ice cream. Cy had really pulled out the stops. Across the fences, his Santa Gertrudis cattle grazed peacefully and stared at the crowds of people who'd come to enjoy the food.

All the powerful people in the county had shown up for Parks's legendary barbecue. Even the children were invited. It resembled, more than anything, a family reunion.

"Is that the Coltrains' little boy, Joshua?" Sara exclaimed, indicating a blond-headed little boy in jeans and cotton shirt and boots running from another small boy with dark hair and eyes.

"Yes, and that's J.D. and Fay Langley's little boy, Jon, chasing him."

"They've grown so fast!" she exclaimed.

"They have," he added, smiling at their antics. "Children must be a lot of fun. Their parents seem to dote on them."

"I imagine they do."

She was staring after the little boys when she spotted a familiar face. Jared Cameron was standing by one of the long tables talking to Cy Parks. With him were Tony the Dancer…and the female attorney, Max, standing with Jared's arm around her.

Sara felt as if she'd just walked into a nightmare.

Seven

At the same time Sara spotted him, Jared glanced her way and saw her with Harley Fowler. His green eyes, even at the distance, were blazing.

She averted her eyes and kept walking with Harley to where Lisa was sitting with Gil on her lap. She didn't dare look the way she felt. Jared Cameron had every right to hang out with his gorgeous attorney. It shouldn't have made Sara feel betrayed. But it did. The realization shocked her.

Lisa smiled as they joined her. "Have a seat. I could have left Gil in his playpen, but I don't really like being away from him, even for a few minutes."

"I wouldn't, either," Sara said. "He's a little doll."

Gil smiled at Sara shyly and said, "Pretty."

Sara and Lisa burst out laughing.

"Horsey, Mama, horsey!" Gil demanded, bouncing.

Lisa put him on one knee and bounced him while he laughed happily.

"He's going to be a ladies' man when he grows up," Harley drawled. "He's starting early!"

Lisa laughed. "You may be right. He likes Sara."

"Everybody likes Sara," Harley said smoothly, winking at her.

"Not everybody," Sara murmured as Jared Cameron walked toward them with Max curled close in his arm. He was smiling at Max, but his green eyes shot daggers at Harley and Sara when he came closer.

"Should you be up so soon after major surgery?" Jared demanded, glaring at Sara.

"Major surgery?" Sara gasped. "I had my appendix out! The incision was barely four inches long!"

Jared's eyes narrowed. "It ruptured," he pointed out.

"Why does he get to make comments on your surgery?" Lisa asked innocently.

"Because I took her home with me and Tony and I nursed her back to health," Jared said curtly. "We have a vested interest in her recovery."

"Like it put you out! Tony did all the work!" Sara retorted.

Jared held up his hand with all the plastic bandages on it.

"You didn't try to pick up Morris, did you?" Lisa asked the newcomer.

Jared looked around him, exasperated. "Am I the only person in this town who didn't know that he bites?"

"Looks like it," Harley chuckled.

"I hate cats," Max muttered. "They're scary, and they have fangs, like snakes."

Sara wished the other woman had been around when Morris was staying at Jared's house. She'd have loved watching him stalk the slick lawyer. He loved to attack people who were afraid of cats.

"Hi, Sara," Tony said, thickening his drawl for the group.

He was wearing his suit and his sunglasses, and he looked really big. "You doing okay?"

Sara had gotten used to him being as articulate as Jared in the privacy of the Cameron ranch. Only now did she realize what a compliment he'd paid her by not putting on what was obviously an act for the masses.

"I'm much better, Tony, thanks," she replied, and gave him a genuine smile.

Max was looking more uncomfortable by the minute. "We aren't going to eat outside, are we?" she asked uneasily. "I mean, there are flies!"

"They only land on bad people," Sara promised.

Seconds later, two huge black flies came to rest on Max's arm. She screamed, hitting at them. "Get them off!" she exclaimed.

Tony glanced at Sara and grinned. "Sound familiar?" he teased.

She burst out laughing, remembering her own horror at the yellow hornet that had landed on her shoulder at Jared's house.

But Max thought Sara was laughing at her and, without a pause, she swung her hand and slapped Sara in the face.

There was a sudden silence around them. Cy Parks, who'd been directing the cowboys cooking the beef, strode up to the small group with blood in his eye.

"Are you all right, Sara?" he asked in a menacing tone.

"I'm…fine," Sara replied. She had a huge red mark on one cheek.

Cy turned to Max. "I've never asked a guest to leave my home until now. I want you off my property."

Max fumed. "She laughed at me! I was covered up in flies and she thought it was funny!"

"She was laughing because the same thing happened to her at our place with a yellow hornet," Tony said, and he looked menacing as well. "I reminded her of it."

Max flushed. "Oh."

Jared hadn't said a word until then. But his eyes spoke volumes. "You can apologize to Sara before I take you back to the ranch," he told Max, and he wasn't smiling.

Max backed down at once. "I'm very sorry," she told the younger woman. "I hope I didn't hurt you," she added in a condescending tone.

Cash Grier joined the small group. He wasn't smiling, either. "If you'd like to press charges," he told Sara while he glared down at Max, "I'll be delighted to arrest her for you."

"Arrest me!" Max exclaimed.

"For assault," he replied coldly. "In Jacobsville, you don't strike another person physically unless you've been attacked physically. It's against the law."

"Yeah, you'd think a lawyer would know that, wouldn't you?" Tony put in his two cents' worth.

Max seemed to be suddenly aware of her whereabouts and her vulnerability in this small town. She laughed nervously. "Surely that won't be necessary…?"

Cash looked at Sara. "Sara?" he questioned softly.

Sara took a deep breath and gave Max her best glare. "I won't have you arrested," she said quietly. "But if you ever touch me again, I'll show you how much I learned in Chief Grier's self-defense course last fall."

"It won't happen again," Jared replied. He took Max firmly by the arm. "Thanks for inviting us," he told Cy, "but we have to go."

Tony grimaced. "Yeah. Sorry," he added, smiling at Sara. "That barbecue sure smelled good."

"Can't you stay?" Sara asked Tony gently.

He lit up like a Christmas tree at her tone.

Jared muttered something under his breath and Max protested as his hand tightened bruisingly on her arm.

Tony glanced at his boss and sighed. "No. I got to go, too. See you, Sara."

She smiled. "See you."

The three walked away with stiff backs. Sara could have kicked Max. She'd ruined everything.

"Thanks, Chief Grier," Sara told the town's police chief.

He shrugged. "You were my star pupil," he replied. He grinned. "I wish you'd pressed charges, though. I would have enjoyed locking her up."

"Locking who up?" Tippy Grier asked curiously, joining her husband. The "Georgia Firefly" as she'd been known in modeling circles was still gorgeous, with long reddish-gold hair and green eyes. She smiled at Sara, and then frowned when she saw the red marks on her cheek. "What in the world happened?" she exclaimed.

"Jared Cameron's lawyer hit her," Harley said angrily.

"A man hit you?" Tippy gasped.

"A woman," Sara corrected. "It was because of the flies."

Tippy stared at her, wide-eyed. "Flies. Right."

"No," Sara laughed. "I mean, she thought I was laughing at her because she attracted flies."

"Good riddance, I say," Harley muttered, watching Jared's Jaguar peel out and roar away. "The poor flies will probably drop dead now."

Sara was disappointed, because she'd hoped that she might have a chance to dance with Jared. But she hated herself for the thought. He'd been horrible to her about Harley, and now he'd sided with Max. But Tony had defended her. Sweet Tony.

"Who was the big fella with Jared?" Cash asked curiously.

"Tony the Dancer," Cy answered before Sara could.

Everybody looked at him.

He realized at once what a slip he'd made. "I heard Jared call him that," he said at once.

They still looked at him. He'd used Jared's first name, something he never did with strangers.

He cursed. "Just pretend I didn't say a word, and let's go and eat barbecue," he muttered. He bent to Lisa, smiling, and picked his little son up in his arms.

"Daddy!" Gil enthused, hugging his father around the neck.

The burned arm was still a little weak, but it didn't show. The look on his face as he held the little boy was indescribable.

"Gil's growing," Tippy said, smiling at the child.

"So is our Tris," Cash replied. "She's two now. Rory's twelve. He's crazy about his niece." Rory was Tippy's younger brother.

"Speaking of Tris," Tippy grinned, looking past her husband's shoulder.

Rory had little Tris up in his arms and was carrying her around, laughing. She looked just like her mother, with red hair and green eyes, and she was wearing a pretty little green-patterned cotton dress with white shoes. She was holding on to Rory for all she was worth, talking to him.

Rory, taller now, had dark hair and green eyes, and he obviously doted on the little girl.

"She can walk, you know," Cash told the boy with a smile.

"She likes it when I carry her, though," Rory replied, grinning. "Isn't she just the neatest thing in the world?" he added, kissing the little girl's hair.

"You're spoiling her," Tippy laughed.

Rory shook his head. "No, I'm not. I just carried her away from the ice cream. She talked Randy into giving her a bowl of it, but I made him take it back."

"Wanted ice cream, Rory," Tris pouted. "Bad Rory."

He only chuckled.

Tippy held out her arms for Tris, who got a tighter hold on her uncle. "No!" she said. "Want Rory!"

Cash looked down at his wife musingly. "So there."

She laughed, pressing close against him. "All right, Tris," she told her daughter. "Rory, when your arms get tired, bring her back."

"Okay, sis." He went off toward the fenced pasture where horses were grazing.

Harley excused them and drew Sara along with him to the tables where plates of barbecue and beans and rolls were being served up.

"You sure you're all right?" Harley asked, concerned.

Sara nodded. "It was a shock, that's all."

"I don't like that smarmy lawyer," he muttered darkly. "But she and her boss do suit one another. They're both bad company."

Sara didn't answer him. She was remembering the hard look Jared had given Max. He hadn't liked the woman's reaction to Sara. That was comforting. But her face still stung.

The Latin music played by the Mariachi band had everyone who could walk streaming up onto the wooden dance floor Cy had built for the occasion. Strings of large Japanese lanterns provided light, after the sun went down, and there was a crowd swaying to the rhythm.

Matt Caldwell and his wife, Leslie, were doing a spirited *paso doble* while Cash and Tippy Grier looked on from the sidelines. They exchanged mischievous glances, got up, held hands and moved onto the dance floor.

"Bet you can't do a tango," Cash chided.

Matt gave him a wicked grin. "You lose. Hey, Paco!" he called to the band leader. "Tango!"

The band leader and his band all laughed, stopped playing, measured the rhythm and then sailed into a Tango number that was all fire and passion.

Everybody except the two couples evacuated the dance floor, expecting a real competition.

They got one. It was a duel, and both couples put on their best form for it. As the music built to a crescendo, both couples stopped at the same time, in lingering poses, as the band finished the number.

But it was a draw, as the dancers had figured it would be. They laughed and shook hands as the audience went wild with clapping and cheering.

"Pity we don't have trophies," Cy Parks drawled.

"Next time, we have to have a waltz contest!" Harley called. He'd been studying the dance for months, and he was good at it.

"I learned to waltz in Austria," Cash called to him.

Harley flapped his hand at the police chief.

The music started again, this time a lazy two-step. Just as Harley turned to take Sara onto the dance floor, he was bypassed.

Jared Cameron lifted Sara gently into his arms, carried her onto the wooden dance platform and eased her to the floor.

"My turn," he said softly, and he smiled in a way that made her heart race.

She slid her free arm around his neck and looked up at him with her breath catching in her throat.

Harley, for one instant, thought about separating them. But when he saw Sara's face, he knew it would be almost a betrayal to interfere. Subdued, he went back to the buffet table for a beer.

"I didn't think you'd be back," Sara said to his chest. He was so much taller that her head barely came to his chin.

His big, warm hand contracted around hers. "Didn't you?" He tilted her chin up so that he could see her cheek. "At least it isn't bruised," he added quietly. "I've never wanted so badly to manhandle a woman. Max needs to take some classes in anger management."

"She thought I was laughing at her."

"Tony explained it." His hand tightened. "You keep your

distance from Tony," he added firmly. "He's not what he seems to be. He could hurt you."

"He would never lift a hand to me," she protested at once.

He stopped dancing for an instant and looked down into her wide eyes. "I don't mean physically."

She frowned. "He's very sweet to me."

He started dancing again. "You remind him of his sister."

"Yes. He said she died."

He made a slow turn, one that drew her very close to his hard-muscled body and made her tingle all over. "Tony has issues you're better off not knowing about."

"Cy Parks knows both of you."

"I've lived here several weeks," he said carelessly.

"That isn't what I mean."

He raised an eyebrow. "I've known Cy for a while."

She was really curious now. Most people knew that Cy Parks, Eb Scott and Micah Steele had been professional mercenaries, soldiers of fortune, before they settled down in Jacobsville. She knew next to nothing about Jared Cameron. She wondered what secrets he was keeping.

He saw that curiosity in her eyes and just smiled. "Never you mind," he told her, drawing her closer. "I don't plan to waste the evening with walks down memory lane. I'm much more interested," he added huskily, "in making new memories."

His hand slid gently up and down her spine in sensuous little forays that made her feel boneless. It worried her that she didn't want to protest the near intimacy of his hold. If he ever turned up the heat, she knew she wouldn't be able to resist him. She couldn't help but remember what Max had told her about Jared's easy conquests and his indifference to them afterward.

"I had Tony drive Max to the airport," he said after a minute.

Her heart skipped. "She's gone?"

"Yes. She's gone." He didn't mention the vicious things

Max had to say about Sara and Jared's interest in her, or the threat he used to get her out of town. Tony wasn't too keen on leaving Jared alone while he escorted the lawyer to the airport, either. It had been a battle.

"Is Tony coming over, then?" she asked.

He stiffened. "Yes," he said, but he didn't sound happy about it. "I meant what I said. You don't need to start looking at Tony as a prom date."

"I didn't go to the prom," she said absently. "And it's not your business who I look at. I came with Harley," she added firmly.

He drew back so that he could see her eyes. "And you're going home with me," he said softly.

How she wished that her excitement hadn't shown when he said that. She couldn't walk off with another man when Harley had brought her here. It would have been unthinkable…

"Sara," Harley said from beside them, grimacing, "I've got something to do for the boss. It can't wait."

"I'll drive her home," Jared told the younger man. "No problem."

"Sara, is that all right with you?" Harley asked gently.

She nodded. "It's okay. What is it? Or can't you say?"

Harley shrugged. "I really can't," he replied. He forced a smile. "We'll do this again, Sara."

She smiled back. "Of course."

He nodded to Jared and walked off toward the parking lot, looking forlorn even from behind.

Jared was smiling.

Sara frowned. "Did you have anything to do with that?"

"You mean, did I ask Cy to occupy Harley so that I could take you home? Of course I did. I don't like competition."

She was gaping. "Excuse me?"

His arm contracted. His eyes were strangely darkened as he met her own. "I'm possessive," he said softly. "Territorial."

"About...me?" she asked, unbelieving.

"Of course about you," he muttered.

"But Max is beautiful," she began.

"Max is the past," he said bluntly. "She knows it."

That was thrilling. Exciting. Her whole face lit up. He was serious!

He stopped dancing and traced her mouth with a long forefinger, teasing her lips apart in a sensuous tension that grew by the second. "You're tired," he whispered. "You've done too much. You need to go home, and I have to take you because Harley left early."

She nodded, wordless.

He caught her by the hand and tugged her to Cy and Lisa. They said their goodbyes. Jared asked Cy to tell Tony where he'd gone. He put Sara in the Jaguar, buckled her up and revved off toward her small house.

They didn't exchange a single word during the short drive. The tension between them was so thick it was almost tangible. Sara felt hot all over. The feel of Jared so close to her had removed all her inhibitions. She couldn't think past wanting to kiss him until her mouth hurt.

He cut off the engine in front of her house and turned to her. "We've reached the point of no return," he said curtly. "Either we go ahead, or we stop seeing each other. I'm too old to stop at kisses."

She stared at him helplessly, all her upbringing urging her to tell him to leave, to go inside by herself. All her life, she'd done the right thing, the safe thing. But she loved this man. If she said the wrong words now, she knew she'd never be in his arms again. The thought was torture. Then she caught herself. She was being overly worried. He wanted to do some heavy petting. Of course. He wasn't a kiss-at-the-front-door sort of man. And if things got too hot, well, she'd just find an excuse to get up. Easy.

He got out of the car, opened her door and locked the sleek vehicle before he followed Sara up onto her porch. Nervously she unlocked the door and went inside. She reached for the light switch, but he was right behind her. He stayed the movement, locked the dead bolt and suddenly swept her up into his arms and brought his mouth down on her soft lips.

The sofa was only a few feet away. It was long and wide, just right for two people to lie on. Sara felt his weight with a sense of destiny. It was the most glorious thing she'd ever felt, all that hard, warm muscle down the length of her body. She seemed to throb like her own runaway heartbeat while Jared made a midnight snack of her mouth.

Before long, she was as anxious as he was to have her blouse and bra out of the way so that his hands, and then his mouth, could explore the softness of her warm skin. By the time he slid his hands under her skirt and against her bare legs, she was shivering all over.

She felt his body vibrate, as if he was as electrified as she was. He whispered something under his breath that she didn't understand. Apparently it wasn't too important, because only seconds later, she felt him against her in a way that was as new as it was frightening.

She started to protest, but it was already too late. His mouth ground into hers as his body suddenly invaded the most secret place of her own. The delicious sensations she felt when they began were now absent as she felt him insistent and demanding, his big hand under her hips, holding them steady as he pushed down hard. He groaned as he felt the soft barrier give. His control was gone at once. He drove for fulfillment; abstinence and too many beers had robbed him of self-control. He felt the rush of pleasure like a hot wave over his body, leaving him to shudder in a tense arch that was like rain after the baking desert.

When he regained his control, he felt her trying to get away from the crush of his body. He was aware of broken sobs. Trembling. Audible misery.

He lifted his head. He couldn't see her in the darkness of the room, but his hand touched her face and felt the wetness.

"Please," she sobbed, pushing at his chest.

He was shocked at his lapse. He hadn't really meant to go this far, not the first time they were intimate. But it was too late now. He moved away, fastening his slacks. He heard her move, heard fabric against skin. At least she'd stopped crying.

"I'll get the light," he said gruffly.

"No!" She was standing now. "No," she added in a more controlled tone. "Please don't."

"Why not?" He moved closer to her. "We made love. What's so horrible about it?"

She was shivering with self-revulsion. "Please go," she whispered.

"Sara…"

"Please!" she sobbed.

He drew in an angry breath. "Small town girls and their damned hang-ups," he muttered. "What now? Do you think you'll go to hell for sleeping with a man you haven't married?"

It was so close to what she'd been taught all her life, that she didn't even bother to reply.

"I don't believe this!" he raged. "I can't be the first man to—" He stopped dead, remembering the barrier that he'd dealt with. "I was the first," he said slowly. "Wasn't I, Sara?"

"Please go," she pleaded tearfully.

He drew in a long breath. "Tell me you're on birth control," he demanded.

"I never needed to be," she bit off.

"Great!" he burst out, furious. "That's just great! And you

see me as a meal ticket, don't you? If I made you pregnant, you'll have a free ride for life! Except you won't," he added coldly. "I don't want children ever again. You'll have a termination or I'll take you to court and show everyone who lives here how mercenary you are!"

He was talking about a possibility she hadn't even considered. She'd tried to stop him. Why did he expect every woman to be prepared for sex? Was that the way people thought in big cities? Were they all prepared, all the time?

"Don't worry," she said through her teeth. "I promise you, there won't be any horrible consequences. Now will you please go home?"

He started for the door, still furious. But he paused with it open and looked back toward her. "I didn't mean to hurt you," he said uncomfortably.

She laughed hollowly. "My whole life has been nothing except pain. Why should this be any different?"

She turned and went into a room down the hall, closed the door and audibly locked it.

He left, frowning, curious about the remark. He didn't want to think about how much he'd hurt her. He honestly hadn't planned to seduce her, but she wouldn't believe him. She was hurt and shocked and outraged. Probably she'd been taught that premarital sex was a sin, and now she was going to punish herself for falling victim to demon lust.

He turned the lock on her door so that it would engage when he went outside and pulled the door shut.

He stood on the porch, feeling the cool breeze touch his sweaty face, cooling him. He'd never lost control like that in his life. He was furious at himself.

While he was debating his next move, the ranch truck pulled up beside his car. Tony leaned out the window.

"She okay?" he asked his boss.

"She's fine," Jared lied, unlocking the Jaguar. "Let's go home. I want a drink. It's been a damned long day."

"You can say that again," Tony replied. "You won't believe the hell Max raised at the airport."

He'd believe it, he thought. His whole evening had gone from bad to worse, and he wasn't about to tell Tony any of the details. Two women in his life, and he couldn't deal with either of them. He wished that this whole charade was over.

Eight

Sara didn't sleep at all. She took a shower and changed into a clean nightgown. Then she sat in front of her mirror and looked at the fallen woman there. Her grandfather would be ashamed of her. So would her father. They hadn't raised her to be careless with her morals.

She wasn't sure what to do. She knew there was a morning after pill, but she'd have to go to a doctor she knew to ask for it. Everybody in town would know what she'd been doing. The shame was too great for the risk. But what if she conceived? She was only at the beginning of her cycle. Wasn't that a bad time to get pregnant? But some women weren't regular. She wasn't. Would that make a big difference?

Jared hadn't even asked first. He'd taken what he wanted. Maybe she'd done something to make him think she was willing. She should have told him in the car that she was innocent. She'd thought he meant that he wanted to have a nice petting session in her house, not that he expected her to go the whole way with him. Had he thought she was agreeing to sex?

She was sickened by her lack of protest. It had been so sweet to lie in his arms and feel him wanting her. Nobody had ever wanted Sara, not in that way. Her grandfather had cherished her, but she'd been in such a condition when she and her mother first came home from overseas that she wasn't really expected to live in the first place. The group that had sponsored the family's trip had been kind enough to arrange for a medical flight back to Texas for Sara. As a result of her injuries, she had slight brain damage. People who knew her were aware of it. They never made fun of her when she couldn't match socks or clothes, when she forgot little things as soon as she learned them. She had trouble remembering much of the past as well. The doctors had said she was very smart and that she would be able to compensate. But now she wasn't so sure.

Maybe, she comforted herself, nothing would happen. She really hadn't enjoyed what Jared had done to her. Didn't that mean she wouldn't conceive?

She should have read more books, she told herself firmly. She knew too little about her own body, or what men and women did in the dark. At least she knew now what women had been talking about in whispers all her life. Sex was painful and quickly over with. It was only fun for men. Women endured it to have children. Now she knew that she'd never want it again. She knew the truth.

She went to bed. For the first time in years, though, she didn't have nightmares.

Jared felt guilty all day. He was shocked at his loss of control. He was sorry for the things he'd said to Sara, but she should have told him up-front that she had no experience of men. Most women knew how to take care of themselves in intimate situations. If he'd known Sara was completely innocent, he'd have used something and he wouldn't have hurt her so much.

He laughed coldly. Sure he would have. He hadn't had control of himself for those few, electrifying minutes on her sofa. He'd wanted her so much that he couldn't contain it.

Tony hadn't said anything to him about it, but he kept looking at Jared as if he suspected something. It didn't help to remember how fond Tony was getting of Sara. Sara liked Tony, too.

"You aren't yourself today," Tony commented at lunch, for which they had a nice paella that he'd concocted.

Jared moved restlessly, but he didn't reply.

"Max didn't leave town."

That got his boss's attention. "What?!"

Tony compressed his lips. "She's upstairs."

"I told you to take her to the airport!"

"I did," Tony said shortly. "But short of bodily carrying her onto the plane, I couldn't think of a way to get her out of the terminal."

Jared almost exploded. Just as he started to speak, Max lounged into the dining room in a gray silk pantsuit.

"Lunch? I'm starved."

"I told you to leave," Jared shot at her.

"You didn't mean it," she said complacently. "You're always throwing me out. Then the next day you call to apologize and ask me back again. I saved you the steps in between."

She was right, and Jared hated knowing it. She helped herself to paella and coffee. Nobody said anything else at the table.

Jared wasn't a drinker. He hardly ever touched alcohol. But remembering what he'd done with Sara sent him to a liquor bottle. Halfway through the afternoon, he was well on his way to staggering.

Max cornered Jared in his study, surprised at the amount of whiskey he was consuming. It had to be something rough, she thought. He hadn't had this much to drink since his daughter's death. "Something's gone wrong, hasn't it? Come on," she coaxed. "Tell me."

He glared at her. "I can handle this myself."

"Handle what?" She pursed her lips. She knew him very well. There was a pattern to his behavior that she recognized. A new woman. The hunt. The seduction. Then the need to extricate himself from the woman. "Don't tell me," she purred. "You let that hick girl seduce you, didn't you?"

He looked shocked.

"I thought so," she continued. "It was easy to see that she was after you. She watched every move you made. She wore seductive clothes. She did everything except wear a sign to show you that she was willing. No man could have resisted her."

She made him feel less guilty. She was right. It was Sara's fault. He'd been seduced, not the reverse. The alcohol helped him see the truth.

She saw the wheels turning in his mind. "And now you're worried about consequences."

He gave it away without knowing.

She nodded. "Don't worry. I'll take care of everything. You just attend to your current situation and leave it to me."

"Don't hurt her," he said as an afterthought.

"That's a joke. I won't have to."

"Okay." He went to find Tony. He felt a weight lifted from his shoulders. It would be all right. If Tony noticed that his boss was half lit, he was kind enough not to say anything about it.

* * *

Sara was back at work on Monday morning, feeling guilty and ashamed, as if what had happened showed on her face.

"Bad weekend?" Dee asked gently. "We all have them, from time to time."

"I went to the barbecue at the Parks's place," she replied. "The food was great."

Dee grinned. "Did Harley have a good time, too?"

"Harley had to go run an errand for his boss just after the dancing started," Sara said sadly. Harley would have saved her if Cy hadn't separated him from Sara.

"Mmm-hmm," Dee murmured.

Something in her tone disturbed Sara. She glanced at her boss. "What?"

"Did you know that Jared and Cy Parks grew up in the same town?"

Sara dropped the stapler she was holding and scrambled to pick it up again. "How do you know?"

"My cousin works for Cy on his ranch. He knows all the gossip. Yes, Cy had a place in Montana, and so did Jared Cameron." She stopped putting used books into boxes for resale. "Jared asked Cy to remove Harley from the field," she added.

Sara had always liked Cy Parks, until now. But he couldn't have known what a near-tragedy he'd contributed to. He probably thought Jared was seriously interested in Sara. According to Max, Jared was never seriously interested in any woman. Especially, she recalled sickly, once he'd had her. Her eyes closed in misery.

"Harley was topping cotton he was so mad," Dee continued. "He almost quit his job. He said you were a babe in the woods and Jared was a wolf in disguise."

"Jared was a perfect gentleman," Sara lied, and made it look convincing.

Dee stared at her for a minute and then visibly relaxed. "Thank goodness. I was worried…silly of me. I have to run to the bank to get some change for the drawer. Want coffee from the doughnut place?"

"Yes, please, black. No cream or sugar."

"That's new. You're sure?"

"I'm getting back to the basics, even in coffee. I'll hold down the fort."

Dee smiled gently. "Okay."

After Dee left, Sara felt as if the world was collapsing around her. It was a crisis that compared in intensity only to that episode in her past. She'd survived that, she reminded herself. She could survive anything, after that.

But minutes later, Max parked one of the ranch trucks outside the bookstore and strolled in, looking smug and arrogant. "Jared sent me," she said curtly. She took out an envelope and handed it to Sara. "It's a check for ten thousand dollars. He said there had better not be any complications from what happened Saturday night." She nodded toward the envelope. "There's more than enough in there to pay for a termination. And if it's not necessary, then you've still got a nest egg for the foreseeable future. Jared won't be here much longer."

"Won't…be here," Sara stammered, shocked by the unfolding nightmare.

"He's been down here waiting for the authorities to get their hands on three illegal aliens who came up from South America to kidnap Jared and hold him for ransom."

"Ransom?"

Max pulled a magazine from her briefcase. It was a national financial journal. There, on the front cover, was Jared Cameron. The story inside was revealed in a sentence: Oil magnate target of terrorists after firefight at South American pipeline…

Sara gasped.

"You can keep it," Max said easily. "To remember him by."

"But why did he come here?" Sara asked blankly.

"Because some of the team of mercenaries that helped him destroy the original terrorist cell that targeted his oil pipeline two years ago live here," she replied. "The survivors aren't willing to give up. They figure if they can nab Jared, they'll recoup what they lost when they failed to hold on to his oil pipeline in South America. They demanded millions for it, and he sent in mercenaries instead. He pulled out when the oil companies were nationalized, but the terrorists still want the money. Now they want revenge as well. They were just apprehended today near Victoria."

"Then he's safe," Sara said dully.

"He is. And he can go down to Cancún with me for a long holiday," she added. "His headquarters is in Oklahoma, but he has another house in Billings, Montana, and vacation homes all over the world. He's worth millions. The terrorists knew that his corporation would pay any amount of money to get him back. He's something of a financial genius." Her eyes narrowed as she smiled. "Hardly a match for a little bookseller in outback Texas, is he?"

Sara just looked at her, with the anguish she couldn't hide all over her face.

Max's expression hardened. "You'd better realize that he means business. If you turn up pregnant, you'd better get a termination. You don't want to know what he could do to you and your reputation."

Sara didn't answer her. She couldn't. She just stared.

Max shrugged. "You've been warned." She stopped at the doorway. "You shouldn't look so tragic. Women have fought their way into his bed for years."

"What for?" Sara asked with deliberate scorn.

Max looked as if she'd been doused with water. "You don't mean that you didn't enjoy…?"

"I'd rather stay single for the rest of my life than go through that again, ever," Sara said with a sob in her voice.

Something in Max that had been buried for a decade sat up and shivered. She searched for the right words. "You've never…?"

Sara swallowed hard. "My grandfather said that women who give their bodies cheaply are bound for purgatory."

Max's thin eyebrows pulled together. "Sara," she began hesitantly, "how old are you?"

"What does that have to do with…?"

"How old are you?"

Sara swallowed. "Nineteen."

Max felt the blood going out of her face. She was using a cannon to shoot a bird. She drew in a long breath. Well, at least it hadn't been statutory rape. But she was sure Jared didn't know how old this child was. He'd never have touched her.

"I'm sorry," Max told her. "I'm really sorry."

She turned and went out the door.

Sara dried her tears and went back to straightening the books on their shelves. Jared was a multimillionaire who owned an oil corporation and he was only here at the ranch to set a trap for the terrorists who wanted him for ransom. Sara had thought he was here forever. When he held her close and kissed her, she thought he wanted her forever. She was wrong on both counts. He could buy as many women as he wanted. Sara wasn't even in the running, except that he'd wanted her. Or, maybe he'd just wanted a woman and she was handy. She really did need to grow up.

Max was solemn and quiet when she went back to the ranch. Jared noticed.

"What's wrong?" he asked.

She looked up at him. "She's nineteen, Jared."

He had to sit down. Nothing had ever hit him quite so hard.

She sat down across from him in an armchair. "I told her what was necessary…"

"You what?" he asked, aghast.

She held up a hand. "Being kind to her isn't an option. What if she decided to accuse you of forcing her? You could lose millions. Your reputation would be in ashes. What sort of life would it be for a child, if she had one, living in this small town asylum with a mother who barely made minimum wage and could hardly afford to clothe her?"

Jared wasn't thinking about money. He was remembering the throb in Sara's voice in the darkness. She hadn't been leading him on. She hadn't realized what he meant. She didn't know that she was agreeing to have sex with him. And she was nineteen years old. He felt guilt like a rush of hot acid in his gut.

"When are we going to Cancún?" Max asked, to divert him.

He turned and looked at her, but he didn't see her. "I haven't thought about it."

"A few days on the beach would do you good," she coaxed. "You can put this place behind you."

He was staring at her. "Why Cancún?" he asked.

She hesitated. "It's got lovely beaches. There are Mayan ruins nearby."

His eyes had narrowed. "You'd better come clean."

She frowned. "I'm not doing anything dishonest," she said. "There's a consortium that handles pharmaceuticals. They want to invest in our corporation."

"Name them."

She frowned more. "Well, I don't really have just one name. They call themselves the Reconquistas."

"When did you speak with them?"

"Last week. Why?"

"Law enforcement just apprehended three terrorists in Victoria, heading this way," he said furiously. "And you don't know why?"

She looked stunned. "You can't mean…!"

"They're part of the consortium that smuggles narcotics, Max," he told her flatly. "If you'd come to me in the first place, I would have told you. But you were seeing dollar signs, weren't you?"

She flushed. "It never hurts to make more money."

"It never hurts to fire people, either," he said pointedly. "You'd better start looking for another job."

"You're not serious," she laughed. "You fire me all the time, but you always call me back."

He looked resolute. "Not this time," he said in a cold tone. "You've done enough damage."

"Me?" She stood up, fuming. "I've done enough damage? What would you call seducing a nineteen-year-old virgin?"

The last word drifted away as she noticed Tony standing fixed in the doorway, with eyes that promised mayhem.

Jared saw him and grimaced.

Tony marched right up to him. "Is it true?" he demanded.

Jared couldn't even find the words.

"That sweet woman," Tony said coldly, "who never hurt anybody, after the tragedy of her past almost destroyed her, and here you come to put the last nail in her coffin!"

"What do you mean, the tragedy of her past?" Jared asked.

Tony didn't reply. He looked more dangerous at that moment than Jared had ever seen before. "I'll never tell you. And the minute this standoff ends, I'm through. I won't work for a man like you."

He turned on his heel and went right back to the kitchen.

Max swallowed the hurt. She and Tony had both hit rock bottom, it seemed. "Well, it looks like you and your conscience will have a long time to get to know each other, doesn't it?"

She stopped by the kitchen to ask Tony to drive her to the airport. He agreed curtly. Jared went back into his study and slammed the door. He'd never felt so ashamed in his life.

The next morning, when Sara went to work, she noticed a strange beat-up van in the parking lot. It had been there just as she drove out of the parking lot the day before. In fact, it had pulled in just after Max walked into the bookstore. Sara hadn't seen anybody in it the day before, and she didn't see any people in it now. Maybe it broke down there and the owner had left it until he could get a mechanic to tow it. She went into the bookstore.

"Hi, Dee," she called.

Dee smiled. "Hi, yourself. I'm off to the bank. Want coffee?"

"I'd love it."

"I'll pick us up a doughnut apiece, too." She stopped at the door. "That old van's still there."

"Maybe it broke down," Sara murmured.

"I'm amazed anyone would risk driving it in the first place," Dee chuckled. "I'll be quick."

"Okay."

She'd no sooner driven away than three foreign-looking men walked into the bookstore. They glanced at Sara and nodded before they walked down the aisles, one of them peering into Dee's open office.

Sara didn't usually have premonitions, but she felt something odd about the men. She remembered what Max had said about terrorists. These three were tall and swarthy and disreputable-looking. They were wearing jeans and T-shirts, and they had very prominent muscles. She was in the bookstore alone, with no weapons except the pocketknife she used to open boxes with. She wouldn't stand a chance against even one of them, much less three, despite Chief Grier's handy self-defense for women course. She could scream, of course, but the bookstore was temporarily the only business in the strip mall.

They might have been arrested in Victoria, but it was obvious that they'd made bail. She knew the look of the people who lived in her area. These three were from overseas. And she didn't need a program to know why they were in town. They were after Jared. Max had come to the bookstore in a ranch pickup and had a solemn conversation with a woman. They might have had high-tech listening devices. If they knew who Max was, and they'd overheard what she said to Sara, maybe they figured Sara was a softer target than Jared, with his bodyguard.

She pretended not to see them, while her mind worried over possible courses of action. There was one. It was a long shot. If she stabbed herself with the pocketknife and they could see blood, and she pretended to be unconscious and tried to look dead, they might be startled into leaving. It would be risky to carry a wounded woman off for ransom, wouldn't it? Especially if she looked as if she were dying…it would slow everything down.

I'm probably crazy, she told herself. They're just tourists or ranch hands searching for something to read. Right, she added, and that's why they're looking outside to make sure nobody's coming and heading straight for me!

She knew where the appendicitis incision was. It was her best hope of missing any essential organs. They came around the counter, towering over her.

"You come with us," one of the men said in accented English. "We see you with the lawyer. You are Cameron's woman. He will pay for you."

"I am nobody's woman. I will die before I go with you!" she said, and, giving up a silent prayer, she jabbed the pocketknife into the incision, through her blouse. "Oooh!" she cried, because it did hurt.

She crumpled to the floor with blood on her hands and shirt. She sighed heavily and held her breath. She looked dead.

The men hesitated. They'd planned well, and now their hostage had committed suicide right in front of them!

While they hesitated, Harley Fowler got out of his truck and headed for the bookstore. He was wearing a sidearm, a six-gun that he carried when he was working fence lines, in case he encountered a rattler or some other dangerous animal. The men made a quick decision. They ran for it. They ran so fast that they almost knocked Harley down in the process.

Harley didn't understand why three men were running for the van. Then he thought about robbery. Sara and Dee were here alone. He darted into the bookstore.

Sara was on the floor, blood pouring from her side. She looked up at Harley, gasping for breath. "It worked," she mumbled. "I hurt myself, though. Can you call 911 please?"

He grimaced as he saw the blood. "Yes, I can." He flipped out his cell phone and pushed in the code, holding it to his ear with his shoulder as he pulled Sara's shirt aside and looked at the wound.

He put pressure on it to stop the bleeding and spoke into the cell phone between his shoulder and his ear. He had an ambulance sent to the bookstore. He managed to hold one hand on her wound and close the phone with the other and slide it back into his pocket.

"You'll be all right, Sara," he told her. "Any man who'd do this to a woman should be shot! I should have stopped them!"

"They didn't do it, Harley, I did," she said weakly. "They were going to kidnap me. They thought Jared Cameron would pay ransom for me. What a joke!"

"Why would they think that?"

"His lawyer, Max, came to buy me off yesterday," she said miserably. "They must have followed her here."

"You aren't making sense."

The wound hurt. She moved and flinched. "Look at the magazine on the counter, Harley," she told him. "You'll see."

"When the paramedics get here, I will," he replied, but he didn't move his hands. He didn't dare.

Dee and the ambulance arrived at the same time. She ran into the store, red-faced and fearful.

"Oh, my goodness!" she exclaimed. "Sara!"

"Three men. They were in that old van, I think," she told Dee. "They were going to kidnap me for ransom."

"Ransom? Dear, you must be feverish…"

Harley picked up the magazine and looked at it, frowning as he handed it to Dee.

They exchanged a worried glance.

The paramedics loaded Sara on the gurney.

"I'll go with her," Harley said. "Dee, you'd better call Cash Grier, in case they come back."

"I'll do it right now." She picked up the store phone.

"I'll be all right. Honest," Sara assured Harley.

He didn't answer. He was too worried.

The wound wasn't bad. Dr. Coltrain had to sew her up. He did it, after giving her a local anesthetic, shaking his head. "Couldn't you have dialed 911?" he asked.

"I'd never have made it to the phone. There were three of them, heavily muscled, with accents, and not Spanish ones. I heard accents like that in Africa," she whispered.

"Why were they after you?" he asked.

"They were going to take me for ransom."

"Oh. Who do you know with that kind of money?" Coltrain teased.

"They followed Jared Cameron's lawyer into the bookstore," she murmured, feeling drowsy now that the excitement was all over. "I guess they thought I had a connection to him that they could exploit. There's an article about him in the new financial magazine. His photo's on the cover. He's down here trying to avoid being kidnapped by South American terrorists who made a try for his oil pipeline."

"The excitement of living in Jacobsville, Texas," he replied as he stitched her up. "When I was a kid, this place was like the end of the world. Never any excitement."

"Maybe he'll go away and we'll get back to normal."

He only mumbled.

Sara was sitting up on the examination table when Cash Grier walked in.

"Harley said three men attacked you in the bookstore," he said without preamble. He looked solemn. "Three prisoners escaped from the Victoria jail yesterday about noon. They were Arabic, according to the police chief up there. At least, they spoke what sounded to him like Arabic."

"Yes," she replied. "They were in a ratty old van. They followed Jared Cameron's lawyer to the bookstore in one of the ranch trucks. They thought I was important to Mr. Cameron. What a joke!"

He didn't laugh. "Did they say anything to you?"

"Only that they thought I had a connection to him. They must be really desperate for a hostage."

"Did one of them stab you?" he asked.

She grimaced. "You aren't going to believe this."

"Try me."

"I stabbed myself. I made them think I was committing

suicide. They hesitated when I fell on the floor and pretended to be dead. Then Harley showed up and they cut their losses and ran for it. Good thing Harley was wearing his .45 on his hip today!" she added. "He always does when he rides fence lines."

Cash's dark eyebrows arched and he smiled gently. "Well, aren't you the mistress of improvisation?" he said with respect.

She grinned. "It seemed the only chance I had. There were three of them. You always said there was no shame in running if you were up against impossible odds."

"Yes, I did. You spooked them, I gather."

"Want to hire me?" she asked saucily. "You can teach me how to shoot a gun and next time I won't have to resort to stabbing myself. I can shoot them instead."

"We've put out a BOLO on the van," Cash assured her.

"It will stick out," she said. "It really is ratty."

Harley stuck his head in the door. "How are you?"

She smiled. "Dr. Coltrain sewed me back up. I'm fine."

"You couldn't have screamed?" he asked.

"Who would have heard me?" she retorted. "We're the only business left in the strip mall."

"She has a point," Cash told the younger man.

Just then, his radio beeped. He talked into the radio mike on his shoulder. "Grier."

"We got them," Assistant Chief Judd Dunn told him. "We're bringing them in now."

"On my way," Cash replied. "Clear."

He turned to Sara, grinning. "And that's a nice day's work. Stop stabbing yourself," he added firmly. "I'm sure there's a law against attempted suicide."

"Never again. I promise," she assured him.

He winked and left. Harley moved into the cubicle and held Sara's hand.

"What a relief to find you in one piece," he said gently.

Sara smiled at him. He wasn't the only person who was relieved.

There was a terrible commotion in the corridor. Seconds later, Tony the Dancer walked into the cubicle.

Nine

Tony glanced at Harley, who was holding Sara's hand in his.

"I heard those three assassins went after you," Tony told her, worried. "They followed Max, didn't they?"

"I think they did," she admitted. "But how did they know her?"

"Our Web site mentions all the people who work for the corporation," he replied. "I'm sure the would-be kidnappers are computer literate. Most terrorists are these days. You okay?"

She smiled at him. She nodded.

"What did they do to you?" he asked, noting the dried blood on her blouse.

"They didn't do anything. I stabbed myself where I had the appendectomy and played dead on the floor. They didn't want a dying hostage, I figured. Then Harley showed up with his .45 and spooked them while they were deciding what to do about me. They ran. Chief Grier said his men just stopped them and they're under arrest."

Tony let out a breath. He glanced at Harley and smiled. "You do look like a gunslinger," he said.

Harley chuckled. "I never get any practice on living targets," he said. "Pity they ran."

"Wasn't it just?" Sara murmured. She grimaced.

Copper Coltrain came back into the cubicle, raising his eyebrows at the newcomer.

"This is Tony Danzetta," Sara introduced him. "He works for Mr. Cameron."

Coltrain nodded. So did Tony.

Harley checked his watch. "Damn! Sara, I was on my way to pick up some butane and fencing for Mr. Parks when I stopped by the bookstore for a minute to see you. I've got to go."

"Could you call Dee and tell her I'll be there as soon as Dr. Coltrain releases me," she began.

"In a pig's eye you will," Coltrain snapped, his red hair seemed to flare up. "You'll go home and stay in bed for two days. You'll start an antibiotic as well, to protect against that wound getting infected." He hesitated. "You don't need to be on your own."

"Chief Grier and his men have the would-be kidnappers in custody," she repeated.

"Sara, that isn't what I mean," he replied.

"She won't be alone," Tony said quietly. "I'll take her home and get the prescription filled. Then I'll take care of her until she's well."

"But, your boss," Sara began.

"I'm quitting today," he returned, avoiding her eyes. "If they've got the kidnappers, he won't need me. He doesn't need protection anymore. If he does, he can hire somebody else. He's rich enough."

Sara sensed a confrontation, and she was sure she didn't

want to know why Tony had quit. She was almost certain it had something to do with her.

She flushed scarlet as she considered what Tony might have found out from Max.

Coltrain saw the flush and Tony's tight lips and drew a conclusion. "Mr. Danzetta, I need to take one more look at the incision. Will you wait outside, please? You, too, Harley."

"I'm just going. Get better, Sara," Harley said softly, smiling.

"I'll do my best. Thanks for what you did."

"It wasn't much. See you."

"I'll be right outside," Tony added, following Harley out into the hall.

Coltrain closed the door of the cubicle. His eyes were quiet and intense. "You don't have to say it. I read faces very well. What do you want to do?"

She started to deny it. She knew better. Coltrain was a force of nature. "I can't kill an ant," she said.

He scowled. "Who asked you to?"

She pulled the envelope with the check out of her pocket and handed it to him, nodding when he started to open it.

Tony the Dancer heard the curses outside in the hall. He opened the door and went back in, daring the doctor to throw him out.

"What?" he asked.

Coltrain, red in the face with bad temper, handed him the envelope.

He cursed as darkly as the doctor had. "A firefight in Africa that damned near killed her, and now this," he muttered.

Sara and the doctor gaped at him.

He cleared his throat. He looked at Sara. "You don't remember me, do you?" he asked.

She shook her head, feeling again the sadness that came with remembering her past.

Tony moved a step closer and stuck his hands in his pockets. "I was with a group of American mercs who were fighting to restore the rightful government in the province where your parents were missionaries," he said quietly. "We'd just driven into town, chasing after a rebel group that killed two of our men. We saw the explosion. And we found you and your parents."

She stared at him, trying to reconcile her memories. "Yes. Some mercenaries buried my...my father," she said huskily. "And one of them carried me to a truck and got me and my mother to safety, to the mission headquarters."

"That was me, Sara," Tony replied quietly.

She smiled sadly. She hadn't recognized him. But then, she couldn't remember much of that long-ago life. "I lost some of my long-term memory. I can't quite match colors, and I forget names..."

"You're smart, though," Tony replied. "It doesn't show. Honest."

Coltrain drew in a long breath. "It's a small world, isn't it?" he asked.

Tony nodded. "Cy Parks was in another group of mercs, working with us. He walked right into the gunfire of a machine nest and took it out. One of the men who died had set the explosion in the mission that killed Sara's father and injured her."

Sara was spellbound. "I never knew," she said softly.

"You never needed to," Tony told her. He looked at Coltrain. "When can you tell if she's pregnant?"

Sara gasped.

Coltrain took it as a matter of course. "In a couple of weeks," he replied. "Maybe three. I could do a blood test now, but we might get a false positive. You need to shoot your damned boss," he added without missing a beat.

"I'm tempted," Tony said curtly. "But it's too late now. What's done is done. I'll take care of her, no matter what."

Sara fought tears and lost.

Tony pulled her face to his shoulder and held it there while she cried. "Now, now," he said gently. "It's all over. Everything's going to be fine."

Coltrain clapped Tony on the shoulder. "I'll write the prescriptions for an antibiotic and some pain medication. You can make sure she takes it properly."

"You bet I will," Tony replied.

Sara felt like royalty. Tony was a wonder. He cleaned the place until it shined like a new penny, rearranged her uncoordinated shelves in the kitchen and made dinner. He also doled out pills and did the laundry.

Afterward, he called Dee and gave her a progress report.

Sara was aghast when he told her, late that night. "You told her you were staying with me?" she asked.

He glowered at her. "At least Dee doesn't have a dirty mind," he informed her.

"I do not have a dirty mind," she protested.

He drew the covers up over her, in the plain, discreet pajamas she was wearing. "I want to tell you a story," he said, sitting down on the edge of the bed beside her. His dark eyes were quiet and sad. "I had a sister, who was three years younger than me. We lived in foster care. Our old man drank and knocked us around a lot. Our mother was long dead. They took us away from the old man and we shuttled from foster home to foster home, where we were mostly barely tolerated. At one of the homes," he added coldly, "there was an older boy who liked the way my sister looked. I warned him off, but he was persistent and she was flattered that a boy liked her. She was only fourteen, you see." He drew in a long breath and looked down at the floor. "Long story short, he got her pregnant. She was so ashamed, so scared, that she didn't know what to do. The boy found out and told her he'd make her sorry if she didn't get rid of the kid. He wasn't going to be rooked into paying child support for sixteen years because she was too stupid to get the pill and use it."

"What a nasty boy," she muttered.

"She was too ashamed to tell the foster parents what she'd let him do, and too afraid of the boy to have the child. I was moved to another foster home while all this was going on, so she couldn't tell me, either. So she went out one night, after everybody was asleep. They found her washed up on the riverbank the next afternoon."

"Oh, Tony," she said gently. She touched his arm. "I'm so sorry."

He grimaced. "She was all I had."

She slid her little hand into his big one and smiled at him. "No. I'm your family now," she replied. "You can be my big brother."

He looked down at her with eyes that were suspiciously bright. "Yeah?"

She squeezed his hand. "Yeah."

He drew in a steadying breath. "Well, we'll be part of one amazingly dysfunctional family, if you still consider Jared part of it."

She glared. "He became a stranger when Max handed me that check. And we're not going to let him be in our family anymore, either."

He didn't believe that she'd stopped caring about Jared. She was just hurt. So he smiled and nodded his head. "Suits me."

He squeezed her hand and let it go. "You need to get some sleep," he said, standing. He smiled down at her. "I'll be a better family to you than my ex-boss was," he added coolly. "That's for sure."

The memory of how close she and Jared had become, until the end, made her sad. She'd cared for him more than she wanted to admit. His betrayal was almost more than she could bear.

"Don't brood," Tony said firmly. "It won't change anything. We'll deal with whatever happens."

"I'm not getting rid of a child, if the test comes up positive."

He smiled. "I never thought you would."

"We won't tell him," she muttered. "He can go back to his houses all over the world and have fun with Max."

"Nobody has fun with Max," Tony told her. "She's got a one-track mind. All she thinks about is money."

"That's sad. I mean, it would be nice to have money. But I'm happy living the way I do."

"So am I, kid," he told her. "Money's poor company if it's all you've got."

She smoothed the cover over her belly, wondering. "He loved his little girl," she said out of the blue, and felt sorry for him all over again.

"He did," Tony had to admit. "But he discovered it far too late. Now he's alone and afraid to risk having another child. He'd be vulnerable."

She laid back against the pillows. "Everybody's vulnerable. You can't escape life."

"Yeah," he had to agree. "I know."

She didn't expect to sleep, but she did. It was comforting having Tony down the hall. People would probably gossip about her, but she'd live with it; with the pregnancy, too, if she had to. Her friends wouldn't snub her, and it didn't matter if her enemies did. She frowned. She didn't have enemies. Well, unless you counted that conceited rancher who couldn't take no for an answer.

Tony brought her breakfast and went to work baking them

a nice pound cake. But just before lunch, he walked in with her portable phone, his big hand over the mouthpiece.

"Who do you know in New York City?" he asked, curious.

"No one… New York? Give me that!" She was almost on fire with excitement as he handed her the phone. She wrenched her newest set of stitches grasping for it and groaned before she spoke into the receiver. "Sara Dobbs," she said at once.

"Miss Dobbs, I'm Daniel Harris, an editor with Mirabella Publishing Company. I wanted to tell you that your story is delightful, and the drawings are exquisite. We'd like to publish your book!"

Sara sat there with dreams coming true. Tears rolled down her cheeks. She fought to find her voice. Yesterday her world had felt as if it were ending. Today…today was magic!

"I'd love that," she managed finally, and then listened while he outlined the process that would ensue, including an advance against royalties that would be forthcoming.

Tony lifted his eyebrows while he listened unashamedly to her conversation. She was so animated that he wouldn't have been surprised to see her levitate right up to the ceiling.

She hung up, finally, and handed him back the phone. "They bought my book. They bought my children's book! They're going to publish it! And I get paid!"

He laughed. "Well!"

"I can't believe it!"

"What's this book about?" he asked, curious.

She told him, going into detail about the puppies and their adventures. "I have to call Lisa and tell her. She'll be so thrilled. I'll call Tom Walker, too," she added. "His dog was their grandfather—old Moose, who died just recently."

"I'd love to see this book," Tony replied.

"I just happen to have a copy," she told him, and pointed

to the small desk in the corner of her bedroom. "I made a duplicate, in case it got lost in the mail."

He sat beside her and went through the drawings, exclaiming over their beauty. "I never knew anybody who could draw like this," he murmured. "You're really good."

"Thanks, Tony. I'm overwhelmed. I never dreamed it would even sell, and certainly not so quickly."

He glanced at her. "You know, life evens out. Something bad happens, and then you get something good."

"My grandfather used to say that." She leaned back against the pillows. "My mother hated him. He talked my father into the mission to Africa, something he'd always wanted to do, but never could. Mama didn't want to go. She thought Africa was too dangerous, but my grandfather and my father made her feel guilty enough to back down. She blamed Grandad for everything that happened. She went out of her way to embarrass him, to make him pay for Daddy's death." She shook her head. "The only person she really hurt was herself."

"You poor kid," he said gently. "I thought I had a bad life."

"Everybody has a bad life, up to a point," she replied, smiling. "But somehow we survive, and get tougher."

"So we do."

She'd just finished a cup of coffee when the door opened and Jared Cameron stalked in. His face was unshaven. His eyes were bloodshot. He looked worn-out and irritated. He wasn't smiling.

He stood over her, glaring. "Why didn't you call me? Why didn't Tony call me? You were targeted because of me!"

She felt uncomfortable with him, after what had happened. She couldn't meet his eyes. "We didn't think you'd want to know."

He cursed fiercely. "The police chief said the kidnappers followed Max to your bookstore. I didn't send Max to see you!" he raged.

Her sad eyes managed to meet his. "I guess she forged your name on the check, huh?"

He went very still.

That did make her feel a little better, but not much. She pulled the envelope out of the bedside drawer and tossed it to the foot of the bed where he was standing. "You'd better have it back," she said. "I don't take bribes."

His high cheekbones went a ruddy color as he picked it up and looked at it. "Damn Max!" he said under his breath.

"And I'm not having a termination," she added fiercely. "You have no right to try to force me to jeopardize my soul!"

He looked at her as if he didn't understand what she was saying. But slowly it came to him, and he seemed even more ill at ease. "I don't want another child," he bit off.

"Then why didn't you stop?" she demanded hotly.

The flush got worse. "I didn't mean it to go that far," he said curtly. "I swear to God I didn't."

It didn't help much, but it helped a little.

"I thought you were older," he added heavily. "Nineteen years old. Dear God!"

That helped a little more.

He stuck his hands into his pockets. "I fired Max."

"I'm not surprised."

"Which one of those SOBs stabbed you?" he added abruptly.

She blinked. "None of them," she said. "I stabbed myself. It was the only thing I could think of. I was alone and there were three of them. I thought they wouldn't want a dying hostage."

"You did what?" he exploded, horrified.

"I had a pocketknife. I stabbed myself where Dr. Coltrain

did the appendectomy. It bled a lot, but I didn't hit anything vital. It was all I could think of."

He winced. "If Max hadn't taken it on herself to interfere, they'd never have tracked her to you," he said. "I could have choked her when she told me."

"She didn't tell you about the check, I guess?"

"No," he replied curtly. "If she had, she'd never work again. I make a bad enemy."

She knew that already, from personal experience. She studied him quietly. "I thought you were just a comfortably well-off rancher," she said slowly. "That magazine story said you own oil corporations."

He frowned. "What magazine?"

"Max showed it to me," she said. "You were on the cover."

He let out a short breath. "It just keeps getting better and better," he gritted.

Tony came into the room, angry. "How did you get in here?"

"I walked in the front door," Jared shot back. "You should have called me!"

Tony glared at him. "Wouldn't you be lucky if I did?"

Jared glanced from Tony's hard face to Sara's hard face. He grimaced. "It isn't doing your reputation much good to have Tony hanging around here day and night," he said.

"See? He's got a dirty mind, too," Sara told Tony.

"I have not!" Jared gritted. "I hate to see you being gossiped about."

"Then don't listen. It's a small town," she pointed out. "There's usually not much excitement going on around here. Gossip is how we get through life."

Jared seemed to draw inside himself as he looked at Sara. All his regrets were in his green eyes. He glanced at Tony. "Give us a minute, will you?"

If he'd demanded, Tony would have dug in his heels. But

it was hard to argue with politeness. He shrugged. "Okay. I'll be in the kitchen, Sara."

"Okay," she replied.

Jared stuck his hands deeper in his pockets and looked down at her. "When will you know for sure?" he asked.

She fought a scarlet flush. "Dr. Coltrain says it's too soon to be sure. Two or three more weeks, I think."

"Damn the luck," he cursed through his set teeth.

She glared at him. "You go right ahead and curse," she said. "But all of this is your fault."

His eyes were sad and full of guilt. She was so young. "I know that, Sara," he said quietly. "It doesn't help much."

She sagged back against the pillows. She didn't know what she was going to do. Her conscience wouldn't let her take the easy way out, although she was pretty sure that he wanted her to.

"Don't torment yourself," he said after a minute. "You did nothing wrong, except trust me. That was a mistake. I haven't had a lot to do with women in the past few months. I just lost it. I'm sorry, if it helps."

It did, a little, but it was too late for an apology to be of much use. "Nobody ever made such a heavy pass at me," she murmured, not meeting his eyes. "I thought you just wanted to kiss me."

"I did," he said heavily. "But kisses lead to other things. I thought you were older, more experienced."

"You wish," she said curtly.

He sighed. "Well, we'll deal with it when we have to," he said after a minute. He looked down at her quietly, his green eyes searching, curious. "I should never have let them talk me into coming here," he told her. "Tony wanted the extra protection that some of his old comrades could provide. I didn't expect to have you drawn into this."

"Neither did I," she said. She stared at her fingers. "I guess it was hard on you, living in a little hick town, with no suitable women around to date."

He made a rough sound in his throat. "Stop that," he said shortly. "You weren't a substitute, Sara."

"Max said you love women until you seduce them, and then you just throw them away," she returned, staring straight at him.

His high cheekbones colored. "Damn Max!"

"If you're filthy rich, I expect you can buy as many women as you want," she continued conversationally.

"I don't buy women," he informed her. "I just don't want to get married."

"I don't think there's much danger of that, with Max carrying payoff checks around to all your girlfriends."

"I told you, I didn't tell Max to do that! It was her idea," he added. "She said she'd handle everything, and I was drunk enough not to care how."

Her eyebrows arched. "Drunk?"

He looked rigid. "You asked me to stop, and I couldn't," he growled. "How do you think I felt? I read the situation wrong and threw my conscience to the wind. Then Max told me how old you were." He winced. "Nineteen. Dear God!"

"Well, I'm not exactly a child," she shot back, growing angry herself. "And I'm no stranger to violence."

"People hit you with books in the bookstore, do they?" he asked, in a condescending, faintly amused tone.

She looked him in the eye. "A rebel paramilitary unit in Sierra Leone tossed a grenade into the clinic where my father was dressing wounds," she replied, watching the shock hit him. "I was standing beside him, holding a bowl of water. I was just ten, it was the only way I was able to help. My father died. I was concussed so badly that I had brain damage. That's why I can't match socks and earrings," she added. "I was right in the path of the grenade. Fragments penetrated my skull. One's still in there," she told him. "They were afraid to try to take it out."

His face was white. Absolutely white. "Why were you there?"

"My grandfather talked my father into doing a stint at missionary work. Dad had been a medic in the army and he was a lay preacher. He and my grandfather forced my mother into going. I begged to go, too. I thought Africa had to be the most exciting place on earth," she added in a dull, quiet tone. "Well, it was exciting, I guess."

"What happened to your mother?"

"She drank herself to death, after she used every low trick she could think of to embarrass my grandfather, to make him pay for Daddy's death. She grew famous locally. It's why I was innocent," she added bitterly. "I was afraid to go out with local boys, because she'd slept with some of them. Everybody thought I was like her. Everybody except Grandad."

Jared winced. "You didn't tell me any of this," he accused.

"We were friends," she replied heavily. "Just friends. I knew you'd never want somebody like me for keeps. I'm nothing like Max, or the women who chase after you. I don't care about money, I don't like diamonds, I'd never fit into high society and I'm brain-damaged. It would never have been my idea to get involved with you physically," she added coldly, "because I knew from the outset that there would be no future in it."

His teeth were grinding together. He'd felt bad before. Now he was sick to his stomach. Somewhere along the road to get rich, he'd lost his way. He had everything he'd ever wanted, but he had no one to share it with. He was alone. He would always be alone, surrounded by women who liked expensive jewelry and travel. And by bodyguards hired to protect him from people who wanted his money enough to risk anything to get it.

"It's going to ruin your reputation, having Tony live here with you," he pointed out.

"What reputation?" she muttered. "Thanks to you, I'm a fallen woman. If I do get pregnant, it's not something I'll be able to hide. Everybody who sees me will know what I've been up to. You'll be off in Las Vegas gambling, or sailing a yacht in the Mediterranean. At least Tony cares about me."

"There are things about Tony that you don't know," he said flatly.

"Yes, and there are things about Tony that you don't know, either," she retorted. "Tony got me to the hospital in time for them to save my life in Africa. I don't remember him, of course. A lot of my childhood was removed along with the damaged tissue in my brain."

His face was almost frozen in place. Nothing had gone right for him since the death of his daughter. He'd destroyed the life of the young woman in that bed. He'd disgraced and shamed himself. He didn't know what to do. But he knew that he needed to do something. He couldn't walk away and let Sara face this alone, not even with Tony for company. He'd have to have a nice talk with Tony, who hadn't bothered to tell him what he knew about Sara. All this misery might have been prevented.

"Don't you have a board meeting or a conference or a yacht race to go to?" Sara asked when he didn't speak. "I'd hate to delay you in any way from your business."

His eyes almost glowed red. He was just about to open his mouth and let her have it with both barrels when Tony walked in, carrying the phone.

"Sorry, Sara, but it's that guy from New York again," he said, handing it to her.

Jared frowned. "And just who the hell do you know in New York?" he demanded suddenly.

Ten

His own words shocked Jared. He was jealous. He didn't want to be.

Sara, oblivious to his thoughts, was torn between telling Jared to mind his own business and talking to the editor who was going to buy her book.

"Hello?" came a voice from over the telephone.

She put it to her ear. "This is Sara," she said.

Jared glared at her.

"Miss Dobbs? It's Daniel Harris here, at Mirabella Publishing Company."

"Yes, Mr. Harris?"

"I wanted to ask if you could do us a colored drawing of just one of the puppies to use in advertising. Also, we're going to need some ideas for a title. The contract will be on its way to you later this week. You aren't agented, are you?"

"No, I'm not," she said worriedly. "Do I need to be?"

"Of course not. You can have an attorney look over the contract for you, if you have any worries. We're offering you a standard royalty contract, with an advance—" he gave her the figure, and she gasped "—and then thereafter you'll get a percentage of the royalties when the book is on the shelves. We would also like for you to do some publicity, signings and so forth; but that will be when the book is published. Tentatively we're scheduling it for next spring. Sound okay?"

"Oh, yes," she said, beaming. "Mr. Harris, I'm just overwhelmed. I don't know how to thank you."

"It's a good book," he replied. "We're proud to publish it. If the terms are okay with you, we're sending the contracts down by courier. If you could send us the single drawing by next week or the week after, that would be fine."

"Yes, I can do that," she agreed, without mentioning her condition. She gave him her street address, trying not to let Jared's black scowl unnerve her.

"We'll be in touch."

"Thanks again," she replied, and hung up.

"Who's Daniel Harris?" Jared demanded.

Her eyebrows levered up. "What business is it of yours?"

The scowl darkened. "You're living with an ex-mercenary and handing out your home address to strangers in New York."

"Well, I am getting to be quite the vamp, aren't I?" she asked, and blinked her long lashes at him.

His teeth set audibly. "Who is he?"

She just glared, but he didn't back down an inch. "All right! He's an editor. I sold my children's book to him."

"Book?"

"The one I was working on? Lisa Parks's puppies?"

"Oh."

"They bought it. They're sending me a contract to sign."

"I'll have an attorney look it over for you," he offered.

She sat up. "Max isn't touching my book! Or my contracts!"

His expression lightened. "You're jealous."

She flushed. "So are you!"

He looked odd for a minute. He blinked. "Yes," he said finally.

That floored her. She just looked at him, dumbfounded.

"You might be carrying my child," he said after a minute, and something odd flashed in his eyes. "I'm territorial."

"It's my child, if there is one," she shot back. "You're not taking me over."

He was thinking, scheming, planning. It was in his expression. "I'm good at hostile takeovers."

"Remember me? The uncouth savage from Outer Cowpasture?" she prompted. "Imagine showing me off at cocktail parties! Think of the embarrassment when I open my mouth and drawl at your circle of friends."

"I don't have friends," he said coldly.

"Why not?"

He shrugged. "I never know if they're seeing me or my money."

"Fortunately I don't have that problem. Being poor has its advantages." She thought for a minute. "Well, I won't be as poor as I was, I suppose. If the book sells, I mean."

"If it's publicized enough, it will sell."

She gave him a wry look. "Don't even think about it. I can do my own publicity."

"I have a firm of publicists working for me, making up ad campaigns for the corporation and its divisions," he said.

"I don't work for your corporation."

"I thought we were family," he began.

"Tony and I are family. We just voted you out," she told him.

He moved closer to the bed. "You'd leave me alone in the world, with nobody?"

"You've got Max."

"I fired Max."

"I'm sure she won't be hard to replace," she said cattily. "And I'm sure you have a whole houseful of beautiful women ready to step into her shoes in other ways," she added meaningfully.

He avoided her eyes. "I'm a man," he said curtly. "Men have needs."

"Yes. I noticed," she said deliberately.

He moved restlessly. "I told you, I didn't mean for that to happen!"

She colored. "Great! If there's a baby, we can tell him he was an accident."

"Don't you dare!" he exploded.

She felt embarrassed at the statement, which she hadn't meant. He just made her mad. "I like babies," she said slowly, putting her hands flat on her stomach. "But it's scary, thinking about having one. They're so little…"

"When Ellen was born," he recalled quietly, "they put her in my arms. I'd never seen anything so tiny, so perfect." A sad smile touched his hard mouth. "I counted little fingers and toes, kissed her little nose, her feet. I never loved anything so much…"

He stopped and turned away, walking to the window. He looked out over the kitchen garden. It took him a minute to get his emotions under control.

Sara felt guilty. He'd loved his little child. He was afraid to have another one, afraid of losing it. He was closing up inside his shell for safety.

"Lisa and Cy lost their first baby," she said softly. "It was born with several rare birth defects. The doctors couldn't save it, and they had specialists all the way from Dallas. Lisa said it wasn't meant to be. They grieved for years. They were afraid to try again, too. But when she got pregnant again, everything went perfectly. She and Cy are like children themselves. They're crazy about this child and talking about having more. You can't hide from life," she concluded quietly. "I know. I've tried to. I have nightmares, remembering how my father died. I blocked it out for years, but sometimes now I can see it. I was conscious for just a few seconds after the concussion hit me. He was blown apart…" She had to stop. The memory was nightmarish.

He came back to the bed, standing over her. "I wish you could have told me about it," he said softly. "You haven't had it easy, have you?"

"Neither have you," she replied.

He drew in a slow breath. "I've lost my nerve," he said after a minute. "I don't think I could cope with losing another child."

"Neither did Lisa and Cy, but it didn't stop them from trying again. Life doesn't come with guarantees. Sometimes you just have to have faith."

"Faith," he scoffed. His face was hard, closed. "I hated God."

"He doesn't hate you," she said gently. "He doesn't punish people, you know. We have free choice. He doesn't control every second of our lives. Bad things happen. That's just the way life is. But faith is how we cope. Especially in small towns."

"You're only nineteen," he said quietly. "How did you come to be so wise, at such an age?"

"I had a hard life as a child," she replied simply. "It teaches you things you wouldn't learn in a protected environment." She searched his eyes. "I had a best friend at the mission in Africa. I watched her die of a fever. All the medicines we had couldn't cure her. One of our best workers, a nice boy named Ahmed, was gunned down two feet from his front door by rebels. He was smiling when he died. He said he was going to heaven now, and we weren't to grieve." She shook her head. "In Jacobsville, you can walk down the streets after dark and not get shot. I think of that as miraculous. People here just take it for granted."

He sat down beside her on the bed. "Where we sunk wells in South America," he said, "there were people living in conditions that you couldn't conceive of if you hadn't been there. Women were old by the age of forty, men were missing fingers, teeth, eyes. Children died in infancy of diseases we can prevent here. I felt guilty for making a profit from oil, when all those conditions were going on around me. I set up a foundation, to provide small grants to people who wanted to start businesses of their own. Women, mostly, who could weave cloth and keep chickens and a cow so they had eggs and milk and butter to sell. You'd be amazed at how far that little bit of money went."

She was fascinated. "But they sent kidnappers after you," she said.

He nodded. "The government nationalized all the oil companies. I pulled my people out. I'd already foiled one kidnapping attempt when I went down with our corporate attorneys to try to work the situation out. Do you know what a narcoterrorist is, Sara?"

"Yes. I've read about them. They grow coca and process it in factories on site, and sell coca paste to drug lords who market it in the U.S. and elsewhere," she said. "They control politicians."

"They always need money, for bribes and weapons," he said. "They've discovered that kidnapping wealthy foreigners is a quick, easy way to get cash. It's a bold move, sending people up here to try to nab me. But there was a raid just recently that cost them several million in operating cash. They thought I'd be easy to kidnap. Their mistake."

"Tony said that's why you came here," she replied. "A lot of his former comrades live in Jacobsville."

He nodded. "But it didn't work. They tracked me here without attracting attention. They might have succeeded, if you hadn't been canny enough to panic them." He shook his head, smiling softly down at her. "You're brave, Sara. I don't know a single other person, except maybe Tony, who'd have had the nerve to do what you did."

She felt warm inside. She shouldn't. He'd said terrible things to her. Besides, there was the possibility of a child. She looked up at him steadily. "So the kidnappers are in custody. Those worries are over. Right?"

His lips made a thin line. "They didn't actually kidnap anyone," he said. "Cash Grier is holding them right now on a weapons charge."

She felt her heart skip. "A weapons charge?"

"They had an AK-47 in the van and no permit," he replied. He frowned. "Actually I don't think you can get a permit for an automatic weapon as a private citizen. I'll have to ask Cash. Anyway, it's illegal in their case. But they didn't carry you out of the store or even lay hands on you." He sighed. "So there's a good chance that they're going to get out on bail as soon as their high-priced American attorney gets them to a bail hearing."

"The judge can set a high bail, if he or she is asked to," she began.

He smiled cynically. "Drug lords have so much money that even a million dollars is like pocket change to them. It won't help."

"But if they get out, won't they just try again?"

His expression changed. "Worried about me?" he asked in a soft, deep tone.

"I can worry, even if you're not family anymore," she returned pertly.

He laughed softly. The trap didn't feel like a trap. Maybe he'd been too grief-stricken to think of a child on his own, but this one had fallen right into his lap. Well, he'd helped it to, and he shouldn't feel happy about losing control with Sara, all the same.

She was watching his expression change, unable to follow what he was thinking. He seemed to be more comfortable with her now than he had several minutes ago. That didn't mean he was happy about their situation.

"What will you do?" she asked, because she really was worried.

"I don't know," he replied. "I think I'll go talk to the police chief." He frowned. "Now there's an odd bird," he said conversationally. "Someone said he was a Texas Ranger once."

"He was something else, once, too," she mused.

"The sniper thing?" he scoffed. "Gossip, I imagine."

"No," she said. "It's not. A Drug Enforcement Administration agent's little girl was kidnapped by the former head of one of the Mexican cartels last year. They threatened to kill her if the feds didn't back off their raid on a local drug warehouse. Cash Grier took out two of the kidnappers and the DEA agents got the rest and rescued the child. He made the shots in the dark from over six hundred yards away." She lowered her voice. "They say he was a covert assassin once."

His eyebrows lifted. "And he's a small town police chief?"

"He's happy here," she told him. "His wife, Tippy, used to be a model. They called her the 'Georgia Firefly.'"

"Well!"

"They have a little girl named Tris." She gave him a smirk. "So, you see, not everybody dislikes living in Outer Cowpasture."

"Touché," he replied.

"Maybe he has friends who could get those three guys on some sort of terrible federal charge," she murmured. "We never found out who the DEA agents were," she added. "One of them does undercover work, so he wasn't identified. The other, the child's mother, was a DEA agent, too. Her husband bought property here, but they're living in Houston until the end of the school year because of their daughter. They didn't want to put her into a strange school midyear."

"Do you know everything about everybody here?" he asked curiously.

"Sure," she told him. "Everybody does."

He glanced at the door, where Tony was just entering with soup and sandwiches on a tray. He glared at his ex-boss. "She needs to eat her lunch."

Jared got to his feet. "I was just leaving." He smiled down at Sara. "Eat it all up, like a good girl."

She flushed. "I'm not a kid."

He sighed. "Compared to me you are," he said quietly, and he looked lost.

"My mother was nineteen when she had me," Tony said abruptly.

Jared glanced at him, curious.

Tony shrugged. "It isn't the age, it's the mileage," he clarified, meeting the other man's eyes. "She's got almost as much mileage as you have. She just looks younger."

"I suppose so."

"I like babies," Tony said, setting the tray across Sara's legs.

Jared withdrew into his safe shell. He didn't say a word.

"Try not to get killed," Sara told him. "I'm in no condition to go to a funeral."

He laughed. "I'll do my best."

Tony glanced at him. "They'll try again," he said. "The minute they make bail, and they'll make it."

"Yes, I know," Jared replied. He pursed his lips. "I've had an idea."

"What?" Tony asked.

Jared glared. "Oh, sure, I tell you, and you tell her, and she tells everybody in Jacobsville."

"I only gossip about people I like," Sara protested.

"And pigs fly," he returned. "I'll come by tomorrow and check on you."

"I'll be fine," Sara protested.

He glanced at her belly with an unreadable expression. "I'll come by anyway."

He turned and left without another word.

"We could have offered him lunch," Sara told Tony. "Even if he isn't part of our family anymore."

"He'd curdle the milk," Tony muttered.

Sara laughed and finished her soup.

Jared went straight to Police Chief Cash Grier's office when he left Sara's house.

Cash was on the phone, but he hung up when Jared walked in and closed the office door.

"I haven't let them out yet," Cash told him, anticipating the reason he'd come.

"They'll skip town the minute they can make bail," Jared replied.

"In the old days, I'd have thrown them out the back door and charged them with attempted escape."

Jared glowered at him. "Civilization has its price."

Cash sighed. "Spoilsport."

Jared sat down in the visitor's chair without being asked. "They'll be as much a danger to Sara as they are to me," he said. "We have to find a way to prove they're kidnappers."

Cash's dark eyebrows went up. "We could stuff you in their van under a blanket and catch them at the city limits sign," he suggested dryly.

Jared chuckled. "That's just what I had in mind."

"It would be entrapment, I'm afraid," Cash replied, leaning back in his chair. "We'll have to find a legal way to keep them locked up."

"Suppose we have Tony the Dancer arrested for breaking and entering?"

Cash blinked. "Are we having the same conversation?"

"You could put him in the cell with the three kidnappers," he continued. "Tony could offer to help them get me, for revenge."

Cash whistled. "And I thought I was the only dangerous person in town."

"I didn't inherit what I've got," Jared told him. "The first company I started was a security business. I hired my men and myself out to oil companies as protection against terrorist attacks. An elderly oil tycoon with no dependents took a liking to me, taught me the business and left his company to me when he died. Eventually I sold the security company and parlayed the oil business into a worldwide corporation."

"So that's how you know Tony the Dancer."

Jared nodded. "He was the first man I hired, in the days before he worked for a legitimate authority. He still does odd jobs for me, from time to time."

Cash pursed his lips. "Then I suppose you know about his real background?"

Jared chuckled. "I check out everybody who works for me. His dossier was, to say the least, impressive."

"Yes, and how fortunate for him that he's not wanted in the States," Cash replied. "The only man I know who's a target for assassination in more countries than Tony is an undercover DEA agent named Ramirez."

"I know him," Jared said unexpectedly. "He worked for me, too, in the early days."

"He worked for a lot of people. He's involved in a case right now, so if you see him anywhere, pretend you don't know him."

"Isn't it risky for him to go undercover again?" Jared asked, curious.

"It is in Texas. He helped bring down the late drug lord,

Manuel Lopez. But he's not known locally, except by a few of us with ties to mercenaries. His name was never mentioned when his partner's child was kidnapped by drug smugglers here last year."

"I understand you brought down some of the kidnappers."

Cash nodded. "Some skills never get rusty." He leaned forward. "Who talks to Tony, you or me?"

"It had probably better be you," Jared said heavily. "He'd enjoy cutting my throat right now because of Sara."

"You didn't put Sara in the hospital," Cash replied, misunderstanding.

"No, but I may have gotten her pregnant," he said uncomfortably.

Cash's good humor eclipsed. His black eyes flashed at the man across the desk.

"We're all capable of making ungodly mistakes," Jared said quietly. "I don't think I've ever been around an innocent in my whole life. In recent years, women are as aggressive as men when it comes to sex."

"Not all of them," Cash said in an icy tone. "And Sara's only nineteen."

"I didn't find that out until it was too late," he said. "She seems older than she is."

"Considering her past, that isn't surprising."

Jared nodded. "I didn't know about that, either." His eyes held a sad, faraway look. "My daughter died eight months ago," he said. "I've grieved until it was an effort just to get out of bed in the morning. I don't understand how, but Sara brought the sunlight back in for me. I never meant to hurt her."

"I'm sorry," Cash said. "I know what it is to lose a child."

Jared met his eyes. There was, suddenly, a bond between them, forged of grief.

"Tony seems very fond of Sara."

Jared's face hardened. "Well, I'll take care of that when the time comes. If she's pregnant, that's my child. No way is he raising it."

Cash's eyebrows arched.

Jared cleared his throat. "He's not going to be able to settle down, anyway."

"You need to meet a few people around town," Cash told him. "Starting with Eb Scott."

"Eb Scott lives here?" he exclaimed.

"Yes. He's got a state-of-the-art training center for military and government resources," he said. "A lot of ex-mercs work for him."

"I'd never have expected Scott to be able to settle down."

"Most people said the same about me," Cash replied, smiling. "I think it comes down to what's important to you. It used to be work, for me. Now it's Tippy and our baby. And Rory," he added. "My brother-in-law." He chuckled. "He's twelve years old."

"It's still work that gets the major portion of my time," Jared replied. "But just recently I've begun to wonder if I don't have my priorities skewed." He studied his boots. "There aren't many women around like Sara. Of course, she's years too young for me."

"Judd Dunn, my assistant chief, is married to a young woman who was twenty-one at the same time he was thirty-two. They have twins and they're very happy. It depends a great deal on the woman. Some mature sooner than others."

"I guess they do."

Cash got to his feet. "I think I'll go have a word with Tony."

"I think I'll stop by the flower shop and start working on my campaign."

"Campaign?"

"Tony's not marrying Sara," Jared said shortly.

"That would be her decision," Cash cautioned.

"Yes, well, he can't afford as many roses and chocolates as I can, so let's see him compete!"

Cash knew when to shut up.

Sara was curious to see Cash Grier at her door. It must have something to do with the would-be kidnappers, she thought.

"How's it going, Sara?" he asked, smiling. "Feeling better?"

"A lot, thanks. Why are you here?"

"I have to talk to Tony." He moved closer to the bed. "You wouldn't mind having someone else stay with you for a couple of days, would you?"

"Why would you ask that?"

"Well, I'm going to have to arrest Tony for breaking and entering," he began, "and I don't want you to be here alone."

"Arrest…?"

"Now, calm down," he said. "It isn't for real."

"What isn't for real?" Tony asked, carrying two cups of coffee. "We can talk in the living room," he told Cash. "Sara, will you be okay for a few minutes?"

She couldn't put two words together.

Cash put his finger to his lips, walked out with Tony and closed the door, leaving Sara worried and quiet.

"But I didn't do it to steal anything," Tony was protesting. "I had to feed the cat!"

"It isn't for real," Cash insisted. "We want you to have to be thrown in with the kidnappers. Jared's having you arrested. You're furious at him. You want to get back at him. They'd love to help, I'm sure."

Tony put his coffee cup down. "Okay, now, you're starting to scare me. Have you been drinking?"

Cash chuckled. "Not today." He leaned forward. "Here's

the deal. I have to turn the men loose. All I'm holding them on is a weapons charge. I can't convince a sane judge to set a million dollars bail for a weapons charge. They're going to skip town the minute the cell door opens. If they do, they may try to grab Sara again, or they may go after Jared. Either way, it's going to lead to tragedy."

Tony pursed his lips. "Oh. I get it. You want me to lead them into a trap so that you can charge them with kidnapping."

"That's exactly what I want."

Tony's eyes narrowed. "Jared put you up to it."

"He did," Cash confessed. "He's worried about Sara."

"Not enough to keep himself from seducing her," Tony said angrily.

"I heard about that, too. He's sorry he did it. But if you have plans to help her raise the baby—if there is a baby—you're in for the fight of your life," he added. "He's just starting to feel possessive about her."

Tony scoffed. "He goes through women like a sword through tissue paper," he said coldly.

"Like a man who's afraid to risk his heart twice, I would have thought," Cash replied solemnly. "He told me about his little girl."

Tony's hard demeanor softened. "Yeah. That was rough. She was a sweet kid. He didn't spend nearly enough time with her, but he loved her. She loved him, too. Hell of a tragedy."

"Let's not have another one," Cash said. "Help me get these guys off the street before they do something stupid. Sara might not be so lucky a second time. And they wouldn't hesitate to kill her, after she foiled their plan so deftly."

"I thought about that, myself."

"It's only going to be for a couple of days," Cash said, "but we need somebody to stay with Sara. I thought maybe Harley Fowler…"

Tony's dark eyes twinkled. "Did you? I was thinking that Jared might be willing to sacrifice himself."

"Let him stay with Sara?"

Tony nodded. "It might be just the thing to get them both to sort out their priorities. And you could have extra patrols on the house, too. Just in case."

Cash grinned. "I like the way you think."

Tony just chuckled.

If making the decision was easy, telling it to Sara wasn't.

She looked utterly tragic. "But you can't put Tony in jail!" she cried. "I thought you were my friend!"

Cash grimaced. Tony was standing beside him in handcuffs.

"It isn't what you think, Sara," Tony agreed.

"Jared Cameron put you up to it, didn't he?" she demanded, and Tony grimaced, too.

She was almost in tears when the front door opened and Jared walked in carrying a suitcase. Sara spotted him, picked up a vase on the bedside table, drew back and flung it at him past the two stunned men. It shattered near Jared's shoulder.

"You get out of my house!" she yelled.

Cash looked at Tony. "Are you sure asking him to stay with her is a good idea?" he asked.

Eleven

Jared managed to look disgusted. "Is that any way to treat the father of your child?" he demanded.

"I'm not having a child!" she yelled, red-faced.

"How do you know?" he retorted. "It's too early for a pregnancy test."

"He's got you there," Cash interjected.

"You shouldn't be getting so upset, Sara, it's not good for you," Tony said worriedly.

"He's absolutely right," Jared said, putting down the suitcase. "I'm going to take care of you while Tony's away."

"You make it sound like he's going on vacation," Sara muttered. "He's going to jail!"

"Yes, I know."

She frowned. "You know?" She looked from him, to Tony, to Cash Grier. She wasn't stupid. "Oh."

"It's the only way," Tony told her. "Otherwise, you'll never be out of danger."

"You're sure you aren't going to keep him?" she asked Cash.

Cash smiled. "I'm sure. We'd better get going."

"I'll be back before you know it," Tony told Sara. He paused beside Jared. "You be careful, too. There may only be three of them, or there may not."

"I know that, too," Jared replied. He smiled wryly. "Don't forget who taught you surveillance techniques."

Tony chuckled. "I wouldn't dare. See you, Sara."

"See you, Tony."

Cash nodded and walked him out the door.

Jared watched them leave, his hands deep in his pockets.

"What did you mean about surveillance techniques?" she asked.

He turned. His green eyes were mischievous. "The first business I ever owned provided private security. Tony and I worked together until we could train assistants."

She studied him quietly. "And what did you do before that?" she asked.

"I was a cop in San Antonio."

Her lips fell open. "For heaven's sake! And you own an oil corporation now?"

"I've had a lot of help along the way. Most of it from Tony," he told her, stepping gingerly around shattered pottery. "We were always best friends until you came along."

"Well, you know why that happened," she muttered.

"Yes, I do. No need to remind me." He accidentally stood on a piece of ceramic that broke again. "Where's a broom?"

"In the closet in the kitchen," she began, but he was gone before she could ask anything else.

He came back with a broom and a dustpan and cleaned the floor as naturally as if he'd done it all his life.

"Were you in the military, before you were a policeman?" she asked, curious about him.

"Army," he said. "I was in special forces. So was Tony." He poured the broken pieces of what had been a vase into a nearby trash can and propped the broom and dustpan beside it. "He was best man at my wedding."

He'd never talked to her like this before. It was fascinating. "Did you love your wife?"

"Yes, when I married her," he said. "We both came from ranch families. My father got kicked in the head by a bull and died soon afterward. My mother grieved herself to death. Marian's parents died in a tornado outbreak. We'd known each other most of our lives. We were friends. I suppose we thought friendship was enough. It wasn't."

"Why did she leave you?"

"She found someone she loved," he said simply. "She took our daughter, Ellen, with her. She was a wonderful mother. Ellen was happy with her. I wasn't home much, but when I was, Ellen was always welcome to come and stay with me. My permanent home is in Oklahoma," he added, "where my corporation headquarters is."

"But you bought a ranch here," she said, mystified.

"I told you at the cemetery that I needed a change," he said. "I meant it. I was grieving for Ellen and upset over Marian's suicide just afterward. I thought new surroundings would help me get past the depression."

"The surroundings don't matter much," Sara said gently. "Pain and grief are portable. They go with you."

He glanced down at her and smiled warmly. "There's that odd insight again. You really are old for your age."

"And getting older by the day," she replied.

He moved to the bed and sat down beside her. He was

wearing jeans and a chambray shirt, open at the neck. He looked very sensual with his hair faintly ruffled and his nice tan.

Without warning, his big, lean hand pressed gently on her flat stomach. "I made a hell of a fuss about it. But maybe it wouldn't be a bad thing, if you're pregnant. I'll be a better father this time around."

"You can come and visit anytime you like," she told him.

He frowned. "My child isn't being born out of wedlock."

"Well, he won't have much choice, because I am not marrying you," she said firmly.

"Why not?" he asked, and seemed really intent on her reason.

She colored and averted her eyes. "Because I don't ever want to have to do that again."

He lost color. He knew his heart had stopped. "Sara, it was your first time and I was in too much of a hurry," he said softly. "I hurt you because I rushed it."

Her face was red by now. She couldn't possibly look at him. She clasped her hands together and picked at her thumbnail nervously.

He tilted her embarrassed face up to his. "I won't ever hurt you again," he promised. "It gets better. Honest."

She grimaced.

She was so young, he thought sadly. Probably he should never have touched her. But she made him feel young and vital and full of fire. She brought feelings of nurturing and possession to him. He'd never wanted a woman for keeps. Even his wife had been a footnote in his life. But this woman was magic. Sheer magic.

He thought back to their first meeting, and inspiration struck. "You could have your own bookstore," he said.

Her eyes widened. "My own…?"

"We could even build a child activity center into it. The baby could play while you worked. And if customers with children came in, they could play there while their parents browsed. There could be a snack shop with fancy coffee."

She was melting. Just the thought of her own place was tantalizing. "Really?"

He smiled at her enthusiasm. She couldn't even hide it. "I could delegate more, and travel less. We could have more than one child."

She looked into his eyes with all her longings showing there. Children. A home. A business. Max. She scowled and glared at him.

"What?"

"Are you sure you fired Max?" she wondered aloud. "Tony says you're always firing her, but she always comes back."

"This time it's permanent," he assured her. He drew in a long breath. "I'm through with the playboy life as well. I thought a few encounters would be a cure for loneliness. It wasn't. It only made me feel cheap."

That was a powerful admission, she thought. And he did seem sincere.

His big hand pressed gently against her stomach. He looked at it, his eyes quiet and full of wonder. "You know your body better than I do. What's your gut feeling?"

"I…I don't know," she faltered. "Really. It's too soon."

He smiled. "Well, either way, we'll cope. If you aren't pregnant, we'll spend some time getting to know each other before we start a family. We'll have plenty of time." He pursed his lips. "And Tony will have to find himself a new source of entertainment, besides looking after you and cooking," he said, and felt guilty and elated all at once. If she really was pregnant, Tony was right out of the running as a potential husband.

She frowned. "Tony will be all right, won't he? There are three of those men. They're all big and muscular, and they can't watch them all the time while they're in custody at the county detention center." Which was where they would be taken, because the city didn't maintain a jail.

He chuckled. "I've seen Tony take on six guys and walk away grinning," he told her. "It's the best idea we could come up with," he added, tugging the sheet up over her belly tenderly. "We can't risk having them make bail and come after you again."

She grimaced. "Life used to be so uncomplicated until you came along," she sighed wistfully.

"You're too young to appreciate monotony," he returned. He bent and kissed her gently on the forehead. "Try to get some sleep. I have a few phone calls to make, then we'll talk some more about the future."

She could have argued that there might not be one, but it was sweet to pretend. She smiled at him and agreed.

Tony was muttering, furious, as he was put into the general quarters in detention, wearing an orange jumpsuit and flip-flops. He glowered at everybody around him.

"I didn't even take anything!" he yelled at the guard who'd delivered him. "I was just feeding the cat."

"Tell it to a judge," the deputy replied wearily.

"You bet I will!" he raged. "He just wants me out of the way, so he can walk off with my girl. You tell Jared Cameron that when I get out of here, I'm going to drive a truck over him!"

"Terroristic threats and acts carry a felony charge," the amused deputy called over his shoulder.

Tony gave him a four-fingered salute.

One of the men in the dormitory was giving him odd looks. Tony stared at him belligerently. "You got a problem?" he demanded.

The man was about his own age, tall and muscular, with a mustache and tattoos over both arms. "Sounds like you got one," he said with a hint of a foreign accent. "Somebody locked you up for nothing, huh?"

Tony moved to a chair and sat down. "Something like that."

The man took a chair beside him. "Jared Cameron? I think I heard of him."

"Most people have," Tony muttered. "God, I wish I had a smoke!"

"Can't have cigarettes in here, my friend," the other man chuckled. "But I could get you some weed, if you got anything to trade."

"Do I look like I got anything to trade?" Tony demanded. "What are you in here for?"

"Weapons charge," the man said easily. "But me and my boys, we'll be out as soon as we have our bail hearing."

"Lucky you," Tony told him. "I'm in for breaking and entering. It's a felony."

"Not a big one," his companion said.

Tony stared at him. "It is if you're out on probation," he said.

The man grimaced. "Ah. I see. Too bad."

"Yeah. Too bad." His eyes narrowed angrily. "Jared Cameron better hope I get the death penalty for it, because the day I get out of here, he's a dead man. I know his routine, the layout of his house, everything!"

"How is that?"

"I was working as his bodyguard," Tony scoffed, "until he took a fancy to my girl and stole her from me. Now he wants me out of the way."

The man looked down at the floor. The room smelled of foul odors. Tony wondered if any of these people had ever been introduced to soap. One was obviously coming down from a drug-induced high, shaking and threatening people. Another was staggering drunk. Nobody looked as if he was a stranger to the criminal justice system.

"You know," the other man began casually, "you could make a lot of money and get even with Cameron at the same time if you wanted to."

Tony was all ears. "I could? How?"

"I know some people who would pay a lot of money for him."

"He's no pushover," Tony warned.

"Yes, but he is now lacking his bodyguard," the man persisted. "Before he can hire another one, it would be a good time to apprehend him."

Tony stared at the man. "Yeah. It would, wouldn't it?"

The man got up. "I got to talk to my friends about it. But I think I could get you in on it, if you're interested."

"I got no money for a lawyer and Cameron didn't even offer to help me," Tony muttered. "In fact, I think it was him who told the police I broke into the girl's house. Some boss!"

The other man was grinning now. "You want to get even, yes?"

"Yes."

"We will talk more later."

Tony shrugged. "Well, I'm not going anywhere. Not right away, at least."

That night, the jailer came and took Tony out, mumbling something about an attorney wanting to talk to him about his arrest.

Cash Grier was waiting in the interrogation room. He turned as Tony was escorted inside and the door closed, with the guard standing on the other side of it.

"Any luck?" Cash asked him.

Tony grinned. "Their ringleader wants me to help them put the snatch on Jared. He's been talking his two companions into it. One of them thinks I'm a plant. The other has, basically, the IQ of a plant."

Cash chuckled. "So you're in?"

"Seems so. I expect them to double-cross me the instant they see Jared in their sights, of course."

Cash thought for a minute. "We'll have Sara call a bail bondsman for you. We'll pay him without letting anyone else know. When you and the three outlaws get out, we'll have you wired and a homing device placed in their van. As soon as they grab Jared, we'll have them for attempted kidnapping and give them to the feds."

"Not a bad plan."

"You really think so? Thanks," Cash said with enthusiasm. "I don't actually know any feds, you understand, but I can look them up in the phone book."

Tony was laughing. "And they give you real bullets, do they?"

"I haven't shot anybody in a year, at least," Cash said with mock dismay.

"Just don't shoot me, when you show up to get those other guys. I weigh five pounds more than I should because of bullets they can't take out."

"I have a couple of my own that never left," Cash replied. "Okay. I'll go. I'll talk to Jared and have a couple of my officers standing by. Don't do anything until they actually have Jared in their van," he added cautiously. "We have to have charges that will stick."

"You keep an eye on Sara as well," Tony told him. "These guys don't act like they're hitting on all six cylinders. There's no telling what they may try next."

"I noticed. You know," he added seriously, "you look pretty good in orange."

Tony's eyes narrowed. "No fair picking on innocent victims of crime."

"Oh, that's rich, coming from you," Cash chuckled. "I'm leaving."

"Tell Sara not to worry about me."

"I can tell her, but it won't do any good. She likes you."

He shrugged. "I like her, too."

"We'll find a way to separate you from the kidnappers at the bail hearing so we can get you wired. I've already done their van."

"They may look for a homing device," Tony pointed out.

"They can look all they like," he replied. "They'll never find this one. See you."

"Yeah. You, too."

It was a very good plan. Tony was wired just before he left with the three men, now dressed again in their civilian clothing as Tony was. They seemed to trust him.

But once they were in the van, the driver spoke in an Arab dialect on his cell phone, blissfully unaware that Tony spoke that particular dialect.

The leader of the kidnappers told his contact that they were on their way to get the woman Jared loved. Somehow they'd found out that Jared was staying with Sara. They were going to hold her long enough to make him give himself up to them, then they were going to kill her. They would kill Tony, too, because he could become a liability once the girl was dead. They would kill Jared eventually, the minute they had the ransom in their hands. They already had airplane tickets. It would be a matter of hours. The contact could meet them at the airport in Belize where they usually hooked up.

Tony cursed the change of plans. He couldn't warn anybody. If he repeated what the kidnapper had said, they'd know he spoke Arabic and he'd be dead. If he didn't, Sara would be in terrible danger. Jared was with her. It would be an easy matter to take both of them.

He had to pretend that he hadn't understood a word and

act nonchalant. "Don't you guys kill Cameron," he cautioned belligerently. "He's all mine!"

"Be assured, we have no plans to kill him. We only wish for the ransom he will bring." He told the driver to slow down as they approached Sara's house.

"Hey," Tony murmured, looking out the windshield. "That ain't Cameron's house!"

"He isn't in his house," the leader of the three men replied. "Cameron is with your girlfriend."

"Don't you hurt her," Tony warned.

"Relax, my friend!" the other man laughed. "We intend only to take Cameron hostage. Then you and the girl will be free. I give you my word."

Which was as good as his sense of fashion, Tony thought sarcastically, but he only nodded and pretended to believe the man. While he was nodding, he was considering his options. He was not only wearing a wire, he had a hidden gun in an ankle holster and a commando knife in a sheath inside his slacks. He had a watch with a pull-out garrote. All that, combined with advanced martial arts training, should stand him in good stead if he had the opportunity to act.

"You taking Cameron out of the country after you nab him?" Tony asked.

The three men were intent on the sparse lighting of the small house just ahead. "Yes, yes," the leader said, distracted. "We have a base in Peru, where we can hold him until the ransom is paid."

Tony doubted that Jared Cameron would be alive after the ransom was in their hands.

"Stop!" the leader told the driver. "You stay and wait for our signal," he added. "We will take the bodyguard with us. Be vigilant."

"Of course," the driver replied.

The leader slid open the side panel of the van and motioned the shorter man and Tony out behind him.

"You will go first," he told Tony. "Knock on the door and pretend that you have come to check on the woman."

"Not a bad plan," Tony said, grinning, because this plan would give him room to act. "You guys are smart."

"You must not harm Cameron," the leader told him firmly. "We need the ransom very badly. Later, we will give him to you, once we have the funds."

Tony pretended to mull over the suggestion. "Okay. But you better give me a crack at him."

"We will. Of course we will," the leader said. He was now holding an automatic weapon. So was his companion.

It was going to be tricky, Tony mused, but he'd been in tighter spots. "You guys better get out of sight," Tony told them, hoping Cash Grier was listening closely to what he said to the hidden microphone.

"We will be just around this corner," the leader said. His face went hard. "We will have you in our sights, also. For insurance."

"In other words, I get shot if I try anything funny," Tony replied. "Hell, I want the guy as much as you do!"

The leader seemed to relax, a little. "Very well." He motioned to the second man and they went, light on their feet, around the corner of the porch.

Tony knocked on the door. He heard footsteps coming. They weren't Jared's footsteps. He would have known them anywhere. He had to hide a grin.

The door opened. Tony dived through it as Cash Grier slammed the door. Outside there was gunfire.

"Quick reflexes," Cash remarked to Tony.

"I've, uh, had a little practice over the years. How about Jared and Sara?"

"When we heard your plan over the wire," Cash replied,

"we got them out of the house. They're at Jared's. Nobody here but old Morris the cat, and we put him in a closet, just in case."

The shooting ended.

"All clear!" a voice called.

Cash and Tony went out onto the porch, where four Jacobsville police officers and a man in a suit were leading the two would-be kidnappers toward the front door. In the yard, the wheel man was standing in front of his van, handcuffed, with two other men in suits holding guns on him.

"Nice operation," Cash told his men. "I knew that extra training in hostage negotiation would come in handy."

"Hostage negotiation?" Tony exclaimed. "They've all got guns!"

Cash looked sheepish. "Well, you negotiate your way and I'll negotiate my way."

The officers chuckled. So did Tony.

They had tape of the kidnappers confessing. Federal marshals were escorting them to Dallas, where they'd face federal charges. Their kidnapping days were over.

Tony was back at the ranch the next day, but Jared was sending him on to Oklahoma to make sure the house was ready for occupants. And also to make sure no more would-be kidnappers were lurking around.

"You take care, Sara," Tony told her gently, and bent to kiss her on the cheek. "I expect we'll see each other again."

"I hope so." She hugged the big man and kissed his lean cheek. "Thanks for everything."

"No problem."

He shook hands with Jared. "I'll put Fred and Mabel to work getting the house set to rights. I assume you're not coming home alone," he added with a grin.

"You assume right," Jared said with a tender, possessive

look toward Sara, who was just going back inside the house to make sure old Morris was all right. Tony had brought him over after all the excitement was past.

Tony stuck his hands in his pockets. "I've got to go back to my day job," he said. "I'm tempted to give it up, but it's comfortable."

"You're too young to want to be comfortable," Jared replied. "Besides, you have to keep those reflexes honed." He smiled mischievously. "You might be the next target for kid-nappers looking for ransom." He looked past Tony at the sleek Jaguar sports car that had been lodging in the huge garage with Jared's classic automobiles. "That car could get you some unwelcome attention."

"You're just saying that because you don't want me to take it away," Tony shot back.

"You could always get a newer one," Jared suggested.

"I don't like the newer ones. I like that one."

"Damn!"

"Listen, we signed papers," Tony reminded him. "It isn't as if I stole it."

Jared pursed his lips. "There's a thought," he began.

Tony wagged a finger at him. "You report this car stolen, and you'll never make it home to Oklahoma without being arrested for possession of at least one Schedule I substance. I swear!"

"All right, all right," Jared muttered. "You did see it first at the auto show."

"Damned straight, I did." He hesitated. "You take care of yourself. And if there is a baby," he added, "I get to be the godfather."

Jared opened his mouth to speak.

"I know at least one shaman who can do nasty spells back home in North Carolina," he interrupted.

"You're from Georgia," he shot back.

"My foster parents are from Georgia. I was born in Cherokee, North Carolina."

"Yes, but your real father wasn't."

Tony gave him a glare. "We don't talk about him."

"You need to," Jared said solemnly. "You have to deal with it one day."

"I'm going to Oklahoma." Tony put his sunglasses on. "Right now."

"Nice shades."

"That's what my boss said."

"You didn't! You wouldn't swipe his sunglasses…?"

"Of course I didn't swipe them. I won them."

"How?"

"He had a full house, I had four aces," he said smugly. "He threw the deck at me and walked out."

"Serves him right for getting suckered into playing poker with you," Jared said. He held out a hand. "Be safe."

Tony shook it. "You, too. I'll be in touch."

Sara came back with Morris in her arms, just in time to watch him drive away in a classic red sports car which, Jared told her, belonged to Tony.

"If Tony's leaving, why am I still here?" she asked Jared worriedly. "The bad guys are in Dallas by now, and I'm very fit."

He drew her to him, quiet and somber. "You're still here because we have things to talk about."

"Such as?"

He was oddly hesitant. "Come here."

He picked her up, Morris and all, and carried her into the living room, dropping down onto the sofa with her. Morris, uncomfortable, jumped down and went in search of food.

"We haven't known each other for a long time," Jared began quietly. "But I think we're basically the same sort of people. You're no doormat, and you're smart. You'd fit right in back in Oklahoma. Most of my friends are working people, just as I used to be. I don't travel in high social circles. In the past I spent a lot of time on airplanes, but that's going to stop. Whether or not you're pregnant doesn't matter right now. I'm going to delegate authority and start living my life for something other than making money."

"That sounds serious," she said, and her heart was hammering away in her chest. His eyes held a warmth she hadn't seen there before.

"It's very serious. I'm a good deal older than you," he began, "and I've had, and lost, a family. You could stay here and marry someone younger. Harley Fowler, maybe."

"I don't love Harley," she said softly, searching his eyes. "He's my friend. As for our ages," she added, "I'm more mature than a lot of women, because of what I've gone through."

He traced her mouth with a long forefinger. "Yes, you are," he agreed quietly. "Which leads to the next question."

"Which is?" she probed.

"Will you marry me, Sara?"

Twelve

Sara just looked at him, with her heart plain in her eyes. "Do you love me?" she asked, hesitating.

He smiled tenderly. "Yes," he said. "Of course I love you." He hesitated. His dark eyebrows lifted. "Well?"

"I loved you the minute you walked into the bookstore," she replied breathlessly. "I didn't really think you were an ogre, you know."

"Maybe I was, sort of," he returned, smiling. "But you've reformed me. So what do you think about getting married here and moving back to Oklahoma?"

"I don't mind where we live, as long as we're together," she told him. "But Morris the cat has to come with us." She paused. "Do you have pets?"

He laughed. "Do I! I've got saddle horses, cattle dogs, two huge Persian cats, an emu and an Amazon parrot."

"Oh, goodness," she exclaimed. "Why do you have an emu?"

He traced her mouth. "Ellen wanted one," he said simply. "I'd never even seen an emu, but a rancher I know was experimenting with them. We got Ellen a baby emu. She was crazy about him. We named him Paterson, after the Australian poet, and raised him with two border collies. The collies chase cattle, and the emu runs right along with them." He laughed. "It's quite a sight."

"I imagine so."

"We'll have cat furniture set up for Morris. After a few days of being spoiled, he'll adjust."

"What about your cats?"

He shrugged. "They'll all spit and fuss for a week, then they'll curl up and sleep together at night."

She smiled. It was usually the case when two sets of cats met. "We could be married here?" she asked, still having trouble believing it.

"Of course."

"I could wear a wedding gown, and carry a bouquet?"

"You can even have a photographer," he replied. "So that we have nice pictures to prove that we're married."

"That would be nice."

"We'll fly up to Dallas. You can have a gown from Neiman Marcus."

"I could buy something off the rack," she protested.

He brought her small hand to his lips and kissed the palm. "I'm fairly notorious," he said. "There will be news coverage. You wouldn't want me to look like a cheapskate on national television, would you?" he asked reasonably.

She laughed. "Nobody would think such a thing."

"Ha!"

Her head was spinning. She couldn't believe how quickly it had all happened. But there was that other thing, that worrisome thing...

He was watching her expression closely. He knew what the problem was. They were alone in the house. Old Morris had wandered off into the kitchen. He was safely established, for the time being. He pursed his lips as he looked down into Sara's worried face.

"There's no time like the present," he murmured.

"Excuse me?"

He bent and drew his mouth tenderly against Sara's. "Don't think," he whispered. "Don't worry. Just let go."

While he was talking, his hands were moving over her in soft, light caresses that made her mind overload. She wanted to tell him something, but he'd unbuttoned her shirt and his mouth was already on her breasts.

She gasped at the sensations. They weren't like last time. He was insistent, and expert. As the heated minutes sped past, she was as frantic to get her clothes out of the way as she had been to escape him the last time he'd touched her this way. But the sensations she was feeling now were explosive, overwhelming. She arched up to his ardent mouth and sobbed as his hands found her under the concealing cloth and created exquisite waves of pleasure.

She was under him. She felt the cold leather under her bare back, the heated weight of his body over and against hers. His mouth trailed down her body and back up again, in soft, arousing kisses that trespassed in all sorts of forbidden areas.

He asked her something, but she was already too far gone to hear him. Shivering, aching for satisfaction, she drew her legs up to ease his path, she arched up to his devouring mouth. It was the closest to heaven she'd ever imagined.

When she finally felt him, there, she dug her nails into his hips and held on for dear life as he buffeted her on the sofa. She was aware of the ceiling overhead, and the sound of his rough breathing, of her own frantic little gasps, as the pleasure began to build.

It was like climbing, she thought breathlessly, from one level to the next and the next and the next, and the pleasure increased with every fierce downward motion of his hips. She was dying. She couldn't survive. The pleasure was so deep and throbbing that it was almost pain. She strained for some goal she couldn't quite reach, her hips darting up to meet his, her body arched in a strained posture that was painful. She was almost there, almost there, almost…there!

He pushed down, hard, and she felt the world drop out from under her as a wave of white-hot pleasure racked her slender body and held her, motionless, in its vise-grip.

He lifted his head seconds later, drenched in sweat and barely able to get a whole breath. She was shivering in the aftermath. Her soft eyes were drowned in tears of joy as she lay under him, satiated.

"Now do you understand what was missing, the last time?" he whispered tenderly.

"Oh, yes." She locked her arms around his neck. She was trembling. "Is it always like this?"

"No," he murmured, smiling as his hips began to move again. "It gets better."

"You're kidding…!"

It was the last remark she was able to make for some time.

The wedding was beautiful, Sara thought, amazed at the media that gathered to watch Jared Cameron merge his oil empire with an unknown little bookseller in Jacobsville, Texas. One of the newswomen just shook her head, having covered stories that Jared featured in years ago. This little retiring Texas rose didn't seem at all the type of woman he'd marry. But then he looked down at his new bride, under her veil, and the look they exchanged made everything clear. Love, the reporter thought, was truly an equalizer.

Harley Fowler congratulated them with a bittersweet smile. Sara hugged him and thanked him for all he'd done, especially scaring away the kidnappers in the bookstore. He wished them well. Sara was very fond of him, but she'd never felt romantic toward him. He knew it, and accepted it.

All the mercs showed up at the wedding, along with just about everybody in town. Sara felt like Cinderella at the ball. And now she was going away with her very own version of Prince Charming. She'd never been so happy.

Several days later, Sara had packed up everything, including Morris the cat, and Tony had arranged for Sara's possessions, plus Morris, to travel to the house in Oklahoma City, where Jared lived most of the time. Morris rode in a chauffeured limousine, with one of Tony's old comrades, and Jared's new bodyguard, Clayton, at his side.

"Morris will never get over that," Sara told her new husband.

"It was the safest way I could think of," Jared replied, smiling. "Clayton will take great care of him. Tony trained him. He's good."

"We won't have to worry about kidnappers again, will we?" she worried.

He drew her gently into his arms. "*We* won't worry. We'll let Clayton worry. That's what he gets paid for."

"I thought Tony worked for you all the time," she commented.

"He was borrowed, for this assignment," he told her, and didn't offer any further information.

"He's rather mysterious, in his way," she said.

Jared raised an eyebrow. "You have no idea how mysterious," he assured her.

"Tell me."

He chuckled. "Not now. We've got work to do. You have to help me pack, now that we've got you covered."

"I'll miss Jacobsville," she said.

"I know you will, honey," he replied. "But you'll get used to it. Life has to be lived. You can't sit by the road and watch it pass."

"Maybe when we're old," she began.

He nodded. "Yes. Maybe when we're old."

"It was sweet of Dee to give us those rare World War II memoirs for a wedding present, wasn't it?" she asked.

"Yes, it was. And sweet of you to pack up all your grand-father's collection to bring with us. I'll only read one a week, I promise," he said when he saw her expression.

She frowned. "That reminds me, are you a sports fan?"

"I love soccer," he replied.

She beamed. "It's my favorite sport!"

"In that case, we'll make plans to go to the next World Cup."

"We could? Really?"

"Yes." He drew her against him and kissed her. "I love you."

She smiled. "I love you back."

"No regrets?"

She shook her head. "I'm going to take very good care of you."

He kissed her eyes closed. "And I'm going to take very good care of you." He rocked her in his arms. "Just for the record, any unusual nausea?"

She drew back and looked up at him, grimacing. "I'm afraid not. In fact, something monthly started up this morning. I'm sorry."

He kissed her. "We won't rush things," he said gently. "We'll grow together before we start a family. We'll travel. We'll go shopping. We'll find a nice location for a bookstore."

"You meant that?" she exclaimed.

"Of course I meant it," he said, smiling. "You can have anything you want, Sara."

She moved into his arms and pressed close. "Most of all, I want you, for all my life. I love you very much."

He swallowed hard and his arms closed around her. Grief had almost destroyed him, but this sweet, gentle woman had brought him back into the sunlight. She was his world now. He rested his cheek on her soft hair. "I love you, too, baby. I'll make you happy and keep you safe, all my life," he promised.

And he did.

* * * * *

IN THE ARMS OF
THE RANCHER

JOAN HOHL

Joan Hohl is a bestselling author of more than sixty books. She has received numerous awards for her work, including a Romance Writers of America Golden Medallion award. In addition to contemporary romance, this prolific author also writes historical and time-travel romances. Joan lives in eastern Pennsylvania with her husband and family.

To:
My new editor, Krista, and her assistant, Shana.
Welcome to my imaginary world!

Prologue

He needed a break, and he was going to take one. Hawk McKenna stood in the sunlight slanting from the west onto the covered porch that ran the width of his ranch house, his hand absently resting on the head of the large dog next to him.

Though the sun's rays were warm, there was a nip in the early October breeze. It felt good to Hawk after the long, hot, hard but productive and profitable summer. Yet he knew that before too long, the mild autumn would be replaced by snowflakes swirling, driven by harsh, bitter cold winds.

When the deep snows came, Hawk knew the

work on the ranch would be just as hard as it had been during the summer. No, he thought, smiling wryly as he gazed around him at the valley in which his ranch was nestled, the work in the deep snows of winter entailed numb fingers and toes and being chilled to the bone. All things considered, he'd rather sweat than freeze.

The idea of what was to come sent a shiver through him. He must be getting old, Hawk mused, stepping from the porch into the fading sunlight. But as he was only thirty-six, perhaps it wasn't so much his age as it was tiredness. Other than a run into Durango, the city closest to the ranch, for supplies, he hadn't been off the property in months.

Nor had he been in any female company in all that time, other than that of his foreman Jack's nineteen-year-old daughter and his wrangler Ted's wife.

Not exactly what Hawk had in mind for female company. Ted's wife, Carol, while very nice and pretty, was…well, Ted's wife. And Jack's daughter, Brenda, was even prettier but far too young, and she was becoming a pain in the ass.

A year or so ago, Brenda, who had hung around the ranch every summer since Jack had come to work for Hawk, had begun trailing behind Hawk. Her sidelong, supposedly sexy glances were beginning to grate on his nerves.

He wasn't interested. She was a kid, for cripes' sake. Not wanting to hurt her feelings, Hawk had tried dropping subtle hints to that effect, to no avail. She had gone right on with the sly, intimate looks, at moments even deliberately making physical contact, while making the touches appear accidental.

Frustrated, not knowing what to do other than be brutally honest by telling her to act her age and knock off her flirting, Hawk had approached Jack about her behavior. Treading as carefully as if he were negotiating a mine field, Hawk had asked him what Brenda's plans were for the future.

"Oh, you know kids," Jack said, grimacing. "They want everything. They just can't decide what in particular."

Hawk sighed. Not much help there. "It's over a year since she graduated high school. I thought she was planning to go on to college?"

"She now says she isn't sure." Jack gave him a probing look. "Why? Has she been making a pest of herself hanging around here?"

Drawing a slow breath, Hawk hedged. "Well… she has been kinda getting underfoot."

Jack nodded his understanding. "Yeah, I noticed," he admitted with a sigh. "I've been meaning to say something to her about it, but you know girls… They get so dramatic and emotional."

"Yeah," Hawk agreed, although he really didn't

know girls, as in kids. He knew women, knew as well how emotional they could be. He worked hard at avoiding the dramatic ones.

"I'll talk to her," Jack said, heaving a sigh before flashing a grin. "Maybe I can talk her into spending the winter with her mother, as she always did while she was still in school." He chuckled.

Hawk shook his head. Jack and his former wife had not divorced amicably. Although Brenda had spent only the summers with Jack while she had been in school, mere days after receiving her diploma, she'd taken off, telling her mother she wanted to be on her own, *free.*

Well, Hawk mused, if being on her own and free meant living with her father while bugging the hell out of him, she had succeeded too well. "You handle it any way you want," Hawk said, not bothering to add that Jack had better handle it, and her, sooner rather than later. "Maybe a father-daughter heart-to-heart will help."

"Will do." Jack started to turn away.

"Hold up a minute," Hawk said, stopping Jack short. "I'm going to take off for a couple weeks for a little R and R. Can you hold down the fort, and Boyo?" Hawk ruffled the hair on the dog's head.

Jack gave him a look. "You know damn well I can."

Hawk grinned. "Yeah, I know. I just like riling you now and again."

"As if I didn't know," Jack drawled. "You tellin' me where you're going and when?"

"Sure. No secret. I'm going to Vegas as soon as I can make room reservations. I'll let you know where I'll be staying." He paused before going on. "When I get back, you and Ted can take some time off. While I'm gone, you can decide who goes first."

"Good deal." Jack grinned and went back to work.

Relieved, Hawk drew a deep breath of the pine-scented mountain air. The dog looked up at him expectantly. "Not this time, Boyo," he said, ruffling the dog's thick hair. "You'll be staying with Jack."

If a dog could frown, Hawk thought, that was exactly what the big Irish wolfhound was doing. With a final hair ruffle, he turned to the porch steps.

A smile on his lips, Hawk walked into the house, picked up the phone and began punching in numbers.

One

Kate Muldoon was behind the hostess station, checking the reservation list, when the restaurant entrance door opened. A smile of greeting on her lips, she glanced up to see a man just inside the door and felt a strange skip beat in her chest.

The first word to jump into her mind was *cowboy*. Kate couldn't say why that particular descriptive word came to mind. There wasn't a pair of boots or a Stetson in sight. He was dressed the same as most patrons, casually in jeans that hugged his hips like a lover, a pale blue button down shirt tucked into the narrow denim waistband, the sleeves rolled up to mid-forearm.

His height was impressive. Kate judged him to be six feet five or six inches tall at least, maybe more. He was lean, muscular and rangy. He had a head full of thick, straight dark, almost black, hair with strands of deepest red glinting under the lights. It was long, caught at his nape and was tied with a narrow strip of leather.

He was striking—sharply defined features, a squared jaw and piercing dark eyes. His skin was tanned, near bronze. Part Native American, perhaps? Maybe.

But he wasn't what she would call handsome, not in the way Jeff was….

"May I help you?" Kate asked brightly, pushing away errant thoughts of her former lover.

"I don't have a reservation, but I'd like a table for one, if you have it." His voice was smooth, low, rather sexy and alluring.

Telling herself to grow up, Kate said, "Yes, of course. If you'll follow me." Scooping up a menu, she ushered him to a small table for two set in a corner between two curtained windows.

He arched a dark brow with visible amusement when she slid out a chair for him. "Thank you."

"You're welcome," she replied, handing him the

menu. "Tom will be your server today." Feeling oddly breathless, she added, "Enjoy your dinner."

He smiled.

Kate felt the shivery effects of his smile all the way back to her station. Ridiculous, she chided herself, dismissing thoughts of the tall man when she noticed a line of unexpected guests waiting for her.

Greeting and seating the hungry patrons who had suddenly shown up snared Kate's focus. After seating a party of four nearest the corner table, she heard the tall man quietly call to her.

"Miss?"

The shivery effects began all over again. Sighing through her professional smile, she stopped at his table. "Can I get you something?" she responded, noticing his half-empty beer glass. He smiled, this time with a suggestive hint. Kate felt the shiver turn into an unnerving shimmering heat.

"Is Vic in the kitchen this evening?"

His question threw her for a moment. She didn't know what she had expected, but an inquiry about her boss wasn't it. "Yes, he is," she answered, instantly regaining her composure.

"Would you give him a message from me?"

"Yes, of course." What else could she say?

"Tell him Hawk would like to talk to him." He smiled again, revealing strong white teeth.

"Hawk…just Hawk?" she asked. Lord, the man had a killer smile.

"Just Hawk," he said with a soft laugh. "He'll know who you mean."

"Uh…right. I'll tell him," Kate said, turning away to head for the kitchen. It was a good thing Jeff had immunized her against men, she thought, pushing through the swing door to the kitchen. That kind of man would get under an unwary woman's skin in a hurry.

That was one appealing package of femininity, he mused, his gaze fixed on the subtle yet intriguing movement of her hips as she pushed through the door to the kitchen. Of average height, she was all woman from the riot of loose curls in her long dark hair to her slim ankles, and everywhere in between. And he had noticed she wasn't wearing a ring on the third finger of her left hand.

Of course, that didn't necessarily mean she wasn't married. Hawk knew of many men as well as women who didn't wear their bands of commitment. Cramped their style, he supposed. He was wondering if she might be one of those women when a familiar voice broke into his musing.

"Hawk, you old dog, when did you get into town?" Vic Molino came to a stop next to Hawk, a big smile of welcome on his handsome face, his right hand outthrust.

Rising, Hawk grasped the hand and pulled the shorter man into a buddy embrace.

Stepping back, Hawk flicked a hand at the empty chair opposite his. "Got a minute to talk…or are you too busy in the kitchen?"

Vic grinned. "Always got a minute for you, Hawk. How the hell are you?" He arched his dark brows. "It's been a long while since your last visit."

"Yeah, I know." Hawk grinned back. "Been too busy making money. Now, before winter sets in, I aim to spend a little of it."

"I hear you." As he spoke, a server came to a stop at the table. Vic smiled at him. "I'll take care of this customer, Tom, but you'll still get the tip." He lowered his voice dramatically, as if to prevent Hawk from hearing him. "And he's a big tipper."

Tom smiled. "Thanks, Vic." He turned to leave but Vic stopped him before he could take a step.

"One thing, Tom. You can bring me a pot of coffee." He shot a glance at Hawk. "You want a fresh beer?"

Hawk shook his head. "No, thanks. I'm going to have wine with dinner, but I would like a cup of coffee."

"Coming right up, sir," Tom said, hurrying away.

Hawk glanced around the dining room. "Business looks brisk, as usual."

"It has been good," Vic said, a touch of gratitude in his voice, "even with the slump in the economy." He pulled a frown. "I didn't even get a vacation this year."

Hawk gave him a droll look. "Poor baby. Lisa cracking the whip over you, huh?"

Vic flashed a white grin. "Never. My bride is too much in love with me to find fault."

Hawk felt a touch of something—longing, an empty sensation. Surely not envy for his friend and the bride he'd married over five years ago.

"In fact," Vic went on smugly, "Lisa's too happy at the present to find fault with anyone." He paused, waiting for the look of confused curiosity to bring a frown to Hawk's face.

"Well," Hawk said. "Where's the punch line?"

Vic gave a burst of happy laughter. "She's pregnant, Hawk. After all this time, all the praying and hoping, we're going to have a baby."

Hawk lit up in a smile. "That's wonderful, Vic. When's the baby due?"

"In the spring. She's in the beginning of her second trimester."

"Damn! Damn, that's great, for both of you. I know how much you've wanted a child." Even as he congratulated his friend, Hawk again felt that twinge of empty longing. He brushed it off as he shook Vic's hand.

"Yeah," Vic said, grinning like a kid. "We were almost at the point of accepting that there would never be a baby for us."

Grinning back at him, Hawk raised his glass of beer. "Well, here's to perseverance." Bringing the glass to his lips, he downed the beer remaining in it. As he set the glass down, the hostess came to the table with a full fresh pot of coffee.

"Tom was busy at another table," she explained. "So I brought this over. Is there anything else, Vic?"

"No thanks." Vic shook his head. As she started to turn away, he stopped her by taking her hand. "Wait a minute. I want you to meet an old friend."

"Okay." She smiled at Hawk.

He felt an instant of breathlessness. He stood up as Vic rose from his chair.

"Hawk," Vic said, "this lovely lady is Kate Muldoon, my hostess and Lisa's and my friend." He smiled at her. "Kate, Hawk McKenna. We've been friends since college, and he's been Lisa's friend since our wedding." A teasing gleam shone from his eyes. "I suspect she'd have grabbed him if she'd met him earlier."

"Right," Hawk drawled, offering his long-fingered hand to her. "Nice to meet you…Kate?"

"Of course," she answered. "Hawk?"

"Of course," he echoed.

"Have a seat, Kate," Vic said, rising to grab an

empty chair at the next table while beckoning to someone.

Kate shook her head. "I can't, Vic. There are custom—"

"Yes, you can," Vic interrupted. "You haven't had a break yet."

Kate gave him a dry look. "I started working only two hours ago."

"Long enough," Vic said, turning to the young woman who had come to a halt at the table.

"You employed the imperial wave, sire?" the woman said, her blue eyes fairly dancing with amusement.

Vic laughed as he watched her give a quick glance at Hawk, her eyes widening with surprise. "Hawk!"

"Hi, Bella." Hawk said, getting to his feet just in time to catch her as she flung herself into his arms. "Subdued as ever, I see." Taking her by the shoulders, he set her back a step to look at her. "And beautiful as ever."

"I bet you say that to all your friends' sisters," Bella said, laughing. "You look great, Hawk."

"Thanks." Hawk smiled. "So do you."

"If this ritual of mutual admiration is over," Vic said, "I'd like you to take over at the desk for Kate for a while."

"Sure." Bella gave Hawk another quick hug before turning away. "Will I be seeing you while you're in town, Hawk?"

"Of course." Hawk smiled.

"Good." Bella smiled back. "Take your time, Kate. I can handle the ravenous crowd."

"Thanks, Bella," Kate said. "I'll only be a few minutes."

Her soft, almost smoky-sounding voice, along with her smile, caused an even stronger searing sensation in Hawk's stomach and sections south.

"So," Vic said, "how long are you going to be in town this time, Hawk?"

"I haven't decided yet. I have a room for a week." Hawk shrugged. "After that…depends."

"On what?" Vic laughed. "The weather?"

Hawk grinned. "Yeah, the weather. You know how much it concerns me." He shook his head. "No, actually, if I'm tired of the whole scene at the end of a week, I'll head home. If not, I'll make other arrangements."

"And where is home, Hawk?" Kate asked.

"Colorado," Hawk said. "In the mountains."

She laughed. "Colorado is full of mountains."

A tingle skipped the length of his spine. He drew a deep breath, willing steel to chase the tingle from his back. "I'm in the southwest corner, in the San Juans, a double jump from Durango."

"A double jump?" she said.

Vic answered for him. "Hawk's got a horse ranch in a small valley in the foothills there," he said. "I gotta tell you, this guy breeds and trains some gorgeous horseflesh."

"And I'm damned good at it, too," Hawk drawled around a quick smile.

Once again he felt that strange reaction to the conversation, a reaction he had never felt before. Hawk wasn't sure he liked it.

They chatted for a few moments longer. Then Kate excused herself to get back to work.

Unaware of his surroundings, Vic, or the soft sigh he expelled, Hawk watched Kate walk back to the hostess station, head high, her back straight, as regal as any queen.

"Attractive, isn't she?"

Vic's quiet voice jolted Hawk into awareness. "Yes," he said, shifting his gaze to his friend.

"And you're interested." It was not a question.

"Yes," Hawk admitted without hesitation.

"A lot of men are." Vic shrugged.

"I did notice she was not wearing a ring on her left ring finger." Hawk lifted his brows. "Is she attached?"

Vic shook his head. "No."

"Why do I have the feeling that if I said I wanted to ask her to have dinner one evening with me, you'd tell me she'll refuse?"

"Because she very likely would." Vic gave him a half smile. "She always does."

"She doesn't like men?" Hawk felt a sharp pang of disappointment.

"She used to," Vic answered cryptically.

Hawk's eyes narrowed. "Are you going to explain that murky statement, or am I going to have to call you out?"

Vic grinned. "Pistols at dawn, eh?"

"No…" Hawk drawled. "My foot in your rear right here in front of all your customers. So you'd better start explaining."

"There was a man…" Vic began.

"Isn't there always?" Hawk said in disgust.

"The same as there's always a woman with bitter men," Vic said. "Isn't there?"

"I wouldn't know." It was not a boast. Hawk had never been in love. He had no experience of how a relationship gone sour could rip a person up.

"You're a lucky man." Vic sighed. "Well, Kate knows in spades. She was head over heels with a guy, enough to let him move in with her after they got engaged."

"He dumped her for another woman?" Hawk asked at the thought of any sane man dumping Kate.

"No, worse than that. Not long after he moved in with her, he became abusive."

Hawk stiffened, his features like chiseled rock. "He what?" His voice was low, icy with menace.

"Not physically," Vic said. "Verbally, which is just as bad, if not worse. Bruises heal pretty quickly. Emotional scars take a lot longer."

"The son of a bitch."

"That's my take on him."

Hawk was quiet a moment. "I'm still thinking of asking her to dinner one night." He frowned at Vic. "What do you think?"

"Well…" Now Vic was quiet a moment. He shrugged. "It can't hurt to give it a try."

"You wouldn't mind?"

"Why would I mind?" Vice shook his head. "I think it would do Kate good to get out… She hasn't been since she tossed the creep out." He grinned at Hawk. "And I know you'd never do anything to hurt her."

"How do you know that?"

Vic's grin grew sinister. "Because if you did, I'd have to kill you."

Hawk roared with laughter. "Get outta here and get me something to eat…and make it good."

Standing, Vic leveled a stern look at Hawk. "You know damn well everything I cook is good. Excellent, even."

"I know," Hawk admitted. "So, go cook."

Moments later he was served a glass of red wine. Soon after the wine, the server set a steaming plate of pasta before him, with a short, folded note on the side. Hawk opened the note and chuckled. Vic had written just seven words.

Kate's days off are Monday and Tuesday.

Two

Kate didn't have time to think of anything except greeting and seating customers for over an hour. When she again returned to her station, she was both disconcertingly disappointed and pleased.

She needed a breathing break. What Kate didn't need were the thoughts of the attractive Hawk McKenna, which immediately flooded her mind.

He was just another man, she told herself. And yet he invaded her mind and senses the minute activity around her slowed. Shaking her head, as if she could physically shake the thoughts aside, she busied herself by fussing with the station. She straightened the large menus and made a production out of studying the names not crossed off on the long list of reservations. The few parties left on the list were not due to arrive for a while.

Sighing, she glanced up from the list, right into the dark eyes of the very man she had been trying her best not to think about.

She managed a professional smile. "How was your dinner, Mr. McKenna?"

He gave her a slight frown. "I thought we had agreed on Hawk and Kate."

"Okay. How was your dinner, Hawk?"

"Superb, as Vic's dinners usually are."

Kate felt the effects of his breathtaking smile all the way down to her curling toes.

"That's true," she managed to articulate around the sudden tightness in her throat. "Vic is a very talented chef. One of the best."

"I know." He nodded, a shadow of his smile lingering at the corners of his too-attractive mouth. "He was taught by another very talented chef…" He paused for effect. "His mother."

Kate laughed. It felt good to laugh with him. Too good. She quickly sobered. "I know," she said, sneaking a glance around him in hopes of finding a waiting patron. The entryway was empty.

"You expecting someone special?" he asked, obviously not missing her swift look behind him.

"No." She shook her head. "Why?"

Hawk studied her a moment. Kate felt strangely trapped, as if pinned to a board like a butterfly or some other species of insects.

"You're afraid of me, aren't you?" He was frowning again, this time in consternation.

"Afraid? Me?" She gave a quick and hard shake of her head. "That's ridiculous." She raked a slow look down the length of him, the long length of him. "Should I have a reason to fear you?" Kate was babbling, and she knew it. She just didn't know how to stop. "Do you mean me harm?"

"You're right. That is ridiculous, Kate." There was a note, a bit angry, a bit sad, in his soft voice. "I mean no harm to any woman. Why would you even think that?"

Kate bit her lip and closed her eyes. "I…I don't know…I…"

"Yes, you do." He cut her off. He drew a deep breath.

"That bastard really did a number on you, didn't he?" His voice was low, as if to make sure no one could overhear him.

Kate froze, inside and out. How did he know? Who told him? Vic, it had to have been Vic. The mere thought of Jeff, his nasty temper and his accusations caused a cold sensation in her stomach.

Dammit, she thought. She had believed she was over it, free of the memories.

"Kate?" Hawk murmured, his soft tone threaded with concern.

Steeling herself, Kate looked him square in the eyes. "My personal life is not open for discussion, Mr. McKenna. I'd like you to leave, please. I have a party of four due any minute."

As if on cue the party swept into the lobby, laughing and chattering. His face unreadable, Hawk stepped to one side, standing firm.

Kate conjured a pleasant smile and turned to face the new arrivals. "Good evening." Lifting four menus from the neat pile, she added, "Right this way."

After the patrons were seated and perusing their menus, Kate started back to the hostess station. Spotting Hawk—how could she miss him?—leaning against the side wall, she couldn't help noticing again how tall and lean and...

Don't go there, Kate, she advised herself, trying and failing to ignore the tiny twist of excitement curling around her insides.

She began feeling edgy as she approached the station. There wasn't a single person waiting in the foyer. She lifted her chin, prepared to glare at him for still being there.

Hawk didn't move but remained standing there,

leaning one shoulder against the wall, his gaze fixed on her, a small, enticing smile curving his masculine lips.

His smile set off a new sensation in her body, one so intense she reached for anger in defense.

"You still here?" she said, inwardly cringing at having stated the obvious.

Hawk glanced down, then at the wall he was lounging against, then at her. "I do believe so. At least, it looks like me." His smile broadened, his eyes grew bright with a teasing light.

Kate suppressed a shiver of awareness as he pushed away from the wall and strolled to stand directly in front of her.

"Will you have dinner with me Monday or Tuesday evening?" he asked softly.

Nonplussed, Kate stared up at him. Surprise kept her silent. Raking her mind for a reply, she decided that she simply couldn't brush him off. He was a good friend of Vic's, besides being a customer. Still…the nerve of the man. She scowled at him while fighting a sudden urge to agree.

Foolish woman. She didn't even know him, trust him. She was afraid to trust any man, other than her father and Vic. Yet she was tempted to say yes to him.

"How did you know I was off Monday and Tuesday?" she said in a sad attempt at irritation.

He cocked his head.

She couldn't blame him, when the answer was so evident. Damn him. "Vic," she answered for him.

"Yes." Hawk nodded. "I can be trusted, Kate," he said, voice soft, tone sincere. "And Vic will vouch for me. I promise not to step out of line."

Dilemma. What to do? Kate knew what she wanted to do. It had been so long, months since she'd been to dinner with a man.

Looking up at him, she stared into his dark eyes, seeing admiration and concern…for her.

Hawk leaned closer, against the station, his voice a bare, husky whisper. "Word of honor, I'll be good."

Kate relented. "Okay, Hawk, I'll have dinner with you Monday evening."

"That has got to be the hardest I have ever worked to get a date. What time and where can I pick you up?"

There was no way Kate was giving him her home address. "You can meet me here. Is seven-thirty okay?"

"Fine. I'll see you then." He raised a hand as if to respectfully touch his hat, which wasn't there. Grinning at her, he lowered his hand, gave a quick wave, turned and strode from the restaurant.

Bemused by his attractive smile, salute and even more so his laughter, Kate stared after him, kind of scared, kind of excited. Had she done the right thing in accepting his invitation, or should she have refused? Should she stay firmly hidden behind her barrier of mistrust for men?

Fortunately, Kate was temporarily relieved of the weight of the conundrum by the door opening to a family group exactly on time for their reservation.

By eleven forty-five, Kate, along with the other employees and the boss, had finished getting the place cleaned, the tables set and everything ready for the next day, Saturday, one of their busiest days.

As he did every night while the other male employees escorted the waitresses out, Vic walked Kate to her car, which was parked in the employees section of the parking lot. Kate used those few minutes to question Vic.

"Why did you tell your friend Hawk my days off?" She kept her voice free of inflection.

Vic slanted a wary look at her. "He asked. Are you angry at me for telling him?"

"No." Kate shook her head as she came to a stop next to her car.

"Just annoyed with me," he said. "Right?"

Kate met his direct gaze and smiled. "A bit, yes," she admitted. "You know how I feel about…" She paused, giving him a chance to speak over her.

"Yes, Kate, I know how you feel about men in general and what's-his-name in particular. And I respect that." He shrugged. "But Hawk isn't any man in general, and not just because he's my friend. Hawk's one of the good guys, honey." He grinned. "You know, the ones who wear white hats in the cowboy movies." His grin widened. "Besides, I warned him that if you happened to accept his invitation, and he got out of line, I'd have to kill him."

Kate had to smile. "Well, I…um…I did agree to have dinner with him Monday evening."

"Good. It's time for you to get out and about again. Flirt a little. Hawk will love it, after being stuck in the mountains all summer."

"I'm sure I'll enjoy his company, Vic." Kate said. "But I don't believe I'm ready to flirt yet, if ever again."

"Well, if not this time, then sometime. Just relax and enjoy a little." He glanced at his watch. "Now, I'd better be getting home to Lisa…before she starts getting suspicious."

"As if." Kate laughed. "Thanks, Vic. I'll see you tomorrow."

He waited until she had slid into the car, locked the doors and started the engine. With a quick wave, Vic headed for his own car.

Kate sat for a minute before pulling out of the lot. Although Vic's recommendation helped, she still felt a little nervous about the date with Hawk.

Drawing a deep, determined breath, she released the hand brake and drove away.

* * *

Two more days until Monday.

Excitement and trepidation pushed at her mind. Fortunately for Kate, Saturday evenings and Sunday brunches were always the busiest times in the restaurant. She barely had time to take deep breaths between greeting and seating patrons, never mind long enough to let herself indulge the nervous twinges playing havoc with her stomach.

Kate was relieved when it was finally time for her break Sunday evening.

She felt her entire body tighten with nerves when Vic joined her in the small employees' break room next to the noisy kitchen.

"Instead of enjoying a quiet break," he said, eyeing her critically, "you look as if you just heard terrifying news." His tone was only half kidding. "Would you like me to get in touch with Hawk and tell him you've changed your mind?"

Yes. The word immediately slammed into her mind. But Kate gritted her teeth, damned if she would chicken out.

She gave her head a quick shake. "No. I'll confess I'm a little nervous." She tried on a smile; it didn't fit. "But I have no intention of backing out of the date. I'm going to go and I'll enjoy the evening, as well." What a liar, she chided herself.

Vic's slip tightened as if to suppress a smile. She

could tell he knew exactly how ambiguous she felt about spending the evening with Hawk…or with any other man, come to that.

Fortunately, Vic changed the subject and Kate managed to maintain her composure until quitting time.

Monday, 7:25 p.m.

Kate stood next to the hostess station, chatting with Bella. She was early. She had arrived at the restaurant soon after seven. She was also nervous. She felt foolish about her anxiety, but there it was, like it or not.

Bella was seating customers. Kate was casting quick glances at the doorway, chiding herself every time she did, which by now was too often.

Kate glanced up as Bella returned to the station, just in time to see the young woman's face light up with a bright smile.

"Hi, Hawk," Bella said, quickening her step to launch herself into his open arms.

For an instant, a heartbeat, Kate felt the strangest emotion. She couldn't describe it exactly, but then, she didn't want to examine it, either, refusing to even think the word *envy*.

She allowed another word into her mind. *Breathtaking*. Hawk looked absolutely breathtaking. This evening he was dressed casually elegant in dark gray slacks, a crisp white shirt, no tie and a navy blazer.

Kate was relieved that she had taken extra time with her own attire. She had chosen a frilly-collared, long-sleeved sage blouse, a long, swirly nutmeg skirt and three-inch heels. While the days were still warm and even sometimes hot in October, the evenings dropped into the fifties and even the forties, so she had brought the same smooth fleece shawl that she had worn at work the previous night.

Bella swung out of Hawk's arms as a party of two entered. Hawk switched his dark gaze to Kate.

"Hi." His voice was soft, enticing.

Kate had to swallow before she could manage a rusty-sounding response. "Hi."

He slid a long glance the length of her body. "You look lovely."

She swallowed again. "Thank you. "Y-you look lovely, too." Good grief, Kate thought, feeling foolish. Had she really said that?

Hawk strolled to the hostess station, a smile flickering on his temptingly masculine lips. "Hungry?"

Watching his lips move, Kate felt as if the bottom had fallen out of her stomach. And in that moment she was hungrier than she'd ever been in her adult life. Yet the last thing on her rattled mind was food.

"Yes." She tried to unobtrusively wet her parched lips. "Are you?"

His eyes narrowing, he watched the slow movement of the tip of her tongue. "You have no idea," he murmured, reaching out a hand to take hers.

"W-where are we going?" Kate felt a flash of annoyance, not at Hawk, but at herself for the brief stutter again. Damn, she didn't stutter. Never had, not even briefly.

Hawk grinned. "Right here. Vic's creating something special for us."

"Here? We're staying here for dinner?" Kate had to laugh. "Why?"

His brows drew together in a dark frown. "You don't like Vic's cooking?"

"I love Vic's cooking," she protested. "It's just, well, I thought you would want to…"

"What I want, Kate," he declared, "is for you to feel comfortable with me, and I figured you would here." He smiled, then added, "With Vic to defend you."

"Right," Vic drawled, leading them to the same corner table for two that Hawk had been given a few days before. "As if I could defend her against you. I'm a chef, not a warrior."

"Cute. You're the one who works with knives." Hawk shot Vic a wry look as he held a chair for Kate. "Wine?" he asked, folding his long body onto the chair opposite her.

Pondering their odd exchange, Kate nodded. "Yes, thank you." She glanced at Vic. "What do you recommend with the meal? White or red?"

"White for you," Vic said. "I think nothing too dry, nothing too sweet. You're both at my mercy with the meal tonight."

Hawk smiled dryly. "Right. I'll have the red. Room temperature.

"You know each other very well, don't you?" Kate said as Vic retreated to his kitchen.

"Hmm." Hawk nodded, taking a sip of his water. "We roomed together at college."

"Did you serve in the military?" Her question, seemingly coming out of nowhere, brought his eyebrows together in a brief frown.

"Yeah, after college I served in the air force. What made you ask that?"

Kate shrugged. "Vic called you a warrior, so I assumed that's what he was referring to."

His brows smoothed as he gave a soft chuckle. "I flew a Black Hawk chopper, but that wasn't what Vic was referring to," he said. "The warrior reference was to my heritage. You see, my father is Scottish, but my mother was a full-blooded Apache Indian."

"Was?"

"Yes, my mother died giving birth to my younger sister, Catriona." His smile was bittersweet. "I was two and never got to know her. All I have of her are pictures of her lovely face."

"I'm sorry," Kate said, at a loss for any other words of sympathy.

The bitter tinge vanished, leaving only the sweet. "Kate, it was a long time ago. I'm thirty-six years old. Though I'd have loved to have gotten to know her, I'm over it."

Somehow Kate doubted his assurance, but she didn't push. "Catriona. That's different," she said, changing the subject.

"It's Scottish for Catherine."

"What about your father?"

"He, with help from my mother's parents, raised me and Cat. After college I joined the air force. And after Cat graduated two years later, she moved to New York, and then Dad moved back to Scotland, where he owns several business holdings." A server appeared and Hawk took his glass. "He and his second wife raise Irish wolfhounds."

"Oh," Kate said. "They're really big and kind of mean, aren't they?"

Hawk's head was shaking before she finished. "They are big, but certainly not mean. I have one. His name's Boyo, and he's a pussycat." He hesitated before clarifying. "Of course, he can get ferocious if I'm in any way threatened. The breed is very protective of his people."

Kate had to laugh. "His people?"

"Oh, yeah." He laughed with her. "Boyo believes I belong to him."

They grew quiet when their meal was served,

enjoying the sumptuous dinner Vic had prepared for them.

"Dessert? Coffee?" Hawk asked when they had both finished eating.

Kate shook her head. "No thank you. I'm too full for even coffee."

"Good." Hawk drew a quick breath. "It's nice here, but…" He took another breath. "I have tickets for a show on the strip. Would you like to go?"

Kate was quiet a moment, stilled by a little flicker inside, a combination of anxiety and expectation. As she had before, she drew a quick breath and made a quick decision. "Yes, thank you. I would."

Hawk shot a look at his watch, pushed back his chair and circled around the table to slide Kate's chair back for her to rise.

"We'd better leave. It's after nine and the show starts at ten." Hawk waved for their server. He said, "Check, please," when the server hurried over.

"No check," the server said. "Vic said this meal is on the house."

"Tom, you tell Vic I said he's a sweetie," Kate said, smiling as the young man's cheeks flushed.

After quick goodbyes to Bella, they exited the restaurant.

Three

Taking Kate's elbow, Hawk steered her to the first parking space in the parking lot. Noting the make-shift Reserved sign tied to the light pole in one corner of the lot, Kate raised an eyebrow and looked up at him.

Hawk grinned at her. "It's good to be the king," he declared quoting from an old Mel Brooks movie.

The car he guided her to was midsize. After she was seated, Kate watched, a slight smile on her lips, as he crammed his long body into the seat behind the wheel. Settled in, he slanted a look at her.

"This king needs a bigger carriage."

"You do appear a bit cramped in that seat."

He rolled his eyes dramatically. "You have no idea." He heaved a put-upon sigh. "At home I drive a big-boy truck, with a large seat and lots of legroom."

"This car is easier to fit into a parking space," she said.

"Granted, but…" He smiled at her, smugly, as he started the engine. "I don't have to park it. I'm going valet." He paused an instant before adding in a gotcha tone, "So there."

Kate lost it. Her laughter poured out of her with genuine amusement. She couldn't recall the last time she had laughed so hard, with such ease. It was even better that Hawk was laughing right along with her.

As promised, he drove them to the valet parking at one of the casino hotels. The show, by a comedian Kate had never heard of before, was in one of the smaller entertainment rooms. The room was already full when they were escorted to their table just ahead of the burst of applause as the comedian strolled onto the stage.

The man wasn't merely funny; he was hilarious…and he worked clean. He didn't tell jokes. He told life, everyday things that just about every person in the room could relate to and appreciate.

The few times Kate shifted a quick glance at Hawk during the show, she found him laughing, too. One time he winked at her.

A simple wink, and yet it made Kate feel warm all over. Silly woman, she chided herself.

Now, the show over, Kate moved to get up. Hawk stopped her with a shake of his head. "Want to go into the casino, play awhile before we leave?" he asked.

Kate hesitated. Then, remembering this was one of Jeff's favorite gambling sites, she shook her head. "Not tonight. I hurt from laughing," she said, smiling at him to soften her refusal. "He was very funny."

"Yes, he was," Hawk agreed, leading her outside. He handed over his parking ticket to the valet before adding, "And you're a lousy liar."

Kate opened her mouth, but before she could utter a protest, he said, "No insult intended."

"What would you call that remark?" Kate didn't attempt to conceal her annoyance.

The valet area was crowded with people waiting for their vehicles. Hawk moved closer to her. "Kate," he said, his voice low, private, "I'm not unconscious. I saw the flicker in your eyes when you uttered that lame excuse. For some reason of your own, you don't want to go near that casino." He raised one dark brow. "Care to tell me why?"

He stood there, so close to Kate that she could smell his cologne and the pure masculine scent of him, and the tang of wine on his breath, teasing her lips. It played havoc with her nervous system.

"No?" He smiled.

She smiled, surrendering to his smile. "It's a silly thing, I guess," she said, sighing. "I didn't want to go in there, because that is one of Jeff's favorites." She shrugged. "I prefer not to run into him."

The instant she finished speaking, as if she had conjured him up, Jeff's practiced, cultured voice sent shivers of revulsion through her.

"Well, Kate. Beautiful as ever," he said, his voice and smile much too smooth. "Imagine seeing you here. I thought you didn't like the casinos." He acted as though Hawk wasn't there.

"You thought a lot of things, Jeff," she returned, her voice as cool as she could make it. "Most of them wrong...no, all of them wrong."

Jeff's pale blue eyes went cold; his smooth voice grew a jagged edge. "Not all of them." A leer twisted his lips as he ran a quick look over her. "I wasn't wrong about your response in the bed...."

"If you'll excuse me," Hawk interjected in a menacing drawl, sliding one arm around Kate's waist. "The car's here, Kate."

Relief washed through her, but only for a moment. Jeff caught her by the arm, keeping her from moving away with Hawk. She stiffened, angry and embarrassed.

Jeff glared up at Hawk. And *up* was the word, as Hawk had a good six inches on the man. "Who the hell do you think you are?" he demanded.

"I don't think who I am," Hawk said. "I know who I am. And I don't want to know you." His drawl vanished, a soft warning taking its place. "Now, little man, take your hand off my lady."

"Little man! Your...your lady..." Jeff sputtered in anger. "You dare—"

Hawk sighed. "I. Dare. Anything." He enunciated very softly. "Now, back it up, buster, before I'm tempted to get real nasty."

To Kate's near amazement, Jeff took a step back, looking not at all like a cock of the walk, which was how he regularly portrayed himself. She watched him stare narrow-eyed at them as Hawk helped her into the car. But he blinked and took another step back as Hawk turned to stare back at him.

Although Kate couldn't see Hawk's face, she thought his expression must have looked meaner than hell, for turning on his heel, Jeff quickly strode back into the casino.

Turning her head, Kate watched, expecting to see a man ready to explode with anger, as Hawk came around the car and slid behind the wheel. To her utter surprise, she saw the brightness of inner laughter in his eyes and a grin on his rugged face. Amusement danced in his voice.

"I bluff at poker, too."

It started as a chuckle from Kate and developed into full laughter. "You're something else," she said, her laughter subsiding.

"Oh, lady, you don't know the half of it." Hawk slid his glance from the wheel after starting the car to toss a smile at her.

The tension of the previous minutes drained from Kate's body, leaving her relaxed and comfortable. For the first time since throwing Jeff, cursing and arguing, out of her apartment, and her life, she felt at ease in the company of a man.

Kate couldn't quite decide if that was good or not. She knew too well that being at ease with a man was not the same as trusting one. At this point in time, she wasn't sure she would ever again be able to trust a man, any man. It was sad, really, that one nasty male… She gave a mental shake. Forget him, she thought. He wasn't worth the effort it cost her to dwell on him. Resting her head back, she allowed her thoughts to drift.

They drove for several minutes, Kate content and mellow, before Hawk broke the mood.

"Er…Kate, are we going to drive around aimlessly for the rest of the night, or are you going to tell me where you live?"

Kate knew the mood was too good to last. "I

parked my car at Vic's," she said, straightening from her near lounging position.

"Um," he murmured, making a turn at the next intersection. "We're a little past his restaurant."

Kate gave him a startled look before glancing around at the area. She frowned when she didn't recognize where they were. "How little?"

A smile twitched the corners of his mouth. "Oh, only a couple miles or so," he said. "You looked so comfortable, I hated to mention it. Fact is, I wasn't certain you were awake."

She felt her cheeks grow warm and was glad for the dark interior of the car. "I wasn't sleeping but I was drifting a bit. It must be the wine."

"All two glasses of it," Hawk drawled. Then he sobered. "Were you thinking about that clown who was giving you a hard time?"

"His name is Jeff," she said, tossing off the name as if it didn't matter, and it truly didn't.

"He grabbed your arm." His voice had changed. It was now close to a growl, almost scary. "And if he tries something like that again, touches you again when you're with me, his name will be sh—er—mud."

She had to chuckle at his quick word switch. "I do know the word, Hawk."

"I know. Everybody does." He shrugged. "My father is a stickler for speaking politely in front of or to a lady. I feel the same way he does."

"That's nice." Kate said as he drove into the restaurant parking lot. He came to a stop next to her car in the otherwise empty lot.

Unfastening the seat belt, she turned to face him, offering her hand for him to shake. "Thank you, Hawk, for a lovely evening."

Although he took her hand, he shook his head. "I'm following you home, Kate."

"But…"

That was as far as he allowed her to get. "It's late, so I'll follow you and make sure you're safely inside." His voice was firm; he would brook no argument.

Shaking her head, she sighed and didn't argue. She got out of his car and into her own. True to his word, Hawk stayed on her tail, nearly tapping her bumper, until she pulled into the parking area of her apartment complex.

Once again he parked next to her. He got out of his car as Kate stepped from hers.

"I'll see you to the door," he told her.

"Really, Hawk, it's not necessary," she protested. She might as well have saved her breath. Without replying, he strolled beside her to the entranceway.

"Thanks again, Hawk," she said once more offering her hand to him.

"You're welcome." He took her hand and used it to gently draw her close to him. "Will I see you again?"

"Yes," was all Kate was capable of saying due to her suddenly dry throat.

"Tomorrow evening?"

She swallowed, hesitated before repeating, "Yes."

"Good." A mixture of relief and satisfaction colored his voice. "I'll pick you up here at seven-thirty, okay? We'll do something fun."

She nodded, her heart skipping when he raised his hand to cradle her face, his thumb slowly stroking her cheek. "That creep was right about one thing, Kate," he murmured, gently lifting her chin with the heel of his hand. "You are one very beautiful woman."

Now Kate's heart wasn't skipping; it was thundering.

"Hawk...I..."

"Shh," he murmured, lowering his head to hers. "It's all right. I won't hurt you." His breath whispered over her lips an instant before his mouth brushed over her mouth in what was not a kiss, but more a promise. "Good night, Kate." He stepped back. "Now, go inside and lock up."

Barely breathing and not thinking at all, Kate went inside, unlocked the lobby door and ran up the stairs to her second-floor apartment, completely forgetting the elevator.

As Hawk slid behind the wheel of the rental, he glanced up at the building just as lights went on in the second-floor front apartment.

Staring at the glow through the sheer curtains on the windows, Hawk propped his elbows on the steering wheel.

Kate.

Surprisingly, as his lips had barely touched her own, there was still a shimmering trace of her taste on his mouth, an unfamiliar twinge in his chest. He rather liked it. Smiling as a shiver raced up his spine, Hawk switched on the engine and drove back to the hotel he'd booked on the Vegas Strip.

Not twenty minutes after leaving his car key with the valet, Hawk was in bed, lost in fantasies of Kate, her lithe, equally naked form close to his.

Hawk woke suddenly, his skin chilled beneath a fine film of perspiration. He was cold, hot and frustrated. He hadn't even realized he'd fallen asleep, only to suddenly awaken right at the most intense part of his fantasy dream. He was aching with need.

Knowing he had to take drastic measures to cool the passion pouring through him, he dragged his body from the bed and headed for the bathroom.

Damn, he hated cold showers.

Kate stood at a side window, one hand flicking the curtain aside an inch or so. Gliding her tongue over her lips, she watched until she could no longer see the car.

She could taste him.

Ridiculous, Kate told herself and let the curtain

fall back into place. That mere brush of his mouth over hers had been the furthest thing from a kiss she had ever experienced. She walked to the bedroom. Why in the world would she think she could taste him? Testing, she again slid her tongue along her bottom lip and snivelled.

No, it wasn't ridiculous; she really could taste him, and she liked the taste very much. Kate feared that a real deep kiss from Hawk could very likely be addictive…like rich dark chocolate.

A real deep kiss from Hawk. She replayed the thought inside her head. Swallowing to moisten her suddenly parched throat, she began to undress, her hands fumbling with the simple routine. She mumbled a mild curse to herself.

She had just managed to remove her blouse when the phone rang.

Hawk? Kate froze, her heart beating wildly. It rang again. Not bothering to look at the caller ID, she snatched it up, nearly dropping it. Drawing a quick breath in an attempt to keep a tremor from her voice, she said, "Hello."

"Who was he?" Jeff snarled.

Kate went cold and stiff. "That is none of your business." She wouldn't so much as say his name.

"Yes, it is," he snapped back at her. "You're mine and you know it."

"I never was yours," she said icily. "And I broke up with you months ago, as you well know."

"You were in a snit." He was back to the snarl. "And—"

"No," she said, cutting him off. "You were being verbally and emotionally abusive…again."

"I'm not giving up, Kate. I know you love me." His voice was suddenly soft, cajoling, "I'll get you back."

"I've been patient up until now, Jeff," she stated flatly, finally saying his name, anger stirring in her voice. "If you bother me again, I'll report you to the police. And this time I mean it."

"Sure," he said in honeyed tones. "You mean it every time, which only tells me you don't mean it."

Kate drew a deep breath in an attempt to control her anger. How in the world had she ever thought that syrupy tone was attractive? Now it repulsed her. *He* repulsed her.

"I have only three words for you, Jeff," she began.

"Yeah, I know," he replied smoothly, interrupting her. "Like I told you, you love me."

"Go to hell." She hung up on him.

Kate stood trembling, staring warily at the phone as if it might attack her.

Damn him. Damn him. Damn him.

She had had enough. Tomorrow morning she would see a lawyer about reporting him to the authorities and would take out a restraining order against him.

Although Kate had never done so before, in case there happened to be an emergency in her family, she was so uneasy that she disconnected the landline and turned off her cell.

After she was ready for bed, she still felt shaken by the call and so she checked the locks on the front door, even though no one could go beyond the lobby without a card key. Then she double-checked the locks on the patio door and on every window.

Kate lay in bed for some time, unable to sleep. When she finally drifted off, she drifted right into a dream. Not of Jeff and fear, but of Hawk and unbelievable pleasure.

He came to her softly, murmuring of the exciting delights to be found in the joining of their bodies. She sighed in her sleep, her body moving in sensual restlessness.

She wanted, needed, ached for his touch, the feel of his mouth taking passionate control of hers, for his hard body possessing, owning, her own.

Kate woke, trembling, quivering deep inside her body, her breathing harsh and uneven. She kicked the covers away from her perspiration-slicked body. Never had she had a dream so real, so vivid that it actually brought her close to release in her sleep.

Her breathing slowly returning to normal, she

sat up, staring into the dimness of her bedroom, her mind and senses still reeling.

While it was true that it had been some time since she had been intimate with a man—she would not think his name—it seemed unreal to Kate that a dream of a man she had so recently met and knew practically nothing about, not simply a dream of a fantasy man, could affect her to her very core. Her thoughts ebbed as sleep claimed her once more.

To her surprise, Kate woke later refreshed, if still a bit anxious.

What was with her, anyway? Kate asked herself, musing on her unusual reaction to Hawk. Yes, he was extremely attractive and fun to be with, not to mention sexy as hell. But he was just another man…wasn't he?

Shying away from the thought, Kate centered her attention on the business at hand. Going to the phone, she reconnected the landline and dialed Vic's home number.

Lisa was happy to oblige with the name of a good attorney, as she had been after Kate to swear out a restraining order against Jeff ever since Kate had thrown him out of her apartment.

Minutes later, Kate had an appointment for the next morning with the attorney Lisa had recommended, an older-sounding man named Edward Bender. It was a start.

Four

Even though she knew the time of Hawk's arrival, Kate jumped when the buzzer rang from the intercom in the lobby. Fortunately she had just finished swiping her lashes with the mascara wand, or she would have had a very strange black streak across her temple.

Grabbing her purse and a Black Watch plaid wrap that complemented her off-white dress, she flipped the button and spoke into the wall-mounted receiver.

"Hawk?"

"Yes." His sexy, low voice gave her an all over tingly sensation.

"I'm coming right down."

Without waiting for a response, Kate switched on a night light, locked the door and headed for the elevator.

She had felt an attraction to him from the moment he had walked into Vic's, standing there all tall and lean and ruggedly masculine.

On the other hand, even from the beginning Jeff had appeared almost too handsome, cultured and charming. Almost too good to be true. Of course, before long, his real character had come through.

Kate snorted derisively as she pressed the elevator button. Handsome, cultured and charming was an act hiding Jeff's true nature.

As Kate stepped inside the elevator, an old adage of her mother's came to mind. *Handsome is as handsome does.* Well, for Kate, handsome had proved to be a nasty jerk when things didn't go exactly the way he wanted them to go.

"Hi," Hawk said as the elevator doors parted. "You look lovely." His eyes held a teasing gleam. "How did you know the Black Watch was my favorite of the clan plaids?"

Kate laughed. "I didn't. It just happens to be my favorite, too. And hello yourself." She grinned.

"Where are we going this evening?"

Shaking his head, Hawk cupped her elbow and led her to the car. "I thought we'd pick up where we were, before we were so rudely interrupted. Do you avoid all casinos or just the one we almost went in last night?"

"Just that one," she said and buckled her seat belt. "But I don't go to casinos very often." She smiled. "As the old song goes, I work hard for my money. But I do play occasionally."

"Table games?" He arched his brows.

"No, I play the machines only." Kate arched her brows back at him. "What about you?"

"Poker, Texas hold 'em," he answered, shrugging. "And some blackjack now and again. Ready to go?"

"Whenever you are," Kate said, and he pulled out of the lot.

He was quiet for a moment as they drove. "I don't know what scent you're wearing but I like it...a lot."

Kate grew warmer and more tingly. "Thank you, Hawk. It's the only scent I wear."

"Whenever or wherever I smell it, I'll think of you." He flashed a smile at her.

Kate was certain everything inside her was melting. She told herself she had better be careful, because this man wasn't merely dangerous, but he was dynamite. Compared to Hawk, she thought, Jeff wasn't even a firecracker.

Playing with firecrackers was one thing, but playing with dynamite... Kate shivered.

"Are you cold?" Hawk asked, noticing her shiver even though he never took his eyes from the road. "I can turn on the car heater." He reached to do so.

"No…no." Kate shook her head while offering a weak smile. "I'm fine, really, and we're almost to the strip." Jeez, she thought, if he turned on the heater, she'd melt right there in front of him.

"It does seem strange," he said. "In October here in Vegas in the afternoon, the temp can go into the seventies and even the eighties, yet in the evening it can drop down into the fifties and forties."

"It's different where you live?" she said, wanting to know every little thing about him, about his life.

He grinned. "It depends what part of the state you're in. In Denver it can get very warm during the day and cooler in the evenings. But in the mountains where I live, while we might get some warmth in the daytime, it can get damned cold at night."

"I like the mountains," she said, unaware of the wistful note in her voice.

"You're not from here originally?"

"No." She shook her head. "I'm from Virginia, near the Blue Ridge Mountains. My father runs a small horse farm."

He slanted a quick smile at her. "There you go. We have something in common."

"Horses?" She laughed.

"Hey, don't knock it. It's a start."

Kate couldn't help wondering exactly what he meant by a start. A start of what? He was only going to be in Vegas for a while, wasn't he?

Hawk surprised her by avoiding the Strip, driving to one of the older hotel casinos in town, one she had never been inside before. That is, old in comparison to the unbelievably expensive palaces forever under construction.

Kate liked it even better than the much more elaborate pleasure palaces with which Vegas abounded. For one thing, it wasn't nearly as crowded as the others.

"So," Hawk said, "what do you want to do?"

Kate was quiet a moment, glancing around her. "I think I'll wander around a bit—" she flashed a smile at him "—until one of the machines calls to me."

"Fine," he said. He paused before adding, "I think I'll wander to a blackjack table. Suppose we synchronize our watches and meet right here in, say, an hour?"

Grinning, Kate looked at her wristwatch. "Right. If I don't see you before, I'll see you then."

They had no sooner separated than Kate began to feel lonely. Silly, she chided herself, checking out the lines of machines as she strolled around.

In a bid to distract herself from thoughts of Hawk, she sat down at a machine at the end of a row. She spent several minutes studying the instructions on the three-coin machine before feeding a twenty into the money slot. She racked up eighty credits in the credit window.

Kate had played the machine for almost the full hour when she became aware that someone new had taken the machine beside her. She did not spare a glance at the person.

"Hello, Kate." Jeff's smooth voice gave her a start. "I saw you sitting here all alone and came to keep you company."

Jeff, here? Kate could hardly believe it. This casino was not the kind he frequented; he preferred the glitzy new ones that drew all the celebrities. The thought that followed sent a chill down her spine.

Was he following her, stalking her?

Scared but determined not to reveal her fear to him, Kate turned a cold look on him. "I'm not alone. I have company, and even if I didn't, I would never want yours."

"Now, Kate, we both know you don't—"

That was as far as she allowed him to go. "You know nothing, Jeff, but I'll enlighten you." She drew courage from the cool tones she had achieved. "If you aren't gone from my sight within the next few seconds, I will begin screaming for security."

"You wouldn't dare," he said. "You forget I know you hate making a scene."

"Perhaps," she admitted, "but I'll gladly make an exception in your case." She made a show of glancing at her watch. "You have exactly two seconds to disappear." She didn't look away from her watch. "One...two..."

He was off the stool and moving away from her, swearing a blue streak. Shaken by the encounter, she drew a calming breath, and the minute he was out of her sight, she hit the pay-out button and walked away with five dollars more than she'd started with.

She was hurrying back to the place where she'd agreed to meet Hawk when she spotted him at a blackjack table. She hesitated a moment but then decided to approach him, certain Jeff wouldn't try anything again so long as Hawk was near.

Coming up behind him, Kate laid a hand on his shoulder to let him know she was there. "Hi. I see you're winning." There were several stacks of chips in front of him.

"Yeah." He turned to smile at her. "You ready to leave?"

"No hurry," she said. "I'd like to watch awhile, if you don't mind me standing in back of you as you play."

"Not at all," he said, managing to keep an eye on the play of cards at the same time. "I'm not superstitious. Fact is, I like you there."

Feeling inordinately pleased and warmed by his

comment, especially after that unpleasant encounter with Jeff, Kate lightly flexed her fingers on his shoulder. The warmth flowed stronger when he raised a hand to cover hers briefly, his fingers lacing with hers.

The feeling of his touch remained on her even as the evening continued. Would his touch bring such torrid dreams again? She hoped it would banish those nightmares that only Jeff could inspire.

Five

The idea was to tire himself out enough to sleep. Hawk knew that was the only reason he found himself back at the poker tables until after two in the morning. As he had earlier in the evening, he won. But that wasn't the purpose.

He didn't even doze off, not until after four. Hell, he thought, prowling around the spacious room, popping the top off a can of light beer, he might as well have stayed at the poker tables. He stopped at the floor-to-ceiling window to stare at the glaringly bright lights along the Strip. On the street below, the traffic, both human and vehicular, was almost as heavy as in the afternoon or evening. He took a swig of the cold beer. Obviously there was more than one town in the country that never slept.

His thoughts swirled continuously, every one about Kate. Hawk sighed, "Kate." He didn't realize he had whispered her name aloud or finished off the beer. Shaking his head at his wandering mind, he tossed the can into the wastebasket.

He wanted to be with her so badly, he ached with the wanting, the raw need. His back teeth hurt from clenching them together. There were other women in Vegas; there had been plenty of them in the casino and the restaurant yesterday morning. Several of them had cast unmistakable looks of availability at him. He had ignored them.

Just any woman wouldn't do. Hawk was always selective when it came to the females he spent time with, despite the fact that he so seldom left the ranch.

This time around was different. Hawk was coming to the reluctant conclusion that the only woman he wanted to spend his time with was Kate.

And Kate had man problems, dammit.

She appeared to resent the oily guy more than fear him…but one could never really know what another person was thinking, feeling. Vic had said Kate had thrown the creep out of her apartment for verbally abusing her. And last night he had been far from pleasant.

Hawk frowned. Was the jerk harassing her? Had he been harassing her since she dumped him? Hell, that was months ago now.

When Kate had joined him at the blackjack table earlier that night, she had seemed different than when they had separated, he to play the tables and she to play the slots. It had been nothing overt or obvious. She had been quieter and slightly more reserved, not at all the woman who had laughed so easily earlier.

The wheels in Hawk's mind were rolling full speed. Had that creep approached her again between the time they parted and when she joined him at the blackjack table? Had she come to him for protection? Hmm, it was possible, and now that he thought about it, probable.

Confused by her sudden change in mood, he had slightly withdrawn. He had had such high hopes for a kiss, a real kiss, with her before she went into her apartment building.

Hope in one hand and spit in the other.

The old saying of his father's slipped through his mind. Hawk rejected the very idea that he gave up hope. Sliding beneath the covers again, he thought he had better get some sleep if he wanted to be sharp enough to catch any slight change in her attitude, because he *could* see her tomorrow.

This time he was unconscious within minutes.

* * *

Kate entered Mr. Bender's office with a heavy step that morning. The lawyer was older—close to sixty she judged—and he appeared to be the classic prototype of an old-fashioned gentleman.

She told him her problem. In turn, Mr. Bender had questions.

"Did he ever hit you, even the lightest slap?"

"No." Kate shook her head. "But…I must admit there were times when he was the most angry, swearing…I began fearing he might."

"I see. Did he ever threaten you?"

"Not outright," she said, "but in a vague, oblique way." She sighed. "I don't know how else to describe it, but he frightens me."

"Now, don't you worry, Miss Muldoon. The law will take care of this…" He hesitated, his lips pursed as if from a sour taste. "This lowlife."

Sighing with resignation at her predicament, Kate pushed herself through the revolving door.

Directly into reality. Her cell phone rang. Kate hesitated, eyeing the instrument as if it might leap into the air and bite her. It wasn't a number she recognized.

Thoughts whipped through her head, one tripping over another. Jeff…the bastard. She knew; she knew he'd track her to the lawyer's. He must have followed her.

What to do?

The phone rang for the third time. Kate opened the phone, determining to rip a verbal strip off him.

"Hello?" Her mouth was bone-dry; her voice, sharp with impatience. She fully expected to hear Jeff's angry voice in response.

"Kate?"

A silent sigh of relief slipped through her lips. "Hawk! I, uh, I'm glad to hear it's you. I had a lovely time last night," she said, trying to forget the unwanted and unwelcome appearance of Jeff, and the doubts assailing her now.

"I'm glad." Now she could hear the relief in his voice. "I wondered whether something had upset you."

"Well, you wondered wrong," she said, her tone firm. "It's been a very long time since I laughed the way I have with you these past two evenings, Hawk. It felt good." Too good.

In all honesty, and as much as she would have liked to deny it, she felt shaky at the awareness it was him on the line. She felt as if everything was smoldering inside her—and breathless, shivery. She had felt somewhat the same at first with Jeff almost two years ago. This time the feeling was stronger, more intense. No, she didn't like it at all.

She had believed herself immune to any other charmer. For Jeff had been charming and gallant for many months, right up until she had agreed to him moving in with her, his ring on her finger. For a while she had been content. Her contentment had lasted all of three months. A bitter taste filled her mouth. First Jeff had become possessive, questioning her every move when they weren't together. Then he had become verbally abusive, cursing, accusing her of being with other men, even Vic.

The warm sensations that had been inside Kate faded to cold determination. She could not, would not, go through a situation like that again.

He jumped on her last remark. "In that case, lunch?"

She had no choice but to smile, and it did feel good, dammit. And she couldn't resist, didn't want to resist, even though she feared she'd regret it.

"I've got to stop by my apartment to change. Do you want to meet me there?"

"Sure. What time?"

Kate glanced at her wristwatch, noting it was not quite twelve-thirty. "Would forty-five minutes work? You realize I'm not going to even ask whether Vic gave you the number."

He chuckled in reply. "See you then."

Within fifteen minutes, Kate was entering her apartment. Slipping off her jacket as she went, she headed for her bedroom. She removed the rest of her suit, hung it back in the closet and made a beeline for the bathroom, wanting to wash up before applying fresh makeup.

She smoothed her hair with a brush, giving it a healthy sheen. Makeup was fast and easy. She kept it light, natural looking. Back in the bedroom she was reaching into the closet for one of the outfits she wore only to work when the buzzer sounded on the intercom.

Hawk? Kate shot a look at the bedside clock. Only thirty-five minutes had passed since she'd talked to him. Pulling on a lightweight robe, she went running to the intercom.

"Yes?" she said on a quick breath.

"Ready for lunch?"

A flutter tickled her stomach, clutched at her throat. "Err…" she said, "not quite. Sorry."

"That's okay, I'll wait."

"You don't have to wait in the lobby," she said, feeling uncertain that inviting him up was wise. Still, she did. "I'll buzz the lock on the lobby door. I'm in the second-floor front apartment. Just walk in. I'll be ready in a few minutes."

"Gotcha."

That was what she was afraid of, and if he did have her, what did he intend to do with her?

Thinking she must either be nuts or self-destructive, Kate unlocked the front door and, turning, dashed back into her bedroom, shutting the door behind her.

She heard the front door open and Hawk call out, "I'm here, Kate. Take your time. I'm in no hurry."

In the process of fastening her belt, Kate had to smile. Hawk was—or at least appeared to be—so nice, pleasant. But then appearances, she reminded herself, were deceiving. She sighed, fully aware that she knew that better than most.

When she entered the living room, Hawk was standing with his back to her, perusing the books on her five-shelf bookcase. He looked gorgeous from the rear.

"See something you like?" she asked, her face growing warm from merely thinking about his tight rear.

He turned to smile at her before replying. "Now I do." He ran a slow look over her, which parched her throat and moistened other places she didn't care to think about at the moment.

"Ready to go?" she asked brightly, perhaps a bit too brightly.

"Ready for anything," he said in a tone that was darn close to a purr. "What about you?"

So am I. The thought zapped into her mind and she immediately zapped it back out. "Uhh…" She stalled, trying to think of a reply, then improvised. "Well, if you don't mind, I'm not ready for lunch…at least not in a restaurant." She dragged up a facsimile of a smile. "I'll be spending most of the rest of the day in a restaurant."

He shrugged. "Okay, what would you rather do?"

She didn't have to think about that one. "It's such a mild and beautiful day. "I'd like to spend some time outside. What do you think?" Kate watched as he pondered her suggestion for all of a few seconds.

"I think it's a great idea," he said and arched one brow. "Do you like hot dogs?"

Kate had to smile. "I love hot dogs, especially dogs loaded with chili."

"Well…" he said slowly, "how about we drive to town, park and stroll around the outside of the casino hotels. Some of the grounds are beautiful. When we're ready, we can go into one of the hotel food courts, have our dogs and, if we still have time, maybe check out some of the upscale shops."

Kate came to a halt, staring at him as if he had two heads.

"What?" Hawk said, frowning.

"You like to shop?" She managed a fake note of awe.

His frown turned into a wry expression. "I wouldn't go so far as to say I like it, but I don't mind shopping occasionally…like two or three times a year." He grinned at her.

Even as she shook her head in despair at him, Kate grinned back. "Okay. Let's roll before you change your mind."

"Good idea." As if unconscious of his move,

Hawk curled his hand around hers, laced their fingers together and led them out the door.

Kate's hand tingled with warmth as they rode the elevator to the ground floor. When the doors slid apart, she immediately felt both chilled and angry all over at the sight that met her eyes.

Jeff… What was he doing there? Her earlier fear coursed back. She could hardly miss his hand reaching for the buzzer to one of the apartments. She felt Hawk stiffen beside her, as if readying for a fight, either verbal or physical.

"What are you doing here, Jeff?" she said, trying to tell Hawk to keep his cool by squeezing his hand.

Without taking his hard-eyed gaze off Jeff, Hawk tightened his grip on her fingers.

"I came to invite you to brunch," Jeff answered, his tone of voice demeaning. "But I see you obviously have already eaten."

Steel infused Kate's back and her head lifted, propelled by pride and anger at the insult in his double entendre. A low, almost growling sound in his throat, Hawk took a step forward.

"Don't," she said, yanking his hand to hold him back. "He's not worth your time and energy." She looked at Jeff with distaste. "I saw a lawyer today. He is going to swear out an order of restraint against you."

"You bitch," Jeff snarled. "And you think that

should worry me?" His laugh was harsh, demeaning. "I should have taught you who's boss long ago."

Kate felt the simmering anger inside Hawk with
the tremor that flashed through him from his rough
hand in hers.

"You gutless bastard." Hawk's voice was very
soft, controlled and somehow terrifying. He again
took a step forward, loosening his fingers to draw
his hand away from hers.

Kate clasped his arm with her free hand, holding
him in place next to her.

"I'd advise you to leave, Jeff, while you are still
in one piece," Hawk growled.

Though Jeff sneered and put on an act of bra-
vado, as if unimpressed with the six-foot-six-inch
Hawk, he cast a disparaging look at Kate as he
turned, yanked open the lobby door, then paused to
glance back this time in clear fear and anger. He
glared at Hawk. "You have no idea the trouble
you're going to be in." He sneered. "I have friends
in this town."

"Yeah, yeah," Hawk drawled, obviously neither
impressed nor intimidated. "And all of them in low
places, I'm sure. You know what you can do with
your threats and your friends. Get lost."

His face looking like it was about to cave in on
itself, Jeff tore out of the lobby. The swiftness of his
steps as he headed for his car was proof that the

bigger man had more than intimidated him. He had scared the hell out of him.

"Son of a bitch," Hawk said softly between his teeth, harsh anger in his voice. Tension hummed through his taut body. He made another move, as if to follow after Jeff.

"Hawk, please don't," Kate said, tugging his hand.

He paused, but his hard-eyed gaze remained fixed on the other man until he drove away. Only then did he shift his gaze to her. "I'm not a violent man, Kate," he said, his voice still threaded with anger. "But I'll take only so much, be pushed only so far…."

"Not today," she said, smiling in hopes of cooling his temper.

"No?" Hawk raised one brow. "Says who?" The tension and anger were gone; his eyes teased her.

"Me…I…" She shook her head. "Whatever. I'm ready for a walk in the sunshine… I need a breath of fresh air after that nasty encounter."

Hawk's expression was sober, but his eyes continued to tease. "Okay, but this jaunt better be good."

"Or?" Kate asked in challenge.

"Or it won't be," he said, grinning, an invitation for her to join him.

Her relief palpable, Kate laughed.

The tension gone, they had a brief tug-of-war

over whose car they were going to use. Hawk won with the simple offer to drop Kate off at work afterward.

The hours they spent together seemed to fly by. They talked practically the entire time, except while they were devouring the chili dogs, sharing one order of French fries and sipping on iced tea.

In a boutique in the Forum Shops at Caesars, they discussed the array of colorful cashmere scarves since Hawk was considering giving one as a Christmas gift to his sister, Catriona. Kate didn't hesitate giving him her opinion.

"This is beautiful. Perfect for winter," she said, holding up a scarf in swirling shades of forest green, russet and antique gold.

His lean fingers lightly stroked the length of the soft material.

As if he were touching her, a tingle slid the length of Kate's spine in time with the stroking of his fingers. She drew a quick breath before asking, "Yes? No?"

He nodded. "I think you're right. "It's perfect. Is there anything else you want to look at?"

"No." She shook her head.

"You wouldn't like one of these scarves for yourself?"

"I'd love one," she said ruefully. "But my clothing budget doesn't stretch to cashmere anything."

From the expression that flittered over his face, Kate was afraid for a moment that he was going to offer to buy her one of the gorgeous scarves. She softly sighed with relief when he shrugged.

"Are you ready to go, then?"

"Yes," she said, glad he hadn't made an offer she would have to refuse, even one involving a simple, if very expensive item.

Kate was happy to get outside again and barely noticed where they were walking until they were in sight of where Hawk had parked the car. It was only then that she glanced at her watch for the first time since they had left her apartment complex.

An odd sensation, almost like sadness, settled on her as they drove to Vic's restaurant. Their day together was almost over. Kate doubted there would ever be another one, as he would soon be leaving for his ranch, his vacation over.

"I had a lovely day, Hawk. Thank you," she said when he brought the car to a stop in the restaurant lot. This time she waited until he opened the car door for her.

"You're welcome, Kate." His hand on the door handle, Hawk looked at her as she emerged from the car, an endearingly soft smile curving his tempting mouth. He leaned toward her. Without a thought, she met him halfway.

Hawk's kiss was as soft as his smile and gentle, with no sudden hungry pressure or demand.

Naturally, Kate wanted more, a lot more. Obviously, Hawk did, too. A low groan of protest slipped into her mouth as he reluctantly drew away.

Moving back, away from her, he dragged a deep breath into his body. Looking her straight in the eyes, he said, simply, "When?"

Kate didn't need to question him. She knew exactly what he meant. The heat radiating through her body was a dead giveaway. He wanted her. Always honest with herself, she acknowledged she wanted him just as badly. But… Why did there always have to be a but? Nevertheless, there it was. Feeling she had known him forever didn't change the fact that she had met Hawk less than a week ago, and she didn't really know the inner man, the unvarnished person.

Oh, Kate was well aware that there were women who "hooked up" with a man the same day or night of meeting him. Yet as hackneyed as it sounded, she was not one of those women.

"Kate?"

At the soft sound of his voice, Kate blinked to meet his direct stare.

"I'm sorry, Hawk," she said, disappointment tingeing her tone. "I…I'm just not sure…I…"

"Shh," he soothed, raising a hand to glide a finger along the curve of her cheek. "It's all right. I can wait." A self-deprecating smile played over his lips. "Well, I think I can wait." His smile turned teasing as he added, "I'll suffer in silent agony."

Kate had to laugh, but she felt like crying. "You really don't need to come back for me tonight. Vic will drive me home."

There it was, her feeble declaration of independence. Hawk stared at her for a moment, but she knew he had understood. She was feeling pressured and was asking him to give her some room.

He gave her a wry smile and circled the car to the driver's side. "May I call you tonight, after you get home from work?"

"Yes, of course." She glanced at her watch. "I've got to go, Hawk, or I'll be late."

"Tonight," he said, standing by the open car door.

"Tonight," she echoed, softly sighing as he slid behind the wheel and swung the door shut.

Kate made it to Vic's just in time, not that Vic would have said anything if she had been a few minutes late. While he was easygoing—the employees didn't even have to clock in—she was a nut about punctuality. Although she admitted she had plenty of human flaws, being late wasn't one of them.

Big deal, Kate thought, hanging her jacket on the coat rack in the employees' break room. So she was never, or hardly ever, late for anything. What was so great about that? She would be better served by being tough rather than prompt. If she were tough, she would have had Jeff hauled into court for abuse and harassment long ago.

But, no, she hadn't done that. She had tried reasoning with him. Ha! A lot that had got her. She should have realized early on that there was simply no reasoning with the self-indulgent, narcissistic jerk.

And Kate knew Jeff would ignore any restraining order and would do exactly as he pleased, which meant the continued harassment of her, especially after Hawk returned home.

There was only one thing she could do. Though Kate had thought of it many times, she now felt certain she had to leave Vegas. She had put off the decision because she liked it here, liked her job and the people she worked with. And she loved Vic, Lisa and Bella like family.

No, as much as she wanted to stay, she couldn't take a chance of putting her friends in danger. Kate heaved a sigh of regret and hurried to the hostess station to relieve the older woman who worked part-time handling the lunch patrons.

She was afraid the day would drag by. It didn't. The restaurant was so busy, time just flew. Kate also expected Hawk to amble in for dinner. He didn't. So, of course, not only was she disappointed, but she couldn't help but wonder where and with whom he might be spending his evening.

After they closed the restaurant, Vic walked Kate to his car. "Are you all right, Kate?" he asked, sounding concerned. "You've been awful quiet tonight."

"I'm fine," she answered, managing a smile for him. "At least I will be after tomorrow."

Vic frowned, opening the car door for her. "What's happening then?"

Kate sighed. "Jeff's been bothering me again," she said, touching his arm reassuringly when she saw him grow stiff. "It's all right, Vic. Nothing happened. Hawk was with me at the time."

Vic cocked an eyebrow. "And nothing happened? Hawk didn't do anything?"

She smiled, if faintly, looking at her hand on his arm. "He couldn't. I held him back."

Vic actually laughed. "Yeah, right. Honey, if Hawk wanted to go for him, you wouldn't have been able to hold him back."

"I said please." She gave him a sweet smile and fluttered her eyelashes at him.

"Yeah." Vic nodded. "I can see that would have stopped even Hawk." Shaking his head, he ushered her into the car. Although she knew he was bursting with questions, Vic didn't voice even one as he drove her home.

She had no sooner entered her apartment than the phone rang. Hawk. Dropping her purse onto a chair, she hurried to the phone and snatched it up.

Six

"Hello?" Somehow she managed to keep her voice calm, concealing the eagerness she felt.

"I'm sorry, Kate."

She froze, hand gripping the receiver. "I won't speak to you, Jeff."

Before she could hang up on him, he went on. "Please, Kate, listen. I mean it. I'm so sorry for what I said to you today in the lobby. I was just so shocked to see you step out of the elevator with that man, I…" He paused as if to catch his breath.

Kate frowned. He had made an odd noise. Was he crying? Jeff? Ha! Was she crazy?

He babbled on. "Baby, I can't—"

"I told you before, over and over again, not to call me that," she said, cutting him off.

"I know, and I'm sorry. I forgot. Geez, Kate, I love you so much, I can't stand it."

"Jeff. Restraining order," she said, striving for patience. "I have nothing to say to you except leave me alone."

"Damn you, Kate!"

The call waiting signal beeped. Relief washed through her.

Hawk.

She had to get rid of Jeff. "I have another call. I'm going to hang up."

"*Kate*, you will be *very* sor—" Kate pressed the flashing button. Drawing a quick steadying breath, she said, "Hello?"

"Hi." His voice was soft, intimate.

Shivering in reaction to the nasty note in Jeff's voice, Kate dropped onto the chair beside the phone table and curled into herself, trying to contain the shakes. "Hi, yourself," she said as calmly as possible. "Have a nice evening?"

"You want the polite answer or the truth?"

She dredged up a quivering smile. "The truth." Or maybe not, she thought, but it was too late to change her mind.

"Well…" He exhaled a very long sigh. "I ate

dinner…alone. I went to the pool…alone. I played some poker. I won…alone." He sighed again, so sad and forlorn. "I took a nap…alone." That last comment was followed by a groan.

Kate was holding her hand over her mouth to keep from laughing—or was it sobbing?—out loud.

He went on. "I had a late snack…alone. I played blackjack…alone." Now, as if he was having difficulty controlling his voice, a sliver of humor broke through. He cleared his throat. "I won again…alone. You get the picture?"

She opened her mouth.

He didn't wait for an answer. "Dammit, Kate, I was missing you like hell the whole time."

Kate couldn't hold it in any longer; instead of sobs, laughter poured out of her.

"Sure, you can laugh," Hawk groused, very close to chuckling. "You had friends and customers around all day and evening to talk to. You were probably even flirting with some of those nice old gentlemen I've noticed watching you as you walk away from the tables."

"What?" Kate blinked. Confusion overrode a lingering fear. "What are you talking about?" She drew an easier breath. "What nice old gentlemen?"

"The ones with the nice old ladies who aren't paying attention," he shot back at her, pausing before clarifying. "I mean, those regular patrons I've seen there every time I've been there."

"The regular old gentlemen customers watch me walk away from their tables?" How funny, she mused. She really hadn't known.

"Sure they do," he answered. "The younger men do, too, when their dates or wives aren't paying attention." He gave a short laugh. "I've been sending quite a few glares their way."

"Really?" she asked, pleased and surprised. "Why?"

"I had rather hoped I was the only one watching the gentle, sensuous sway of your hips," he murmured.

Oh my. Kate grew warm—no, hot—all over. She drew a deep, silent breath and let it out softly, all thoughts of Jeff banished.

"Kate?"

"Yes, Hawk?" Her voice was little more than a whisper of air through her suddenly dry lips.

"When?"

She swallowed to moisten her dry throat and took a look at her watch. "Hawk, it's nearly one o'clock in the morning."

"Yeah, I know…and I'm starving."

For you.

He didn't need to say it. Kate heard it loud and clear. Not allowing herself to hesitate, consider, she murmured, "I am, too, Hawk." Starving and scared.

"So?" His voice was quiet, calm, without a hint of pressure.

Kate wet her lips, swallowed again and said, "How soon can you get here?"

"Twenty-five minutes or so, maybe less if the traffic has thinned," he responded at once, sexual electricity sizzling in his tone.

"I'll be counting the minutes."

"I'm on my way." He hung up.

Determined to push Jeff's not-so-veiled threats from her mind, Kate replaced the receiver and disconnected the phone cord from the wall jack. Digging her cell phone out of her purse, she turned that off, too, before rising to go into her bedroom.

Hawk had said around twenty-five minutes or so. That was just enough time for her to have a quick shower and slip into something a little more comfortable. Simply thinking about that made her smile as she undressed and headed for the bathroom. Tossing off her clothes, she stepped into the shower, careful not to get her hair wet.

Kate was excited but nervous, as well. She hadn't been with a man in some time, and in all truth, she had never thought the act of sex was the end all and be all it was made out to be.

What if she disappointed Hawk? On the other hand, what if he disappointed her? An image of him swam into her mind. Somehow she doubted he could disappoint any woman.

Why was she taking this course now, with this particular man? She had had offers before, many times. Why Hawk? Oh, sure, he was very attractive, masculine and made her laugh.

He made her feel safe and secure.

Was that enough reason to go to bed with a man? They were practically strangers…and yet. Kate shook the thoughts away as she stepped out of the shower and stuffed the wet towel and her clothing into the wicker laundry basket in the closet.

Why was she analyzing her reasons? She was thirty-one years old; she didn't need reasons to go to bed with a man. What she needed was the man, this man, simply because he turned her on something fierce.

She opened a dresser drawer and reached for a nightshirt. No. Why bother? she thought, slipping into her silk, wide-sleeved, knee-length robe. If you're going to do it, do it right, she told herself, staring into the mirror to smooth her hair.

Makeup? Kate shook her head. No. No artifice. This was the way she looked. It was take it or leave it, Mr. Hawk McKenna.

The intercom buzzed. Kate froze, frowning at her reflection. Maybe she should quickly apply a bit of makeup, if only blush.

No. No backing out, she thought, backing away from the dresser and walking to her bedroom doorway. Drawing a deep breath, she rushed to the intercom to buzz Hawk through the lobby door.

The next instant she nearly panicked. Good grief! What if it wasn't Hawk? What if it was Jeff, coming to back his threats up physically?

The doorbell rang. Standing rigid, Kate said softly, "Hawk?"

His answer came back as softly. "Who were you expecting? The big bad wolf?"

Close, she thought. Dragging a smile to her lips, she unlocked the door and opened it for him, one brow arched. "Aren't you? The big bad wolf, I mean." Swinging the door open wide, she moved back.

Stepping inside, he shut the door, locked it, tossed aside the windbreaker he carried and stood there, leaning back against the door frame. His heated gaze took note of every inch of her body. "I wish I were," he murmured, closing the short distance between them. "You certainly look good enough to eat."

"Hmm…uh…would you like something to drink?" Her throat was dry; her voice low, raspy.

His mouth took hers, ending her question. His kiss was every bit as soft, gentle and undemanding as before…for a moment. With a soft growl deep in his throat, Hawk parted her lips with his tongue, delving, tasting every part of her mouth before plunging deep inside.

Afraid her legs would fail her, Kate grasped him at the waist, hanging on for dear life. His kiss was hot, devastating. Drowning in sensations, she slid her hands up his chest and curled her arms around his neck.

Without releasing her mouth, Hawk slowly rose to his full height, taking her with him. Her feet dangling a foot or so off the floor, he carried her into the bedroom, closing the door with a backward thrust of one foot.

Still he held her lips and her mind in thrall as he lowered one hand to the base of her spine, drawing her hips in line with his own.

Hawk's purpose was apparent and successful. Kate felt the hard fullness of him. Lost in the fiery world of sensuality, needy and wanting, she held her hips tightly to him.

"I know," he said at her sudden movement, ending the kiss to allow them both to breathe, pressing into her body.

Kate drew a deep breath before trying to speak. "What do you think we should do about it?" she said, surprising herself with her brazen response to him. Never before had she felt like this, and certainly never with…oh, the hell with *him*. He was a nothing compared to Hawk. No, he was a nothing, period.

"I suppose I could think of a few things," he drawled, his lips a hair's breadth from hers. "We could start with losing our clothes." His tongue tickled the corner of her mouth.

She hadn't known a touch so simple could cause such a burning reaction. Kate couldn't wait to find out what else she hadn't known. Eager to learn, she cupped his head with her hands, and whispering, "More, please," she roughly drew his mouth to hers.

Hawk was quick to comply. This time his kiss wasn't as long, but it was just as powerful. Breathing deeply, harshly, he murmured, "I'm going to burst out of these jeans if I don't get them off soon."

Having no idea that the smile was seductive, Kate lowered her arms and stepped back, looking directly at the spot he indicated.

"This I want to see," she murmured.

Shoes, socks and pants were removed and kicked aside before he answered.

"Well, I didn't mean literally." His gaze devoured her as he dug into a pocket of the discarded jeans, withdrew a foil packet and laid it on the nightstand.

Kate's breaths were coming out of her body in tiny puffs. Her throat felt parched. Curious, she shamefully lowered her gaze to his boxer shorts, her breathing halting altogether at the sight and size of the bulge there. She tried to swallow, was unable and had to try again. She never even saw him pull off his golf shirt.

"Not fair," he said, his own voice sounding desert dry. "I'm doing all the undressing."

Raising her glance, she gasped for breath at the sight of the width of his flat, muscled chest. She blinked as it and he moved closer. She looked up and immediately down again as he pushed down the boxers and kicked them aside.

Good grief! The man was big, absolutely beautiful in form, and perfectly proportioned. Reluctantly returning her gaze to his face, she found him watching her, as if studying her reaction to his nakedness.

"You're…you're beautiful," she whispered, staring into his smoldering gaze.

"Men aren't beautiful." There was a trace of pleasure in his voice at her compliment.

"Sure they are," she said, a wave of her hand brushing aside his rebuttal. "At least you are." She hesitated a moment before blurting out, "Anyway, *I* think you are."

Hawk stepped up close to her, his hand reaching for the belt of her robe. "I disagree with you, but I confess I did like hearing it." The belt knot loose, he gently parted the sides of her robe to glide a slow look over her body. "Now, that's my definition of beauty." Slipping the silky cloth off her, he let it drop to the floor.

Kate was hot and cold. She was shivering on the surface of her body, but a fire blazing inside.

"Hawk?" It was the only word she could manage from her dry throat. It was enough.

"Anything you want, Kate. Anything," he murmured, throwing back the bedcover and sweeping her into his arms to lay her in the middle of her bed. The next instant he was beside her, drawing her to the heat and hardness of his body.

"Another kiss," she said, moving with him as he flipped onto his back, drawing her over his chest. His hands cradling her face, he slowly drew her lips down to his. His tongue was ready for the meeting of mouths, laving her lower lip, driving her wild for more.

Feeling like a column of flames burning only for him, she shuddered at his intimate exploration of her body…every inch of her body. And all the while he murmured to her about what he would do next, sending her anticipation, excitement and tension higher and higher.

Her breathing as rough as his, moaning softly, Kate matched him kiss for kiss, stroke for stroke, thrilling at the sound of his own deep-throated moans.

"That feels so good," he whispered when at last

she took him in her hand, marveling at the thick length of him. "But be careful. Don't go too far."

"Are you sure?" Kate didn't need to ask him what he meant; she knew very well. Still, obeying an impish urge, she wriggled down his now sweat-moistened body and took him into her mouth.

Hawk's body jerked as though he had been touched by a live wire. "Kate…I…" His voice gave way to a groan and he arched into her as she laved him with her tongue. "Damn, Kate. You've got to stop now." His voice was ragged yet his hands were gentle as he grasped her shoulders and pulled her body up the length of his.

"I thought you might like that," she said, the same impish feeling driving her to tease him.

"Like it?" Heaving a deep breath, he rolled both of them over until he was on top of her. "Oh, you have no idea. I loved it."

"But…" she began, enjoying teasing him.

"But I want to be inside you," he said, settling his body between her legs.

Kate sighed as she watched him tear the foil packet, sheath himself. She arched her hips as he slowly, too slowly, slid himself inside her, joining them as one.

Dragging harsh breaths into her chest, Kate sighed with pure pleasure as he began a steady rhythm, slowly building the tension coiling inside her.

Catching him by the hips, she pulled him deeper inside her quivering body, needing more and more of him until, with a soft cry, the tension snapped, flinging her into a shattering release.

A moment later she heard Hawk exhale a gritted "whoa." And felt the shudder of his body as he exploded within her.

With a heavy sigh, Hawk settled on top of her, his face nestled in the curve of her neck. Drained, satiated, Kate idly stroked his shoulders, his back, and kissed his forehead in thanks for the pleasure he had given to her, a pleasure she had never before experienced.

She sighed with utter contentment.

"Yeah," he said in complete understanding. "That has never happened before. An orgasm as strong as that," he murmured close to her ear, which he proceeded to nibble on. "I thought the top of my head would blow off."

"If it does, you'll clean it up," she said, tilting her head to give him better access to her neck, where he was dropping tiny kisses.

Chuckling, he lifted himself up so he could look down at her. "You're something else. You know that?" Without giving her time to respond, he kissed her in a way that was every bit as hot and arousing as before.

Where did the man get his stamina? Kate wondered hazily. Feeling him growing again against the apex of her thighs, she went warm all over. How was it possible for him to be ready again so soon? she mused, every bit as ready as he was. She moved against the hardness pressing against her.

"More?" he asked, his tone soft and hopeful.

"Oh, yes, please." Kate surprised herself with her immediate and pleading answer.

This time Hawk took his time. Slow and easy, he caressed, stroked, kissed every inch of her, lingering on her breasts with maddening attention.

Moving sensuously against him, moaning low with pleasure, she speared her fingers through his long hair, holding him to her as she arched her back.

"Like that?" he said, flicking his tongue over one tight nipple.

Kate was barely able to speak but she managed to sigh, "Oh, yes." Without warning him, she pushed against him until she could slide out from beneath him.

"What—"

"Shush," she said, turning on her side to face him. "I want to play, too." Leaning against him, she gently kissed one of his flat nipples.

Hawk sucked in a breath, then let it out on a laugh. "I did say we could do anything you want. My body's your playground for the rest of the night."

Gliding one palm down his chest, Kate laughed, too.

"Sounds tempting, but I doubt I'll last that long."

Her teasing hand found its destination. "From the size of you, I doubt you can last that long."

Hawk's hand was also moving, curving over her small waist and rounded hips to the apex of her thighs. He drew a quick gasp from her with his exploring fingers.

"Oh my God!" she cried. "Hawk, stop. I can't wait much longer. I want you now."

"That's good." His voice was raw. "Because I can't hold out much longer, either."

Rolling her onto her back, he slid between her thighs and entered her. Within moments they cried out their release simultaneously.

It took longer this time for Kate to come down from the sexual high. Slowly her breathing returned to normal. She smiled as Hawk flipped onto his back, his breathing still labored.

"That was fantastic," he said, turning his head to grin at her.

Although Kate blushed, she felt a sense of deep satisfaction and just a bit of pride. She felt so very pleased, in fact, that she returned his compliment with complete honesty.

"Know what? I've never, ever experienced anything even vaguely like that." Pleasantly exhausted, she curled up against his warm, moist body and closed her eyes.

"Hey, don't go to sleep on me," he said, sitting up. "Well, you may go to sleep on me, but not until we've cleaned up under a shower."

Kate groaned in protest as he took her by the shoulders to sit her up next to him. "Hawk, please. I don't want a shower. I just want to sleep."

"Oh, c'mon, my Kate," he coaxed, sliding off the bed with her in his arms. "A quick wash, and then you may sleep till it's time to get ready for work tomorrow." Cradling her in his arms, he strode into the bathroom as if he weren't a bit tired.

He let her legs slide to the floor. "You have the silkiest skin," he said, stroking his hands over her shoulders.

"Thank you." Kate shivered with the thrill of his words and his caress. "Can we get a shower now? I'm freezing and still sleepy."

Hawk heaved a deep sigh. "Oh, okay," he groused, picking her up again and stepping into the shower stall. He turned the water on full blast, and for a few minutes it was very cold.

"Hawk!" she yelped as her shivering intensified.

He wrapped his arms around her shoulders, drew her against his still warm body. "Better?"

She sighed when she felt the heat of him and the warming water. "Much better. Now let's get this over with."

True to his promise of a quick wash, he impersonally soaped and rinsed them both. Picking her up by the waist, he lifted her out of the shower, set her feet down on the shower mat and joined her there.

Kate was the first to dry off. Dashing into the bedroom, she pulled a thigh-length, baseball-style nightshirt from a dresser drawer and slipped into it. She was diving under the rumpled covers as he left the bathroom.

Smiling gently at her, he reached for his boxer shorts and sat on the edge of the bed to put them on. When he grabbed his jeans, she stopped him.

"What are you doing?" she asked.

He slanted a curious look at her, as if his actions should be obvious. "Getting dressed."

"Why?" She frowned.

"Why else?" he answered, frowning back at her. "So you can get the sleep you were whining about."

"I was not whining," she said indignantly. "Anyway, I thought you'd stay, sleep with me." She was beginning to feel hurt and, ridiculously, used.

Hawk went dead still. "You want me to stay the night?" Hope coated his voice.

"Isn't that what I just said?" She smiled.

"You talked me into it." Smiling back, he dropped the jeans to the floor and crawled into the bed, beside her. "I'm sleepy, too." With that he settled, spoon fashion, behind her, smiling when he heard her soft sigh.

Warm and cuddling, they were both asleep within minutes.

Seven

Kate woke, immediately aware of three things: the bed beside her was empty, the clock on the nightstand read 11:42 a.m. and the tantalizing aromas of fresh coffee brewing and bread toasting were drifting into the bedroom.

She felt wonderful, better than she had in over a year or even longer. There was no tightness or tension inside her, no dread of what the day might bring.

She sat up and stretched, and discovered the ache in her thighs. She was stiff, and understandably so, after the workout she had indulged in with Hawk.

Standing by the bed, she noticed his clothes and shoes were gone. Well, at least she didn't have to worry about walking into the kitchen and finding him naked!

Hawk. Kate smiled at the mere thought of him. He was a fantastic lover and a gentle friend. He made her laugh and it felt so good just being with him.

So, go to him, she told herself. Enjoy being with him before he goes back to the mountains. Walking a bit stiffly, she went into the bathroom. After washing her face and brushing her teeth, she looked at her hair in the mirror. Disaster. Too hungry to care, she went back to her room, thinking that Hawk could just deal with it, messy or not.

Pulling on a different robe, one that actually was warm, she slid her feet into satin mules and headed for the kitchen. Hawk was standing at the counter, two plates, a knife, butter and a jar of marmalade in front of him, carefully removing two pieces of golden-brown bread from the toaster.

"Good morning, Hawk," Kate said quietly. "Did you sleep well?"

Turning to look at her, Hawk threw out one arm in an invitation for her to join him. "Good morning, Kate. I love your do," he said teasingly. "I slept very well, thank you," he added, curling his long arm around her shoulders when she stepped up beside him and tangling his fingers into her flyaway curls. "You?"

"Yes. Deeply. I don't even remember dreaming." She raised her brows. "Is one of those pieces for me?"

"There's a price," he said, smiling down at her.

"Hmm." She hummed as though considering his offer. "And the price is?"

"A kiss," he said at once.

"Oh, all right," she said impatiently. "But you should be darned glad I'm hungry." She raised her mouth to him, her lips parted.

Wrapping his other arm around her to draw her tightly against him, Hawk accepted her silent offer. Expecting one of his deep, ravishing kisses, Kate was pleasantly surprised by his sweet and gentle morning greeting.

"The toast is getting cold," he said, releasing her to tend to the bread.

Kate made a production of pouting.

Hawk laughed. "Don't start anything. You have to be at work in about three hours."

They laughed together and it struck Kate that they laughed together a lot. She and the jerk had rarely laughed easily—or together.

They sat at the kitchen table and chatted about things, common things, important things, until they had finished their toast and two cups of coffee each.

Then Hawk shoved his chair back. "I'm going to get out of here to give you time to do whatever you have to do before going to work."

He pulled her into a crushing embrace and kissed her until her senses were swimming. She was breathless and thrilled when he stepped back from her to draw a deep breath.

"Do you want me to help you with the dishes?" he asked after a moment.

"You don't have to help, Hawk." She wore a suggestive smile. "But you could give me another kiss…if you don't mind."

"Mind?" He drew her back into his embrace. "I'll show you how much I mind." He took her mouth, owned it for long seconds before again releasing it, stepping back, drawing another deep breath.

"I'll see you tonight at dinner, okay?" he said in a dry croak. "Right now I'd better get outta here before I do something I'd never be sorry for." Turning, he strode from the room, her laughter following him to the door.

After setting the kitchen to rights, Kate went back into the bedroom to remove the sheets from the bed and wash them. She paused beside the bed, then began making it instead. The scent of Hawk was on her sheets, and she wanted to sleep between them again, surrounded by his masculine smell.

Kate was all but ready to go to work when the intercom buzzer sounded.

Hawk? She frowned when she realized that his name was the first thing to flash into her mind. Well, she told herself, it was understandable.

Going to the intercom, she pushed a button and said, "Yes? Who is it?"

"Florist," a young male voice answered. "I have a delivery for a Ms. Kate Muldoon."

Hmm, she thought. Hawk? Already? Suddenly she flushed with pleasure. "I'll be right down," she said into the intercom, grabbed her purse to extract several dollars for a tip, then opened the front door and ran down the steps, too eager to wait for the elevator.

A young man stood on the other side of the lobby door, smiling at her. She flipped the lock and opened the door. "Hi. Is that for me?" she said, eyeing the large cellophane-wrapped bouquet he held in one hand.

"Yep. Enjoy your flowers."

"I will," she replied handing him his tip and closing the door behind her as she stepped back with the bouquet.

Back in her apartment, Kate went into the kitchen. Setting the pale green glass vase on the countertop, she carefully removed the cellophane to reveal dark red roses.

"Oh, my," she said, unaware she had whispered aloud. The roses, her favorite flower, were just beginning to open, and each bloom looked perfect.

Suddenly realizing she had pulled the florist's card away along with the cellophane, she rummaged until she found it. Her pleasure turned to anger as she read the card.

> *Kate,*
> *I am so very sorry for my obnoxious behavior last night and recently and before, when we were together. It's just that I love you so much, the fear of losing you made me wild and I reacted badly. I know that but I beg you to please forgive me. I love you and know you love me, too. And, please don't go to a lawyer. You'd lose.*
> *Jeff*

Kate's first thought was, How did he get all that on that small card? Her second thought was, The son of a bitch.

Her anger growing into full-blown fury, she tore the card into tiny pieces, dropped them into the kitchen trash can and tossed the beautiful roses in on top of them, slamming the lid shut.

Shaking, she forced herself to take deep breaths and slowly let them out until she had calmed down.

Her gaze landing on the wall clock, Kate strode from the kitchen. She had to go to work.

Hawk made an appearance mere minutes before her meal break. The sight of him as he entered the restuarant and strolled to the hostess station, where she stood, brought a sigh of sheer relief from the depths of her being. Everything would be all right now. The thought startled her. But only until he went back to Colorado, she reminded herself.

"I'm going to miss you when you're gone," she blurted. With her surprising words, an idea popped into her head. Ridiculous, she thought, mentally shaking her head. Forget it.

"Thanks, Kate." Hawk smiled back, not a bright smile but temptingly, slumberous one. "I'm going to miss you, too. You are going to join me for dinner, aren't you? I'm not heading to Colorado this second."

Still recovering from the force of his smile, Kate had to swallow before she could answer.

He picked up two menus and arched a brow. "Will you join me?"

"Yes, yes, I will." Circling around the hostess station, she led the way to a table.

"Is something wrong, Kate?" he said after he'd seated them both. "You seem far away, distracted."

"I am somewhat. I…" she began, halting when

the server came to take their order. She raised her brows at Hawk. Strangely, he appeared to know what she was asking of him.

"We'll both have the special of the day," he said, glancing at her. "Wine?"

Looking up at him, she smiled. "No wine. I'm working." She looked at the server, Gladys, a middle-aged woman with a great sense of humor. "I'll have coffee, Gladys. Before dinner, please."

"Got it," Gladys said, turning her gaze on Hawk. "What about you, Mr. McKenna?"

"Yes, ma'am," he said. "I'll have coffee, also."

Gladys was flushed with pleasure from his respectful address when she moved away from the table.

"What's the matter, Kate?" His voice held concern. Hawk paused before continuing. "Is it something I can help you with?"

Go for it, a small voice inside her said. Kate drew a deep breath, then explained everything that had happened.

She concluded by saying, "I tore up the card and threw it in the trash and dropped the flowers in with it. Hawk…I…" She stopped when Gladys came to the table, bearing a tray with their coffees, cream and sugar.

"Your dinners will be here shortly," Gladys informed them.

Kate added cream to her coffee, gnawing on her lip as she reconsidered her decision to share her idea with him. She was certain that if she did, he'd think she'd slipped over the edge of reason.

"Hawk...I...what?" he said, gently nudging her.

Kate opened her mouth, closed it again, swallowed, then softly and quickly asked, "Hawk, will you marry me?"

Hawk was thrown for a loop by Kate's proposal. He stared at her in dead silence for a moment. She had just finished relaying the details of the harassment and the threats that Jeff, the jerk, had been using to frighten her. And then she tossed the proposal at him out of left field.

"Kate—" he began, but she cut him off.

"No." She was shaking her head. "I'm sorry. I don't know why..." The arrival of Gladys at their table with their dinners silenced her.

She started again the moment Gladys moved away.

"Hawk, forget what I—" she began, but he cut her off.

"No, I want to discuss this matter with you," he said, raising his hand, palm up, to keep her from talking. "Let's eat our dinner. We'll talk afterward."

Kate didn't say a word. She fidgeted. She drank her coffee in a few deep swallows. She picked at her food with a fork but ate little of it.

Watching her, Hawk silently decided that was enough. Reaching across the table, he laid his hand over hers, ending her mutilation of the fish on her plate. She glanced up at him, which had been his purpose.

"Kate." His voice was soft, gentle. "The poor fish is already dead. Calm down and eat. The food is delicious." He smiled. "You don't want to hurt Vic's feelings, do you?"

She exhaled and he could see the tension drain out of her rigid body. "Okay," she said, offering him an apologetic smile. He accepted it with one of his own before returning his attention to his meal.

Hawk cleaned off his plate, along with two rolls from the basket Gladys had set on the table with their dinners. He was pleased to note that Kate had consumed over half of her meal and part of one roll.

"Dessert?" he asked, wiping his mouth with his napkin. "More coffee?"

"Coffee. No dessert," she said, offering him a tentative smile.

He smiled back, feeling relaxed, hoping she would relax also. "Coffee it is." Before he could so much as glance around to locate Gladys, she was there, a coffee carafe in hand. She refilled the cups, collected the dinner plates and was gone again, leaving them alone.

As there were diners at the next table, Hawk kept his voice low. "Okay. What's the deal?"

"Forget it," Kate said, once again shaking her head. "It was a stupid brainstorm. That's all."

"C'mon, Kate," he said, lowering his voice even more. "We were lovers last night. You can tell me anything, even your stupid brainstorm." His smile was sweet. "I promise I won't laugh."

His efforts paid off when she returned his smile.

"Okay. Thanks, Hawk." Kate took a deep breath, as if drawing courage into herself and quickly blurted out, "I asked you to marry me to get out of Vegas for a while and away from Jeff. I'm sorry. I am at the end of my rope and scared. I didn't give a thought to the fact that I'd be using you, and that was unfair of me."

"Why not just report Jeff to the authorities?" Hawk asked reasonably.

"I did." Kate shuddered. "I should have done something when he continued to bother me after I tossed him out. I realize that now. But I was so sure he'd eventually give it up and leave me alone. I thought the restraining order would finish it." She drew a tired-sounding breath. "My mistake and now I'm paying for it."

Hawk was shaking his head. "But you talked to that lawyer yesterday. Call him or the police and tell them Jeff has threatened you."

She shook her head. "You don't understand. Jeff told me he has contacts, friends, some in court, so to speak. This is Vegas. Some of those friends might not be so friendly."

That gave him pause. His expression turned stony.

"So you decided to skip town for a while…with me?"

"No." She heaved a sigh. "The idea that stormed my brain was to ask you to marry me and remain married for a while, maybe four months or so, and to make sure Jeff hears about it. I guess I was hoping that after a time, he'd give it up and find someone else to abuse."

"Uh-huh," Hawk murmured, pondering her explanation. "And did your brainstorm come with any information for me as to how this would work?"

Kate frowned. Damned if she wasn't gorgeous, even with a scowl on her face. "Such as?" She was now staring at him through narrowed eyes.

"Hey, kid, don't look at me as though you want to strangle me." He narrowed his eyes right back at her. "You started this, you know."

Closing her eyes, Kate seemed to deflate. "Yes, I do know. I'm sorry, Hawk. Just forget it. I know I have no right to dump my troubles in your lap."

Deciding he was a damn fool, Hawk smiled and said, "I didn't say I wouldn't do it, Kate. I just want to know what exactly you had in mind."

Eight

Kate was stunned and couldn't find her voice for a moment. "I…uh…as I said, I was thinking about a temporary arrangement, say four to six months."

Hawk's brows went up in question. "You're not suggesting we get married and stay here in Vegas for that amount of time, because if—" That was as far as he got before she cut in.

"No, of course not," she quickly said. "I know you have a ranch to run."

"That's right," he said before she could say any more. "And I'm going to have to get back soon." He only paused a second before continuing. "Look, I was thinking of leaving this weekend…."

"Oh…" she replied, disappointed.

"No, don't go jumping to any conclusions, Kate. Let me finish. Okay?"

She nodded in agreement and flicked a hand, indicating he should continue.

"Good." He smiled.

Kate felt some of the tension leak from her spine. She smiled back at him.

"First of all, though I said I was thinking about flying out this weekend, I don't have to go. I have an open-ended ticket." He paused again, this time to take a swallow of his cooling coffee. "Now, tell me what you have in mind."

"Thank you, Hawk," she said and rushed to convey the details before he could change his mind. "If you're agreeable to my proposal, I thought we could get married here in Vegas, making sure Jeff hears about it. You could then go back to Colorado immediately if you wanted to."

Hawk narrowed his eyes at her. "And you stay here in Vegas? That's not going to convince anybody."

"No, no. If you'd prefer I didn't go with you, I would find another place to stay. Maybe my father's farm in Virginia, although I'd really rather not go there."

"Why not?" he asked. "It seems reasonable to me for you to go there without the farce of a wedding."

Kate was starting to feel queasy. He wasn't going to agree to her plan, which she was starting to think was a bad one from the beginning. Smothering a sigh, she went on to explain.

"My mother died when I was in high school," she said, her voice dull. "I didn't go to college as planned but stayed home to keep house for my father. I liked the work. Cooking, cleaning, keeping the farm accounts on the computer." She paused to sip her coffee.

"You didn't resent not going to college?" Raising his coffee to his lips, Hawk watched her over the rim of his cup.

"Oh, for a while, sure, but I accepted it." She smiled. "I didn't want my father to do everything around the farm and the house by himself."

"No siblings?"

"No, at least not then. I now have two, a brother, Kent, and a sister, Erin."

Hawk smiled in understanding. "Your father remarried, and you found out you were not an exception to the rule."

Kate frowned. "What do you mean? What rule?"

"That two women can't live in harmony in the same house."

"I did try," she said defensively. "Well, maybe I didn't try hard enough." She gave him a wry smile. "I had everything the way I wanted it." She sighed. "But you know the old saying…a new broom sweeps clean."

"Hmm…" Hawk nodded. "So you took off for parts unknown. Right?"

"Yes. My father had insisted on paying me, and since I really had nothing much to spend money on, I had quite a bit saved." She shrugged. "I had a car of my own and took off to see something of the country. I landed, all but broke, here in Vegas and got lucky." She smiled. "Not in the casinos but by meeting Vic."

"And your brother and sister?" he asked, lifting a brow.

"Oh, I hung around, gritting my teeth, until after Erin was born. She's the youngest."

"You don't like kids?"

"I love kids," she said. "I just didn't want to spend years raising another woman's kids, or even helping, to tell the truth."

"Okay, so you don't want to go back to Virginia," he said. "And that brought on the idea to go back to Colorado with me?"

"Hawk, really, let's just forget it," she said, now feeling sorry for presenting the idea. Pushing her chair back, she stood up before he could rise to help her. "Look, Hawk, I'm an idiot. Just forget I said anything. Okay?"

"No," he replied mildly. "I'm still ready to hear

the rest of your plan. I'll be waiting in back tonight when you go for your car."

"But, Vic will be there," she protested.

"So?" Hawk shrugged, drawing her gaze to his wide shoulders. "I'll say hello and good-night." He grinned. "That is, if I may follow you home."

Like the fabled phoenix, Kate's hopes rose from her ashes of defeat. "All right, Hawk. Not only may you follow me home, but you may come in for a drink."

"Now you're talkin'," he said. "You'd better get on the ball before Vic fires you."

"As if," Kate shot back at him as she hurried back to the hostess station.

Hawk left soon after. He didn't stop at the hostess station but rather touched his fingertips to his lips and blew a kiss at her. "See you later," he called, striding from the restaurant.

Kate couldn't wait. She wanted this over with. Her nerves felt like a mass of tangled live electrical wires. Fortunately, the rest of the night passed swiftly. There was only one hitch.

Close to quitting time, Kate's cell phone beeped with a text message. It was from Jeff and contained the same garbage as before: I'm sorry. Forgive me. I love you. And I know you love me. So don't do anything stupid, and call off the lawyer.

Exhaling, she lifted her hand to delete the message, then paused, deciding to keep it instead. She'd show the message to Hawk. Maybe, just maybe it might convince him to help her.

Hawk was leaning against his rental car when she walked across the parking lot. Good heavens, he was one hunk of a man. Kate felt a chasm yawning inside her, a crevasse of longing and want. Being with him last night had been more than she had ever imagined making love with a man could be.

Love? Kate nearly staggered at the thought and came to an abrupt stop. No. She shook her head and straightened her shoulders. Love was an illusion; she had learned that the hard way. What she and Hawk had shared had been sex, great sex, but sex all the same. And in all honesty, she wanted to share it with him again.

"Hey," he called, drawing her from her musings. "Why are you just standing there?" Pushing himself upright, he started toward her. "Are you all right?"

"Yes," she answered, getting herself moving again. "I'm fine. I...er...was thinking."

"Where's Vic? I thought he always walked you to your car." The gentleness in Hawk's eyes had been replaced by a frown.

"He's doing some paperwork. He was going to escort me out here, until I told him you would be here." Smiling, Kate unlocked and opened her car door. "I think I'll go home now," she added, sliding behind the wheel before glancing up at him. "Are you going to come?"

Hawk groaned. "Oh, lady, that is a loaded question, especially as I'm feeling loaded for bear already."

Cringing inside due to the unintentional double meaning of her question, Kate flushed with embarrassment. She felt foolish and not too bright. Not having a clue how to respond, she turned the key in the ignition, firing the engine to life, and began backing out of the space.

Laughing softly, Hawk strolled back to his car. Kate saw him squeezing his long body inside as she drove past him and into the street.

Although Kate couldn't tell if he was following her during the drive home, Hawk pulled his vehicle alongside her car just as she was stepping out of it. The devil was still smiling.

"I amuse you, do I?" she asked, swishing by him to the entrance to the building.

"Oh, Katie, you have no idea what you do to me," he said, standing close to her, whispering in her ear.

Kate's heartbeat seemed to skip and her breathing grew shallow. Inside the lobby her hand trembled, so she had trouble getting the key into the lock.

"You want me to get that for you?" Hawk's expression was somber, but amusement laced his voice.

"No, thank you," she said through gritted teeth, stabbing the key into the lock, turning the knob and striding through the lobby to the elevator.

Hawk was blessedly quiet until the elevator doors slid shut, closing them in together. "You angry at me?"

Growing warm inside, Kate shot him a glaring look. "Are you trying to make me angry?" Her attempt to sound harsh failed miserably.

The elevator jerked to a stop, the doors slid apart and Hawk stepped out of the car, turning to hold a hand out to her. "You want to come?" he said, his lips twitching with laughter.

Ignoring his hand, head held high, Kate walked past him, saying smartly, "Grow up, McKenna."

His lips no longer twitching, Hawk roared with laughter. He laughed all the way through the living room to the kitchen, where Kate stopped, spun around and placed her hands on her hips.

"Do you want a drink or not?" she demanded, trying mightily to control her voice.

"Yes, ma'am," he replied nicely.

Kate shook her head. "You are something, Hawk," she said, her mock frown giving way to a flashing smile.

He strolled to her, shrugging off his jacket and

tossing it over a chair on the way. Coming to a halt in front of her, he lifted the wrap from her shoulders, sent it flying on top of his jacket and raised her head with his hand to rub his rough thumb over her parted lips.

"You think so, huh?" he said, low and sexy. "Well, I think you're something, too. Something special."

Oh…oh…Kate's senses were going crazy. Her lips tingled from his touch, burned for the taste of his mouth on hers. Her entire body ached for his. Hawk. His name echoed through her mind. Hawk.

Closing her eyes to shield herself from the heat glowing in his, Kate gave herself a mental shake, telling herself to get it together. Before anything else, they had to talk, discuss the suggestion she was now sorry she had ever thought of, never mind mentioned to him.

"Uh…a drink," she said, her heart racing as she stepped back and turned to the refrigerator. "What would you like? Beer, wine or something stronger?"

"What are you having?" He smiled. She feared his smile was for her sudden ineptness.

"Well, as I don't often drink beer and never drink the stronger stuff, I'm having a glass of wine." *And I can't get to it soon enough,* she thought. Opening the fridge door, she withdrew a bottle of white zinfandel. "What can I get you, Hawk?"

"Do you have any red?" He was close, too close, peering over her shoulder.

"Yes, on the rack at the end of the countertop." Kate sighed with relief when he moved away from her.

They carried their wine into the living room. Kate motioned for Hawk to have a seat, while she kicked off her shoes before curling up on a corner of the couch. Her pulse rate increased when he chose to settle at the other end of it.

"Okay," he said, taking a swallow of his cabernet. "Tell me exactly what you had in mind."

Kate set her glass on the table next to the couch because her hands were shaking again. "I did, Hawk. I asked you to marry me."

One of his brows shot up. "Kate, tell me what you had in mind," he repeated concisely. "Were you thinking of a convenience marriage, one that is purely platonic?"

"Oh, no," she said at once. "I'm... I wouldn't dream of asking that of you. I had thought, as we seemed to be getting along so well, we could deal with each other for maybe four to six months."

"Live together, work together, share the same bed for half a year? Then go our separate ways, still friends, no harm done?"

Feeling her face grow warm and wanting to look away from his direct, riveting gaze, Kate held her head high, drew a steadying breath and answered, "Yes."

He was quiet for a moment, a long moment, staring into her eyes as if searching her soul. Kate held her breath.

"Okay, you've got a deal." Smiling, Hawk raised his glass to her in a silent salute.

A tremor still rippling through her body, Kate grasped the stem of her glass and returned the salute. "Thank you." Her voice was rough, barely there. She gulped a swallow of wine.

His nearly empty glass in his left hand, Hawk slid down the length of the couch to her. He held out his right hand. "Shake on it?"

Shivering, almost giddy with relief, Kate set her glass aside and placed her palm against his. His fingers curled around her hand. They shook, and then with a light tug, Hawk pulled her to him. He murmured, "A shake and a kiss. That will really seal the deal."

After reaching across her to set his glass next to hers, he drew her into his arms and captured her mouth with his own in a searing kiss.

Sealed indeed. The thought, recognizable if fuzzy, floated through Kate's mind. Or was she herself floating? She didn't care, not while Hawk was igniting a fire deep inside her with his devouring kiss.

When Hawk drew his mouth from hers, Kate

found herself stretched out on the long couch, with Hawk stretched out next to her, or rather practically on top of her.

How did she get into that position when she didn't remember moving? How had Hawk managed the move without her noticing? Did it matter at all?

No. The answer was there, at the forefront of her mind. The only thing that mattered was that she was there with Hawk, secure and safe in his arms.

"That was some seal," he murmured close to her ear, stirring all kinds of delicious sensations throughout her entire body. "But maybe we should do it again…just to make sure."

He didn't give her time to answer. She didn't need time. Kate's lips were parted, ready and eager for the touch of his mouth to hers.

A second later there was a muted beep. Breaking off the kiss, Hawk raised his head to frown at her. "Was that your cell phone, or am I hearing things?"

Heaving a sigh, Kate pressed her palms against his chest. "Yes, please let me get up."

He groaned. "Can't we ignore it?" Still, he shifted, sliding from the couch to the floor.

Scrambling over him, she searched around for her purse, which she'd dropped absentmindedly when she'd come in. Finding the purse on the chair just inside the door, she dug out her cell, certain about who was calling before she looked at the display.

She was right. Softly echoing Hawk's groan, she returned to where he was lying on the floor, now with his hands behind his neck, cradling his head.

"Don't tell me," he drawled. "The sky is falling and we must run and tell the king."

Flipping to the text message she'd received earlier from Jeff, she handed the phone to him.

Hawk skimmed the text message and snorted, but before he could speak, she took the cell phone from him and flipped to the text message she'd just received, then handed the cell back again.

Before reading the new message, Hawk jack-knifed to sit up. Shaking his head, he skimmed the text message. Then, tilting his head, he glanced at her and said wryly, "This clown has a one-phrase song, doesn't he?"

"Yeah," Kate answered, sighing. "He always has. Cyrano he's not. More Scarface. Now, do you see why I'm ready to skip town, so to speak?"

"Yes, but can't this lawyer you've hired take care of it?"

"Hawk, you've read those text messages. If Jeff has the powerful friends he claims to have and I feel certain he does, I really don't believe he'd spend more than a few hours in the lock-up, if that."

Hawk smiled. "Look, Katie, actually don't look so down and defeated. We've just sealed a contract of sorts. We can be in Colorado within a week."

"It will seem awful quick to everyone." She tried a smile and was pleased when it worked. Hawk was very reassuring. "I'll talk to Vic tomorrow at work. I'll explain the situation to him."

"No, you won't." His tone was flat, adamant.

Kate blinked. "Why not?"

"We're going to pull this off like the real thing," he said in the same tone as before. "You know, love at first sight, head over heels, the whole razzle-dazzle. We do have this physical attraction going for us. I'm sure we can appear the picture of not-so-young love."

"I beg your pardon," Kate said indignantly. "Speak for yourself when it comes to age, mister."

Hawk grinned. "You know what I mean, woman. Neither one of us will see our early twenties again. Hell, I won't see my early thirties again."

Suddenly relaxed and easy with him, Kate nodded. "I suppose you're right. That would be the best way to go about it. While I do want the news of our marriage to get back to Jeff, and it will, the chances of the truth getting to him as well are too high even if I tell only Vic."

"I know." Hawk nodded. "Vic would tell Lisa, and who knows where the information would go from there."

"You're right," Kate agreed. "I certainly wouldn't want Jeff showing up at your place."

"Ahh…Katie, you won't have to worry about that. I'm certainly not afraid of him. Besides, I'm a crack shot with a pistol or rifle. I have a foreman and a wrangler who are almost as good with a weapon as I am. Added to that, I have a dog, a very big dog that can bring down a wolf…or a man if necessary."

Kate stared at him warily, not sure if he was putting her on or not. "You wouldn't…" She didn't finish; she didn't have to. Somehow she knew he would if necessary.

"Shoot a man?" he asked. "I did, while I was in the air force. I didn't like it. It was him or me. Sucker lived."

Kate could accept that answer. She nodded. "Okay, we do it your way. I'll simply say it didn't work out when in four or six months I return to Vegas…if I decide to return to Vegas." Before she could as much as raise a hand, she yawned.

"The mood's gone, isn't it?" Hawk looked and sounded disappointed, but his smile held understanding.

"I'm afraid so," Kate admitted. "I'm very tired. Stress, I suppose."

"I can imagine, being bugged and frightened by that SOB." He got to his feet. "Okay, I'm leaving now. I'll meet you at the restaurant tomorrow. We should be together and have our act together when we talk to Vic. That work for you, Kate?"

"Yes, Hawk, that works for me."

He went to the door, Kate behind him. At the door he turned to gaze into her eyes.

"One kiss?" he asked.

Her answer came with the lift of her head. His kiss was warm and gentle and comforting.

"Sleep well, Kate."

"You, too, Hawk."

Right, Hawk thought. He'd be lucky if he slept at all. What had he just committed himself to? Marriage? Sure, he had thought maybe someday, with the right woman. But he had never met that right woman.

Pulling into the line of cars at the valet service at his hotel, Hawk unfolded himself from the car, handed his keys to the valet, accepted his receipt and strolled into the casino.

Since he was positive he wasn't going to sleep well, Hawk decided to pass some time playing poker. Within less than an hour, and with the loss of a couple hundred-dollar bills, he pushed away from the table and went to his room.

Standing sleepless once more at the floor-to-ceiling window overlooking the busy Strip, Hawk sipped the beer he had removed from the small in-room bar, contemplating his future, at least the next four to six months of it.

Starting tomorrow afternoon he had to play a man madly in love with Kate Muldoon. He smiled. Well, it shouldn't be too onerous. Kate was a lovely woman, easy to be with, a comfortable companion and fantastic to be with in bed. In truth, she was a wonderful woman to make love with.

Love.

Was it possible for a man used to being on his own for the most part ever to find real love…if there was such a thing? And, if he should find that woman, would she be willing to spend the major part of her life stuck with him in the lee of mountains located in the back of beyond?

Hawk sighed, wondering if Kate, never mind any other woman, would even last as long as four months.

Hawk was, at that point in time, firmly stuck between anticipation and a strange sensation of something he couldn't put a name to.

A wry smile shadowed his mouth. If nothing else, Kate being at the ranch should discourage Brenda, the daughter of Hawk's foreman, Jack, from her intentions, whatever they were, in regard to him.

Nine

Fortunately Hawk had warned Kate that the ride would be bumpy after they left the macadam road. His truck was a big workhorse, and it had been comfortable up until he turned onto the private dirt road.

"Almost home now," he said, smiling at her while keeping his eyes on the excuse for a road. "Are you okay?" Obviously he had noticed her death grip on the handle mounted above the door window.

"I'm fine," Kate answered. "Or I will be as soon as we're there and I can move around again."

"Won't be long now." He hazarded a quick glance at her. "I imagine you're tired."

"A little," she said wryly. "It's been a pretty hectic day."

He laughed. "It's been a hectic week."

"Yes." A tire hit a pothole, and Kate's butt lifted from the seat for an instant, landing with a painful jar to her spine.

To her mind, they couldn't get off this miserable road fast enough. But, all things considered, the past week had gone by smoothly and swiftly.

The day after Hawk had agreed to her marriage idea, he had shown up at the restaurant moments after she had arrived for work. Together they had sought out Vic. They both knew he had to be convinced that they had almost immediately fallen in love, which wouldn't be a snap, as Vic was a very shrewd man.

The performance began with Hawk asking Vic if they could talk in private. Readily agreeing, though eyeing both of them with a curiosity bordering on suspicion, Vic led them into his small office.

"What's up?" he asked, getting directly to the point.

Encircling her waist with his arm, Hawk took over. "I'm stealing your hostess away, Vic."

Vic looked from one to the other, his suspicions now completely awakened. "What exactly do you mean by stealing Kate?" His gaze settled on her. "You want the day off to spend with the warrior here?" He indicated Hawk with a jerk of his head.

Pulling her closer to him, Hawk answered for her. "No, Vic, she doesn't want the day off to spend with me. Kate's going to leave to spend the rest of her life with me at the ranch."

"What the hell?" Vic exclaimed, his expression a mixture of shock and disbelief. "What are you talking about, Hawk? Is this some kind of a joke?"

"You know me better than that, Vic," Hawk answered. "I wouldn't joke about something this serious. I love Kate, I'm going to marry her as soon as possible and I would like you to be my best man."

His expression now oscillating between delight and confusion, Vic stared at Kate. "Is he serious? No, I can tell he's serious. What about you, Kate?"

"I'm very serious, Vic," she said, her voice soft but rock steady. "I love him." Kate turned to gaze up at Hawk in what she hoped was close to adoration. In truth, it wasn't difficult....

She had no time to contemplate the questions rising to nag at her mind. Without further probing, Vic let out a whoop and snatched Kate from Hawk to give her a big brotherly hug.

"Of course I'll be your best man, chump," he told Hawk. "Hell, I always was the best man."

"Not in this lifetime or any other," Hawk retorted, extending his right hand to Vic. "We want to get married as quickly as possible." He pulled Kate gently from Vic and back into his arms. "Don't we, Katie?"

"Yes, we do," she whispered, lowering her eyes and easily managing a soft sigh.

Vic was grinning and rubbing his hands together. Kate thought she could almost see the wheels rolling inside his head. "Okay, I have an idea."

Kate smiled. Vic always had an idea and was usually dead right with it.

"Go on," she said.

"I was sure you would," Hawk drawled.

Vic looked at Kate. "Were you thinking of getting married in one of the hotels or chapels?"

"Lord no," Kate yelped.

Vic smiled happily. "I was hoping you'd say that. Now, would you like to be married right here, in the restaurant, with the customers as witnesses?"

"Yes!" Kate and Hawk declared in unison.

"Then go do what you have to do," Vic said, flicking a hand to send them away. "I'll take care of everything."

"But…" Kate protested, "don't you need me at the hostess station?"

"We'll manage." Vic hugged her again. "Go. Be together. I have things to do, people to talk to, the first one being Lisa."

"Oh, that reminds me," Kate said. "I must call Lisa to ask her to be my matron of honor."

"I'll take care of that, too." Vic grinned. "She is

going to be so excited. I can't wait to tell her. So, kids, get lost. Come back for supper."

Kate and Hawk went shopping, though not together. She went shopping for a special dress. He, she found out later, went shopping for wedding bands…plural. Kate couldn't have been more surprised days later, when after Hawk placed a gold band on her finger, Vic handed her a matching band to slide onto Hawk's finger.

It was a beautiful wedding. After sending Bella shopping for decorations, Vic had drafted all the employees, and any of the customers who wanted to help, to festoon the restaurant with yards of white tulle and dozens of white silk flowers. Everyone had enjoyed every minute of the fun, and when they had finished, the decorations had looked so good, Vic had decided to keep them up permanently.

Kate smiled in remembrance of the serious, fun but long wedding day. She and Hawk had left the party, still in full swing, just in time to catch the flight to Colorado that he had booked them on.

Now, tired to exhaustion, Kate was relieved when Hawk steered the truck onto a smoother surface before coming to a stop in front of a large ranch house with a deep porch that ran the entire width.

Pulling the hand brake, Hawk heaved a deep sigh

and turned to smile at her. "I'm dragging, Kate. What about you?"

"I feel the same," she said, sighing as deeply as he had. "Why are there lights on in the house?" she asked, frowning. "I hope you don't have company, because I'm light years away from entertaining tonight."

"I only rarely get company, Kate, and never without forewarning." Pushing his truck door open, he jumped to the ground. "I contacted my foreman to ask him to turn on the lights for us."

"Oh, okay." She turned to open her door only to find him coming to a halt beside it. He offered his hand to help her out, and she gratefully accepted, knowing full well there was no way she'd jump out the way he had. She'd be happy if she could walk straight after the long and bumpy ride from the small airport.

Kate didn't need to walk. Hawk swept her up into his arms, drew her from the truck and carried her up the porch steps. He paused to turn the doorknob and nudge the door open with one foot before carrying her into the house, which would be her home for the next four to six months.

"You left the truck door open," she said after he set her feet firmly on the floor.

"Yeah, I know." Hawk smiled. "Welcome home, Kate. And make yourself at home. Walk around to get the stiffness out of your muscles. Explore the place while I get our bags from the truck."

Kate was happy to move about; she even did a few quick stretching exercises before exploring. She was standing in a large, comfortably decorated living room, her attention riveted on a beautiful Indian woven rug, which took up most of one wall. The living room flowed into a smaller room, the dining room, which opened to a large eat-in kitchen. A hallway ran from the living room to what she surmised were the bed- and bathrooms. She fell in love with the place at first sight.

Kate was still standing there admiring the woven rug on the wall when Hawk entered, lugging their bags.

"What do you think so far?" Hawk raised his eyebrows and dropped their luggage to the floor with a thud.

"I like it." Kate smiled a bit nervously. "Very much what I've seen of it so far."

"Good." He didn't return her smile as he studied her expression. "You're nervous, right?"

Kate nodded. "A little, yes."

He moved to her side and lifted her head as he lowered his to brush his lips over hers. "There's no need to be, Kate," he said. "There's no rush about anything, and that includes sleeping arrangements. Anything you want or need, just say it. I'll do my best to provide."

As the nervous anxiety she'd been caught up in drained from her, Kate smiled and rattled off her present wants and needs.

"Let's see," she began, smiling up at him. "I want and need a shower, a change of clothes, food, a glass of wine and ten hours of sleep, not necessarily in that order. Actually, I believe I'd like the food and wine first. No wait, I need a bathroom first."

Hawk was laughing as he waved a hand at the hallway. "The first bedroom on the right," he said after catching his breath. "It's mine and I have my own bathroom. I'll pour the wine and rummage in the fridge to see what's available. Take your time."

"Thank you." Before heading for the hallway, Kate scooped up her carry-on bag from where he had dropped it. She entered the first door on the right.

Hawk's bedroom was spacious, big enough to hold a tallboy chest of drawers, a double dresser, a wall of sliding closet doors, a man's club chair and, in the middle of it all, a king-size bed. She stared at the bed, which was covered by a puffy comforter, for several long seconds until necessity made her turn away.

Intending only to avail herself of the facilities and wash her hands and face, Kate looked longingly at the shower for a few moments.

Oh, she could hardly wait. But first, carefully

lifting from her suitcase the gorgeous off-white dress she had found in one of the upscale shops in Hawk's hotel, she shook it out and neatly draped it over the back of the club chair. Quickly stripping off her jeans, sweater and underwear, she stepped into the shower. She gave a long sigh of pure pleasure as the water flowed over her tired body. Oh, it was sheer heaven.

Kate could have stood under the spray forever if it hadn't been for the water beginning to run cold and for the fact that Hawk was waiting for her.

After drying off and quickly blow-drying her hair so that it was only slightly damp, Kate pulled out the panties, nightgown and lightweight, thigh-length robe she always packed in her carry-on bag. Digging out a brush, she smoothed her riot of curls the best she could. As she left the bedroom, she decided she owed it to Hawk to sleep there that night and every night, and she realized that she wanted to, as well. Kate quietly walked barefoot to the kitchen.

Although she didn't know how Hawk heard her enter, he must have, because he turned, raising that one brow as he gave her robed figure and still damp hair the once-over.

"I couldn't resist your shower," she explained. "I felt kind of yucky."

"Yucky, huh?" He smiled, warming her from the outside in. "You smell good…like soap or shampoo."

Kate returned the smile. "Both, I think." She inhaled. "Something else smells good."

"It's what my father always calls comfort food. I'm heating soup and making grilled cheese sandwiches."

"Tomato soup," she said, inhaling again. "The best comfort food."

He shot a quick grin at her. "It's about ready. Have a seat."

Kate was about to ask him if there wasn't something she could do to help when she glanced at the table and found that it was set for two, with wine in stemmed glasses and water in sturdy, heavier glasses.

"It looks like you're pretty handy in the kitchen," she observed, seating herself at the table.

"I've been here alone, except for the occasional guest or two, for almost ten years." Carrying two soup bowls, he crossed to the table and set one in front of her and the other at the place setting opposite.

"Ten years," she repeated, surprised.

"I quickly learned to cook and take care of myself."

He smiled, turning to the countertop to pick up two luncheon plates. "I've got a shelf full of cookbooks and I use them, too."

"Books…books, damn," Kate said, grimacing. "I packed up all my books to go with the things I put into storage." She glanced at Hawk, to find him watching her in apparent bemusement. "Like Jefferson said, 'I cannot live without books.'" She quoted the author of the Declaration of Independence. "And I'd wager the closest bookstore is in Durango. Right?"

"Most likely. I've never checked," he drawled. "But don't fret, Katie. There's always Amazon. Besides, I've got a bookcase jammed with both fiction and nonfiction hardcover keepers." He smiled. "You can spend the winter curled up with a book, warm and safe from the elements."

"Not on your life." Kate gave him an indignant look. "I never intended to have a vacation here. I haven't the temperament or the patience to lounge around all day while other people work." She paused for a breath, noticing Hawk appeared mildly taken aback by her outburst.

Kate lowered her voice. "I'm sorry," she apologized. "But I want to help out with whatever I can. Be useful, you know? Don't forget, I was raised on a working farm."

His lips twitching, Hawk held up his hands in surrender. "Okay, if that's what you want, I'll put you to work." The twitch gave way to a smile. "So, now, do you want to negotiate salary?"

Kate's head snapped up, chin thrust out; her spine stiffened. "Are you looking for a fight?"

Leaning back in his chair, Hawk erupted with laughter. When he could breathe again, he teased, "Ahh, Kate Muldoon McKenna, you are a fiery one, aren't you?"

Kate flushed and smiled at the same time. Hearing him call her McKenna sent a tingling chill through her. After the past crazy days reality finally hit her. This wasn't a dream or make-believe. She was Hawk McKenna's legal wife, if only on a temporary basis. *His*. In a weird way, after knowing him not even two full weeks, Kate kind of liked the idea.

The ghost of his smile still played over his mouth. "What's going on in that busy mind of yours?"

Kate returned his smile. "I was just thinking how strange it sounded to hear you call me Kate McKenna," she said.

"You'll get used to it." He chuckled. "What you'll hear after I've introduced you to my men is Ms. McKenna whenever they address you."

"How long will that last?" she asked, frowning. "I'd much rather they call me Kate."

"Oh, they will in time." He grinned. "They'll have to get used to you first. Take your measure."

"In other words, they're going to be judging me." Kate wasn't sure she liked that idea.

His lips quivered. "Sure, they'll want to make sure you're good enough for me."

"Good enough!" Kate said, anger sparking until she saw him silently laughing at her. "You are a devil, aren't you? Well, I'll show you and your men how good enough I am."

"I already know," he reminded her. "As for my men, go to it...after we've taken a few days for, as my foreman called it, honeymooning."

Kate rolled her eyes.

Hawk laughed.

Together, they cleared away the supper dishes, all but the wineglasses. When the kitchen had been set to rights, he asked, "As you already had your shower, food and wine, are you now ready for sleep?"

"The shower, food, wine and conversation gave me my second wind. I'm not nearly as sleepy as before." She held her glass out to him. "I'd like to have a little more wine, crawl into bed, prop myself up against some pillows and relax while I finish my drink."

Hawk half filled both glasses before saying, "There are two other bedrooms and a central bath on the left side of the hall, opposite my bedroom. Have you decided where you're going to sleep?"

She gave him what she hoped was a sexy, come-hither smile. "My toiletries bag is in your bathroom."

He sent a smile back at her that heated her blood as it tap-danced up her spine. She reached for her glass. He held it aloft.

"Lead on, Kate. I'm right behind you."

She set off for the hallway.

He followed her. "And, since the word *behind* is out there, you have a very enticing one."

In retaliation, Kate wiggled her hips. With a low wolf whistle, he followed her into his bedroom.

Hawk plumped the pillows for her, waited while she crawled into the bed then handed the glass of wine to her. "Comfortable?" he asked.

"Very," she replied, snuggling against the pillows. She felt almost lost in the wide expanse of bed. "Oh, Hawk, this is heaven."

"Not yet, but I have hopes," he said, his gaze seeming to touch her in very delicate spots.

Kate drew a quick breath. "Oh, my." She took a quick sip of the cold wine in hopes of dousing the heat shimmering through her.

"My sentiments exactly." Inhaling, he turned away, setting his glass on the dresser. "I'm going to have a shower. I won't be long."

Reclining against the pillows, too warm all over, Kate kicked the comforter and top sheet to the bottom of the bed. Raising her left hand to take another sip of wine, her gaze caught on the gold band circling her third finger. Unlike Hawk's plain gold ring, the band he had chosen for her was covered with pavé diamonds.

It was beautiful and felt oddly right on her finger, as if it belonged there. Taking more swallows of wine, she continued to gaze at the ring, contemplating the intrinsic, sacred meaning behind the exchange of marriage bands.

Dear Lord, what had she done?

Catching her lower lip between her teeth, her gaze locked on the ring, she felt the sting of incipient tears in her eyes. In her determination to get away from one man, a nasty, possibly dangerous man, she had talked a good man, a decent, wonderful man, into a loveless marriage. It was terribly unfair of her. He deserved better.

The tears overflowed her lower lids just as Hawk, a towel wrapped around his hips, came into the room. He stopped short by the side of the bed.

"Tears," he said, his voice and expression concerned. "Are you feeling regrets?"

"No… Yes, but it's not what you think," she said, sniffing.

Without a word, he walked to the dresser, opened a small side drawer and withdrew a man's snowy-white handkerchief and a foil-wrapped packet. Moving around to the side of the bed she was lying on, he handed the hankie to her and laid the packet on the nightstand.

"Now, what is this 'no…yes'? It's not what I think it is?" Holding the towel with one hand, he took the glass from her trembling hand and set it on the nightstand, next to the foil packet.

Blinking to disperse the tears, which didn't work, she sniffed again and brought the hankie to her nose. "I…I'm sorry. I had no right."

Holding on to the slipping towel, Hawk carefully sat on the edge of the bed, next to her. "If I heard correctly, you mumbled that you had no right." Taking the hankie from her hands, he mopped away the tears. "No right to what?"

Kate sniffed twice, drew a couple deep breaths and shakily answered, "I had no right to talk you into this farce." She sniffed once more. "I'm sorry."

"Kate." Hawk's voice was soft, soothing. "You didn't talk me into anything. If I hadn't wanted to do it, you could have talked your head off, and I'd have said, 'No, thank you, but no.'"

"Oh…" She blinked again.

"Right. Oh." He smiled. "Now, in case you haven't noticed, I'm shivering here. That's because I'm cold. Move over and share the warmth."

Kate shimmied over to let him in.

His gaze skimmed the top of the bed, from her head to her waist. "Where's the sheet and comforter?"

"I was already warm, so I shoved them to the bottom," she admitted. "I'll get them."

"Stay put," he said, turning to grab the covers with his free hand and pull them up and over most of her. "Do you want your wine?"

"No, I'm finished for tonight." Kate quickly lowered her eyes as he lifted his rear off the bed to yank off the towel and toss it to the floor.

"I've had enough, too," he said, sliding into the bed, next to her. "Why are you looking away, Kate? You've seen me naked before."

"Yes, I know," she said, her voice barely a whisper. "But that was before we were married."

Silence. Dead silence. Kate was getting jittery. All of a sudden laughter rumbled in his chest before roaring from his throat.

"Kate, oh, Kate, you are a joy to be with." Rolling to and over her, he cradled her face with his big hands and kissed the nervousness out of her.

She didn't respond, well not verbally. But she kissed him back as if her very sanity depended on his kiss. Then again, maybe it did.

Their lovemaking was even more intense, more exhilarating than before. This time Kate and Hawk reached the summit together.

Completely exhausted, refusing to get out of his bed for any reason, she curled her arm around his waist when he returned from the bathroom, rested her cheek on his still moist chest and closed her eyes.

Hawk slid his fingers into her loose curls, holding her to him. "Good night, Kate." He kissed her hair.

Kate sighed with contentment. "Good night,

Hawk." Closing her eyes, she immediately began to drift.

The marriage was consummated. It was her last thought before drifting into a deep sleep.

Ten

Hawk had set aside four whole days for them to honeymoon. They didn't spend the entire four days in bed, or even three days. But they did spend three of those days in the house, hanging out, reading, eating, having sex, unbelievable, breathtaking sex.

The fourth day they went outside. Unlike the mild, warm October days in Vegas, in the mountains there was a definite chill in the air in the afternoon and the nights were cold, a harbinger of approaching winter.

Hawk had mentioned showing her his horses, at least some of them. She had no idea he had so very many. Kate supposed she should have realized this, as Vic had told her that Hawk bred beautiful horses.

It was a glorious autumn day. There was a nip in the air, but the sunshine was brilliant in a gorgeous deep blue sky. The leaves on the mountain's deciduous trees had begun to fall but the sight was still spectacular.

Caught up in the beauty of this valley nestled in the mountain range, Kate was startled when Hawk, curling his hand around hers, broke her reverie.

"We're having company, Kate," he said, turning her a half step.

In the near distance Kate saw two men riding toward them. "Your men?"

"Yeah," he answered, raising a hand in a welcoming wave. "Coming to meet the Mrs., so please stay in wife mode."

"Well, of course," she said, both hurt and mad, glaring up at him. She could have saved herself the display of annoyance, because beneath the wide brim of the Western hat he had settled on his head before leaving the house, his gaze was fixed on the riders. She now knew the reason he had at times reach to touch a brim that wasn't there while he was in Vegas.

Before he had donned his hat, Hawk had plopped one on her head. Now she was glad he had, as the wide brim shaded her eyes from the dazzling sunlight.

The two riders slowed to a walk as they drew near her and Hawk and pulled up a couple of feet in front of them. Jumping down from his mount, a middle-aged man of medium height and with a sturdy body strolled over to Hawk, his hand outstretched.

"Mornin', Hawk. Ted and I came to meet the wife. I hope we're not intruding."

Hawk gave them a droll look. "Figured," he drawled, turning to her. "Kate, I want you to meet my foreman, Jack, right here, and Ted, the fellow next to Jack, is the best wrangler in the state."

She smiled and nodded at both men. "Jack, Ted, I'm pleased to meet you both." She noticed that Ted was younger than Jack, taller and as slim as a whip.

"Nice to meet you, ma'am," the men said in unison. "We were wonderin' when the boss here was goin' to find a good woman to keep 'im in line," Jack added.

Kate laughed. "Needs to be kept on a short leash, does he?" she said, grinning up at Hawk.

"Yessum, Ms. McKenna," Ted chimed in. "The boss here has a tendency to work too hard."

"That's right," Jack confirmed. "Forgets there's more to livin' than babyin' horses."

Kate laughed, already liking the men.

"Okay, you two, knock off the comedy and get back to work." Hawk interjected. "I'll be with you in a little while."

Both men chuckled, then remounted and rode off in the direction of a pasture with a good number of horses moving around in it. Jack called back, "Take your time, Hawk, if you have better things to do."

Hawk shook his head. Kate smiled. "I like your men, Hawk," she said. "They seem very nice."

"They are good men," he said. "You'll be seeing them again this Saturday. We've invited them to a reception, of sorts."

Kate shot a startled look at him, but he continued speaking.

"Ted and his wife, Carol, and Jack and his daughter, Brenda, will be here Saturday evening, after we've packed it in for the day. Jack's been divorced for close to seven years now. Brenda has spent most of her summers here, at least five, during those years. Carol's a lovely woman. She and Ted have been married two years." He arched that same brow again. "Okay?"

"Okay what?" she asked. "Okay that we have a reception or okay that Ted and Carol have been married two years?" Somehow she managed to keep a straight face.

Now he shook his head in despair at her. "Can you ride?"

"Yes, I can." She put on a haughty expression. "Rather well, too. But first I have a question."

"Shoot," he said.

"Do you…we…have the makings for a party on Saturday night?"

"Plenty of stuff in the pantry and freezer," he answered. "And plenty of beer, wine and soft drinks. Do you have any favorite foods?"

"I'll give it some thought." She smiled. "Now I'm ready for a ride."

"Good." Taking her hand, he led her to the stables. "Let's saddle up, and I'll give you a short tour of the place before I get to work with the men."

Walking by Hawk's side to the stables, Kate was struck by the sudden realization of how completely different her life and lifestyle had been since leaving Vegas. Where she used to sleep in because of working the late hours, now she was up before dawn to prepare Hawk's breakfast. At first, she wasn't too happy about it, but now she enjoyed cooking for him, watching him dig in to the food she had made.

Hawk needed to spend time on ranch chores despite the honeymoon, and he always showered before dinner. He came to the table smelling of shaving cream and pure male. Before the first week was over, Kate was showering with him while the evening meal simmered.

"So, what do you think?"

The sound of his voice drew her from bemusement and Kate glanced up to look at the horse he was saddling. He had picked out a gentle roan mare for her and told her Ted had named the mare Babycakes. Kate was happy with his choice and the name. She was surprised when she saw the horse he saddled for himself. It was the biggest horse she had ever seen, other than draft horses.

As they trotted side by side to the pasture, one of several she later learned, she felt like a child on a pony next to Hawk on the tall, sleek animal.

As they circled around, both she and Hawk waved to Jack and Ted as they worked the horses, before heading on to the pasture beyond.

With the sunlight playing on their sleek coats, the horses looked beautiful, well kept and cared for. "Have you always been a horse man?"

Hawk smiled. "Yes, I fell in love when my father bought me my first horse, a filly." He slanted his head, his smile morphing into a grin. "And here comes my second animal love." Pulling up his mount, he jumped down and turned just as a large animal streaked by Kate's horse and leapt straight at Hawk.

"Hawk, watch out…" Kate cried just as the animal made the jump. Fear caught her breath. Gulping in air, she couldn't believe her eyes or ears.

Hawk was on the ground, laughing. She could now see that the animal on top of him was a very big dog. The dog's tail was swishing back and forth a mile a minute, its tongue lapping every inch of Hawk's face.

"Yeah, Boyo, I love you, too, but get off me now. You're crushing my ribs."

To Kate's surprise, the dog immediately jumped to the side, as if he understood every word. Hawk ruffled the dog's wiry-looking coat before getting to his feet. Walking to the side of her horse, he grinned up at her.

"Boyo?" was all she said.

He laughed. "Yep, Boyo. It's Irish slang for *boy.*" The dog came to stand next to him. Hawk placed his hand on the dog's large head. "This is the Irish wolfhound I told you about."

Kate gave the dog a dubious glance. "Does he resent competition?"

Hawk caught on at once and grinned at her. "No, or at any rate, he tolerates it, and that includes every person on the property."

The sigh Kate exhaled wasn't all show. "That's a relief. He's kind of frightening."

"Nah," Hawk said, shaking his head. "He's a pushover for anyone willing to scratch his head."

"I'll keep that in mind," she said.

Nevertheless, she made sure she didn't ride too close to Boyo on the way back to the stable. This time Kate noticed a large white circle between the stable corral and the pasture.

She looked at Hawk. "Is that a helipad over there?"

"Yes, I put it in for rescue purposes, in case of an emergency with either the people or the animals."

"Do you own the chopper?" she asked as she dismounted.

"No, I use a rescue service," he explained as he jumped off his horse. "But I could fly a chopper. I flew a Black Hawk in the service, and I practice now and again."

"Cool," she quipped, giving him a high five.

Kate learned that her wariness of the dog was unnecessary once they were in the house. Boyo nudged her leg with his long snout twice until she hesitantly lowered her hand to his head to give him a brisk scratch. He was immediately her best friend. Kate fell in love with the big, ferocious-looking baby.

Kate spent the next few days getting ready for the reception. While Hawk was outside working with his men, she prepared numerous dishes. Some she had found in his cookbooks; others she had learned from her mother.

She was nervous Saturday evening, before their guests arrived. Hawk came into the house and brushed his mouth over hers on his way to the bathroom for a shower. As he swept by, she caught a whiff of fresh air, horse, sweaty male and Hawk's personal scent. For a moment, she was tempted to join him in the shower.

Kate gave a heartfelt sigh. Living with Hawk was so good…but it was not permanent. The physical life they shared in bed almost every night was wonderful. His sudden quick kisses made her head spin. She knew she wasn't falling in love with him, because she was fathoms deep already.

She knew Hawk loved kissing her, making love with her, but she also knew he was skeptical about the very word *love*. He simply didn't believe in romantic love, the forever after kind. She wished…

The realization of time passing sent her back into the kitchen. Hawk was beside her in record time. "How's it going? Can I do anything to help?"

"Fine and no," she answered, stirring the mouthwatering, aromatic beef barbecue, one of her mother's recipes.

"Lordy, that smells good, and I'm starving." He caught her chin in his hand to turn her to face him. "Hungry, too," he murmured, kissing her senseless.

Kate shoved him away after a few heavenly minutes. "I've got to get this together," she said, grabbing a breath between each word. "Pitch in, lover."

Hawk gave a fake shudder. "Oh, Katie, hearing you call me lover turns me on."

"Later," she said, flashing a smile at him. "Right now I do believe our guests have arrived."

"I'm going to hold you to that," he said, moving away from her.

"I certainly hope so," she replied, laughing as he tossed a wicked grin back at her.

The reception was wonderful. Everyone chattered, laughed and even sang. Kate liked Carol at once. She was young but mature with a great sense of humor.

After Carol, Hawk led Kate over to Jack to introduce her to his daughter. Brenda was a pretty girl, in her late teens, Kate judged.

With a murmured "excuse me, ladies," Jack wandered to where the men were gathered, Hawk handing out cans of beer.

"I'm glad to meet you, Brenda," Kate said, extending her hand to the girl.

"Likewise," the girl replied, a sweet, miss-innocent smile on her face as she took Kate's hand in a crushing grip.

Managing to keep from wincing in pain, Kate tightened her own fingers harder around the girl's hand.

Glaring at her, Brenda gave in, withdrawing her hand.

Despite the tingle of pain in her fingers, Kate met Brenda's glare with a serene smile. "Now, if you will excuse me, I have to check on the food cooking on the stove."

Oh, boy, Kate thought, making her way to the

kitchen. In her estimation, Brenda was walking, talking, snotty trouble. There was something sly and petulant about her that sounded an alarm inside Kate's mind. But why had the girl targeted her? Hawk's soft laughter came from across the room.

Of course. Kate sighed. Brenda was infatuated with Hawk. Kate couldn't blame Brenda. Hawk was all the things of many women's dreams, but he was way out of the young girl's league.

A sense of foreboding rippled through Kate, a warning of unpleasant things, scenes to come.

The festivities lasted long into the night. Finally, but reluctantly, the party broke up. Kate stood next to Hawk on the porch, grateful for his arm around her to ward off the night cold, still talking to the others as they made their way to their vehicles.

"You throw one hell of a party, lady," Hawk said, praising her efforts once everyone had left. "Thanks."

"You're welcome, and thank you for the compliment, sir." Standing on tiptoes, she kissed him on the side of his sculpted, hard jaw. "Now you may help me clear the mess away inside."

"Aw, gee, Kate," he groused like a kid. "Can't we leave it till morning? I gotta work, ya know?"

But Hawk pitched in right beside her, heaving deep, put-upon sighs every few minutes. By the time they were finished, Kate was laughing. She wasn't laughing a short time later, after they were in bed. She was crying out in delicious pleasure.

Kate had dinner ready for him when he came in to eat as the sun went down the next day. While he dug into his food like a starving man, they did a postmortem of the reception the night before.

"I like your friends," she said, handing the dish of mashed potatoes to him for a second helping. "And I could tell at once that they are friends as well as employees."

Nodding, Hawk swallowed before replying. "They are," he said. "Good thing, too, especially during the winter months. We get together often...." He smiled and took another roll from the bread basket. "If we didn't, we'd likely all get antsy with cabin fever."

Kate laughed and gave him an arch look. "And here, all this time I was thinking you were a loner."

"I don't mind being alone," he said, picking up his coffee cup. "Fact is there are times I prefer it."

"Like when you want to read?"

"Yes, and when I'm watching football."

"Uh-huh." Kate tilted her head, fighting a smile. "Is this your way of reminding me there's a game on tonight and you don't want to be bothered?"

"No, because you don't bother me." Standing, he took both their plates, carried them to the sink and came back to the table with the coffee carafe. "Do you like football?"

"I can tolerate it," she admitted. "But I'd rather read."

He was pensive a moment. "I could go into the bedroom to watch the game on the set in there," he offered, pleasing her with his thoughtfulness.

Kate was shaking her head before he'd finished. "That's not necessary. If I'm into a story, I don't even hear the TV unless it's blaring."

"It won't be." Hawk slanted a slow smile at her. "I could watch the game in the living room and you could read your book in bed," he suggested.

Kate laughed. "No, you may watch in the game in bed. I can't get comfortable reading in bed."

He heaved a sigh. "Will you sit next to me and read if I watch the game while sitting on the sofa?"

"I will if you'll refill my cup," she said, reminding him he was still standing there with the carafe in hand. "Can we get back to our discussion about the reception now that our seating arrangement for tonight has been confirmed?" She grinned.

He grinned back, causing a melting sensation inside her. "Sure we can." He frowned. "Something about it on your mind?"

"Well…it's about Brenda."

Hawk groaned. "What about her? Was she rude to you? Did she insult you in some way?"

"Not exactly." Kate paused, searching for the right words. "I tried to draw her into a conversation. She seemed so, oh, I don't know, almost sullen." She sighed. "She wasn't very responsive."

He drew a deep breath. "I was going to talk to you about Brenda. I should have done it before the party. She is, and has been for some time, a pain in the neck and parts south." He ran his fingers through his long hair, loosening it from the leather thong.

Kate smiled at his ruffled strands of hair. His expression serious, Hawk untied the thong and shook his head, freeing the long locks.

"As I was saying," he went on, ignoring her obvious urge to laugh, "Brenda has been coming to the ranch for a long time. When she was younger, she was a high-spirited kid. Jack and I taught her to ride." He grimaced. "When she arrived here after graduating from high school, a year ago this coming summer, she was different."

"In what way?"

"Kate, the only way to describe it is that she began hanging around me too much." He shook his head. "Understand she had always hung around, but that summer it was different. At first I thought she was just using me to practice her wiles to use on younger men. But it wasn't that. She started *accidentally* brushing against me...with her breasts, touching me, hugging me." His smile was wry. "I'm not stupid. Her actions were not the same as when she was a young girl. She was coming on to me. I did talk to Jack about it before I left for Vegas, and he assured me he'd take care of it. Looks like his lecture went in one ear and out the other."

"And now," Kate said, "I suspect Brenda, the temptress in training, resents the woman you brought home with you from Las Vegas."

Sighing again, Hawk finished his coffee and began to clear the table. Kate got up to help him. "That's the way I figure it," he said. "I suppose I'll have to talk to her, tell her a few home truths."

"Ahh, no, Hawk, I'll talk to her, at the right moment." She knew her smile wasn't sweet. "I'll be gentle, but firm."

The right moment appeared the following week. Kate was on the phone. She had received a call from her father, the fourth since Kate had told him she had married Hawk and moved with him to his ranch in Colorado. She was actually gushing in an attempt to finally convince him she was safe, well and over-the-moon happy.

No sooner had she cradled the phone, with a sigh of relief, when it rang again. It was Vic calling from Vegas. After chatting a bit, enquiring about Lisa, Bella and everyone at the restaurant, she told him to hang on while she searched out Hawk who, fortunately, was working in the stables that day.

At a near run, she went to the stables only to stop short at the low, supposedly sexy sound of Brenda's voice.

"You know, Hawk, it would be fun to take a ride when you're finished here," she said, moving so that the side of her breast made contact with Hawk's arm as he brushed down the mare, Babycakes. "Just you and me. Wouldn't It?"

"Brenda…" he began, strain underlying his tone.

"I don't think so," Kate said, striding forward to wedge herself between Hawk and the girl. "Vic's on the phone, Hawk," she said, taking the brush from his hand. "I'll take over here."

He frowned with concern. "Lisa?"

"No, no," Kate shook her head. "Just a friendly call."

"Good," he said, loping from the stable as he headed for the house.

Kate began applying the brush. She imagined she could hear Brenda getting ready to explode. "I thought you were going for a ride, Brenda." Kate continued brushing. "I'm afraid you'll have to ride alone now." She shifted to level a warning look at the girl. "And in the future…if you get my drift?"

With a snort almost as loud as Babycakes could make, Brenda stormed from the stables.

A few minutes later Hawk startled Kate by silently stepping up next to her. "How can a man walk so damned quietly in those heeled boots?" she demanded.

He grinned. "Practice." He lowered his voice. "Is the temptress in training gone?"

Kate nodded, sighing. "She wants your body."

He tossed his head, exactly as his stallion did. "Who doesn't?"

She rolled her eyes, and changed the subject. "Did Vic want anything in particular?"

"No," he shook his head and gave her a wry look. "He said you sounded okay and told me flat out I'd better make sure you remained okay."

"Or what?" Kate had to laugh. "Vic's in Vegas and we're here. What was he intending to do about it?"

"He said he'd have to come rescue you from me."

"Right," she drawled. "I can just see Vic, running off to the mountains to rescue me, leaving his precious, pregnant Lisa at home alone." Shaking her head as if in despair of the silly men, Kate went back to the house.

Fortunately, they didn't see hid nor hair of Brenda for several weeks. Kate was settling nicely into a routine, inside and outside of the house. She was beginning to feel if she belonged there, in the mountains, in the house, with Hawk.

Dangerous feeling, she told herself. She didn't belong there. She was there simply because of a good and kind man…who didn't even believe in romantic love.

Kate had learned of his attitude one evening while he was watching a game and she was reading a book, a historical romance novel. During half-time, after fetching glasses of wine for them both, he asked her what she was reading. Not thinking anything of his curiosity, she told him, adding a brief resume of the story. To her surprise, he raised a skeptical brow.

"What?" she asked.

"That stuff—fantasy, love till the end of time. You don't really believe in that, do you?"

If she hadn't, she was beginning to, Kate thought. Aloud she merely answered in a teasing tone, "Could happen."

"Uh-huh." Without another word, he turned his attention to the second half of the game.

"You don't believe in love?" Kate said, snagging his attention away from the TV. "What about Vic and Lisa and Ted and Carol? They appear very much in love."

"Okay, yes, I know they are in love, but they have their problems, too. It's certainly not the fairy-tale, happily-ever-after stuff." He shrugged. "Per-sonally, I've never experienced the feeling."

Kate fought against the crushed sensation his words caused inside her. She wanted to cry out against the ache in her chest, the sense of loss and deflation. But she didn't cry out, instead lifted her head and simply said, "Too bad." Picking up her book, she walked away. "I'm going to bed."

The days sped by. They had a light snowfall in early November. The snow didn't last. They gathered at Ted and Carol's house for Thanksgiving. Hawk provided the huge turkey he had in his freezer chest.

As the season turned from chilly fall to cold winter, Kate worked with the horses until Hawk taught her how to keep the records of the ranch and the bloodlines of the horses on his computer.

Two weeks before Christmas, Hawk drove Kate into Durango. He went shopping for groceries and ranch supplies, leaving her to do her Christmas shopping. First she bought gifts for her father, stepmother and the children, and Vic, Lisa and Bella, and had them packaged and sent to Virginia and Las Vegas. Then she shopped for what she thought would be thoughtful but not personal gifts for Hawk.

As a rule, Christmas shopping had always been fun for Kate, but not this year. She simply couldn't get into the holiday mood. By next year she'd be gone—who knew where. She wasn't even sure she had done the right thing buying gifts for Hawk. She didn't even know if he celebrated Christmas.

Glancing at her watch, Kate saw that it was almost time to meet Hawk at the truck. Well, she thought, shrugging, what's done is done. She could always take back the gifts if he didn't want them. The very idea made her sad.

Kate felt a lot better about the whole holiday thing the next week when Hawk dragged a large pine tree onto the porch to dry.

When he set it up in the living room a couple days later, Kate got even more into the spirit of the holiday. If there was only to be one Christmas with Hawk, Kate was determined to make the best of it.

Christmas morning, both Kate and Hawk slept in late. Well, they weren't asleep all morning. Tossing back the down comforter, they worked up a pleasant sweat exchanging certain Christmas gifts.

Later, freshly showered and dressed, they breakfasted on coffee and Christmas cookies as they sat together on the floor to exchange material Christmas presents.

There were small items with Hawk's name on the tags: new tough leather work gloves, a braided belt and a handheld computer game. He was very obviously surprised and pleased with the handmade cable-knit sweater in the Black Watch colors, imported from Scotland, that Kate had ordered for him online.

There and then, he pulled off the sweatshirt he

had minutes before put on, replacing it with the sweater she had chosen for him.

After he had finished opening his gifts, Hawk slid a small pile of presents toward Kate.

As excited as a kid, Kate dove into the pile. Carefully unwrapping each gift, she revealed a delicate handwrought sterling silver bracelet, which she immediately insisted Hawk fasten on her wrist. The next package contained an Amazon.com gift certificate for a hefty amount, which she exclaimed over. The last package held the cashmere scarf Hawk had bought in Vegas, supposedly for his sister. The scarf earned Hawk what he declared to be a teeth-rattling kiss.

One morning a few days later, Kate had been out helping in the stables, and noticing it was time to start lunch, she headed for the house. Upon entering, she noticed at once that the door to Hawk's bedroom was open. Kate clearly recalled shutting the door before leaving the house.

Walking quietly down the hallway, she stepped inside the room, to find Brenda rifling through Hawk's dresser drawers, touching his clothes.

"What are you doing in here, Brenda?" Kate's voice was soft but icy.

"I...I..." The girl stopped trying to answer and glared at Kate. "He belongs to me, you know."

"Really?" Kate smiled.

Brenda flinched at Kate's cold expression, then lashed out in anger. "Yes, he does. He is mine. Who are you but a Vegas tramp who thought she had bagged a rich rancher?" She was breathing heavily. "Well, I'm telling you, bitch, when he's tired of his new playmate, he'll toss you out and I'll have him back."

"You've got a lot to learn, young lady," Kate said, holding on to her temper. "Hawk is my husband. Other than being the daughter of his friend, you mean nothing to him."

"That's a lie," Brenda shouted. "I'll be around long after you've been tossed out."

"Oh, Brenda," Kate sighed. "I think what you need is a swift kick in the ass to jar some sense into you."

"And I've got the boot to do it," Hawk said from the doorway. "Go home, Brenda, and don't come back until you've learned how to act your age."

"Damn you both," Brenda cried out like a spoiled kid, tears running down her face, sniffing, as she ran out of the room. They heard the front door slam.

Drawing a deep breath of relief, Hawk smiled at Kate. "Thanks, Kate. I do believe the message finally got through to her. I appreciate it."

"Anytime, cowboy," she said. "Now, what do you want for dinner?"

He laughed. She joined in with him.

The next day Jack drove Brenda to the airport to put her on a plane. She was going back to her mother's home.

Winter brought with it heavy snow. On the morning of the heaviest snowfall, Hawk confined Kate to the house. He didn't advise her to stay inside, he issued a flat order. The name Jeff immediately sprang into her mind.

"Hawk," the sharp edge of her voice stopped him in his tracks as he headed for the back door.

"Yes?" He turned frowning.

"I'm an adult, a full-grown woman. I will not be ordered around, not by you or any other man." Placing her hands on her hips, she stared defiantly at him.

Hawk's drawn eyebrows rose. "Kate, I'm only insisting you stay inside because I know how treacherous the terrain can become outside in this weather. It's for your own safety."

Kate lifted a hand to flick a shooing motion at him. "You go to work, and leave me to worry about my safety." Without waiting for any argument from him, she stormed down the hallway and into their room to make the bed. She fully expected him to follow her. Her shoulders slumped and she felt like crying when he didn't.

Damn, she didn't know what she wanted anymore. Now there was a rift between her and Hawk, but Kate knew she had to carry on. A deal was a deal. Only their deal was now a mostly silent one. They spoke only when necessary. The quiet wore on Kate's nerves. Tired of it, she went outside to stomp around in the pristine snow, slamming the door behind her.

Hawk was there waiting for her when the cold finally sent her back into the house, wet and shivering.

"Feel better?" He looked tired. He sounded tired.

Kate felt ashamed for acting out like a spoiled kid. "I'm sorry, Hawk, but I will not be penned up in the house, snow or no snow."

"I can understand that," he said, his tone inflectionless. "I don't like it myself. But when I'm working some distance from the house, will you agree to confine yourself to the path the men and I made from the back of the house to the stables? I'm sure Babycakes would appreciate your company."

Kate knew that once Hawk had given her the mare to use while she was on the ranch, he had not taken Babycakes out with him to work.

"Yes, I'll agree to that."

"Thank you." He started to turn away. "I'm going to get a shower before dinner." He glanced back at her. "That is, if we're having dinner."

The shame making her uncomfortable turned to

a flash of anger that zipped through her. "Of course we're having dinner," she said heatedly. "Haven't I prepared dinner every evening since I've been here?"

"Yes, Kate, you have." He gave her a half smile. "Thing is, I've gotten used to coming into the house to be greeted by the delicious aroma of whatever you're cooking. I don't smell a thing today."

Pleased by his appreciation of her cooking efforts, Kate smiled back at him while shaking her head in exasperation. "I made dinner earlier…so I could go romp in the snow. The meal is in the fridge; all it needs is warming up. It will be ready by the time you've finished your shower."

"Oh…okay." His smile now rueful, he retreated to the bedroom.

From that day forward there was a change in Hawk, in the atmosphere whenever they were together. Though he was unfailingly polite, there was very little laughter or teasing, and what smiles did touch his lips were strained.

Kate couldn't help but notice the only time he touched her during the day was obviously accidental. The nights were different, too. His lovemaking steadily grew a bit rough with an almost desperate intensity, driving Kate to heights of breathtaking pleasure she had never experienced, never dreamed could be experienced. Yet when she finally came down from the shattering high she felt empty and alone.

Longing for the easy companionship they had shared before, Kate racked her mind for a reasonable explanation for the change in him. Thinking a breath of fresh air might clear her mind, she took some sugar cubes and an apple then went to the mudroom at the back of the house and pulled on her boots and heavy jacket.

Leaving the house, Kate made her way along the path that was now almost bare due to the sudden shift to milder weather a couple of days ago. Entering the stables, she went straight to Babycakes' stall. The mare was obviously happy to see her as she nudged Kate's shoulder before lowering her head to snuffle at her jacket pocket.

"You know me too well, Miss Babycakes." Laughing, Kate drew two sugar cubes from her pocket and gave them to the eager horse. When the animal was finished with the treat she looked up, her big brown eyes staring right into Kate's as if sensing her unhappiness and silently asking why.

Kate's eyes and nose began to sting an instant before she burst into tears. Once again the mare nudged her shoulder. With no one else to talk to, Kate poured her heart out to her temporary pet.

"Oh, Baby, I don't know what to do." Raising her arms, Kate cradled the mare's large head atop her shoulder. "There's no one else for me to talk to. I don't know Carol well enough and I can't call Lisa, she'd get upset and that's the last thing she needs at this stage of her pregnancy. I won't call my father because I've let him believe I'm so happy and so very much in love."

Kate sniffed and, moving back, she dug in her other jacket pocket for a tissue. She blew her nose. Before she was through, Babycakes nudged her again, as though telling her to go on with her tale of woe.

Smiling, crying, she stroked the long nose, swallowed and allowed the misery to spill out. "There's been a distance between us for weeks now and I hate it." The tears flowed freely. "He told me he didn't believe in love." A sob caught in her throat. "And he told me long ago he enjoyed being alone." The horse whinnied as if in commiseration. "I'm afraid he's beginning to think of me as an intrusion into his life." For a moment Kate closed her eyes, swiping her hand over her wet cheeks.

"I'm a fool, Baby," she murmured. The mare shook her head, eliciting a weepy laugh from Kate. "Yes I am, a foolish idiot. I suggested the bargain as the perfect answer to my problem and now I have a bigger problem, a much bigger problem. I am so deep in love with Hawk I can't bear this coolness between us."

With a final sniff and a final stroke of the mare's long nose, she took the apple from her pocket and fed it to the horse. "Spring's almost here, Baby. I want winter back. I want the Hawk I knew in Vegas back." The mare finished chomping the apple and Kate turned away.

"I want, I want," she muttered, sighing as she left the stable. "And I'm talking to a horse. Sheer idiocy."

While Kate grew more quiet, more withdrawn, Hawk was wrestling with uncertainties of his own. Throughout the past few weeks the coolness in the house had nothing to do with the heating system, and everything to do with the chill between him and Kate.

Riding in late one warm afternoon in the beginning of April, Hawk walked his horse to cool him down. After grooming the roan, he stabled him then walked down the aisle of stalls to the one holding Babycakes, the mare he had given to Kate for her exclusive use while she was at the ranch. Now he couldn't think of the animal as anything other than Kate's.

Stepping into the stall of the gentle chestnut, Hawk took up a brush and began to groom her. Also, without thinking, he began softly talking to her.

"I'm in deep crap, Baby," he murmured, using Kate's nickname for the horse. "And I'm afraid you're going to be mad as hell at me." The horse nickered. "You may not believe it now," he said, as if he had heard a "no way" in the horse's noise, "but you'll understand when your mistress is gone."

The mare shook her big head. Damn, Hawk thought, for all he knew, maybe the horse did understand. Mocking himself for the very idea, he nevertheless continued talking.

"It's my fault she is going," he went on. "I deliberately built a wall of virtual silence between us." The horse snorted. "Yeah, I know, pretty stupid. But, much as I hate to admit it, even to you, I was getting scared. It started after we had a silly argument about her staying inside during the worst weather. As gentle as Kate is with you, Baby, you wouldn't believe how she blew a gasket at me for daring to give her orders."

For a moment Hawk smiled in memory of how magnificent Kate had looked in her defiance of him. Another memory flashed and he sighed.

"But it was the night I laughed at the book she was reading, calling it a fantasy of happy-ever-after and telling her I didn't believe in that kind of thing. She walked away from me, and since then has stayed away from me, there but cool and distant. I could kick myself in the ass. When she walked away a knot settled in my gut. It's been getting tighter and tighter with each passing day."

By pure coincidence, Hawk felt sure, the mare moved her large head, trapping Hawk's head against her long neck. The curry brush fell unnoticed to the ground. Hawk rested his forehead on her smooth coat.

"And now our bargain time is up, Baby. Kate's going to leave us both." A shudder ran through him. The horse shook her head. "I know, you don't want her to go. You think she's yours. Well, I don't want her to go, either. I love her. I—who has never felt anything deep or lasting for any woman—love Kate more than my own life."

Hawk shuddered again and felt a sudden sting in his eyes. Tears rolled down his face. Damn, he never cried, hadn't shed a tear since he was nine or ten. He didn't make a sound but the tears continued to flow until the mare moved her head and he noticed the wet spot on her coat.

"Sorry, girl," he drew a deep breath, scrubbed his big hands over his face and stood up straight. "I don't suppose you have any suggestions? No? I didn't think so." Stepping back out of the stall, he closed the gate. The mare stuck her head out and with a shaky laugh Hawk stroked her face. Her big brown eyes appeared sad.

"I'll see what I can do for the two of us, sweetheart," he promised. "I'll beg her to stay if I have to."

* * *

Stepping out onto the porch for a breather late one afternoon early in April, Kate felt the first mild breeze of spring. The last remnants of happiness and contentment she had enjoyed until recently with Hawk, while working, laughing, making love with him, dissolved like the small patches of snow from the last snowfall.

It was almost time for her to leave. Her six months were up. Sadness welled up in her; tears stung her eyes. Where had the days gone, one after another, fading from month to month? Kate loved spring, but she wanted winter back. She didn't want to return to Vegas or to her father's farm. She didn't want to go, couldn't bear the thought of being away from Hawk forever.

But his coolness, his near silence for nearly two months, said it all to Kate. It was time for her to go, to give Hawk's life back to him.

Tears streaming down her face, Kate squared her shoulders and walked into the house. A deal was a deal. Pain twisted in her chest as she remembered the way they had "double" sealed their deal with a handshake and two kisses.

Going to Hawk's bedroom, *their* bedroom, Kate swiped the tears from her cheeks, impatient with herself for wanting, longing to renege on their bargain.

It wasn't fully six months yet; she could wait until the end of the month. The thought wriggled its way into her head, tempting her to hang on to him every last minute.

Kate shook away the thought. It would only get harder for both of them if she lingered longer. Dragging her suitcases from the closet, she began packing her things. For a moment, she stroked the beautiful scarf Hawk had given to her at Christmas. The tears started again.

Ignoring them, sniffing, Kate continued until she had packed all her belongings but the clothes she was wearing and the those she planned to wear tomorrow, when Hawk, she hoped, would take the time to drive her to the airport.

Hawk entered the house and frowned at the lack of aromatic cooking scents wafting on the air. It was quiet, too quiet. There was no sight or sound of Kate.

He smiled softly, thinking she had probably lain across the bed to take a nap and had overslept. His smile growing sad, he went down the hallway to their bedroom, planning to take advantage of the opportunity to join her on the bed…and sleep had nothing to do with his plan.

The door was partially open. Quietly pushing it in, he stepped inside the bedroom and stopped dead.

Kate was sitting on the side of the bed, her suitcases on the floor next to her, unchecked tears running down her flushed face.

"Kate?" Hawk crossed to her in three long strides. "What's wrong? Why are you crying? And what are your suitcases doing here on the floor?"

She drew a long, shuddering breath and, without looking up at him, said, "I'm leaving, Hawk. The six months are almost up. Will you drive me to the airport tomorrow, please?"

"No." His heart was racing.

Her head flew up and she stared at him. "Oh, well, if you're too busy, perhaps Jack or Ted can take me."

"No." Now he could hardly breathe.

"Why?" She swiped a hand over her red-rimmed eyes.

Hawk couldn't stand seeing her cry. Kicking her luggage aside, he grasped her by the shoulders and pulled her up to face him.

"I don't want you to go, Kate." He heard the pained rawness in his voice and didn't care. "I want you to stay here with me."

"After the coolness between us for two months, you want to extend my stay?" The tears had stopped but her lips still trembled.

"No, dammit!" Throwing caution and possibly his hope of continued happiness away, he gazed directly into her red, puffy eyes and said, "Will you marry me, Kate?"

She blinked, then blinked again. "Hawk, what are you saying? We *are* married."

He shook his head. "I mean, will you stay married to me? Can we renew our vows to each other, for real this time?" He caught his breath. "Kate, I love you so much. If you leave me now, I'll live. But I won't like it."

Kate had the audacity to laugh…right before she threw herself against him, wrapped her arms round his neck and joyously shouted, "Yes, yes, yes, I'll stay, Hawk, because maybe you'll live if I go…but I don't know if I will. I love you." She raised her voice even louder. "I love you, Hawk McKenna. I believe I have from our first kiss."

* * * * *

AT THE
TEXAN'S PLEASURE

MARY LYNN BAXTER

A native Texan, **Mary Lynn Baxter** knew instinctively that books would occupy an important part of her life. Always an avid reader, she became a school librarian, then a bookstore owner, before writing her first novel. Now Mary Lynn Baxter is an award-winning author, who has written more than thirty novels, many of which have appeared on the *USA TODAY* list.

One

What was she doing?

Molly Stewart Bailey couldn't ignore her queasy stomach a moment longer, so she pulled off the highway onto the side of the road. Quickly she turned to see if her unexpected action had awakened her son Trent who was sound asleep in his car seat, his head lobbed to one side. For a second Molly considered jumping out of the car and propping his head back upright.

She squelched that idea as traffic was swishing by her at a rapid rate and in her present state of despair, she was liable to get run over. Still, she paused and continued to look at her son, who favored her, with dark brown hair, smoky blue eyes and clearly defined features.

A friend once told Molly she had the most uncluttered face ever. When she recalled that, it made her smile.

Not today.

Her mind was in too much turmoil; maybe that was why she kept her eyes on her child.

The only feature he had of his father was…

Suddenly Molly slammed the door shut on that thought. Now was the worst possible time to travel down memory lane. As it was, it would take every ounce of fortitude and courage she could muster to do what she was about to do. But she had no choice, even though choices had consequences. In this case, the consequences could change her life forever, and not for the better either.

That was why she had to guard her heart and its secret with every bit of fight she had in her.

Shaking her head to clear it, Molly pulled back onto the highway, soon to realize she was closer to the Cavanaugh Ranch than suspected. Once again she felt a wave of nausea wash through her. So much for her vow never to return to east Texas, much less to this precise location.

But then who could've known her mother would fall and injure her back to such an extent she was now bedridden? Molly stifled a sigh and tried to concentrate on something mundane like her surroundings, the tall oaks decorated in their fall colors of reds, browns and golds, the pines whose limbs seem to reach to the heavens—the ponds whose waters glistened like diamonds, and the meadowlands dotted with fenced-in cattle.

Only she found she couldn't fix her mind on anything other than gaining ground on her destination.

Nothing could usurp the fact that after almost five years she was about to see Worth Cavanaugh again. In the flesh. Cold chills darted through Molly, and she shivered. Stop it! she told herself. She had to get control of her splattered emotions and never let go of them. Otherwise, she was in for a world of hurt for the next couple of weeks, if not longer.

Gripping the steering wheel harder, Molly made the last turn before entering the long strip of graveled road which led to the ranch house atop the hill. Once there, she stopped the car and took several deep breaths, which helped settle her nerves. She'd known this endeavor wouldn't be easy, but she hadn't envisioned it being this difficult. It seemed that every nerve in her body was riding on the surface of her skin.

Not a good thing, she told herself, and not at all like her. As a registered nurse, she prided herself on having nerves of steel. Her job actually demanded it. But the *who* she was about to encounter didn't have anything to do with her job. It was personal. She would soon come face-to-face with the one man she had hoped never to see again, the man who had not only broken her heart but had jerked it out and stomped on it.

"Don't, Molly!" she chastised herself out loud, then quickly glanced in the rearview mirror at Trent. Her self-imposed rebuke hadn't impacted him at all. He was still sleeping soundly. She frowned, realizing that in a few moments, she'd have to awaken him, which would not be to his liking, or hers. When he didn't get his full nap, he tended to be grumpy and oftentimes hard to manage.

Waking up in a ranch setting would most likely right his world quickly, as she'd been telling him about the horses and cattle he'd see every day. She had even bought him a new pair of cowboy boots and hat in honor of this visit to see his grandmother.

Trent had insisted on wearing his new attire today, which brought a smile to Molly's face, recalling how he'd paraded around the house, peering at himself in the mirror every chance he got, a big grin on his face.

Another sigh filtered through her at the same time the smile disappeared. Worth's house stood in front of her, and for a second she was tempted to jerk the gearshift in Reverse and back down the drive. Out of sight; out of mind. That thought was only fleeting as the needy edge in her mother's voice rose up to haunt her, recalling this visit wasn't about her, Molly, but rather her mother.

As long as she kept that uppermost in her mind, she would do just fine. Molly owed Maxine Stewart more than she could ever hope to repay, and not because she was her mother, either. Maxine had stood by her, though she had been kept in the dark about much of what had gone on in her daughter's life these last few years. If for no other reason, Molly would always love her for that.

"Mommy."

Glad for the interruption, Molly flung her head around and smiled at her son who was now wide-eyed and kicking his booted feet. "Hey, it's about time you woke up."

"When can I see the horses and cows?" Trent asked right off the bat.

Molly grinned. "First things first, okay? We'll see Granna, then the animals."

"Granna'll take me."

Molly heard that comment just as she exited the Toyota Camry and came around to release Trent from his car seat. Then helping him out, she said, "Remember Granna can't do anything. She's in bed with a hurt back."

Trent frowned as he jumped to the ground, his eyes scanning the surroundings. Molly followed suit, taking in the lovely manicured lawn close to the modern ranch house. Then her gaze dipped beyond to the sloping grounds where animals grazed in the distance near a blue pond.

"Mommy, look, I see lots of cows."

"Me, too," Molly said absently, turning Trent by the shoulders and steering him in the direction of the side door to her mother's small living quarters. Although Maxine's bedroom and sitting room were part of the main house, Worth had been thoughtful enough to add a private entrance, for which Molly was especially grateful today.

As splintered as she was, she didn't need to run into Worth, not until she'd at least seen her mother and found out for herself how seriously she was injured. Beyond that, Molly intended to take the moments as they came and deal with them no matter how painful or unsettling.

"Mom, we're here," Molly called out, knocking on the door, then opening it.

Maxine Stewart lay propped up on a pillow in her bed, a broad smile on her still-attractive face, her arms reaching out to Trent, who seemed hesitant to move.

"It's okay, honey, go give Granna a hug."

"I'm expecting a big hug, you cutie tootie. Granna's been waiting a long time for this day."

Though Trent still appeared reluctant, he made his way toward his grandmother and let her put her arms around him, giving him a bear hug. Finally pushing Trent to arm's length, Maxine's eyes glistened with tears. "My, what a big boy you are."

"I'll be five my next birthday," Trent said with pride.

Maxine winked at him. "Granna hasn't forgotten. I already have your birthday present."

"Wow!" Trent said with awe.

"Don't get too excited," Molly cautioned. "Next month you'll only be four and a half, which means your birthday's a while off yet."

"Can I have it now?"

Molly grinned, tousling his hair. "Not a chance, boy." Then it was her turn to hug her mother, though through it all, her heart took yet another beating, but for an entirely different reason.

Maxine's once unlined face had wrinkles that were unavoidably noticeable and dark circles under her eyes where none used to be. Her mother appeared frail, so much frailer than she had ever been.

Though Maxine wasn't a robust woman, she'd always been the picture of health and beauty. Friends and strangers who saw the two of them together knew they were mother and daughter because they favored each other so much. Some even told them they could pass for sisters.

Pain. That was the culprit that had so changed and aged her mother. Peering at Maxine closely through trained eyes, Molly didn't see any signs of that pain turning Maxine loose any time soon, not if the X-rays her doctor had sent Molly to peruse were correct. At this point, Molly saw no reason to question the diagnosis.

"Mom, how are you really doing?" Molly asked into the short silence.

"Good."

Molly rolled her eyes. "Hey, remember who you're talking to."

Maxine made a face. "A nurse, I know."

"All the more reason you need to be honest and 'fess up."

"Okay, my back hurts like you-know-what," Maxine admitted down in the mouth, casting a glance at Trent who was busy wandering around the room, fingering this and that.

"That's why I'm here."

"Only not for long, surely." Maxine made a face. "You just can't leave your job. I'd feel even worse if you lost it because of me."

"Hey, calm down," Molly said, leaning down and kissing Maxine on the cheek. "I have a great doctor for a boss. Besides, I have sick days, as well as vacation days, I haven't used. Four weeks' worth, actually."

"Still…"

"It's all right, I promise. I'm not going to do anything that puts my career in jeopardy."

Maxine gave a visible sigh of relief. "I'm glad to hear that." She smiled. "It's so good to see you and Trent. You're a sight for my sore eyes." Maxine faced her grandson and her smile widened. "He's grown so much since I last saw him."

"He's growing much too fast," Molly said with a crack in her voice. "He's no longer my baby."

"That's not so." Maxine looked back at Molly. "He'll always be your baby just like you'll always be mine."

Tears welled up in Molly's eyes, but she blinked them away, hopefully before her mother could see them. "So tell me what's going on here."

"Are you referring to my job?"

Molly was taken aback. "No. I wouldn't think there's a problem with that."

"I hope you're right," Maxine said, her brows drawing together. "Worth let me hire a part-time helper several months ago, which is good. She's more or less running the house now, with me telling her what to do, of course."

"So is that working out?"

"Yes, but this home needs a full-time housekeeper, especially with Worth thinking about entering politics."

The last person Molly wanted to talk about was Worth. Actually, she'd rather not know anything about him *period.* Under the circumstances, she knew that wasn't possible.

"I just can't help but be a little fearful of eventually losing my job," Maxine said, "especially if I don't start improving."

"Oh, come on, Mom, Worth's not going to let you go. You know better than that."

"Maybe I do, but you know how your mind plays tricks on you and convinces you otherwise." Maxine paused. "I guess what I'm saying is that my mind is my own worst enemy."

"That comes from lying in bed with nothing to keep you occupied." Molly smiled with a wink. "But now that Trent and I are here, that's going to change." Speaking of Trent made her turn to check on him, only to find he was no longer in the room.

"Did you see Trent leave?" Molly asked, trying to temper her building panic.

"No, but he can't go far."

That was when she noticed the door leading to the main house was open. "I'll be right back," Molly flung over her shoulder as she dashed out of the room, soon finding herself in the house's main living area. "Trent Bailey, where are you?"

"Who is Trent?"

Molly stopped in her tracks, and stared into the face of Worth Cavanaugh. For what seemed the longest time, not only did her body shut down, but their eyes also met and locked, though neither said a word. But that didn't matter. The tension was such that they might as well have been screaming at one another.

"Hello, Worth." Somehow Molly managed to get those words through cotton-dry lips.

"What are you doing here?" he demanded in a curt tone, choosing to ignore her greeting.

"I would think that's obvious."

"Maxine failed to tell me you were coming." Instead of curt, his tone was now in the freezer, showing no chance of thawing.

"That's also obvious."

Another silence.

"Again, who's Trent?"

"My son."

Worth's black eyes flickered and his mouth stretched into a

pencil-thin line. "Lucky you," he finally said in a caustic tone, his eyes filled with scorn as they traveled up and down her body.

The word *bastard* was about to fly out of her mouth when Trent rounded the corner, racing to her side. "Mommy, I went to see the moo cows."

Molly pulled him against her, clamping her hand on his shoulder. When he started to squirm, her hold tightened. As if sensing he was in trouble, Trent stopped wiggling and stared up at Worth with open curiosity.

"Trent," Molly said in a tight voice, "this is Mr. Cavanaugh."

Worth merely nodded at the boy, then looking up at Molly said, "I'd like to talk to you alone."

Biting back another choice word, Molly peered down at Trent. "Go back to Granna's room, honey. And don't leave. I'll be there shortly."

"Okay," Trent said, whirling and running back down the hall.

Don't run, Molly wanted to shout, but she knew it wouldn't do any good. Trent was already out of hearing range.

"So how old is he?"

Molly shook her head as though to clear it, Worth's question taking her by surprise. "Almost four," she said, lying with such ease that it shocked her.

"Good-looking kid."

"Thanks."

Instead of receding, the tension between them continued to rise until Molly felt either she or the room would explode. Or maybe both. She sensed Worth felt the same way, as his features seemed to darken by the second.

"How long are you planning to stay?" he asked, the muscle in one jaw moving up and down, something that always happened when he was angry or disturbed.

"I'm not sure." She paused. "Maybe a week. Maybe longer. I'm not sure. Do you have a problem with my being here?"

"Not in the least," he countered in a harsh tone.

"Is there an addendum to that?"

"Yeah," he said in a parting shot, "just stay out of *my* way."

TWO

He'd been blindsided and he hated it.

This was *his* domain, dammit, and he had control over what went on here. Or at least he thought he did. Worth muttered a curse, rubbing the five o'clock shadow that covered a good portion of his face as he continued to stand on the porch outside his room. In the distance, he could see the last remnants of a sun fast sinking into oblivion.

Worth peered at his watch and noted that it was not quite five. He loved the fall of the year, especially October because the leaves changed colors. There was one exception, however. The time change. He didn't like anything about falling backward, robbing him of an hour of light at the end of day. As a hands-on rancher, light was a precious commodity.

At this particular moment, whether it was daylight or not wasn't what his frustration was all about. Time had nothing to do with the gnawing deep in his gut. But he sure as hell knew what did.

Molly.

Back in his life.

No way.

Not possible.

Not happening.

Only it had.

She was in his house.

And there wasn't one thing he could do about it short of pitching her and the kid out the door. He muttered another colorful expletive, but again that did nothing to untie the growing knot in his stomach.

Granted, he'd known he would eventually see her again. To think not would've been ludicrous and unrealistic. After all, her mother worked for him. But since he hadn't seen Molly in nearly five years, he'd begun to think that maybe fate was smiling on him.

Heretofore, during her vacation, Maxine had always gone to visit Molly. He'd assumed that would continue to be the case.

Of course, that was before Maxine had fallen and injured her back to the extent she'd been confined to bed. Molly returning to the ranch seemed to fit the logical order of events, which wouldn't have been as much of a problem, if only he'd known about it.

He didn't like surprises, especially not surprises of this nature. Almost walking head-on into her had definitely been a blow—a blow from which he hadn't yet recovered.

The kid hadn't helped, either.

Worth rubbed the back of his neck, feeling the hard coiled muscles under his fingers. Nothing short of asking them to leave would give him any relief. That wasn't about to happen, at least not for several days anyway.

Meanwhile, he'd just have to put up with the situation. If Molly did like she was told and stayed out of his way, then he could manage. If not… Hell, he wasn't about to go down that treacherous road. It would only make him madder and more frustrated.

He just wished she still didn't look so damn good. Lovelier than even he remembered. And his memory was excellent. Never a day went by that some little something didn't remind him of her. While that never failed to shoot his blood pressure up, he'd learned to shove thoughts of her aside and move on.

Now though, that wasn't doable. He'd most likely see her every day whether he wanted to or not, regardless of what he'd told her. Having gotten over the initial shock somewhat and his head screwed back on straight had brought that reality home. As long as she was on his property, he couldn't avoid her altogether. He couldn't avoid the kid, either.

No doubt about it, she couldn't deny the kid. Looked just like her, which wasn't a bad thing. Molly's dark hair that reminded him of soot, was short and stylish, a perfect backdrop for those smoky colored eyes. And that sultry voice—God, it had always been a turn-on and still was.

Even though he knew she was twenty-seven, seven years younger than he, she didn't look it. With her unmarked skin that reminded him of porcelain at its finest, she could pass for less than twenty.

However, if one were to look closer, her figure bore testimony to her actual age. While remaining thin, with a to-die-for body, he noticed that it was more rounded, even slightly voluptuous in certain places, particularly her breasts and stomach.

Having borne a child was responsible for those added factors. Instead of detracting from her beauty, they merely enhanced it, making her body sexier than ever. Though he was loathe to admit it, he'd have to be dead not to notice. He might be many things, but dead wasn't one of them.

There had been times, however, when he'd wished he were dead. All because of her.

After Molly had run off, leaving him high and dry, she'd killed something vital inside him, which had never been revived. Part of his heart and soul were dead and Molly was to blame.

He despised her for that.

At least that was what he'd always told himself. But seeing her for that few minutes had turned his perfect world upside down—socked him in the gut, actually. Only not for long, he vowed. Already he was remembering her for the liar she really was.

And with that recall, his confidence rebounded. Even though she was staying in a small suite not far from his didn't mean one damn thing, although at first he'd questioned his placement of her and Trent.

Then he'd told himself, what the hell. Where she stayed didn't mean a thing to him. Hence, he'd had Maxine's part-time helper, Kathy, show them to that particular suite, mainly because it was close to Molly's mother.

In addition, he'd reminded himself, she wouldn't be at the ranch long enough to matter where she slept. He knew she was a nurse with some large doctors' group in Houston. Hell, he'd heard Maxine brag about that until she'd finally gotten the message that he wasn't interested in hearing about her daughter.

He often wondered what Molly had told her mother about their past relationship. He suspected it had been nowhere near the truth, which reinforced his anger. A good thing, he told himself. As long as he held onto that anger and hatred, he'd come out the winner.

And to hell with her.

Suddenly Worth heard a phone ring. It was only after the third ring he realized it was his cell. Without checking who was calling, he barked, "Cavanaugh."

"My, you sound like you're in a sour mood."

"Hello, Olivia."

He didn't miss the aggravated sigh that filtered through the line. "Is that all you have to say?"

"What do you want me to say?"

"Hello, sweetheart, would do for starters."

He didn't answer. First, he'd never called her sweetheart and didn't intend to start now. Second, but most important, she'd hit the nail on the head. He was in a sour mood, but now was not the time to tell her why. He simply wasn't up to fighting the war that would occur if he told her Molly was back in town, staying at the ranch.

More to the point, it wasn't any of Olivia's business.

"Okay, you win," Olivia replied in an offhanded manner. "I'll let you pout, or whatever the hell you're doing."

"Did you want anything in particular?" Worth asked in a cold tone, knowing he was being a first-class jerk. Yet he felt no need to apologize.

"What time are you picking me up?"

Worth's mind went blank. "Picking you up?"

"Yes," she said, not bothering to hide her growing irritation. "Remember you promised to take me to dinner tonight."

"Oh, right."

"You'd forgotten all about that, hadn't you?"

He had, but again he wasn't going to admit it. "I'll be there around sevenish."

Another sigh. "You know, Worth, I think you take great pride in being an ass."

Silence.

"And while we're on the subject of dinner," Olivia added,

"don't forget about the party at my house tomorrow night concerning your political future."

"I haven't, Olivia." His tone was weary. "I know my parents are invited along with a possible potential backer."

"At least you remembered something."

With that, she hung up.

That was two women he'd ruffled today. He wondered if his mother was next in line. Probably so, he told himself. On a normal day, he and Eva Cavanaugh didn't see eye-to-eye on much of anything. If she'd stop trying to micromanage his life, that might change. His father, however, was a different matter. They got along fine, at least on the surface, though he felt he had never known what made Ted Cavanaugh tick.

In all fairness, his parents probably didn't know what made him tick, either. One thing he did know was they wanted him to marry Olivia Blackburn. No. They *expected* him to marry her, which was the same as waving a red flag in front of a bull. He didn't live by, or under, others' expectations. Besides, he didn't love Olivia. He'd made the mistake of falling in love once, and he'd never repeat it. Never.

Only problem was, he needed what Olivia could give him and that land she stood to inherit. His parents had deeded him the three hundred acres that adjoined their property, which he'd hoped would be enough to do most anything he chose in the way of ranching. But with his cattle business thriving, he needed more land.

That was where Olivia fit into his life so well. The acreage she'd inherit from her father would give him the room to expand his horse breeding business, a dream that hadn't yet come to fruition.

Ah, to hell with women and the garbage they dished out, his thoughts targeting Molly. What he needed was a drink, he told himself savagely. Something large and strong that would cut through the constriction in his throat that had a stranglehold on him.

He was just about to accommodate himself when his phone rang again. This time he did look at caller ID and saw that it was his mother. He was tempted not to answer it, but he did. Maybe she was canceling the dinner. A smirk crossed his lips. Not a chance that would happen.

"Yo, Mother."

"Is that any way for a politician to answer the phone?"

"I'm not a politician. Yet." He was irritated and it showed.

"You will be," she said in her lofty tone. "Just as soon as you throw your hat into the ring."

"I haven't decided to do that, either."

"I don't know why you take delight in being difficult."

"Mother, if you're going to get on your soapbox about politics, then this conversation is over."

"Don't you dare hang up on me."

Not only could he hear the chagrin in his mother's voice, but he could picture it in her face, as well. Although tall and rawboned like himself, she was nonetheless a very striking woman, with blond hair and black eyes, who commanded attention with her height and flare for fashion. But when she was out of sorts, which she was now, her usually pleasant features turned hard and unpleasant.

"I'll see you and Dad tomorrow night at Liv's around eight. We can talk about politics then, okay?"

"That's not what I'm calling about."

Something in her voice alerted him to be on guard, that the rest of the conversation would not be to his liking. Her next words confirmed that.

"Why didn't you tell me?"

"Tell you what?" Worth's tone was as innocent as hers was accusing.

"That Molly Bailey, or whatever her name is now, is at your ranch."

God, it didn't take long for news to travel, but then in a small town like Sky, Texas gossip was the most popular game in town.

"Because it's no big deal."

"No big deal." Eva's voice rose. "How can you say that?"

"Because it's true. She came to see about her mother."

"I understand that."

"So what's the problem?"

"The fact that she's staying at your place is the problem."

"Mother, I don't want to discuss this."

Eva went on as though he hadn't said a word. "A motel would've been just fine for the likes of her."

Although he had no intention of defending Molly—not for one second—his mother's words set him off like a rocket. It was all he could do to keep his cool long enough to get off the phone before he said something he'd be sorry for.

"Goodbye, Mother. I'll see you tomorrow tonight."

"Worth Cavanaugh, you can't hang—"

"Yes, I can. I've got to go now." Without further ado, Worth punched the red button on the phone and Eva's hostile voice was no longer assaulting his ear.

Women!

He'd had enough of them for one day. That stiff drink was looking more enticing by the second. He was about to walk back inside when he saw her strolling across the lawn. Alone.

Worth stopped in his tracks and watched. Molly was still dressed in the same jeans she'd had on earlier, jeans that fit her rear to perfection. Right now, it was her backside that held him captive—the sway of those perfect hips. Then she turned slightly, giving him privy to the way her full breasts jutted against the soft forest-green sweater.

For what seemed an eternity, his eyes consumed her. Then

muttering a harsh obscenity, he felt his manhood rise to the occasion. Even though he dragged his gaze away from the provocative thrust of those breasts and back to her face, that action did nothing to release the pressure behind his zipper.

She was such an awesome picture of beauty against the gold and orange leaves falling from the trees that his breath caught in his throat.

It was in that moment she looked up and saw him. For the second time in a day, their eyes met and held.

He stared at her, breathing hard. Then cursing again for the fool that he was, Worth pivoted on a booted heel and strode back inside, only to realize that he was shaking all over.

Three

Lucky for her it was Worth who looked away first. For some crazy reason, Molly couldn't seem to tear her eyes away from him, although he was several yards from her. Yet his tall figure appeared clear to her.

And threatening.

Even so, she had been held spellbound by his presence, though she knew that if she were close enough to read those black eyes, they would be filled with animosity.

Thank heaven the moment had passed and he was gone. However, she didn't move. Her body felt disassembled, perhaps like one of the many leaves that were falling from the trees, never to be attached again.

What an insane thought, Molly told herself brutally, storming back into her room. Besides, it was getting down-right chilly despite the fact the sun was still hanging on. Once it disappeared, the temperature had a tendency to drop quickly.

By the time she closed the French doors, she was shivering all over. Not from the chill, she knew, but from her second encounter with Worth. She eased onto the chaise longue, the closest seat, and took several deep breaths to calm her racing heart, feeling lucky to be alone. Trent was with his grandmother who was happy as a lark reading to him. He had crawled into the bed with Maxine and was hanging onto every word she read out of the book.

Before she had ventured outdoors, Molly had stood in her mother's door and watched them, feeling a peace descend over her. Coming here, despite the obstacles, had been the right thing to do. Not only did her ailing mother need her daughter, she needed to get to really know her grandson. To date, Trent and Maxine hadn't had the opportunity to bond, to develop a close relationship that was so unique to grandparents and grandchildren.

Now, however, the doubts were once again creeping back into her mind, following that long distance encounter with Worth. Molly bit down on her lower lip to stop it from trembling while her eyes perused the room where she tried hard to concentrate on the rustic good taste that surrounded her.

She forced herself to take in, and appreciate, the cobalt blue walls and the big four-poster bed that was angled in one corner. The one thing that held her attention was the handmade quilt that adorned the bed. The coverlet picked up the blue in the wall, as well as other vivid colors, resulting in a stunning piece of art.

An armoire occupied the other side of the bedroom. The sitting area where the chaise resided held a desk and chair. No doubt, it was a place where she could be comfortable for a long period of time. But even if her job allowed that luxury, it wouldn't work.

Because of Worth.

Suddenly Molly felt tears fill her eyes, and that made her mad. Lunging off the chaise, she curled her fists into her palms and strengthened her resolve. She wouldn't let her emotions get the best of her again. She had indulged herself before she'd arrived, and that had to be her swan song. Otherwise, she wouldn't get through the quagmire that was already threatening to suck her under.

Yet seeing Worth again so soon after her arrival seemed to have imprinted him on her brain, and she couldn't let go of that image. What an image it was, too. She had never thought of him as handsome, only sexy.

Now he seemed both. He was tall and leathery thin, but not too thin, having toned his muscles to perfection riding horses and branding cattle—the two loves of his life. His short brown hair still had streaks of blond, but she could almost swear that some gray had been added to the mix. His face, with its chiseled features, was definitely more lined.

Neither change, however, was a detraction because of those incredible black eyes, surrounded by equally incredible thick lashes. They were by far the focal point of his face and his best asset.

And he knew how to use them. He had a way of looking at her like she was the only one in existence. And that was a real turn-on, or at least it always had been for her.

Until today.

When she had practically run into him upon her arrival, she'd seen none of that sexual charisma reflected in his eyes. Instead, she'd seen pure hostility and anger that bordered on hatred. Another shiver darted through Molly, and she crossed her arms over her chest as if to protect herself.

From Worth?

Possibly, because he was someone she no longer knew. More noticeable than the physical changes in him, were the changes in attitude. From the first moment she'd met him that fateful summer, she remembered him as having been rather cocky and self-assured for someone who was just twenty-nine years old. But she'd taken no offense at that attitude; actually that was one of the reasons she'd been attracted to him.

While both cocky and self-assured still applied, other adjectives now fit his personality. He appeared bitter, cynical and completely unbending. Though she didn't know the reason for such a radical change, she didn't like it, especially since it was directed at her.

After all, *he'd* been the one who had betrayed her. If anyone had an ax to grind, it was she. Admittedly she did, but she wasn't about to show her bitterness to the entire world.

Maybe she was just the one who continually brought out the worst in him. Around others maybe he was a kinder and gentler soul. That thought almost brought a smile to Molly's face. Worth Cavanaugh was a man *unto* himself, having carved an empire *for* himself in his early thirties. Kinder and gentler didn't make that happen. Hard and tough-skinned did.

Suddenly a sliver of panic ran down Molly's spine. What was she doing here? It wasn't going to work. She hadn't even been here one whole day, and thoughts of Worth had her by the jugular and wouldn't let go.

Molly swallowed convulsively as she eased back onto the chaise, vivid memories of the last time they were together rising to haunt her. If her recall served her correctly, she'd been in the barn that day, looking for Worth most likely.

The why actually hadn't been important. Once there, she'd climbed into the loft and plopped down in the middle of the hay. She remembered closing her eyes, taking a catnap during which she dreamed about Worth. When she finally opened her eyes, she was taken aback to find him leaning against a post, watching her with unsuppressed desire further darkening his eyes.

Since it had been summer and the temperature sizzling, she'd had on only the barest of clothing—a pair of blue jean shorts, a tank top without a bra and flip-flops. The way he'd stared at her, she might as well have been naked.

Heat pooled between her thighs as their eyes remained locked.

She saw him swallow with effort, causing his Adam's apple to bob up and down as he slowly, but surely pushed away from the post and made his way toward her, his fingers busily un-zipping his jeans.

All of that seemed to take place in slow motion as she lay unmoving, her heart pumping so loudly she could hear it in her ears. By the time he reached her, Molly's eyes were no longer on his face but rather on the juncture at his thighs where his erection was thick and hard.

She couldn't speak; her mouth was too dry. She could only watch him lift his arms and pull off his T-shirt, then toss it aside. A gasp slipped past her lips as her eyes covered every inch of his big, beautiful body, settling on his erection that seemed to be increasing by the moment.

Blood pounded from her heart into her head at such a rapid rate that it made her dizzy. Yet she couldn't have removed her eyes from him if someone had threatened her life with a gun. It wasn't as if that had been the first time she'd seen him in the buff, either.

It hadn't. Far from it, actually.

Since her arrival that summer at his ranch, she and Worth had become an instant item. It had been lust at first sight.

When that lust had turned to love, Molly couldn't say. Maybe it had been after he'd taken her that first time. From then on, he hadn't been able to keep his hands off her and vice versa. With summer coming to an end, nothing had changed. Every time Worth looked at her, or came near her, her bones melted.

That day was no exception.

"You're a beautiful man," she said in her sultry voice that now had a crack in it.

He merely grinned, then knelt beside her and promptly removed her clothing.

"Not nearly as beautiful as you," he rasped, his gaze now covering every inch of her flesh.

He bent over and latched onto an already burgeoning nipple and sucked it until she couldn't keep still. Finally releasing it, he moved to the other one and did likewise. Only after he left her breasts and began to lick his way down her stomach did she take action, latching onto his erection, rubbing her thumb in and around the opening.

Worth let out a loud groan as he nudged her legs apart and gently inserted two fingers inside her.

"Oh, yes," she whimpered, her hips going crazy.

"Baby, baby, you're so wet, so ready."

"Please, now. Don't make me wait."

Propping himself on his hands, Worth leaned further over her, then entered her with unerring accuracy. For a moment he didn't move, seemingly to enjoy the way she formed a tight sheath around him, his eyes burning deeply into hers.

Then he pumped up and down until the fiery explosion hit them at the same time. Moments later he lay limp on her with her arms clasped tightly around him.

"Am I too heavy?" he whispered at last, his breath caressing her ear.

"No."

"Oh, but I am." He chuckled, then rolled over so that she was now on top of him.

She leaned down, kissed him, and said in an awed voice, "I can't believe you're still inside me."

"Me, either, especially since all the lead's gone out of my pencil."

She giggled and kissed him again.

Suddenly his gaze darkened on her. "Know what?"

"I know lots of whats," she said in a teasing voice. "One of them is that I love you."

"I love you, too, so much that I got carried away and didn't use a condom."

For several seconds, silence fell between them.

"Are you mad at me?" he asked.

"No," Molly responded, feeling her brows gather in a frown. "It takes two to tango, as the saying goes."

"Right, but I should've been more responsible."

"Shh. It's okay. It's not the right time of the month for me." Molly paused. "At least I don't think so."

"I'm sorry."

"Don't you dare say that. I loved every minute of it. There's nothing to be sorry about."

It was the thought of those words that jerked Molly out of the past back into the present. *Back to reality.* To the pain and hurt that had resulted from that passionate afternoon of lovemaking.

Knowing her face was drenched with tears, Molly went into the bathroom and wet a washcloth with cold water. Though the cloth felt like ice against her skin, it did what she'd hoped it would and that was clear her fogged mind.

She couldn't change what had happened between her and Worth. All she could do was change how she reacted to him now. Though the aftermath of their affair had left deep and lasting scars, she wasn't sorry because out of it had come the blessing of her life—her son.

For that she would never be sorry.

It was then that Molly suddenly heard the sound of an engine. Hurrying to the French doors, she walked onto the porch where she saw Worth sitting in his truck. She was still standing in the cold when the taillights disappeared.

With her teeth chattering, she went back inside, not stopping until she was in her mother's room, facing her son's animated face.

"Mommy, Mommy, come see what Granna gave me."

Squaring her shoulders, Molly shoved the past back under lock and key deep in her soul.

Four

"Oh, Doctor, thanks so much for returning my call."

"Not a problem," Dr. Roy Coleman responded. "I know you're concerned about your mother and well you should be."

Molly winced under the doctor's direct words, but then she was a nurse, for God's sake, so she shouldn't be surprised. Most doctors nowadays didn't tiptoe around the rose bush. They called the problem as they saw it and let the chips fall where they may. Her boss Sam Nutting was cut from that same bolt of cloth.

Somehow, though, she was reluctant to hear the truth because it was her mother, who had always been Molly's lifeline and still was. Her dad had died from heart failure when she was young, leaving them without ample resources. Hence, Maxine had had to work her fingers to the bone for other people in order for them to survive. However, she never forsook her daughter; Maxine always found time to spend with Molly no matter how exhausted she was, or how much she had to do.

"Are you still there, Ms. Bailey?"

The doctor's crisp voice brought Molly back to the moment at hand. "Sorry, I was woolgathering about Mother, actually. Now that I've seen her and the condition she's in, I'm really concerned."

"As I said earlier, you have good reason. She took a nasty fall, which did major damage to her back, as you already know, of course. The main plus, however, is that she has no fractures."

Even though Maxine had slipped in the hallway two weeks ago, it seemed much longer to Molly because she hadn't been able to leave work and come immediately. Her mother had insisted that she not, making light of the accident.

Only after Dr. Coleman talked with her, then sent copies of the MRI did Molly know the extent of the damage to her mother's back. Ergo, she lost no time in rushing to Maxine's side.

"I appreciate you keeping me posted at every turn, Doctor."

"Wouldn't have it any other way. As I told you, Maxine's special, a rare breed. I know she's in pain, yet she suffers in silence."

"Only that's not good."

"You're right. It's not. I don't want her in pain. But Maxine is one of—if not the most—hardheaded patients I have."

"That's why I'm here, Dr. Coleman, to see that she does like she's told and behaves herself."

He chuckled, and Molly liked that. Although she'd never met him, they'd had countless phone conversations. Each time she was more impressed with his sense of humor and his care of her mother.

"I'd like to get another MRI soon, so we can see if the severely strained muscles are beginning to heal on their own.

Meanwhile, I've ordered a corset for her to wear. In fact, I don't want her even sitting on the side of the bed without it, much less walking."

Molly tried to remain upbeat, but under the circumstances that was becoming more difficult by the second. "That sounds like she's going to be incapacitated for a good little while."

"Because of her osteoporosis, she will be."

Molly's heart sank. "So we're looking at long-term recovery instead of short-term." A flat statement of fact.

"Not necessarily. Maxine is so determined that she could rebound much quicker than most, I suspect." Dr. Coleman paused. "However, work of any kind is out for now."

"What about physical therapy?"

"That's coming, but it's too soon. The corset is enough for now."

Molly fought back the unknown fears that were festering inside her. For the moment, the picture was dismal. What if her mother never regained the full use of her body? Maxine had always worked, had always been full of energy. She didn't believe in resting on her laurels, she'd told that to Molly all her life. An honest day's work for an honest day's pay had been Maxine's philosophy.

"You're going to have to help me convince *her* that she can't work, Doctor. So far I don't think you've gotten that across to her. She thinks she'll be mopping floors next week."

"Someone will be mopping floors, but it won't be Maxine."

"Thank you for being brutally honest with me." Molly's sigh was shaky. "Now, I have to be brutally honest with her."

"If you want to wait, I'll drive out to the ranch. We'll gang up on her."

A doctor who made house calls? No way. Yet he had offered, though Molly wasn't about to take him up on that offer. She could handle Maxine, but it wouldn't be easy. No matter. Her mother had no choice but to comply.

"Thank you for your kindness, but let me have a go at it first. If she bucks me, you'll be the first to know."

"Call me any time."

When the conversation ended, Molly held the receiver for a few moments longer, then replaced it, feeling as though she was moving in a daze.

She had dreaded having this session with the doctor because she knew it wasn't going to be encouraging. Since her arrival yesterday, she had come to realize her mother was indeed in dire straits, with no easy fix.

Now this morning, she had the unpleasant task of breaking the bad news to her mother. Molly was just thankful Trent was with Maxine. Bless his sweet heart, he had rarely left Maxine's room since they had arrived, seeming to have forgotten the horses and cattle with which he'd been so fascinated. But then Maxine had played with him non-stop. Knowing Maxine was exhausted, Molly finally had to call a halt to their togetherness.

Putting off the inevitable wasn't going to make things any easier, Molly reminded herself. Squaring her shoulders with resolve, she left her room and headed toward Maxine's, though not without first taking a furtive look around. While she certainly didn't expect Worth to be lurking in the shadows waiting to pounce on her, she still found herself somewhat rattled every time she left her room.

She had no idea what time Worth returned home last night, but she knew it was late, having heard him open the door to his room. It didn't matter where he went or what he did. Their relationship was past history and she had no right or reason to care about his whereabouts. Her aim was to avoid him at all costs.

Only problem with that, she was staying under his roof.

Pushing that unsettling thought aside, Molly knocked lightly on Maxine's door, then went in, only to pull up short. Her mother was asleep while Trent lay sprawled beside her, coloring in his coloring book.

"Hi, Mommy," he said in a soft voice. "Granna felled asleep."

"It's okay, honey." She reached for him and lifted him off the bed, then gathered the books and colors. "I want you to go to our room and color there for a few minutes, okay?"

Trent made a face. "I don't want to."

She smiled. "I know, but again, it'll only be for a few minutes, then I'll come and get you. I want to talk to Granna alone."

"Why can't I stay?" he whined.

Molly gave him a stern look. "Trent."

With his bottom lip poked out, he took the stuff, and without further ado, made his way to the door.

"Don't go anywhere else. Stay put in our room."

"Okay," he mumbled.

Molly stood watch until he was down the hall and the door closed behind him. He was so precious. Rarely did she ever have to scold him, but she didn't want him to hear this conversation she was about to have with her mother. She feared Maxine's reaction would not be favorable.

"Mom," Molly said, gently touching Maxine on the shoulder.

Her mother's eyes popped open and for a moment, she seemed completely disoriented. Then when she apparently recognized Molly, she smiled in relief, only then to frown. "Where's Trent?"

"He's in our room. He'll be back shortly."

"What time is it?" Maxine asked, her frown deepening.

"Almost noon."

"Oh, dear. I can't believe I even went to sleep, much less for that long."

"It's okay, Mother. You need all the rest you can get."

"No, what I need is to spend time with my daughter and grandson before I go back to work."

Molly was quiet for a moment, her mind scrabbling for a way to tell her mother the truth without breaking her heart. "Mom—"

"You're going to tell me I can't go back to work any time soon, aren't you?" Maxine's eyes were keen on Molly.

"That's right," Molly declared with relief.

"No, that's wrong."

Molly's relief was short-lived. "I—"

"I'm going to be just fine. I know I pulled some muscles in my back—"

"That you did," Molly interrupted flatly. "And according to the doctor, your recovery won't be quick or easy."

Maxine's chin began to wobble. "I refuse to believe that."

"It's the truth, Mother, and you have to face it. More than that, you have to accept it. Now if you didn't already have osteoporosis, then maybe things would be different."

"But what about my job?" Maxine wailed. "Worth has been so good to me, but he'll hire someone permanently to take my place. He'll have to, only I can't bear that thought."

"Mom, let's not beat that dead horse again. Worth is not going to replace you."

"Has he told you that?" Maxine's tone held a bit of belligerence.

Molly hesitated. "No, he hasn't."

"So you don't know what he has in mind." Maxine's voice broke.

"Oh, Mom, please, don't worry. It's going to be all right." Molly caressed one of Maxine's cheeks.

"He doesn't know—" Again Maxine broke off.

"The whole story about your back," Molly cut in. "Is that what you were about to say?"

Maxine merely nodded.

"Ah, so you told him what you wanted him to know, what you thought he wanted to hear."

Maxine reached for a tissue out of the nearby box. "I can't believe this is happening."

"Look, Mom, it's not as grim as you think."

"That's because it's not you." Maxine paused, then added quickly, "For which I'm grateful. I couldn't stand it if it were you in this shape."

"Yes, you could. You'd just come and take care of me like I'm going to do for you."

"You can't," Maxine wailed again. "You have a child and a job. And your life. You can't—"

"Shh," Molly said softly. "Enough. I'm not going to give up my life, for pity's sake. Just rest easy, I have a plan."

"What?" Maxine's tone was suspicious.

"I'll tell you later." Molly leaned over and kissed her mother on the cheek. "Right now, I'm going to send Trent back in here unless you want to go back to sleep."

"Not on your life. I want to spend every moment I can with my grandson."

"By the way, I spoke to Dr. Coleman."

Maxine's chin wobbled again.

"Hey, stop it. I'll tell you about that later also. Meanwhile, keep your chin up, you hear? Everything's going to work out."

Maxine did her best to smile. "Send my boy back to me. I have plans that don't include you."

Molly smiled big, then sobered. "Don't let him wear you out. He can, you know."

"You let me worry about that."

When Molly reached her room, she realized tears were running down her face. Brushing them aside, she forced a smile and opened the door. "Hey, kiddo, Granna's waiting on you."

* * *

Would there ever come a time when she wouldn't react to him?

Yes, Molly told herself. As long as she didn't see Worth, life would resume its normal course. Or would it? Almost five years had gone by and never a day passed she didn't think of him. Residing in his house made a bad thing worse.

Right now she didn't have a choice.

As if he realized he wasn't alone, Worth swung around. When he saw who it was, his eyes widened, then a door seemed to slide over those eyes, blanking out his expression.

"Didn't anyone ever tell you it was rude to sneak up on a person?"

Go to hell.

She didn't say that, but oh, how she wanted to. To speak her mind in that manner, however, would only incite a verbal riot, and she didn't want that. Too much was at stake. She merely wanted to talk to him in a civil manner.

"Sorry," Molly finally said in a moderate tone.

"No, you're not."

She hadn't meant to sneak up on him without warning. She just happened to walk by the door leading onto the porch and saw him there, a booted foot propped on one of the iron chairs. He seemed to have been staring into the waning sun, far in the distance, as though deep in thought.

Molly guessed she should have coughed, or done something to reveal her presence, only she hadn't thought about it. She had just walked onto the porch and waited, seeing this as an opportunity she couldn't pass up.

"Look, Worth, I don't want to fight with you," she said at last. She'd meant what she'd said, too, especially when she watched him set the empty beer bottle down on the table, making more noise than he should have, which spoke volumes about his mood.

She couldn't let Worth see the effect he had on her. Not now. Not ever. And entering into another verbal skirmish with him would put the power in his hands, power that could end up destroying her and what she held dear. At all costs, she had to maintain her cool.

"Is that what we're doing?"

"I don't want to play word games with you, either."

He jammed his hands into his pockets which pulled the fabric tighter across his privates. For a moment, her gaze lingered on the mound behind the zipper. Then realizing what she was doing, she jerked her head back up to his face, praying that he hadn't noticed anything amiss.

If he had, he didn't acknowledge it. Instead, he continued to stare at her through those blank eyes.

"What do you want, then?"

"To take my mother's place."

His head bolted back at the same time he went slack-jawed. "As my housekeeper?"

"Yes," Molly said with punch in her tone.

He pitched back his head and laughed. "Get real."

"I'm serious, Worth," she countered with an edge in her tone.

"So am I, and that's not going to happen."

"Why not?"

He smirked. "Come on, Molly, you know why not. You're a nurse, and that's what you need to be doing."

"I can do both. I can take care of the house and my mother."

"What about Trent?"

"I'll put him in day care, and he'll be just fine."

"No."

She ignored that terse rejection and went on, "My mother's mind is her own worst enemy right now. She thinks you're going to replace her."

"That's hogwash. She has a job here as long as she wants one. And I'll tell her that."

"I appreciate that, but I still want to take her place. I can take care of Mom, encourage her and she will see that my job as housekeeper is temporary. This way she won't worry about someone permanently replacing her. She'll know I'm only filling in. Not only that, but I'm good. I grew up helping her clean houses."

Worth looked astounded. "Are you nuts? Besides, you don't have to do that anymore."

"I know I don't have to. I want to."

"Dammit, woman, you haven't changed a bit."

Molly raised her eyebrows. "Oh?"

"Yeah, you're still as stubborn as a mule."

She wanted to smile but didn't. Instead she held her ground. "So are you."

Worth cursed at the same time their eyes collided then held tighter than magnets.

Suddenly the oxygen in the air seemed to disappear, forcing Molly to struggle for her next breath. She could tell Worth was also affected as his face lost what little color it had left. And something else happened, too, though she couldn't identify it.

What it *hadn't* been was hostility. So had it been blatant desire? No. She'd been mistaken. He despised her and that wasn't about to change. She didn't want it to, either, she assured herself quickly, though the undertow of his sexy charisma was pulling on her.

Forcing her panic aside, Molly sucked in a deep breath and stared at him with an imploring expression.

"I'll think about it," Worth muttered on a sour note, cramming his hands further down in his pockets, which pulled his jeans even tighter across that area.

Molly averted her gaze and muttered, "Thank you."

He laughed, but again without humor.

Feeling heat rush into her face, Molly knew she should leave before insult was added to injury. She was about to do just that when his next words froze her in her tracks.

"Why did you run out on me?"

Five

She whipped back around and stared at him, feeling as though she were strangling. "What did you say?" she finally managed to asked.

"Don't play the deaf ear thing on me." Worth's tone was low and rough. "It won't work. You heard every word I said."

"I used to admire your badass attitude," Molly responded with fire. "In fact, I thought you were the stud of all studs because of it."

His eyebrows shot up as though that shocked him.

"But now I know better."

His features darkened. "Oh?"

"That attitude sucks big time."

The look that crossed Worth's face was chilling, and he took a step toward her, only to stop suddenly as though he were a puppet on a string and someone had jerked that string. She knew better. Worth was no one's puppet and never had been. Then she recanted that thought. His parents apparently knew how to pull his strings and get away with it.

"You know I really don't give a tinker's damn what you think about me or my attitude." Worth's voice had grown rougher.

"Then why ask me that question?"

"Curiosity is the only thing I can figure," he said in an acid tone, fingering an unruly strand of light hair that grazed his forehead.

Molly was suddenly tempted to reach out and push it back in place, something she had done on many occasions that long-ago summer. That sensual memory was so vivid she felt like a piece of broken glass was slicing through her heart.

"Your curiosity can go to hell. I'm *not* answering you."

He smirked. "That's because you don't have a satisfactory explanation."

"I have no intention of swimming through the muddy waters of the past. With your cynical judgment of me, I'd just be wasting my time anyway."

No doubt she was on the defensive and probably sounded as cynical as he did, but she didn't care. If she were going to survive and keep her secret from him and his parents, she had to best him at his own game, or at least match him.

Or she'd die in that muddy water.

"What's wrong?" His eyes consumed her. "You look like something suddenly spooked you."

Was that genuine concern she heard in his voice? Of course not. As before, her mind was playing tricks on her. He didn't give a damn about her. He was too much into himself.

"I'm fine," she bit out.

"Liar."

Her head kicked back. "What do you want from me, Worth?"

"What if I said *you?*"

Molly shook her head, trying to recover from the effect those words spoken in that toe-curling, sexy drawl had on her.

"I wouldn't believe you," she finally whispered.

Those dark pools roamed over her while the blood pounded in her ears like a drum. Oh, God, this kind of craziness had to stop or she'd be like putty in his hands again and wouldn't be good for any thing or any one. That was why she hadn't wanted to see him again. She was too weak, too vulnerable where he was concerned. She only had to be in the same room with him and she almost went to pieces.

"You're right, you shouldn't believe me," he said harshly and coldly, "because it's not true."

Molly sucked in her breath and tried to pretend that piece of glass hadn't taken another chunk out of her heart.

"Maybe you'll answer me this."

Molly barely heard him as she was striving to hold onto her wits and dignity under his attack, knowing that she should turn around and walk away, that nothing good would ever evolve from this conversation.

Why bother? She no longer gave a damn, either.

She simply didn't want to reconnect with that part of her life. Not only was it over and done with, it was way too painful to rehash, especially with him. What she and Worth had between them that summer was obviously dead, and to pull the past out of the dark into the daylight was futility at its highest degree.

"I have to go," she said in a halting voice, refusing to look at him.

"Do you love him?"

Shock caused Molly to blink. "Who?"

"Your husband. That Bailey guy who fathered your child."

Oh, dear Lord, if only she'd kept on going, hadn't sought him out on the porch, then they wouldn't be having this insane dialogue, making a bad situation worse.

"Yes," she lied.

His gaze dropped to her left hand. "Are you still married? I don't see a wedding ring."

"We're divorced." She hated lying, but right now it seemed her only recourse. He was like the Energizer Bunny; he just kept on going, kept on asking questions that were, frankly, none of his business.

If she didn't take charge, there might not be an end to his questioning. The more he knew, the more dangerous her presence became. And she was trapped. She couldn't leave because of her mother.

So they had no alternative but to work through their animosity toward each other, so she could remain on the ranch, ideally as his housekeeper. Maybe getting it all out in the open now, once and for all, was best for both of them. Then they could move on with the day-to-day grind of their lives and be less apt to meddle in each other's.

"I could ask you why *you're* not married," Molly blurted out of the blue, then was appalled. All she was doing was adding fuel to an already out-of-control fire. Would she ever learn to keep her mouth shut?

"Yeah, you could."

Silence.

"So why aren't you?" She paused. "I understand you're still seeing Olivia. I thought she would've dragged you down the aisle by now."

"Well, you thought wrong," he declared flatly, glaring at her.

Good. She'd finally hit him where it hurt, as he'd done to her so many times. Then she felt badly. She was above playing these hurtful games. Exchanging barbs only made the situation worse.

"If I'm going to stay here and work—"

"I haven't said you could do that yet," Worth interrupted, narrowing his eyes on her.

"I'm not leaving, Worth. I can't. My mother needs me."

He shrugged. "When it comes down to it, I really don't give a damn what you do."

"As long as I…we stay out of your way," she added, positive she had verbally expressed what he hadn't.

"You got it."

Ignoring the suppressed anger in his voice, she asked, "How about we call a truce? Do you think that's possible?"

"Do you?" His eyes were brooding.

"I'm willing to try."

He shrugged again, his eyes roaming over her, seeming to linger on his favorite spot—her breasts, which upped her heartbeat significantly.

"Whatever," he said without enthusiasm.

Molly gritted her teeth, but swallowed her sharp comeback. "Good night, Worth."

He didn't respond.

"I hope you sleep well," she added.

"Yeah, right," he muttered tersely, then turned his back on her.

Feeling the cold night air close in on her, Molly went back into the warm house, only to reach her room and notice that she couldn't seem to stop shaking.

"Hey, boss, what's up?"

Instead of going back inside the house, Worth had made his way to the barn. He hadn't expected to run into his foreman Art Downing, but then he shouldn't have been surprised. Art never seemed to know when to go home. He loved his job, especially caring for and working with Worth's stable of prime horseflesh. In fact, Worth had determined long ago that Art was more comfortable at the ranch than he was at home with his wife and kids.

Like him, maybe Art just wasn't cut out for family life.

"I was about to ask the same thing," Worth said.

Art lifted his massive shoulders that matched the massive girth around his stomach, and grinned. "Just making sure these beauties are settled in for the night."

All the while he talked, Art was busy rubbing one of the horse's noses.

"They're fine. Go on and get out of here."

"I will as soon as I check one more thing."

"And just what would that be?" Worth asked, glad to have something on his mind besides Molly who spelled trouble with capital letters.

"Making sure everything's ready for tomorrow's delivery."

Worth had bought another stud horse last week and the targeted arrival was the following morning. "Who you kiddin', man? You've had things ready since we bought him."

"You're right there." Art grinned, then rubbed his belly. "I am gettin' kind of hungry."

"Then get your rear home. And don't come back until it's daylight, you hear?"

"Yes, sir." Art tipped his hat then was gone.

Worth knew he might as well be talking to the air. His foreman would be here long before daylight, which made him more valuable to Worth than money could ever buy.

If he did as his parents wished and ran for political office, his time at the ranch would be limited. Thanks to Art, the ranch would continue to run smoothly.

After taking his own tour of the stables and rubbing all the horses and calling them by name, Worth made his way back to the house. Once there, he grabbed another beer out of the fridge, then headed to his suite. Glancing at his watch, he noticed he only had thirty minutes before he was due at Olivia's. She didn't like anyone to be late.

Dammit, he didn't want to go, not to a dinner party. Hell,

he'd just taken her to dinner the night before. However, he had made a commitment he couldn't break, especially as the gathering was designed to introduce him as a possible candidate for the Texas Senate. Still, it was too formal an affair for him. He knew Olivia expected him to dress for the occasion, which meant a sports coat and slacks.

He hadn't told her that wasn't going to happen. He planned on showing up in jeans, a white shirt and a leather jacket. If she didn't like it, that was her problem.

Instead of showering and changing his clothes, however, Worth plopped down on the side of the bed and guzzled half his beer. God, he was mentally tired, and he didn't know why.

Yeah, you do.

Molly.

Sparring with her on the porch had depleted his energy. He didn't know if he could take having her around here indefinitely, especially if she was working as his housekeeper. How ludicrous was that, anyway? So why had he mealy-mouthed around? He should have told her in no uncertain terms that was impossible.

But seeing her again had reopened the wound he thought had scabbed over. He supposed that was what he found most crippling. And frightening. With her arrival, it was like the messy tracks she had left on his heart had suddenly been covered by a lovely snowfall.

Which made him more of a fool than he'd thought. When it came to her, he couldn't use good judgment, and that made him madder than hell. At this point, he didn't need the aggravation of her presence back in his life.

Maybe if she'd still been married and brought her husband with her that would have made things easier. Like hell, he told himself with a snort, bolting off the bed and finishing his beer.

For a second he was tempted to grab another one and

maybe another after that. By then he'd be on his way to getting smashed. The thought of Olivia's reaction to him showing up three sheets to the wind brought a smile to his face.

Then he sobered. Right now he had nothing to smile about. Okay, Molly had upset his apple cart, so to speak, and he wasn't happy about that. But he remained king of this empire. No one told him what to do or how to do it.

So why had he suddenly gone soft?

The first time he'd laid eyes on Molly, she had managed to wrap him around her little finger. But after she had run off, married someone else and had his kid, Worth was so sure he'd feel nothing but contempt for her, if and when he ever saw her again.

Well, the contempt was sure as hell there, but so was another ingredient—an ingredient he refused to name, though it burned like a raging fire in his gut.

"Give it a rest, Cavanaugh," he muttered in a fierce tone, hurrying into the bathroom like a stampede of bulls were after him.

Only problem was, his mind refused to cooperate. In the shower, he squinched his eyes closed under the water, but it didn't help. Instantly, the image of Molly jumped to the forefront of his mind. She was standing in front of him, her eyes gleaming with desire, while she caressed his face, then his body.

Worth groaned, then gave in to the pain that momentarily paralyzed him.

Six

"Mommy, when can I ride a horse?"

Molly pursed her lips. "Oh, honey, I don't think that's going to happen."

Trent scrunched his face. "You promised."

"I beg your pardon, my sweet, but I did no such thing."

"I bet that man will let me."

Molly almost smiled. "Are you talking about Worth?"

"No, that other man."

Molly thought for a moment, then realized Trent was talking about Art, Worth's foreman. She had always thought he was such a nice man and that Worth was lucky to have him, especially when Worth would get upset about something. Art never seemed to take it personally. Instead he would listen, then take care of the situation.

"I saw him on one of the horses from Granna's window." Trent's voice held excitement.

"That's great, but you don't know a thing about riding a horse."

"I could learn," Trent said with a protruding lower lip.

"We'll see, okay?"

"I—"

She gave him one of her looks. "I said we'll see."

Although he didn't respond, Molly knew he wanted to. His lower lip was now protruding and trembling. "I'll talk to Mr. Art tomorrow, but I'm still not making any promises, young man. Is that clear?"

Trent's face instantly changed, and he ran and gave her a hug.

"Come on, big boy, it's time for your bath, then bed."

Again, Trent looked as if he wanted to argue, only he didn't, as though he realized he'd pushed his mother far enough.

Long after Trent was in bed Molly stood at the window, staring at the cantaloupe-shaped moon and Venus close by. What a lovely clear night, she thought. And chilly, too. She turned and glanced thankfully at the gas logs with their bright, perky flames.

Considering the way Worth felt about her, he sure had given her nice quarters. But then the entire ranch house was nice, built for guests and entertaining, which, now that she was old enough to think about it, rather surprised her. Worth wasn't the entertaining type, didn't have that personality, or at least not the Worth she'd known and loved.

Apparently, that Worth was no longer in existence. If anything, he was more self-centered, more spoiled than ever, an entity unto himself, definitely someone she no longer recognized or wanted anything to do with.

On second thought perhaps now she was seeing the *real* Worth Cavanaugh. Maybe back then, she'd been so young, so impressionable, so inexperienced, she simply hadn't recognized those flaws.

Besides, she'd been madly, and obviously *blindly,* in love.

Since that was no longer the case, she had to do what was necessary for her mother, then leave ASAP.

Thinking about her mother suddenly made Molly long to see her. She checked on Trent one more time, then went to Maxine's room. Thankfully, her mother was still awake.

After she had made both of them a cup of flavored decaffeinated tea, Molly eased into the chair by the bed and said without preamble, "I plan to enroll Trent in a day care facility in town."

"What on earth for?" Maxine asked in an astonished voice.

Molly hesitated, which gave her mother time to voice her displeasure.

"Since you're not going to be here long, I want Trent to stay here." Maxine struggled to sit further up in bed, then winced from the exertion.

Molly hurried to her side only to have her mother hold out her hand. "I'm okay. The sooner I learn to move on my own the sooner I can get up and get back to work."

"That's not going to happen any time soon, Mother, and you know it."

"I know no such thing."

"Please, let's not argue about that again."

"Who's arguing?"

A short silence followed her mother's succinct words.

"So back to why you want to put Trent in day care," Maxine said.

"I'm staying."

When Molly's bluntly spoken words soaked in, Maxine gave a start. "What does that mean?"

"It means that I'm not leaving any time soon."

"But I don't understand. What about your job?"

"For now, I have a new one."

Maxine's eyes widened. "Pray tell, girl, you're not making a lick of sense. What are you talking about?"

"I'm going to take your place here as housekeeper."

Maxine gasped. "No, you're not."

"Mother."

"Don't you Mother me in that tone, young lady."

Molly almost swallowed her tongue to keep from making a sharp retort.

Not so with Maxine. She hammered on, "Why do you think I worked my fingers to the bone all these years?" When Molly would have spoken, Maxine held up her hand again. "No. You hear me out. I did that so you wouldn't have to do manual labor, though don't get me wrong, working for Worth is wonderful. The best job I've ever had, not to mention he's the best person I've ever worked for."

Boy, did that admission ever surprise Molly. She would have thought the opposite, but then maybe it was when he was around her that Worth took on a different personality. No doubt, he abhorred the ground she walked on. Well, the feeling was mutual.

Liar, her conscience whispered before she shoved that thought aside and concentrated on what her mother was saying.

"But that doesn't mean I want you doing that kind of work."

"I'm not above doing that kind of work, as you call it," Molly said flatly. "I'm quite good at it, actually, since I grew up helping, and learning, from you."

"That's beside the point." Maxine glared at her. "I'd rather Worth fire me and hire someone else than for you to give up your job in Houston."

"I never said I was giving up my job. I'm just taking my sick leave and vacation time. Once you get your brace and start physical therapy, you'll be good as new in no time. Then I'll be out of here."

Her mother grunted in disbelief, then said with despair in her tone, "I'm afraid I'll never be the same again. What if those twisted muscles don't straighten out and I have to have surgery? If that happens, then I won't be able to walk across the room without a cane or walker. Worth will surely replace me then."

"There you go borrowing trouble again."

"No, I'm just being realistic, something you young people are not."

Molly rolled her eyes in frustration. "Talk about me being hardheaded."

"If I can no longer cut it," Maxine argued, "then what's to keep him from making me second in command?"

"Mom, we've been over this issue several times already."

"I know, and I'm sorry for beating that dead horse," Maxine said in a petulant tone.

"If I take your place, your job won't be in jeopardy."

"No matter. I'm not about to let you do that."

"Too late," Molly said flatly. "It's a done deal."

"I can't believe Worth would approve that. I need to talk to him."

"I'll admit he wasn't overjoyed at the prospect, but I think he'll come around."

"After I get through with him, he won't," Maxine said.

"This is between Worth and me, Mother."

"Please, Molly, don't do this." Maxine's tone had a begging edge to it.

Molly sat on the bed beside Maxine, leaned over and kissed her on the cheek. "Please, *let* me do this. Don't fight me. You've always been there for me, never judged me for shaming you by getting pregnant before I married, then immediately divorcing. It's my turn now to pay you back."

Maxine placed her palms on either side of Molly's face, looked into her face with tear-filled eyes and said in a torn voice, "You're my child, my baby. That's what mothers do— love unconditionally."

Molly fought back the tears. "And that is what daughters do, too."

Maxine dropped her hands and fell back against the pillow. For a long moment both were silent, seemingly lost in their own thoughts.

Maxine was the first to speak. "I thought you were going to marry Worth, you know." Her mother's voice was weak and far off.

Molly almost choked on the pain that suddenly squeezed her heart. "I did, too, Mom, only it didn't work out."

"You never told me what happened." Her mother's eyes drilled her.

Molly licked her dry lips. "I know."

"It's okay." Maxine reached out and grabbed one of her daughter's hands. "If you ever want to tell me about it, I'm here. I've never been one to pry and I'm not about to start now. You've got a precious child and a wonderful career, so it's best to let sleeping dogs lie."

Molly tasted a tear. "You've been the best mother ever and still are." She sniffled, then smiled. "Perhaps one day I'll be able to confide in you."

"But it's okay between you and Worth now, right?" Maxine asked with concern. "I guess what I'm asking is do you still care about him in that way?"

"Absolutely not," Molly responded vehemently. "Granted, we'll never be friends, but we're okay around each other."

Here she was lying to her mother again. But she couldn't help it. Once she had almost blurted out the truth concerning her and Worth, but the words had stuck in her throat. After that, she had talked with a minister in Houston when she'd found out she was pregnant, then entered counseling.

While some people might judge her harshly for her silence concerning the baby's father and fact that she'd lied about marriage, she felt her mother never would, even if she were to learn the truth. Still, there was a part of Molly that just couldn't unburden her heart to her mother, or anyone else.

For now, no loved one or friend was privy to her heart's secrets.

"My, but you're quiet all of a sudden."

Molly shook her head and said, "Sorry." Then she leaned her head sideways and added, "Have you thought about going to a facility while you're recuperating?"

"Have you gone daft, child?"

Molly chuckled. "No, but I had to ask."

"If I have to leave this place, I would go to Houston with you."

"That's certainly an option."

"Only not now. I want to stay right here, get well, then go back to the job I love."

Molly stood and gave a thumbs up. "Together we'll make that happen."

"I knew you were stubborn—" Maxine's voice played out with a forlorn smile.

Molly chuckled again. "I'm going to bed. We both need our rest."

However, when she returned to her room the sound of a car door slamming pulled Molly up short. Without thinking, she dashed to the window, knowing it was Worth returning from another night out. Probably with Olivia again, though she didn't know that for sure. Still, she didn't move, continuing to track his movements, hoping he couldn't see her because the room was practically dark. Only a small lamp burned in one corner.

Molly glanced at the clock on the bookshelves and saw that it was past midnight. If he'd been with Olivia, had they made love? Suddenly her stomach clenched. The thought of his hands and mouth caressing another woman like they had hers didn't bear thinking about. In fact, it made her flat outright sick to her stomach, which was in itself *sick*.

Of course, he'd made love to Olivia, if not other women, as well. After all, it had been almost five years since she'd seen him. A man like Worth, with a heightened sexual appetite, or at least it had been that way with her, wouldn't have remained celibate all that time.

Dammit, it didn't matter, she told herself. But it did, though she was loathe to admit it because such an admission was dangerous to her peace of mind and threatened her sanity.

If she was going to go through with her plan to work for him—and she was—then she'd have to corral her mind and not let it wander down forbidden paths.

When Molly realized she had been indulging, she blinked just in time to see him saunter toward the house. He was halfway there when he looked up at her bedroom.

Feeling her heart leap into her throat, Molly jumped back, out of sight. Had she been in time? Had he seen her watching him? If so, what must he think?

When she mustered up the nerve to peek again, he was gone. Then disgusted with herself and her juvenile antics, she mentally kicked her backside all the way to bed.

She heard the grandfather clock in the hall chime three o'clock, realizing she had yet to close her eyes.

Damn him!

He had seen her all right. And for a second he was tempted to say to hell with everything, stride inside and bound down the hall to her room. Then what? he asked himself.

Make mad, passionate love to her?

Sure thing, as if she'd let him cross the threshold much less touch her. God, what was he thinking when he let his mind and emotions have free rein? Dwelling on the impossible was crazy. More to the point, it made *him* crazy.

Why he hadn't sent her packing was beyond him. It wasn't too late, he reminded himself as he grabbed a beer, then made his way to his room, making sure he didn't pause in front of hers.

But sleep was impossible. He'd already had too much to drink. He'd used the boring dinner party as an excuse to get partially plastered, much to Olivia's chagrin. Boring though it was, something good had come out of it. The man Olivia had invited as a potential backer for his campaign turned out to be someone he'd instantly liked and to whom he could relate.

Ben Gibbs seemed to have felt the same way about him. They had talked at length, and Worth had come away from the conversation positive Gibbs would back him if he chose to run against the incumbent. He had also spoken highly of Worth's parents, which was another good thing.

Other than Gibbs, the rest of the evening had been only tolerable. After everyone had left, Olivia had wanted him to stay. He made up some lame excuse, which didn't sit well with her, and left.

Now, alone in his bed with only his tormented thoughts, Worth almost wished he'd spent the night with Olivia, so he wouldn't think about *Molly* and that kid of hers. For some reason, he couldn't get the boy off his mind.

If only *he'd* gotten Molly pregnant that summer day in the barn when he hadn't used protection, how different his life would've been. He'd have a child—a son no less.

Now, he'd probably never have that opportunity even if he wanted it. According to the doctor, he'd be damn lucky if he could father a child. A horse had kicked him in the groin shortly after Molly had run out on him.

At the time, he'd been so busy nursing his anger and bitterness against Molly the diagnosis hadn't registered.

Having anything to do with a woman after that had been disgusting to him. The emotional wounds Molly had left had been open and oozing.

Now, after having seen her son, the enormity and repercussions of his accident rose up and hit him in the face like the chill from a bucket of ice water. To make matters worse, he hadn't even told his parents. To this day, they still didn't know that he might not ever give them the grandchildren they so coveted.

Dammit, by all rights Trent should have been his.

"You're full of it, too, Cavanaugh," he said out loud, followed by an ugly laugh.

He drained the remainder of his beer, then tossed the empty bottle on the floor at the same time the room swam. Good. Maybe he was drunk enough to fall asleep. Without removing his clothes, he fell across the bed, trying to forget he was nursing a hard on.

For Molly.

Seven

"Mommy, these pancakes are so good."

"I'm glad, honey, but don't you think you've had enough?" Molly smiled at her son. "Five is a lot, even for a growing boy. But you do need to finish your milk."

"Your cakes taste just like Granna's."

Noticing that Trent's mouth was smeared with syrup and butter, Molly grabbed a paper towel, moistened it, then wiped his entire face, while he squirmed. "Be still. You can't go to day care dirty."

"I'm not dirty."

"Yes, you are," she corrected him with a broader smile. "Go brush your teeth, then we'll go."

"Where's he going?"

Stunned that Worth had pulled her stunt and made an appearance without her knowledge sent her heart into a tailspin. Striving to cover that fact, Molly pulled in a deep breath, and looked at him, which only added to her trepidation. It looked as though he'd just gotten out of the shower as his thick hair was still damp and slightly unruly, which always made her want to run her hands through it.

But it was what he had on that had her heart in such a dither. His flannel shirt was tucked into worn jeans that fit his long, muscled legs like a second skin, especially over his crotch, leaving nothing to the imagination.

For a moment her eyes honed in on that private area and set up camp. Then realizing what she was doing, she jerked her head up at the same time she felt heat flood her face.

To make matters worse, she knew what he was thinking. The lines around his mouth deepened, his eyes turned into banked down coals of desire. Their gazes met and held for what seemed an eternity, but in reality was only seconds.

Bless Trent. He was the one who broke the tension that sizzled between them.

"Hey, Worth."

Her son's words brought Molly back to reality with a thud. "Mr. Cavanaugh to you, young man."

"It's okay. He can call me Worth. I want him to."

Trent turned his eyes tentatively to his mother, as if seeking her approval. "Whatever," she said without conviction.

"I love your cows and horses," Trent said to Worth. "I wish I could ride one of your horses," he added down in the mouth.

"Trent." Molly's tone was reprimanding.

Trent pawed the tile floor with a booted foot, his lower lip beginning to stick out. "I didn't do nothing, Mommy."

"He sure didn't." Worth squatted in front of him. "How 'bout I start teaching you to ride today?"

"No," Molly exclaimed in horror.

Both looked at her like she'd just sprouted two heads.

"I'm about to take Trent to day care."

"Why?" Worth asked, standing, his gaze pinning hers.

Though she wanted to squirm, she didn't. She met him eye for eye. "Because I can't see about him and the house, too. And Mother's not able."

"Kathy can watch him."

"I need her to help me."

A grim look crossed Worth's face, especially his lips. "I don't want you doing that."

Molly glanced over at Trent, then back to Worth, as if to say now's not the time to have this discussion."

"Mommy?"

Without taking her eyes off Worth, she said to her son, "Run brush your teeth."

After looking from one adult to the other, Trent trudged off, his little shoulders slumped.

"He's not a happy camper," Worth said into the tension-filled silence.

"He'll get over it."

"Let him stay here, Molly. I'll hire someone to watch him."

"I can't allow that."

"Why the hell not?"

"I'm responsible for running the house—your house—and I don't want to be worried about Trent and what he's into. Furthermore, it's not your place to hire someone to watch my son."

"For God's sake, Molly, that's all the more reason to put an end to this nonsense. I don't want you running my house."

"Are you backing out on your word, Worth?" She glared at him.

His eyes narrowed on her. "Unlike you, I don't do that."

She wasn't stupid; she knew where that remark originated. He had just taken another potshot at her for when she'd walked out on him. "Contrary to what you might think, I don't do that, either."

He sneered, then muttered something under his breath.

She didn't want to know what it was because it would add coals to an already smoldering fire that simmered between them. Until her mother was up and about, Molly reminded herself she must contain her tongue and hold her counsel, or else she wouldn't survive this jungle she'd reentered.

"I was serious when I offered to teach him to ride," Worth said in a more conciliatory tone than she'd heard in a while. "But I was more serious about him staying here."

Fear burgeoned inside her. "Why do you care?"

"He seems to be a good boy, and I know how much Maxine enjoys his company. She talks about him all the time, how much she misses seeing him."

"My mother told you that?"

"You act shocked," he remarked in a dry voice.

"I guess I am." Molly's tone was confused.

"Obviously you don't know it, but I have a great deal of respect for your mother. She's not just my housekeeper. She's a friend and part of my family."

"I appreciate that, Worth," Molly said in a halting voice as she shifted her gaze. "I really do. I know she feels the same about you."

"That she does."

"Again, I so appreciate your patience with her injury."

"When she hurt her back," Worth responded, "her mind must've conjured up the worst possible case scenario because I never had any intention of letting her go."

"She definitely went into the panic mode."

"Under those circumstances, my suggestion is that you spend time working with, and caring, for her, and let the house go."

"I can't do that, Worth. Even though I'm a nurse, and a good one I might add, I'm not a physical therapist. Too, it wouldn't be good for Mother and me to be together that much. Too much togetherness can be a bad thing."

"Don't I know that," he muttered again.

"Speaking of togetherness, how are Eva and Ted?" Not that she cared, she told herself, stunned that she'd even inquired.

Worth shrugged and gave her a strange look. "Same as always—great."

"I'm glad," Molly acknowledged in a stiff tone.

"You never did like them and still don't." A flat statement of fact.

Molly deliberately changed the subject. "When I get back from town, I need to talk to you about upcoming events. I know about the day-to-day run-of-the-mill things. Mom told me your schedule, more or less, that you—"

"Dammit, Molly, put a stopper in it, okay?"

Her mouth clamped shut at the same time her temper flared. "Don't you dare talk to me like that."

"Sorry," he muttered again, shoving a hand through his hair, clearly indicating his irritation.

"Look, Worth, we can't go on like this."

"And how is that?"

"You're being deliberately obtuse, but for the moment I'm going to let that pass."

Worth eyes darkened on her. "Okay, you win."

Molly's breathing slightly accelerated. "On both Mother and Trent?"

"On one."

"And that is?"

"The house."

Her anger rose. "You have nothing to say about Trent."

"Don't you want him here?"

"Of course," she admittedly tersely.

"Then let him stay. I know someone who's perfect to look after him."

"And I'll pay them," she said in an unbending tone.

After having said that, she experienced a hollow feeling in the pit of her stomach like she'd done something terribly wrong and didn't know how to fix it.

Worth and Trent should not be a pair, but if she continued to remain unmovable, then it might raise a red flag, giving Worth cause for thought. She couldn't allow that. Hence, she'd try Worth's plan. If it didn't work out, then she could always insist on reverting to *her* plan and to hell with what Worth said or thought.

"That's fine by me," he said on a sigh.

"So can we get down to other business now?" she asked.

He made a face, then peered at his watch. "Now's not a good time for me. I have to meet with a breeder. How 'bout later, maybe this evening?"

Before you go see your lover. I don't think so. Appalled at her catty thoughts, Molly felt the color drain from her face as she turned quickly around, praying that he hadn't read her thoughts through her eyes.

"Molly?"

The crusty edge in his voice brought her eyes back around. "What?"

For another long moment, their gazes held.

Worth cleared his throat, then said in an even crustier tone. "Will that be okay?"

"I guess so," she responded in brittle tone.

Worth gave her another long look out of suddenly vacant eyes, then left the room. Once alone, Molly sank against the kitchen cabinet for support, wondering how she was going to survive staying there even one more day.

He just couldn't keep a lid on it.

It was as though he'd suddenly developed diarrhea of the mouth. He shouldn't have interfered with her plan to put the kid in day care. The last thing he wanted was to be saddled with her brat.

Not true.

He liked the boy, and that was the problem. He should leave them both alone, have as little to do with them as possible. Only that wasn't *possible* since Molly insisted on working for him.

Damn her lovely hide.

Only she wasn't to blame. He could have put his foot down and said an emphatic *no* and meant it. She wouldn't have had a choice but to comply. After all, she was on his turf with no alternative but to do as he said.

But again, he'd wimped out, and let her have her way, at least on one account.

Worth let go of a string of expletives that did little to relieve that gnawing in his gut. If only she didn't look so good or smell so good, having her around would be easier.

This morning when he'd walked into the kitchen and saw her dressed in those low cut tight black jeans that hugged her butt and legs to perfection, and the white T-shirt that also hugged her breasts and stomach with the same perfection, he wanted to grab her and punish her with hard, angry kisses for the havoc she was wreaking in his life.

Of course, he hadn't made such an insane move, didn't plan to, either. He aimed to keep as wide a berth between them as possible. With that kind of rationale, he'd be fine, or so he hoped. To think she'd only been there four days. That already seemed an eternity.

Realizing he was almost at his parents' house, Worth gave his head a fierce shake to clear it. Molly was poison and he had to stop thinking about her, *stop wanting her.* Around his parents, he had to be constantly on guard; they were much too inquisitive and much too intuitive.

They had never liked her and had made that quite clear. But he hadn't given a damn. He'd liked her. Hell, he'd *loved her,* and would have married her if she hadn't left him.

Bitterness rose in the back of Worth's throat in the form of bile. Swallowing deliberately, he concentrated on maneuvering up the circular drive in front of his parent's antebellum home. About that time, his father walked onto the porch.

Olivia's father, Peyton Blackburn, stepped out, too, just as Worth braked his truck, killed the engine and got out.

He didn't have anything against Blackburn except that he thought he was better than most, but then that seemed a characteristic of many of the well-to-do families in this town. He was sure people said the same about him and his parents.

"Hey, son, your timing's perfect."

At sixty Ted Cavanaugh still posed a striking figure, Worth thought. Tall and slender with a thatch of silver hair and blue eyes, his good looks had turned many ladies' heads. But as far as Worth knew, he'd never looked at another woman besides his mother. From all appearances, they seemed to adore each other.

"What's up, Dad?" Worth asked, then let his gaze wander to Olivia's dad who posed an unstriking figure. Blackburn, in his middle sixties, looked his age, sporting a paunch around the middle and deep grooves in his face. But the main reason Worth thought him unattractive was the scowl that rarely left his face.

Even now, when he appeared to be smiling, he wasn't. Yet when he spoke, his voice was pleasant enough. "We're working a deal, young man," he said to Worth. "It concerns you."

Worth paused, shook Peyton's outstretched hand, then patted his dad on the shoulder. "How so?"

Ted smiled a huge smile and was about to speak when Peyton jumped in. "No, let me tell him."

"Suit yourself," Ted exclaimed in an amicable tone.

"Tell me what?" Worth was curious and it showed.

"I've decided to go ahead and deed Olivia that parcel of land that adjoins yours."

Good for Olivia, Worth wanted to say, but didn't. What he did say was, "That's great, but what does that have to do with me?"

Ted and Peyton both looked at each other, then back at him, stunned expressions on their faces.

"What?" Worth pressed, getting more agitated by the moment.

"It's got everything to do with you, son, since you're going to marry Olivia."

Worth felt his jaw go slack.

Eight

"Dad, we need to talk."

Worth knew his blunt words bordered on rudeness, especially since he'd totally ignored Ted Cavanaugh's comment about marriage. But he didn't give a damn. Who he married was none of his parents' business, and he wasn't about to let them think it was—rude or not.

Blackburn shifted as though uncomfortable, then said, "Ah, look, I'll leave you two alone. I know you've got lots to discuss, especially with all this political stuff brewing."

"Thanks for stopping by, buddy," Ted responded absently.

Blackburn tipped the brim of his hat to both men, then spoke to Worth, "You take care, you hear? We'll talk about the land and the race later."

"Thanks, Peyton," Worth said, "we'll keep in touch."

Once he'd driven off, Ted said, "Come on in. Your mother's waiting to see you. I think she's made breakfast."

"Mother cooking?" Worth asked in a light voice, purposely masking the fury that was churning inside him.

"Hannah's on vacation," Ted said by way of explanation. "Anyway, we figured you'd be by, so…"

Worth's father let the rest of the sentence trail off as they made their way inside, straight to the kitchen, where the smell of bacon and sausage put Worth's stomach on edge. His mother was in the process of setting the table. When they entered, Eva looked up and smiled, then walked over and gave Worth a cool peck on the cheek.

Like his father, she didn't look her age, continuing to hold her beauty. Although tall and rather strapping, she had beautiful skin and hair, hair that held its true color, a natural blond. But there was an air about Eva that was also off-putting.

"You're shocked, I know," she said, waving her hand across the bar where an array of food was set.

"You got that right. How long has it been since you've made a meal?"

"I'd rather not say," Eva replied in a coy tone. "If you don't mind, that is."

Although she smiled, Worth noticed it never quite reached her eyes. Suddenly Molly's face rose to the forefront of his mind. When she smiled, every feature lit.

Now where the hell had that come from? Dammit, Molly should be the furthest thing from his mind.

"Get a plate and chow down, son, then we'll talk."

The last thing Worth wanted to do was chow down. After the comment his father had made in front of Blackburn, his stomach remained in no mood to tolerate food, even if it smelled divine. In order not to hurt his mother's feelings, he filled a plate and forced himself to swallow as much as he dared.

A while later, after the plates had been cleared and the cups refilled with freshly brewed coffee, Ted asked, "Did I open my mouth and insert my foot in front of Blackburn?"

Worth didn't pull any punches. "You sure as hell did."

Eva's eyes sprang from one to the other. "What's going on?"

Ted told her what he'd said.

Her eyes drilled her son. "I don't see anything wrong with that. You do intend to marry Olivia, don't you?" She paused, then went on before Worth could answer. "Although I am surprised she doesn't have a ring and that a date hasn't been set."

Worth barely managed to keep a lid on his temper. "Marriage is not in the cards for me," he said, "at least not any time soon." Probably never, he wanted to add, but didn't. No use throwing gasoline on a burning fire.

"And just why not?" Eva pressed in an irritated tone. "To be a more viable candidate for office, you need a suitable wife. And Olivia is certainly that."

That lid was jarring loose. "Don't you think that's my call, Mother?"

"What about the land?" Ted chimed in. "I thought you wanted to increase the size of your herd of horses."

A vein in Worth's neck beat overtime. "I do, Dad."

Had his parents always been this steeped in his business and he just hadn't realized it? If so, perhaps that was because he was an only child, and they doted on him. No excuse. He refused to let them live their lives through him.

"Look, Art and I are trying to figure out a way to utilize the land I already have," Worth explained. "We're not there yet, but we're making headway."

"Why would you do that when more land is being offered on a silver platter?" Eva asked in that same irritated tone.

"Because I'm not ready to marry Olivia."

"If your tone of voice is anything to judge by, you won't ever be."

"That's entirely possible," Worth quipped.

His parents looked at each other, then back at him. But again, it was his mother who spoke. "Is it because *she's* back?"

Here we go again, Worth thought with disgust. Same song, second verse. "No, it's not because Molly's back."

"I just don't understand you, Worth." Eva's tone was as cold as the look she gave him.

He refused to take the bait, so he kept quiet.

Eva's generous lips thinned. "You know we're concerned. You should respect that."

"That's right, son, you're not being fair to us."

Worth stood abruptly. "The fact that Molly has come to see about her mother is none of your business."

Eva's gaze tracked him. "I still can't believe you'd let her back in your house after what she did to you."

This time Worth's lips thinned. "Don't press it, Mother. I told you Molly's off-limits."

He might as well have been talking to the wall for Eva steam-rolled right on, "You never said how long she plans to stay."

"Mother!"

Eva's hand flew to her chest as though terribly offended. "That's a perfectly legitimate concern I would think."

"She's taking her mother's place as my housekeeper." Hell, he might as well drop the bomb now as later, and let the debris fall where it may.

Ted and Eva gasped simultaneously, then they both started talking at once, which turned into a bunch of gibberish.

Worth held up his hand. "Don't say another word, either of you. I've made my decision and it stands."

"As my son," Eva said with a quiver, "I gave you more credit than that."

"Sorry to disappoint."

"I understand she has a child."

Worth shrugged. "So she has a child."

"I can't imagine her with a brat."

That nixed it. Suddenly fury was an invisible malignancy that threatened to devour him. Yet somehow he managed not to throttle his own mother. "His name is Trent."

"Then he's with her." Eva pursed her lips.

"Yes," Worth said in a tired tone.

"You don't still care about her, do you?" Eva asked in a softer, gentler tone as though realizing she pushed as far as she could without completely alienating her son.

"No." Worth's voice was clipped. "If we don't change the subject, I'm out of here. Is that understood?"

Eva sighed as she cast another look at her husband who merely shrugged his shoulders as if to say, what choice do we have.

"So, Dad, do you really think I have a chance to win the Senate seat if I decide to toss my hat into the ring?"

Ted's heretofore glum features returned to life. "You betcha. Dan Elliot has lost his popularity with his constituents, which means you've got a clear shot at taking the nomination, if not the election."

Worth rubbed his chin in an idle fashion. "I guess the next step is to have a gathering of supporters and test the waters."

"Now you're talking, son," Eva put in. "Once you win that Senate seat, perhaps you'll become so addicted you'll keep right on climbing the political ladder."

"Hold on, Mom. I'm not even sure about this race, much less anything else."

"I think a barbecue would do for starters."

Worth thought a moment. "That sounds so trite and typical, but I guess that's still the best way to go."

"You need to get Maxine—" Eva paused midsentence,

then made a face. "Oh, dear, for a moment I forgot she's out of commission."

"Not a problem. I've got it covered."

Eva's mouth looked pinched. "Well, I doubt that Molly's capable—"

"Mother!"

"Sorry," she said, compressing her lips.

Worth knew she wasn't in the least sorry, but nonetheless she had the sense to let the subject drop. Suddenly he felt the urge to get out of his parents' house before he completely blew his temper and said things he'd regret, not that he had any intention of defending Molly because he didn't. Still, it bothered him that they looked on her as someone they had carte blanche to belittle and get by with it.

Since he had no intention of defending her, he had no alternative but to keep his mouth shut. He couldn't have it both ways.

Suddenly Worth felt like he'd stepped in a bed of quicksand and was being sucked under.

"Look, I gotta go," he said, lunging to his feet and heading for the door. Then he turned and said to his mother, "Thanks for breakfast. I'll be in touch."

By the time he reached his truck, he slammed his hand down on the top and cursed a blue streak.

Believe it or not she had been at the ranch a week. Since Maxine still needed her, she intended to stay on a while longer. To her relief, the last few days had passed uneventfully.

Molly had gone about her business of taking care of the household duties. With Trent content and happy, watched by a young lady named Tammy Evans, she was free to do what needed to be done. With Kathy's physical help and Maxine's verbal input, Molly was pleased.

The house was lovely and her mother had apparently taken

great pride in keeping it that way, which made things easy for Molly. In the beginning, she'd been leery of her temporary position. But after the first day, Molly realized she actually enjoyed doing something different.

Working with the public, especially the *ill* public, was a far cry from working with inanimate objects such as dishes and crystal. Cooking was the part she liked least, never having mastered that craft like her mother. But she guessed it didn't matter because Worth apparently hadn't wanted her to cook for him.

It seemed as if they had fallen into a pattern of avoiding each other, which was just fine with Molly. Oh, they passed in the hall and at those particular times, their gazes never failed to meet, then tangle. Most times she couldn't read his response unless his features were pinched in anger.

She knew he continued to resent her presence, but that couldn't be helped, she told herself as she went about slicing some fruit for lunch. But she knew sooner or later, they would have to talk, not only about the house, but about upcoming parties or events.

In fact, word had gotten around that a barbecue for potential political backers was on the horizon. In due time she supposed he would speak to her about that.

Meanwhile, she would continue to divide her time between her chores, her mother and her son, all of which were full-time jobs. However, she wasn't complaining; the setting was too perfect. Not only did she work inside, but she worked outside, as well. If she had a hobby, it was growing plants. And her green thumb was evident, especially at this time of year. The multileveled porch was ablaze with potted plants filled with vibrant fall colors.

Now, as she continued to slice the fruit, Molly gazed through the window into the bright sunlight, admiring her handiwork.

She wondered what Worth thought, or even if he'd noticed the added pots of plants.

"You've done a great job with the porch."

Molly's heart went wild. Was that mental telepathy or what? She swung around and faced Worth who looked like he'd been ridden hard and put up wet. The lines on his face seemed deeper; his hair was disheveled; his jeans, shirt and boots were covered in dust.

"What happened to you?" she blurted out.

"Art and I have been clearing land."

"Must have been some task."

"It was that and more."

"You look exhausted."

"I am. But it's nothing a shower and a glass of tea won't cure."

She immediately crossed to the fridge and opened it.

"You don't have to wait on me, you know?" His voice was low with a moody edge to it.

She looked back at him, then swallowed. "I know, but I don't mind." Before he could say anything else, she latched on to the pitcher of tea, poured him a glass, then held it out to him.

As though careful not to touch her, he took the glass, then without taking his gaze off hers, put it to his lips and took a big gulp. His stare was all consuming.

Molly wanted to look away, but couldn't. She was mesmerized by the unexpected heat in his eyes and the way he smelled—manly—like clean sweat. Suddenly her palms went clammy and her mouth went dry.

Before he realized the impact he had on her, she whirled around, went back to the cabinet, picked up the knife and began cutting more fruit. It was in a split second that it happened.

The knife slipped and instead of slicing the apple, it sliced her. "Oh!" she cried, just as Worth reached her side, grabbed her finger, and squeezed it until the blood stopped.

"Dammit, Molly," he said in ragged voice.

"Why are you yelling at me?" she cried, looking at him only to realize his lips were merely a heartbeat away from hers, his eyes seemingly dark with need.

She knew in that second he intended to kiss her.

Nine

Only he didn't.

Worth swore, then focused his attention back to her finger that he now held under the faucet, rinsing off the blood. Molly looked on in shocked silence—not because she'd injured herself, but because she had wanted him to kiss her. Disappointment washed through her in waves.

No! her conscience cried. That was insane. She never wanted him to touch her. Physical contact of that nature was forbidden and out of the question. Again, keeping her distance was her only method of survival.

And her hand in his was *not* keeping her distance.

"It's okay," she murmured, tugging at her hand, only he wouldn't let go.

He grabbed a paper towel and gently touched the wound.

"Ouch," Molly exclaimed before she thought.

"Sorry." Though Worth's tone was gruff, his touch was

gentle, which made her quiver all over, especially since he continued to examine the wound at close quarters. Much too close.

When he finally raised his head and looked at her, Molly was hit with a sizzle of electricity. For a second the world seemed to tip on its axis. Clearing his throat, Worth moved his head back.

"I think you're going to live," he said in a husky tone.

Molly managed a shaky smile. "You think so?"

A semblance of a smile reached his lips, which warmed her insides even more. God, she couldn't let herself fall under this man's spell again. She couldn't. It was just too painful. He ripped her soul out once already and stomped on it. She couldn't allow him to do it again. If it were just her—maybe she'd go for it. But it wasn't just about her.

Trent.

He was the one she had to think about. With that sobering thought, Molly jerked her hand out of his, which in turn dislodged the tissue, causing the cut to start bleeding again. Without thinking, she stuck that finger in her mouth.

"Don't do that," Worth all but snapped.

She removed her finger and stared at him. "A little blood never hurt anyone."

"I'll get some ointment and a Band-Aid."

"That's okay. It'll eventually stop bleeding."

"Until it does, what are you going to do?"

She couldn't believe they were having this rather inane conversation about a cut that was certainly not serious. A big to-do about nothing, actually. "Ah, good question," she said at last.

"I'll be right back."

After he had gone, Molly wrapped another paper towel around the wound and leaned against the cabinet, realizing her legs suddenly had the consistency of Jell-O.

As promised, Worth returned in record time and without asking, reached for her hand. If he held her hand a bit longer than necessary to administer first aid, they both chose to ignore it.

Maybe that was because Trent came dashing through the door about that time, only to pull up short, his eyes widening on the scene before him. Instantly, Molly reclaimed her hand and stepped a safe distance from Worth.

Trent's eyes went straight to the bandage. "Mommy, did you hurt your hand?"

"Yes, honey, I did, but it's okay."

"Did Worth fix it?"

Molly forced a smile. "He surely did."

"But you're a nurse."

Worth chuckled, which instantly drew her gaze and made her catch her breath. It had been so long since she'd heard him laugh, her body went into meltdown. He was sex personified, and she couldn't stop herself from reacting no matter how hard she tried. If she weren't careful, she'd be drooling, for heaven's sake.

"You'll learn one day," Worth said to Trent, "that nurses and doctors are the worst patients ever."

Trent's eyes got big again. "Really?"

Worth winked at him. "Really."

"Okay, you two, enough," Molly put in, then focused on Trent. "Go wash your hands. Lunch is almost ready."

Trent hesitated, cutting his gaze to Worth. "Will you eat with us?" he asked.

Stunned at her son's bluntness, Molly immediately said, "I'm sure Worth has other plans. I'll—"

"No, I don't, except to wash up a bit."

Silence fell over the room at the same time Molly darted her eyes back to Worth. He returned her gaze with one as innocent as a new born babe's. Damn, she thought, now what?

She had planned to take her mother lunch, and she and Trent would join her while she ate. Worth had certainly usurped those plans. Not necessarily, she told herself. She could say no to Worth, tell him what she'd had in mind. If the truth be known, he was probably wishing he'd kept his mouth shut. Wonder why he hadn't?

"Oh, boy," Trent said, racing for a chair.

"Hey, slow down," Molly reprimanded. "You know not to run in the house. Any house."

"Sorry," he muttered, his eyes on Worth, who once again had something akin to a smile on his face.

Trent smiled back and Molly's stomach did a somersault. For a brief moment the resemblance between father and son was so obvious she could scarcely breathe, anxiety having another field day with her stomach.

"Molly?"

Worth's voice brought her out of her trance. "What?" Even though she answered, she knew she didn't sound like herself.

"Are you all right?"

"I'm fine," she said stiffly, groping to cover her tracks. "Why do you ask?"

Worth's dark eyes narrowed, but then he shrugged, glancing quickly at Trent whose eyes were ping-ponging between them, as if sensing something was going on.

"No reason," Worth finally said, then changing the subject asked, "What's for lunch?"

"Roast sandwiches, chips and fruit."

Worth winked at Trent. "Sounds like a winner to me. How 'bout you, son?"

Son.

Don't call him that, Molly wanted to scream. He's not your son—he's *mine.* All mine, she told herself savagely and desperately, as she looked out the kitchen window into the meadow, the sun creating a beauty that miraculously calmed her fractured nerves.

"Mommy, I'm hungry."

"Ah, sorry, honey. I'm coming."

Worth shoved back his chair and walked toward her. "Tell me what I can do."

"Nothing," she said in an obviously cold tone.

He paused midstride, his eyebrows kicking up and a scowl darkening his features. "Excuse me," he muttered, then pivoted on one foot and made his way back to the table.

Molly released a pent-up breath, knowing that Worth was not used to having someone give him orders. That was his job, and he expected everyone, especially hired help, to hop to it. The long hot days of their summer together taught her that.

However, for some unknown reason, he didn't make an issue out of her bossiness, most likely because Trent was there, which was a good thing. She wasn't in the mood to take any of his high-handedness.

"What do you guys want to drink?" Molly asked, making her tone as pleasant as possible, mostly for her own sake. She had to prove to herself that she could be with Worth and behave like a rational, in-control woman. No matter what, he must not rattle her.

Several minutes later, the goodies were on plates, on the table and the tea glasses filled. Though they ate in silence, Molly was aware of Worth, how much he turned her on and how much he provoked her. A double-edged sword, on which she hopefully wouldn't fall.

She sensed he was aware of her, as well. When she accidentally looked at him, he was watching her with a mixture of desire and anger.

"Mommy, I'm finished."

Thank God for her son's perfect timing. "I made cookies

for dessert," she said in a higher than normal voice. "You want one?"

"Can I have two?"

Molly cocked her head, then smiled. "I guess so, since you were such a good boy and ate all your sandwich."

"Mr. Worth, you want some, too?" Trent asked.

Molly couldn't help but notice that her son looked at Worth like he was a hero. She could understand that. As always, Worth looked the consummate cowboy, dressed in jeans, white shirt, and boots, and hat.

It was at that moment that she regretted letting Trent remain at the ranch. She should have insisted he go to day care, eliminating the chance of Worth and Trent becoming too chummy.

But it was too late to renege and too late for regrets. She'd just have to be sure to keep them apart as much as possible.

"You bet, I do," Worth said. "Who in their right mind would pass up homemade cookies?"

"Especially the ones my mommy makes." Trent grinned. "They're yummy."

"Thanks, sweetie," Molly said. "Before you dig in, why don't you and I take Granna's meal to her?"

"I want to stay here with Mr. Worth."

Worth raised his eyebrows. "Unless you need the help, we'll stay and eat our cookies."

Which was exactly what she didn't want. Since she'd seen the likeness in them, she couldn't bear the idea of leaving them alone together. Yet she couldn't make a scene about it, either. She might possibly raise a red flag, something she still did not want to do.

"That's fine," she muttered, grabbing her mother's tray and making her way out of the room.

Five minutes later she walked back in the kitchen to find

Worth seemingly hanging on every word Trent was saying. Panic almost paralyzed her, but she rebounded, saying to her son, "Hey you, it's your nap time with Granna."

"Aw, Mommy, I don't want to take a nap. I'm too big. Tammy doesn't make me."

"Since Tammy's off today, you're out of luck." Molly gave Trent a pointed look. "So don't start whining."

He made a face, which she ignored. "I'll join you and Granna in a minute, after I clean up the kitchen." Molly paused and ruffled his hair. "First, though, tell Worth bye."

Reluctantly, he did as he was told.

"See ya, fellow," Worth said. "Hey, how would you like to look at some of my horses, say maybe tomorrow?"

"Oh, boy," Trent shouted, his gaze landing on Molly. "Could I, Mommy? Could I?"

It was on the tip of her tongue to say not only no, but hell no. She didn't say either. "We'll see. Okay?"

Trent knew not to argue, but his reply was glum. "Okay."

Once he left, a silence fell over the room. At last, Worth broke it. "Come on, let's get this mess cleaned up."

"I don't need your help," Molly said in a stilted tone, then realizing how she must have sounded, she softened her next words. "But thanks, anyway."

"Suit yourself," Worth almost barked.

She turned her back and went to the sink, thinking he would leave, only to have him say, "When you finish, I'd like to talk to you."

Molly swung around, her breasts rising and falling rapidly. For a millisecond, his gaze honed in on her chest, which created more chaos inside her. "Ah, can't you talk to me now?"

"No. I want your full attention." His tone was thick and low. "I'll be in the sunroom."

The entire time Molly cleaned up the kitchen, dread hung

over her. And panic. Had Trent said or done something that had made Worth suspicious? God, she hoped not. But Worth had sounded so serious she couldn't help but worry.

By the time she joined him, Molly was a bundle of nerves. "So what did you want?" she asked without preamble.

His eyes seemed like black holes as they pinned her, as though her directness pissed him off. "Sit down. Please."

"I'll stand, if you don't mind."

"If you're trying to test my patience, you're doing a damn good job of it."

"Sorry," she whispered, hoping for the best but preparing for the worst.

"I'm sure you've heard that I've been considering having a political rally here. Anyhow, I've decided to have it and I want to do a barbecue."

Feeling slightly shell-shocked, she peered into his face, knowing her eyes would rival the size of silver dollars. "Is that what you wanted to talk to me about?"

"Yes," he said in a clipped tone. "What else?"

"Ah, nothing. I'll take care of it."

"No, you won't."

"Excuse me?"

"I don't want you messing with all that. Hire someone to cater it."

"Why?"

"Because I said to."

They glared at each other.

"That's what I was hired to do."

He laughed without humor, which raised her ire to the next level. "If my mother were still in charge, would you hire an outsider?"

Worth didn't hesitate. "No."

"Point taken, I hope."

Faster than a streak of lightning on a stormy night, Worth crossed the room and grabbed her arm.

The very air around them seemed to have dried up, making speech impossible.

"Did anyone ever tell you you've got a smart mouth?" he asked.

"Let me go," she demanded.

"When I'm ready," he shot back.

Molly parted her lips just in time to collide with his mouth in a raw, wet, hungry kiss that sent her senses reeling. She clung to him for dear life.

Ten

From some foreign place in her mind, Molly heard Worth groan, then the next thing she knew he had shoved her at arm's length. With his breaths coming in shuddering gulps, he stared down at her, a dark, tortured expression on his face.

Molly couldn't move. She couldn't even breathe. Like him, she was too stunned at what had just taken place. Thank goodness, he hadn't abruptly released her, or she would have fallen to her knees. They were weak and trembling just like the rest of her body that still felt the imprint of his lips adhered to hers. To make matters worse, she continued to feel the way he'd pushed into her, making her aware of his hard and urgent mound. To her horror, it had felt so good, she had pressed back.

What on earth had she done? *The unpardonable.*

As though he read her mind, Worth muttered in a low, agonized tone, "I must have lost my mind."

Those cold, harsh words were the catalyst Molly needed

to strengthen her body and her resolve. She jerked herself free and gave him a bitter look. "How do you think I feel?" she flung back in much the same tone.

"Okay, so it was a mistake," Worth responded, his tone bordering on the brutal. "Still, I'm not going to apologize."

Molly laughed, but it, too, was crammed with bitterness. "You apologize? The great Worth Cavanaugh." She laid the sarcasm on so thick a sharp knife wouldn't have cut it. "Why, that thought never crossed my mind, not for one second."

"Dammit, Molly."

"Don't you dare damn me. You're the one who—" She stopped suddenly, hearing her voice—along with her control—crack. She could easily go to pieces right in front of his eyes. As it was, she was barely keeping body and soul together. But she couldn't let him know that. She feared he would use that weakness to his advantage.

After all, he was fighting on his home turf, which definitely gave him the upper hand.

"Kissed me," Worth finally said, finishing the sentence she'd started earlier.

"That's right," she countered with spunk.

"And I don't know why the hell, either."

"I hope you're not asking me."

"Maybe I am."

"You're wasting your time."

"I'm not so sure about that." He paused and their hostile gazes collided. "You damn sure kissed me back."

"That I did," she admitted, then felt heat seep into her face and scorch it. He was right. She had kissed him back. Had she ever, and even though it had been so long, Molly felt like she had just reentered the gates of heaven. But again, she didn't intend to share feelings so personal even she was having trouble digesting them.

She had tried so hard to keep from stepping into this hornets' nest and getting stung, but she had failed miserably. The truth was, she hadn't stepped in; she'd jumped in.

Jamming a hand through his already mussed up hair, Worth stepped further back, though he continued to stare at her under hooded eyes. "Maybe you shouldn't stay here."

Molly panicked, widening her eyes. "Are you kicking me out?"

"I didn't say that," he said tersely.

"Then exactly what did you say?"

"Dammit, Molly."

"That's the second time you've damned me."

He blinked.

"That's right, and I don't like it. It takes two to tango, Worth. So maybe you should stop damning me and take a look in the mirror."

She watched the color drain from his face as he took a step toward her, only to pull up short when Trent came bounding in.

"Mommy."

Her son certainly had a knack for timing, for which she was grateful. Reclaiming her composure was difficult, but she managed to do it. "What, honey?"

"Granna she needs you."

"I'll be right there."

"I'll go back and tell her."

Molly forced her gaze off Worth and onto her son. "No, that's not necessary. I'm on my way."

"Can I stay with Worth?" Trent asked out of the blue.

Worth's eyes darted to hers, a question in them.

"No, Trent," she said in a scolding tone. "You know better than to ask."

She felt Worth's gaze purposely pull at her. "It's okay. I don't mind if he comes with me."

"Well, I do."

"Mommy, please," Trent begged, pulling on her hand.

"I said no, Trent."

His chin began to wobble, but he didn't say anything. Instead, he turned and ran back down the hall.

No doubt about Worth's reaction to the rejection, either. His features were taut as their eyes sparred. "In that case, I'm outta here."

"No, please, wait."

He pulled up and whipped around, his jaw clenched, indicating he was pissed. Well, so was she, but they both had to get over this incident and move on, or else she *would* have to go.

"I'm waiting," he said in a ragged voice.

"We need to talk specifics about the barbecue."

He gave her an incredulous look. "You've got to be kidding me."

She ignored that, and enunciated her words very carefully. "No, I'm not kidding you."

"Look, I really don't give a damn about the particulars." His gaze held her captive. "Especially right now."

"You know," she spat, "you really can be a bastard."

"So I'm told."

"I'm not going to disappear."

He looked taken aback, then recovered. "What does that mean?"

"It means I'm not leaving." Her tone was soft yet her eyes drilled him. "Short of you kicking Trent and me out, that is."

A scowl twisted his features. "You make me sound like some kind of monster."

"No, I believe I said bastard."

He looked like he wanted to strangle her, probably thinking she'd crossed way over the line. Frankly, she didn't care what he thought. Even for Worth, his obnoxious behavior was a bit over the line.

She was about to make another suitable retort when she was interrupted by Trent.

"Mommy! Granna wants you. She says she's all hot."

"Go see about your mother," Worth said brusquely. "Let me know what's going on, and if she needs anything."

"Now, Mommy."

"I'm coming, son."

At the door, Worth turned. "Call if you need me."

Molly's eyebrows rose at the concern she heard in his voice, but didn't say anything.

"Later," he muttered and walked out.

Molly turned and practically ran to her mother's suite, certain something was wrong, making her feel badly about dallying with Worth. Suddenly, she wanted to yell at someone; she didn't care who. She'd known coming back here would be difficult. She just hadn't known how difficult until now, still feeling the brutal, yet hungry imprint of Worth's lips on hers.

What had she done?

"Mom, are you okay?" The instant Molly asked that question upon entering Maxine's room, she knew the answer. Her mother's face was extremely red, like she'd been stung by fire ants.

Without saying anything further, Molly raced into the bathroom, grabbed a rag and wet it with cold water. Then racing back into the room, she bathed her mother's face. Then she folded the cloth and laid it across Maxine's forehead.

On the beside table was a bottle of Tylenol. She grabbed two tablets, then proceeded to give them to her mother.

"Mom, do you hurt anywhere, like your stomach, for instance?"

"No," Maxine responded weakly. "Just tired."

"I'm calling the doctor. He may have to make a house call."

Five minutes later she was off the phone, assured that if Dr. Coleman was needed, he'd be here, but that he thought Maxine had probably just picked up a bug and would be okay in twenty-four hours or so.

Molly's thoughts ran along the same line, but she'd still wanted the doctor's opinion. By the time their conversation ended, Maxine felt less feverish, and she'd fallen asleep. However, Molly did not leave, choosing to remain in the sitting room with Trent in her lap, reading to him.

It was only after her mother's fever broke entirely and she was feeling much better that Molly left with Trent in tow to find Worth. Whether he liked it or not, she was determined to get his input concerning the upcoming barbecue, as well as her mother's. A week was not long to make plans, and her personality didn't lend itself to waiting until the last minute.

Besides, she wanted to make a good impression. Worth was convinced she couldn't do it. She was convinced she could. Another battle of wills. Besides, proving him wrong would certainly buoy her battered spirits.

"Mommy," Trent whispered, "I like Mr. Worth."

"I'm glad."

A moment of silence followed. "Why don't you like him?"

Molly's chest constricted, and she had no comeback.

She was the stubbornest, most hardheaded female he'd ever known. He'd thought Olivia had that top honor, but she couldn't hold a candle to Molly. After all these years, he had never quite figured her out. Maybe that was one of the reasons she still interested him.

"Get a life, Cavanaugh," he muttered savagely, kicking at a clod of dirt with the toe of his boot. He'd made the rounds of the stables, met with Art and was now heading to the new barn. He hated that his other one had burned down, but since it had, he'd built a state-of-the-art one this time.

It was his pride and joy, too. He loved to spend time there, and he loved to show it off. In fact, he would like to live in it. If he were truly a free spirit, he could move in and be perfectly content.

He liked his home, too. After all, he'd designed and built the sprawling ranch house with the help of Art and several subcontractors. But again, there was something unique about the barn. Perhaps that was because it was spacious and smelled of hay and horseflesh.

Whatever the reason, the massive structure—painted red, of course—had become a sanctuary when he needed it. Like now.

It would be a perfect place to have his barbecue. Thinking about that stopped him in his tracks, and he muttered a curse. He'd been excited about entertaining until Molly took over the housekeeping duties.

The thought of her working as a maid still soured his stomach. She should have been his wife, not his housekeeper. Suddenly, he upped his pace, like the seat of his pants was on fire.

By the time he made it to the barn, his heart was pounding unusually hard, though he prided himself on being in great physical shape. Emotionally, though, he was a cripple—thanks to Molly. She apparently still had the power to turn him like a combination lock, thus exposing his emotions so easily.

He gritted his teeth, picked up the nearby pitchfork, and began spreading hay that didn't need spreading. But he needed something to do with the overabundance of energy raging inside him.

He'd lost his mind.

That was the problem. He'd kissed her. Hell, he hadn't just kissed her; his mouth had practically raped hers, especially when he'd felt the lush roundness of her breasts poking his chest. To make matters worse, his hands had dropped to her hips so that she'd feel his arousal, which made it even harder to let her go.

She'd tasted so incredibly good, smelled so incredibly good, felt so incredibly good that he'd lost all perspective, his body wanting a satisfaction it wasn't getting.

Just when he'd realized what he was doing and was about to thrust her away, she had gone limp in his arms, and had begun returning his wet, savage kisses. She'd even gone so far as to entwine her tongue with his.

Yet he'd eventually done what he'd had to do and that was to put her at arm's length. But that small endeavor took every ounce of fortitude he had in him.

Looking back on it now, he didn't know how he'd done it. Without thinking, his eyes dipped south and he let an oath rip. Whenever he thought about her, or she was around, he went hard. Somehow he had to figure out a way to stop this crazy rush of blood to his groin.

Maybe what he needed was Olivia. She could give him what he wanted in the way of sex. But the thought of touching her after Molly was repulsive and not going to happen.

That added to his fury and frustration. How dare she come back into his life, wagging some other man's kid, and tormenting him this way?

How dare *he* let her?

Eleven

"Mom, how are you feeling?"

Her mother tried to sit up. Molly placed a hand on her shoulder and stopped her. "Don't. I'll do the sitting."

"I'm fine."

Molly rolled her eyes. "Yeah, right."

"Don't use that high-handed tone with me, young lady." Maxine's smile took the sting out of her words.

"Yes, ma'am," Molly countered with mock severity at the same time she felt her mother's forehead and it was indeed cool to the touch.

"See, I told you I was fine. My fever's gone."

Molly smiled her relief. "Guess it was just a twenty-four hour bug, after all."

"Where's Trent?" Maxine asked, looking around.

"He's with Tammy, running around outside."

"My, but that boy seems to have taken to this place like ducks to water."

Molly gave Maxine a suspicious look. "Don't let those wheels of your mind turn in that direction."

Maxine huffed, as though insulted. "I don't know what you're talking about."

"Damn straight you do."

"Why, Molly Bailey, I don't recall ever hearing you say that word."

"I don't often." Molly paused for emphasis. "Unless it's called for, or I need to make a point."

Maxine picked at the blanket on the bed. "So what's wrong with me wanting you and Trent closer?"

Feeling like a terrible daughter, Molly clasped Maxine's hand. "Nothing, Mom, nothing at all."

"Then why won't you consider it?"

"Why don't you consider moving to Houston?"

Maxine went stark-eyed. "And leave Worth?"

"Yes, and leave Worth," Molly replied in a pointed tone.

"Why, he…he wouldn't know what to do without me," Maxine stammered, seemingly appalled that Molly would even think such a thing.

"I'm sure Eva and Ted would help him out."

Maxine narrowed her eyes. "My, but you sound bitter. What have they ever done to you?"

"Mom, look, I don't know how this discussion got started, but let's can it, shall we?"

Maxine looked taken aback and Molly sensed she'd probably hurt her mother's feelings, but she couldn't help it. At this point, she was doing well just to survive remaining on the ranch, especially after what had happened yesterday between her and Worth.

Because of that kiss, her heart remained sore to the touch. And to think she'd convinced herself that Worth couldn't cause her any more pain.

Apparently, she still had a lot to learn about herself.

"I didn't mean anything by that, Molly. Since you've been here, you've seemed different. Uptight might be the word I'm searching for."

"Mother—"

Maxine went on as if Molly hadn't spoken. "I know things didn't work out between you and Worth, and I hate that because I thought you two were crazy about each other."

She paused and took a breath. "And maybe things didn't turn out the way you wanted, getting married, then divorced, but that shouldn't have a bearing on your attitude toward Worth and his family. Frankly that puzzles me, because you don't have a mean-spirited bone in your body."

Before she found herself getting further tangled in that bed of thorns, Molly forced a laugh. "My, but you must be feeling better, Mother dear. I've never heard you deliver such a long speech."

"If you weren't grown, girl, I'd turn you over my lap and give you a good spanking."

Molly laughed for real this time and gave her mother a big kiss on the cheek. "I love you, even though you nose around where you don't belong."

"Huh! There you go, insulting me again."

"Oh, Mom, I'm okay. But you and this place have been a bit of a strain on me, I'll admit."

Maxine's features became whimsical for a moment. "I just wish I knew more about what makes you tick. You're my only child, but sometimes I feel like I don't know you at all."

"Mother, enough."

"Please, just let me get this off my chest, okay?"

Molly held her council.

"You were married and divorced, and I never even met the man."

"That's all water under the bridge."

"To you, maybe, but not to me. He was Trent's father, for Pete's sake. And I don't even know him." Maxine's words ended on a wail.

Oh, but you do, Molly wanted to shout.

Instead, she grabbed her mother's hands, squeezed them, then peered closely in her eyes. "You and Trent mean more to me than anything or anyone else. I know I've brought you pain by not explaining everything to you. But one day, I promise I will. I just can't say when."

Maxine's eyes filled with tears as she squeezed Molly's hands even harder. "Until that day, I promise I'll try to keep my mouth shut and not bug you."

Molly grinned. "Bug me. Mmm, that sounds like you've been around your grandson."

"Speaking of my grandson," Maxine injected on a lighter note, "you've done a splendid job raising him."

"The raising's just getting started, actually."

"Well, so far, so good, my child."

"Thanks, Mom," Molly said in a slightly choked voice. "Now that you've mentioned that boy, I'd best go see about him. First though, there's a matter I need to discuss with you."

"Okay."

"Tell me how I go about planning a barbecue without any help from the host."

Maxine threw her head back and laughed. "First off, you don't ask him. He doesn't have a clue."

"I suspected that."

"Nor does he want one."

"I suspected that, too."

Maxine chuckled again, then sobered. "If only this old back would straighten up, I could have everything done in no time at all."

"Sorry, you're stuck working through me."

"Not to worry. We'll make a great team. It'll be a rally people will talk about for a long time."

"The gossip flavor of the month, huh?" Molly said with a twinge of bitter humor.

"That's right, honey."

Molly got off the bed, leaned over and kissed her mother's still cool forehead. I'll check on you later."

"Send Trent to see me."

"Will do."

Trent and Tammy were walking toward the house when Molly walked out the door. Trent ran to her. "Mommy, can we go to the barn?"

"Oh, Trent," she said with exasperation.

"You promised."

"I did no such thing."

"I saw Worth go in there, but Tammy wouldn't let me go."

"Tammy did the right thing."

The young girl smiled her sweet smile, showing off dimples that made a plain face almost pretty.

"Thank you for today, Tammy," Molly said. "We'll see you tomorrow."

"Yes, ma'am." She turned to Trent who was pouting. "See you, buddy."

"I'm not your buddy."

"Trent! Your manners."

"Sorry," he muttered.

Tammy merely smiled again, then strode off.

When Molly turned toward Trent again, he was making a beeline for the barn. Her anger flared. Since coming here, he'd turned into a wild child.

"Trent!" she called. "Stop right where you are."

He did, but ever so reluctantly. When he stared up at her, he had a belligerent look on his face. They were really going to have to sit down and have a talk. She couldn't allow his insubordination to continue unchallenged.

"Mommy, are you mad at me?"

"Yes, I am."

"I'm sorry.

"You should be," she said, catching up with him.

That was when she realized the barn was in sight. She pulled up short. Would Worth still be there?

"I don't wanna go back inside," Trent muttered, sounding down in the mouth.

Molly thought for a long minute instead of just blurting out, *too bad,* which turned out to be her downfall.

Trent grabbed her by the hand, "Please, don't make me."

"All right, you little scoundrel, you win. We'll go see what Worth's up to. Maybe he'll let you rub an animal."

"Oh, boy!" Trent jumped up and down. "Come on, let's hurry."

"Hold on. There's no need for that."

Still, it was an effort to keep up with her son. By the time they covered the remaining distance to the barn, Molly was out of breath. She grasped Trent's hand tighter in hers, stopping him.

He gazed up at her with a question in his eyes. "What?"

"We can't just go barreling in there like we've been invited because we haven't. That's not nice."

"I got invited yesterday," Trent said in his big-boy voice. "'Member, Mommy?"

"Ah, right." Molly paused, then digging for courage, she called out, "Worth, are you in there?"

"Yeah. Come on in."

The second she saw him, Molly stopped in her tracks, thinking how sexy he looked leaning on the pitchfork with several twigs of hay stuck in his hair. Sheer willpower kept her from walking over to him and pulling them out.

Totally unnerved, her body broke out in a cold sweat. She shouldn't have come here, especially not with him watching her with eyes that seemed to seduce her on the spot.

"Wow!" Trent said in awe, looking around.

Molly dragged her gaze off Worth and stared at the premises herself. "I second that wow."

"You like, huh?" Worth asked, clearing his husky voice.

"It's great." She took a chance and looked at him again. The desire had been tempered. Actually, his features were blank. "But what about the old one?"

"It burned."

Her voice transmitted her shock. "Burned?"

"To the ground."

"Aw, man," Trent said.

Her son's comment was lost as her mind slid back to that summer, to the old barn where they made love for the last time. She could tell from the change in Worth's features that he, too, was thinking about that day.

The day she'd gotten pregnant.

Feeling dizzy, she closed her eyes. When she opened them again, Trent and Worth had gone ahead.

After a few moments, Worth paused and turned. "You coming?"

"Where are we going?" she asked in a slightly quivering voice.

He stared at her for a long moment. "To show Trent some of my prize horseflesh."

"Okay."

She followed, but didn't really get into the scene like the two of them. After she'd seen several horses, they all started to look alike, with the exception of their color.

"I'm sorry if we're boring you."

Molly almost visibly jumped at Worth's rather harsh and unexpected voice, definitely taking umbrage to what he said. "I'm not bored."

His eyebrows shot up. "Couldn't have proved it by me."

"Mommy, aren't you having a good time?" Trent chimed in as they made their way back to the main section of the barn, as if sensing the sudden undercurrent that ran between the two adults.

"I'm having a great time, honey. Only it's time we head back to the house. I have to make dinner and you have to get a bath."

"Is your mother all right?" Worth asked, changing the subject.

"She's fine. I guess it was just a twenty-four hour virus."

"Again, anything she needs, you just let me know," Worth said almost fiercely. "Anything."

"Thanks," Molly said, thinking at least he thought a lot of her mother. Too bad… She slam-dunked that thought before it could take a life of its own.

Worth had rejected her, not the other way around. She had to keep that in mind.

"Hey, buddy, that's off-limits."

Worth's louder-than-usual voice jerked Molly back to the moment at hand to find Trent on the first rung of the ladder leading up to the hayloft.

"Trent!"

He froze.

"Don't you dare go a step further," Molly said. "You have no business up there."

Hanging his head, Trent turned around.

Molly grabbed his hand. "Come on, let's go."

When they made it to the door, she forced herself to look back at Worth who was once again leaning on the pitchfork, staring at her with that smirk of his. Ignoring him, she said, "I'm about to make supper. Will you be joining us?"

"Nope."

His gaze looked her up and down, which made her body grow hot. "I suppose you're going out again." God, what made her say that? Even to herself, her tone sounded waspish. And jealous. Dear Lord, what must he be thinking? Probably that she cared about what he did, which couldn't be further from the truth.

His eyes burned into hers. "As a matter of fact, I am."

"Fine," she said in a prim tone, then walked out, silently cursing herself all the way back to the house.

"Ouch, Mommy!" Trent cried. "You're pulling my arm off."

"Be quiet, and keep up," she demanded, her breath coming in spurts.

Twelve

Molly almost wept with relief.

The shindig was in full swing without any glitches. *So far,* she reminded herself, tamping her excitement because things could change in the blink of an eye. The day after the debacle in the barn, Molly had finally pinned down Worth as to a date, time and guest list for the barbecue.

She couldn't have put the trimmings in place, of course, without her mother's help, especially since they'd had only a week to get ready. But that had been enough time since Maxine was a pro at planning last-minute parties.

As promised, she had directed traffic, so to speak, from her domain, as Molly fondly called her mother's suite.

Surprisingly, Maxine's back had improved much quicker than first expected. The brace and physical therapy combined seemed to be doing the trick. Molly was a bit disappointed, however, that Maxine couldn't join the festivities even for a little while. But the doctor had been afraid it might be too exerting, and Molly had agreed.

Now, as she looked around the premises, Molly was astounded at the number of people who had attended, just about everyone who had been invited. Yet Molly had been prepared. Her mother had warned her and she'd listened.

Most of the guests were now gathered on the multilevel porch, laughing and talking. At various points, tables were set up and decorated, awaiting the arrival of plates filled with all kinds of barbecued meat.

A band set up by the pool was doing its thing. The singer, belting out a country western song, had drawn a crowd. Other attendees were eating, drinking and being merry, which was exactly what the Cavanaughs wanted.

The hired help aimed to please.

Then kicking herself for that sarcastic thought, Molly forced her mind onto more pleasant things, such as the beauty that surrounded her. Yes, God had definitely smiled on the day. She looked up and didn't see one cloud in the sky.

Talk about great temperature. One couldn't have asked for better. Cool, but not cold—light jacket weather—perfect for an outside event.

Tammy was watching Trent, freeing Molly to take care of anything that might arise and might keep things from running smoothly. But she didn't mind the hard work. It kept her from thinking about Worth, looking at Worth and wondering about Worth.

Forbidden.

All the above fit into that category for her. Suddenly Molly felt a pang near her heart that she couldn't ignore. Stopping and closing her eyes, she took a deep, shuddering breath. When she opened them Worth was looking straight at her.

For an instant, she stood transfixed. He was leaning against a tree, seemingly totally relaxed, surrounded by several men who were talking non-stop—probably trying to convince him what a great politician he'd make.

She agreed.

As usual, he had on a starched white shirt, black jeans, dress boots and a George Strait Resistol. He was total eye candy, of which she couldn't seem to get enough.

Although she was sure he'd shaved that morning, his chiseled features no longer bore that out. He had the beginnings of a five o'clock shadow, which merely enhanced his sexy good looks.

Her heart began pounding like she'd been hiking a mile straight uphill. He broke loose from the posse and strode toward her, his gaze never wavering.

She wished she had the nerve, no, the willpower, to turn her back and pretend she hadn't seen him. Even though that wasn't going to happen, she nevertheless stiffened her spine, preparing herself for the worst.

The last few times their paths had crossed the exchanges between them hadn't been pleasant—anything but, actually.

It seemed as though every time he saw her, he was in an angry mood. Yet he looked at her with anything but anger. Desire and fire often lit his eyes, which kept her on edge. Despite the fact that he despised her, he wanted her. He didn't try to hide that. She suspected that was what kept his anger boiling.

She was sure today was no exception. By the time Worth reached her, his features looked like they were carved out of stone, though his tone was surprisingly soft. "Have you sat down at all?"

"No, but then, I'm not supposed to."

"Hogwash."

Her eyes widened.

He leaned in closer, which called attention to his cologne.

God, he smelled so good. For a moment, Molly's head spun, and she wanted to rest her head against his chest and say to hell with everything and everybody. Then reality hit her in the face, and she literally jumped back.

A dark frown covered Worth's features. "For heaven's sake, I'm not going to touch you."

"I know that," she snapped, crossing her hands over her short pink jacket that barely topped the waist of her low cut jeweled jeans. In doing that, she knew she'd slightly bared her waist as her white camisole underneath was also short. Even when Worth's eyes dropped there, and she saw desire heat his dark eyes, she made no effort to lower her arms.

"Then why did you jump?" His muttered question was spoken in a guttural tone.

"Does it matter?" she asked, thinking she should be ashamed of herself for purposely allowing him to see her naked flesh, knowing what it would do to him. What was happening to her? Once aroused, Worth was like a lighted stick of dynamite; he could go off at any moment.

Instead of that frightening her, it excited her.

As if he could read her thoughts, he stepped closer and whispered, "You'd best be careful how you look at me."

Color flooded Molly's face and she turned away, but not before saying, "Ah, I'd best get back to work."

"I want to talk to you."

She whipped back around, careful her facade was back in place and asked, "What about?"

"To tell you what a great job you've done on such short notice."

"Is that a thank-you?"

"You betcha."

His praise took her so by surprise that her mouth flew open. Her reaction brought an unexpected smile to his lips, which made her heart beat that much harder. It had been a long time since he'd smiled—or at least at her. It seemed as if the sun had broken through a dark cloud.

She smiled back.

He rolled his eyes, though his smile widened. "You're a piece of work, Molly Whoever."

She almost giggled at his unwillingness to say her last name, then caught herself, especially when their gazes tangled and held, while sexual tension danced all around them. For a breathless moment, he looked as if he might actually grab her and kiss her again.

She'd like nothing better.

Appalled anew at her thoughts, Molly shook her head at the same time he shook his, putting everything back on an even keel. "I'm glad everything's going well."

"That's because of you."

"And Mother."

"Of course."

For another moment silence surrounded them.

"I want you to sit down, even have a beer."

"Why, Worth Cavanaugh," she said in her most southern drawl, "you know that wouldn't be good 'cause I can't handle spirits all that well."

He threw back his head and laughed. "Don't I know that. The drunkest I've ever seen you was that night—"

As though he realized what he'd said and where this conversation was headed he broke off abruptly, a scowl replacing the laughter. "Dammit, Molly," he said in a savage tone, "you almost ruined my life."

She gave back as good as she got. "And you almost ruined mine."

Another silence.

"Hey, Cavanaugh, get over here. Rip wants to talk to you."

The moment was severed, never to be repaired. Without looking at her again, Worth turned and walked away. Thank God, a table was near by so she could sink onto the bench, or she might have sunk to her knees. Every bone in her body was quivering.

Every nerve.

Molly couldn't let him paralyze her. Wouldn't let him do that to her. The best antidote for her heavy heart was a dose of her child. Trent had a way of putting things back in perspective. Molly was well on her way to finding her son when she almost ran head-on into Eva and Ted Cavanaugh.

"Oh," she said in a faltering tone, quickly moving back. "Sorry."

Though Molly hadn't seen them since her return to the ranch—she'd purposely kept her distance at the barbecue, too—she knew sooner or later her luck would run out. The inevitable had happened. After her encounter with Worth, meeting them face-to-face couldn't have come at a worse possible time.

With them, there was no good time, she thought, feeling a pinch.

The intervening years had been kind to Eva. Oh, she was maybe a bit heavier and had a few gray hairs now mixed in with the blond, but amazingly her face remained virtually unlined. She still carried her large frame with the same confidence as always.

Aging had also been kind to Ted. He was still tall and good-looking, especially dressed in jeans and boots. She couldn't tell if he was losing his hair since he had on a Stetson.

"Hello, Molly," Eva said in her usual haughty tone, which had always irked Molly and still did.

Ted chimed in, "Yeah, Molly, it's good to see you."

Maybe he had a little too much enthusiasm in his voice to

suit Eva because she shot him one of *those* famous Eva looks, indicating he had done something to displease her. Molly knew that when it came to her just being on planet Earth was displeasing to Eva.

Once she had cared. Now she didn't. And the *didn't* felt damn good.

"I hope you two are well," Molly said out of politeness more than anything else.

Eva inclined her head and ran the tip of her tongue across her lower lip. "Do you really care how we are?"

No. As far as I'm concerned, you can butt a stump and die. Molly smiled her sweetest smile. "Of course."

"How much longer do you intend to stay here?"

"As long as it takes."

"For what?"

Eva knew, so Molly wasn't about to indulge her. Now that she was older and wiser and knew the vicious games these two played, she was not about to take a ticket. When the situation called for it, Molly could be a bitch, as well.

"Her mother, Eva," Ted put in, apparently embarrassed by his wife's open hostility.

"By the way, how is Maxine?" Eva asked, though her tone was devoid of empathy.

"You know very well how she is," Molly said without mincing words. "I'm sure Worth keeps you informed."

"Actually," Ted said, "we don't see that much of our son."

Although Molly was shocked at that disclosure, she didn't let it show. Besides, she felt a tad sorry for the elder Cavanaugh. When he was not with his wife, he was a nice man. That summer he'd treated her with dignity and respect until—

"I'm talking to you, Molly."

Molly clenched her hands to her side to keep from slapping both of Eva's cheeks. She was the rudest person she'd ever known and Molly would be damned if she apologized for woolgathering. "What did you say, Eva?"

"I said you're not wanted here."

"Eva!" Ted exclaimed, giving her a hard look. "Now's not the time for this kind of conversation."

"That's all right, Ted, I don't mind." Molly forced a smile. "Eva should feel free to say what she wants."

Eva laughed though it fell far short of humor. "Mmm, not the same cowed young girl you used to be, huh?"

"That's right."

Eva leaned in closer, her features hard. "Make no mistake, honey. You're no match for me and never will be."

"That thought never crossed my mind," Molly drawled in her sweetest tone yet.

Ted pulled on Eva's arm and said between his teeth, "Let it go, dammit."

Whipping her face around to her husband, Eva said, "If you don't like what I'm saying, you can leave." Her glare harshened. "But you ought to be right in here with me. For our son's sake, if nothing else."

"Eva," he said again with considerably less confidence, as though he knew he was fighting a bear using only a switch.

"It's all right, Ted." Molly gave him a real but halfhearted smile. "I'm no longer that young, stupid girl I once was. I can take care of myself."

"Molly, I'm sorry."

"Don't you dare apologize to her," Eva flung at him viciously. Ted merely held up his hands, then stepped aside.

She'd had enough of Eva Cavanaugh, too, and was close to telling her so. Only her mother and her condition kept her quiet. She didn't think Worth would take any rash action like asking her, Molly, to leave, but when it came to his parents, she wasn't sure. That summer had taught her how much he depended on his parents and how much influence they had on him.

"Molly, one more thing."

"I'm listening, Eva," she said calmly, knowing that would get Eva more than anything else.

"I'm sure you know that Olivia and Worth are soon to be married."

"Not to worry, Eva." Molly smiled. "She's welcome to him. They'll make a perfect couple."

With that she walked off.

Thirteen

The party was winding down and for that Molly was grateful. She knew it had been a smashing success, if the mood of the guests was anything to judge by. Everyone seemed to have had their fill of the best barbecue in east Texas and all the booze they could want.

And the hottest band in the county was still playing.

The guests who remained behind were the really happy campers; her instincts told her they had talked Worth into finally throwing his hat into the political ring. Of course, she didn't know that for sure, not being privy to that information.

The way John Lipscomb, Worth's wannabe campaign manager, was slapping Worth on the back was the best indication that changes were in the works.

Molly still felt like Worth would make a good politician, not that her opinion mattered; it didn't. Still, after musing about it, she sensed he'd make a good one. He was such a take-charge person, one who made decisions and stuck to them. Honesty was another *must* quality. Despite his having been less than honest with her, she felt that didn't apply to his day-to-day dealings. In her book, a politician should have those assets and more.

A sigh split Molly's lips as she looked over the grounds and spotted a table with leftover debris scattered over it. She had just taken steps in that direction when a hand caught her arm.

Knowing that touch above all else, her heart lurched and she swung around to face Worth.

"How 'bout a dance?"

For a split second, shock rendered her speechless, then she stammered, "I...I don't think so."

"Why not?" Worth held on tightly, staring at her out of naked eyes.

"It wouldn't be appropriate," she whispered, feeling her insides go loose.

"Baloney."

"Worth."

"If you don't dance with me, it's because you don't want to."

"I—"

He didn't bother to let her finish the sentence. He grabbed her, pulled her close and they began to do the Texas two-step in perfect unison, which wasn't surprising. That summer they had danced many a time together, and Molly had reveled in each step. Perhaps that was because she was in his arms where she had longed to be.

Now, she'd just gotten into the beat of the music when the song abruptly ended.

"Damn," Worth muttered.

She wanted to mutter hallelujah, knowing they were being watched by the remaining guests, his parents and his lover. Not a good thing.

"Look, I need to get back to work."

"You know how that pisses me off."

"What?" she asked innocently.

"Telling me you have to work when you don't."

"Go ask Olivia to dance," Molly said in a weary tone, gently moving out of his arms, then she hurried to the table where the centerpiece was just short of becoming airborne. She had the object in hand when she felt the hairs on the back of her neck stand on end. Someone was behind her.

She whirled around and stared into the lovely face of a strange woman.

"I'm Olivia Blackburn," she said bluntly.

Molly schooled herself to show none of the myriad of emotions that charged through her. God, what had she done to deserve attention from both Worth's parents and his girl in one afternoon?

"Hello, Olivia," she said with forced politeness, having to admit that the woman was lovely in the truest sense of the word. Her hair was red with blond highlights, and her eyes were blue—a rare combination—but a stunning one, nonetheless. And she had a figure to die for. Though short and trim, she had oversized breasts that emphasized her tiny waist.

She would be just the right person on Worth's arm when he did his political thing.

"If you don't mind, we'll dispense with the pleasantries," Olivia said into the heavy silence, her tone nasty.

Molly took offense, but she kept her mouth shut. If Olivia had something else to say, then so be it. She couldn't care less, one way or the other.

"I know why you've come back."

Molly shrugged. "Good for you."

"You're fooling no one. It's for Worth."

"Oh, please," Molly exclaimed in disgust.

"When you two were dancing, I saw how you looked at him."

"Then you saw wrong."

"No way." Olivia's tone now reeked of sarcasm.

Molly sugar-coated her smile, then said, "Surely you noticed, he's the one who pulled me onto the dance floor."

That blunt statement seemed to rob Olivia of words, but only for a second. She rebounded with the force of an alley cat fighting for survival. "You're not wanted here."

"Trust me, I wouldn't be here, if I had a choice."

"Oh, I know you're saying you came back because of your mother, but I know better."

"Really, now." Molly made her tone as insulting as possible, plus she plastered on a fake smile, both of which seemed to spark Olivia's eyes.

"You're nothing but a slut, Molly Stewart, or whatever the hell your name is, and you'll never be otherwise."

"Now that you've gotten that off your chest, is there anything else?" Molly was determined to keep her voice stone-cold even. She wasn't about to let this vindictive witch rattle her cage.

Only she had, Molly admitted silently, feeling perilously close to tears and hating herself for it.

"As a matter of fact there is. Worth is mine, and I intend to marry him."

"Good for you."

Olivia smiled an evil smile. "You're not fooling me. You'll never get Worth back, so you might as well pack your bags, get your brat and leave town."

"Stop it!"

Olivia blinked, clearly taken aback by Molly's sharp tone and words. "Despite what you think, you're no better than me. As for my son, you leave him out of this." Molly took a heaving breath, then hammered on, "As for Worth, you're welcome to him." She paused again. "To my spoils, that is."

Olivia gasped while her hand flew to her chest as though she might be having a heart attack. While Molly didn't wish that, she was glad she'd pierced Olivia's hard heart with an arrow much the same as Olivia had pierced hers.

Olivia's recovery was quick. Stepping closer to Molly, she hissed, "No one talks to me like that and gets away with it. Trust me, you'll pay."

Molly didn't bother to respond. Instead, she whipped around and walked off, not even aware of where she was going until she reached the cool, shadowed barn. For a second, she was tempted to crawl into the loft and sob until she couldn't sob any more. But giving in to her heartache would only make her feel worse.

Suddenly she felt trapped, wanting to flee Sky, Texas so badly her stomach roiled. Leaning against a post, she surrendered to her pain, letting the tears flow.

"Are you okay?"

Fear froze her insides, especially when she realized her intruder was none other than Worth himself. After those rounds with his parents and his woman, *he* was the last person she wanted to see, especially since her face was saturated with tears.

Would this nightmare ever end?

Before she faced him, she dabbed with a tissue she fished out of her pocket. Maybe in the shadows, he wouldn't be able to tell she'd been crying.

Wrong.

"You're not okay," he said more to himself than to her, as he made his way further into the barn.

Panicked that he wouldn't stop until he was within touching distance of her, which she couldn't handle, Molly turned with her arms outstretched. "Don't."

Worth stopped instantly, though she knew taking orders from her, or anyone, went against his grain. Too bad. She'd had it with the entire Cavanaugh clan.

"Leave me alone, Worth," she said in a low voice, feeling drained to the core.

"No."

"No?"

"You heard me."

"I can't take any more," she said, hearing the crack in her voice and knowing he did, too.

He took two long steps, which put him within a hairs-breadth of her. However, he refrained from touching her.

"I know what's going down."

"I don't think you do."

"I'm not blind, Molly."

"It doesn't matter," she countered in a resigned tone.

"Mother and Dad cornered you." A flat statement of fact.

"I don't want to talk about it."

"Well, I do," he said flatly.

Silence.

"What did they say, dammit?"

Anger suddenly flared inside her. "In a nutshell, I should get lost."

He muttered some of the foulest words Molly had heard in a long time. "They don't speak for me."

"Couldn't prove that by me."

Ignoring that shot, he went on, "I also saw Olivia talking to you."

"She also told me to get lost, that you belonged to her."

Another string of curses flew out of his mouth, then he said, "Contrary to what she said, there's no wedding in the offing."

"Maybe there should be. She'll make the perfect politician's wife—all show and no do."

That muscle in his jaw jerked, indicating that he hadn't liked her remark, but he didn't respond.

"I need to go," she whispered, feeling more drained by the moment.

"Despite what you think, they—Mother, Daddy, Olivia—don't speak for me."

"Like hell they don't," she said, whipping her head back and glowering at him. "From the outside looking in, it appears the monkeys run the zoo, not the zookeeper."

"Damn you, Molly." His nostrils flaring, he grasped her by the arms, hauled her against his chest and peered into her eyes.

"I told you not to touch me." Her teeth were clenched so tightly her jaw throbbed.

"Not in those words, you didn't."

"Then I'm telling you now."

"What if I like touching you?"

She struggled. "Let me go."

"No."

"Worth." Her voice broke.

"Worth what?" His also broke.

"This is crazy."

She swore she could see the blood heat up in his eyes as they held hers captive. "God, Molly, I can't think of anything but you."

"Stop it, please," she pleaded, fearing not so much what he would do but what she would do. Right now, she needed to be held and loved, having been battered and beat up since the moment she'd arrived.

Kindness towards her now would surely be her undoing. It would lead to the one thing she could only dream of, but never have.

Him.

"I can't," he whispered, his agony evident.

Then he did what Molly most feared. He sank his lips onto hers in what was a hot, savage kiss that seemed to rip her soul out of its socket. At first, she fought him, then when his tongue warred with hers, she lost all will and gave in.

As the kiss deepened, their bodies went slack until their knees met the floor of the barn. That was when she felt him reach under her camisole and cover a breast. She moaned and without thinking, dropped her hand to his zipper, feeling him enlarge under her hand.

"I want you," he muttered. "I have to have you. Now." It was when he began to unbutton her jeans that she came to her senses, crying out. "No. I can't do this."

One hard push was all it took for him to lose his balance and fall backward. That was all she needed to scramble to her feet and flee from the barn, his string of curse words following her.

She placed her hands over her ears and ran for dear life.

Fourteen

"Well, son, are you, or aren't you?"

Worth rubbed his stubbled chin. He had gotten up and come to his parents' place before he'd showered and shaved. He'd at least taken time to brush his teeth.

"How 'bout a cup of coffee first?" Worth asked, continuing to massage his prickly chin.

"Eva is the coffee brewed?" Ted called out from his place at the breakfast room table.

"Coming."

Worth still didn't know what the rush had been about to get over to his parents' ranch. His mother had called earlier and said they wanted to talk to him over coffee ASAP. He'd just rolled out of bed, bleary-eyed from having drunk too much the night before, trying to forget Molly was down the hall and that he wanted her more than he'd ever wanted anything in his life.

Yet, she was off limits to him.

Someone who gave her word then went back on it was something he couldn't get past or tolerate. Besides, he believed in the old adage that you can never go back and pick up where you left off. It almost never worked.

However, that didn't stop him from craving the pleasure of Molly's company in his bed. He nursed one particular whisker on his chin, letting his imagination run wild. If she were willing to have sex with him, what would it hurt? A good lay for old times' sake?

Wonder what Molly would think about that? He knew. She'd tell him to go straight to hell in a handbasket, and he wouldn't blame her. After all, he hadn't exactly made her stay at the ranch a bed of roses. In fact, he'd been a thorn in her side at almost every turn.

But dammit, she'd deserved it, he kept telling himself. Still, that didn't absolve his conscience, and he didn't like that. Guilt was not even a word in his vocabulary, and he wasn't about to add it now.

"Ah, thanks, Mom," he said, peering up when Eva set steaming mugs of coffee in front of him and his dad.

"Hannah made some scones and blueberry tarts, your favorites." Eva smiled as she leaned down and grazed her son's cheek. "I'm warming them even as I speak."

Worth shook his head with a frown. "Ah, Mom, thanks, but I'm not hungry."

"Sure you are," she said. "Or at least you will be when you smell them. I think they are Hannah's best efforts yet." She paused and smiled her confident smile. "And Lord knows she aims to please you. Above all."

If only his mother would stop her prattle. If not, Worth wasn't sure he could hang in for very much longer. His head was hurting like someone was beating on it with a jackhammer and his stomach was pitching. If he choked down even a morsel of food, and it stayed down, it'd be a bloody miracle.

But how could he tell his parents he'd gotten dog drunk because he wanted to sleep with a woman who had betrayed him, and whom they held in such contempt? He wouldn't, mainly because it was none of their damn business.

"So tell us what you're thinking."

"Yeah, right," Worth mumbled into his mug.

Eva's eagle eyes honed in on him, before saying bluntly, "You look dreadful."

He put his cup down and peered up at her. "Thanks."

"Well, you do."

"Thanks again." Sarcasm lowered Worth's voice.

"Don't play dumb, Worth," Eva said in a scolding tone.

He rolled his eyes. "Let it go, Mother. I'm not in the mood."

"When are you ever in the mood?"

"What the hell does that mean?"

Ted waved his hands. "Hey, you two, time-out. We're a family who's supposed to be civil, right?"

"I'm going after the goodies," Eva said, exasperation evident in her tone.

"Don't pay any attention to your mother," Ted said, his features scrunched in a frown. "She's obviously in one of her moods. It'll pass."

"It had better," Worth countered without mincing words. "I don't like her in my face, Dad."

Ted's lean face drained of color. "I know, son. Just bear with her. She only wants the best for you, and she thinks that's in politics."

"What if I don't agree?" Worth asked.

Eva walked back into the room and placed a plate of piping hot goodies in the middle of the table. Worth swallowed hard and tried not to look at them. Even the smell turned his stomach, but he decided to keep that to himself. Maybe later, he'd try a bite or two, to keep his mother off his back, if for no other reason.

"Want me to help your plate?" Eva asked with a smile, certain she'd won her son over.

"Not right now," Worth responded. "I'm still enjoying my coffee." Which was a lie. Right now, all he wanted was to go back to his ranch, shower and hit the sack.

"So back to what I asked earlier, son, have you made up your mind?"

Worth heard the anxious note in his father's voice and sighed. His mother, for the first time was quiet, as if holding her breath until he answered. "Nope."

Both gave him a stunned look.

"I can't believe you're still dallying," Eva said, anger deepening her voice. "Even though the rally was only yesterday, you still should make a decision."

"It's not that easy. For me it's a huge decision and a huge commitment."

"Why should that bother you now?" Ted asked, his brows drawn together in a frown. "You've never backed down from a challenge yet."

"You know my heart's really in expanding my horse business," Worth pointed out. "Both would be a bit much to tackle at the same time."

Eva flapped her hand. "The chance to breed horses will always be there. Your political chances won't."

"I'm well aware of that, Mother."

Eva's face took on a pinched look. "Are you also aware that if you don't hurry up and marry Olivia you might lose her?"

That was the straw that broke the camel's back. Worth lunged out of his chair, which caused his parents to jump. "I'm not marrying Olivia."

His mother's hand flew to her throat. "What?"

"You heard me."

"Not ever?" Eva asked, her voice coming out in a squeak.

"Not ever," Worth responded in a tired voice.

Silence filled the room for a moment while Eva and Ted stared at each other, their faces registering perplexity and dismay.

"It's her, isn't it?" Eva asked in an acid-filled tone.

Worth folded his arms across his chest. "I don't know what you're talking about."

"Like hell you don't."

"Eva," Ted said, glaring at his wife.

"Well, it's the truth. He hasn't been the same since Molly came back."

"Leave Molly out of this." Worth's tone brooked no argument. "And while we're on that subject, stay away from her. I know both you and Olivia took your shots at her at the barbecue." Worth transferred his gaze to his dad. "That goes for you, too."

Ted flushed while Eva ground her teeth together.

Finally Eva said, "We have every right—"

Worth cut her off. "You don't have any rights when it comes to speaking for me. Neither does Olivia."

"Worth, you're upsetting me," Eva said, "making me fear things that I shouldn't have to fear."

"If it has to do with Molly, you can stand down. Trust me, she hates me and can't wait to leave here."

Eva released a huge breath. "Thank God for small favors."

Worth drained his cup and put it down. "Thanks for the coffee."

"You mean you're leaving?" Eva demanded, wide-eyed.

"That's right. I'll talk to you later. Meanwhile, try to stay out of my life."

He didn't turn back around, but he knew both their mouths were gaped open.

* * *

Molly tiptoed into her mother's room that same afternoon and saw that Maxine was sleeping. She stood by the bed for a second and peered down at Maxine, feeling herself smile. Her mother was definitely on the mend.

The shots the doctor was injecting into her back had worked wonders. Of course, Maxine hadn't been released to do any housework yet. However, her mother was up and walking, alternating between a walker and a cane, which was a praise. It wouldn't be long now until Molly and Trent could leave.

Thinking of her son sent her to the window where she peered outside. She expected to see Tammy and Trent playing, and she did. What she didn't expect to see was Worth.

Only there he was. With them.

He was dressed in old jeans riding low on his hips, hugging his powerful legs and an old cutoff T-shirt that exposed his washboard belly and his navel. In truth, he was a gorgeous specimen.

And the effect on her was galvanizing as she watched the scene play out before her. Worth had brought a colt from the stable and was letting Trent rub on it. But it was Worth on whom she was concentrating.

As soon as possible, she had to get out of this house, out of *his* life for good, which meant she never intended to set foot on this ranch again. Her mother would just have to come and visit her.

Deciding the panacea to her tormented thoughts was work, she turned her back on the window. When called for, Molly could be a lean, mean, cleaning machine. Today was one of those days. Cleaning things, polishing things, making things sparkle not only occupied her mind, but her hands, as well.

Molly had just changed into some grungy jeans, and a T-shirt without benefit of a bra to encumber her efforts. She had pretty much cleaned the downstairs yesterday until it glowed. She felt the upstairs was entitled to the same treatment.

Suddenly, Molly paused in her thoughts, wondering if Worth had decided to run for office, or not. Of course, she would be the last to know unless he confided in her mother, which was possible.

She was delighted Worth and Maxine had such a good rapport. When the time came for her to leave, it would be with a clear conscience, knowing Worth would never let her mother want for anything.

Worth didn't like many people, but to the ones he did, he was loyal to a fault. She was grateful Maxine fit into the latter category.

She just wished she did.

"Can it," she spat out loud, then cut her gaze to the bed to see if her outburst had awakened Maxine. It hadn't. She turned then and went back to her room. The instant she walked in, her cell phone rang.

Surprised but glad at the caller, Molly said with enthusiasm, "Why, hello, Dr. Nutting."

"Hey, kiddo."

His familiarity was just the balm she needed for her battered senses. While he was the consummate elderly doctor in looks, with a thatch of white hair, delving blue eyes and an ever-ready smile, that wasn't his only claim to fame. He was one of the best and most renown doctors in the south, especially when it came to cardiology.

She'd been thrilled and honored when he'd chosen her as his head nurse. Now that he was willing to send her to school to become a physician's assistant, she was humbled and even more eager to please.

"I'm so glad to hear from you, Doctor."

"Same here, young lady." He paused. "So how are things?"

Molly gave him a quick rundown of her mother's condition.

"Ah, so you may be returning sooner rather than later."

"Sounds like you miss me," Molly said in a teasing tone.

"You have no idea. I've come to depend on you too much, I think."

Instantly Molly felt a bout of homesickness come over her. "Is everything going okay? I hope my absence hasn't created undo hardship in the office."

"Nah, but it'll be good to have you back."

"It won't be long now, I promise. I'll keep you posted."

Dr. Nutting chuckled. "I guess I just wanted to hear your voice and hear you say that. Now, I'm feeling much better."

"Me, too," Molly said with a smile and tears on her cheeks. "Thanks for calling. I'll be in touch."

Once the cell was flipped closed, Molly wiped her face, dashed to the laundry room, grabbed her tray of cleaning supplies and headed to Worth's room. Usually, Kathy maintained his space, but since Kathy was off ill and had been since the barbecue, Molly felt she had no choice but to tackle it herself.

Besides, it was a wreck. She'd passed his room earlier, paused and took a quick look inside, having no idea what possessed her to do such a thing. Maybe it was because Worth's bed was a mess, like he'd wrestled with a bear and lost.

Whatever, the room needed attention, and she was the only one available. With her Sony Walkman attached to her jeans and her earplugs in, she cleaned his bedroom proper, then moved to the bathroom.

After everything was shining there, with the exception of the shower, she stepped into it and began scrubbing. Although she didn't get wet, she came close to it, her T-shirt anyway. It got damp and, therefore, clung to her breasts like a second skin.

After finishing that job, she removed her ear plugs just in

time to hear a sound, a sound she couldn't identify, though she panicked. Surely it wasn't Worth having come back in. She was positive she'd be in and out of his room before that happened.

Brightening, she told herself she was just hearing things. Still, Molly didn't see any reason to tarry any longer. That was when she opened the door and stepped out, only to freeze in horror.

"You."

She wasn't sure if she spoke the word out loud or not, so shocked was she to see him naked as the day he was born, standing in front of her, staring at her with fire leaping from his widened eyes.

For a moment, they both just stared, him at her breasts with their rosebud nipples thrusting forward and her at his huge, beautiful, growing erection.

"Molly," he said in a voice that sounded like he'd been gutted, then he reached for her.

But she was too fast for him. Before he realized what was happening, she turned and ran out of the room.

"Molly!"

She ignored the plaintive cry she heard in his voice and kept on running. *Out of harm's way.*

Fifteen

Out of sight; out of mind.

She wished.

Worth had been gone for three days, and the thought of seeing him when he returned gave Molly the weak trembles. Realistically, there was no way to avoid the inevitable, and she knew it. He'd at least told Maxine he was going to Dallas to look at some horses. She hadn't expected him to tell her, of course, nor was she complaining. The less she had to do with Worth, the better.

Still, she found herself jumping when she heard a door open or close, which was ludicrous. On this ranch, someone was coming or going all the time.

But she knew from past experience she would look up, turn a corner or walk into a room and there he'd be.

In the glory of his magnificent manhood.

Only clothed, she prayed.

Whenever she thought about that encounter in his bath, she almost lost it. Her breathing turned labored, her limbs trembled and her mind spun.

None of which was good. Or sane.

In fact, since that incident she'd been a basket case. Oh, she'd done what she was supposed to do, probably to perfection because she was so determined to concentrate. She'd taken care of the house, her son and her mother. Yet she'd felt as if it were someone else doing those things—as if she existed outside herself.

Right now Molly found herself pausing and leaning against the cabinet for support, feeling slightly dizzy. Stress. That was all it was. She was under so much pressure that she felt her insides might explode at any second, which was horribly unfair to her son and to her mother.

She had let Worth get under her skin. *Again.*

The sight of him naked had made her crazy with an aching need that wouldn't go away. Although she knew it was wrong to want him to make love to her, she couldn't control her mind. It seemed to have taken on a life of its own.

She didn't know what to do; that was the problem. The more she was around the ranch, the more under Worth's spell she fell. She couldn't leave. Not yet. But soon.

Meanwhile, she would continue to remind herself what Worth had done to her, how he had ripped her heart out and trampled on it. Now that she had Trent, she couldn't dare let that happen again. Even though he had denied it, she felt sure he would eventually marry Olivia. And she was yearning to make love to him.

What kind of woman had she become?

Since she couldn't bear to answer that question, Molly went back to polishing the piece of silver. She was just about finished when Trent rushed into the room.

"Mommy, Mommy!"

"What, darling?"

"Mr. Worth's back."

Molly's heart took a dive, though she kept her tone even and cool. "That's great, honey."

"He wants to take me riding."

Molly panicked. "Oh, Trent, I don't think that's a good idea."

He scrunched up his face.

"You've never ridden a horse, and Mommy's afraid."

"I'm not," he responded with belligerence. "I'm a big boy. You're always telling me that."

"You are a big boy."

His eyes brightened. "Oh goodie, I can go."

"Whoa, cowboy. I didn't say that."

"Mommy! You're being mean."

"Trent," she responded in a stern tone.

"What's going on?"

If she hadn't had such a tight grip on the piece of silver, she would have dropped it at the sound of Worth's voice. The time she'd been dreading had come. He was back, and as suspected, in full sexual glory, sending little tremors of shock to her chest.

"Mommy says I can't go," Trent said to Worth, his lower lip twice its normal size.

"I—" she began.

"I won't let anything happen to him, Molly."

She didn't want to look at Worth, especially with him standing in front of her, staring at her through eyes that were thankfully unreadable. She just hoped she could do the same thing. She'd rather die than to have him know she'd been thinking about how awesome he'd looked naked.

"Molly."

Feeling like her face had just caught on fire, she drew a ragged breath then forced herself to meet his gaze.

"I said I'd take care of him." While his voice had a gruff edge to it, his eyes didn't. They seemed to have suddenly ignited with heat that told her he wasn't as cool and in control as he appeared, that he, too, was remembering the episode in the shower.

And what could have happened, but didn't.

"I just don't think—" Molly's voice played out under that hot, probing gaze.

"Pease, Mommy," Trent begged.

"Oh, all right. Just don't keep him out long, Worth."

"Your wish is my command."

The old sarcastic Worth was back, but she ignored that and added, "I mean it." She knew she sounded unreasonably controlling, but she didn't care. The thought of the two of them alone was like a knife turning in her heart.

But why punish her child for her sins? She couldn't. Besides, she would be leaving soon, and she wouldn't have to worry about those unexpected twists and turns.

"Yippee!" Trent cried, zipping around and running toward the door.

Before Worth followed, a smile almost broke through his tight lips. "I'd say he's excited."

Molly wanted to respond in kind, but her lips felt glued together.

Worth cocked his head to one side. "By the way, I'm having my parents, Olivia and John Lipscomb over tonight."

"For dinner?" Molly asked in a business tone.

"No. Just for snacks and drinks."

"Consider it taken care of."

Worth deliberately perused her body with that cynical curl to his lips. "I never doubted that." He then tipped his hat. "See ya."

Molly attacked the next piece of silver with such vengeance, she almost broke her hand.

* * *

He'd had a great time with the kid, which was both good and bad. The good was that Trent made him laugh, something that he rarely did anymore. It seemed like the laughter had left his body at the same time Molly had left his life.

That kind of thinking was as crazy as it was untrue. Still, more often than not, he realized he walked around with a surly look on his face.

The bad was that the boy made Worth yearn for a son of his own, a gift that would never be his.

Muttering a sailor's curse under his breath, Worth strode into his room where he shed his clothes. It was much later than he'd thought; hence his parents, et al. would soon be arriving. He prided himself on punctuality; this evening was no exception, even if he dreaded what lay ahead.

Lately, his parents got on his nerves big time. Olivia, too. John Lipscomb, his potential campaign manager, was the only one he looked forward to seeing. Suddenly, Worth felt the need for a beer. Maybe that would put him in a better frame of mind.

But since he was naked, he could forget that. *Naked.* He groaned, that word bringing back memories of that bathroom debacle. He laughed without mirth. Who was he kidding? That memory had never left him; since it had happened, it had haunted him day and night.

Even this afternoon, when he'd seen Molly in the kitchen, polishing silver, he could barely remember what she had on, though he figured it was her usual work attire—a pair of low-cut jeans, belt and tight-fitting white shirt.

In his mind, *she* was naked.

Envisioning her perfect breasts, perfect tush, perfect legs, perfect skin and perfect lush lips had shot his libido into overdrive at the same time his control took a kamikaze dive. His body so burned to take her, he'd barely been able to contain himself.

Worth licked his dry lips, wanting a beer more by the second. Again, he glanced at his watch and noticed he scarcely had time to get a shower and dress before the guests arrived. But this was his house, and if he was late, then so be it.

He *needed* a drink.

With that, he slipped back into his jeans and made his way into the kitchen where he pulled up short. Molly was still there—working.

"What the hell?" he said in a rougher tone than he meant.

"Good evening to you, too."

Though he heard the sting in her voice, she kept her gaze averted. He wondered if that was on purpose since she probably saw, out of her peripheral vision, he was only half-dressed.

"Sorry," he muttered, charging for the fridge and grabbing a beer.

"No, you're not." With her head lowered, Molly never stopped arranging fruit on a tray.

He pulled in his breath and stared at a spot where her hair didn't quite touch her collar, thus exposing a bare place on her neck. He clenched his fists, longing to lean over and lick that soft skin, knowing it would feel like velvet under his tongue.

Then realizing what she'd said, he made a face. "What does that mean?"

"You might say you're sorry, but you're not, especially when it pertains to me."

He was about to open his mouth and tell her that was a damned lie. But then he slammed it back shut, knowing she was right. He wasn't sorry he'd spoken harshly to her. Any contact with her now seemed to bring out the worst in him.

Worth wanted what he couldn't have, and that was her. Every time he saw Molly that fact ate a bigger hole in his gut and made him angry to boot, an anger he took out on her. What a freakin' mess.

"You're right, I'm not sorry."

"What do you want?" she asked in a tired voice.

"A beer, which I got." He paused, then added, "You look ready to drop in your tracks."

"I'm about finished."

"Good Lord, Molly, we're not feeding five thousand tonight."

"I haven't fixed for five thousand, either." Her tone was hostile.

His gaze perused the table full of food. "Sure appears that way to me."

She merely looked at him.

Worth shrugged his shoulders. "Okay, so I don't know a damn thing when it comes to entertaining."

"Enough said," Molly responded with a wry tone.

He took another swig of beer before he asked, "Is Kathy helping you serve?"

"No, she's not feeling well."

"Dammit, Molly, you're not superwoman."

Her head popped back. "Who told you that?"

She sounded so serious that for a second, he was so taken aback, he actually laughed.

It was then his eyes trapped hers and the room seemed to tilt. In one giant step Worth ate up the distance between them and was about to reach for her when she skirted around him and dashed for the door.

He muttered an oath.

At the door, she turned but couldn't seem to say anything, which told him she was as shaken as he, especially since her chest was heaving.

Finally, though, in a surprisingly neutral tone, she said, "Thanks for taking Trent riding. He had a great time."

Worth bowed, then responded in his most cynical tone, "My pleasure."

"Dammit, boy, you beat all."

"Now, Dad, if you don't calm down, you're going to have a heart attack."

"No, he isn't," Eva said. "He doesn't have a bad heart. But he might, if you don't stop playing cat and mouse with your future."

"Your mother's right, Worth," John pitched in, his features and voice filled with undisguised concern. "Push has come to shove. You have to make a decision."

His guests had just arrived, and he was already eager for them to go home. The moment after they were seated in the living room and ordered their drinks, they had done nothing but rap on his ears about whether he was going to run for office or not.

The bad part about it was they were right. If he was indeed going to enter the race, he needed to make up his mind and make it up now. But there was just something inside him that kept him from saying the word *yes* and meaning it definitively.

Which probably meant he didn't have the heart of a politician.

"I'm with them, Worth," Olivia said, sidling up closer to him on the sofa, and grabbing his hand, then bringing it up to her lips. For some reason, his gaze went straight to Molly, who was at the bar mixing John a drink. If she saw Olivia's intimate gesture, she chose to ignore it.

No matter. Worth removed his hand with as much grace as possible, suddenly repulsed by Olivia's touch. God, everything that he'd once held near and dear seemed to have gone down the tubes.

Once Molly had handed John his drink, she said, "Is there anything else I can get you?" She paused and smiled. "As you can see, the table is filled with hors d'oeuvres and plenty of sweets."

"Thank you, Molly," Eva said in a stilted tone. "You've done a great job."

Worth knew Molly well enough to sense she was having difficulty keeping a straight face. He also knew that Molly thought his mother was a snob in the truest meaning of the word.

It was in that moment that his and Molly's eyes accidentally met. Later, he told himself he was nuts, but at the time he could've sworn she had winked at him, as though she knew he'd read her mind.

Then Molly smiled again and said, "I'll be back shortly to check on you."

"That won't be necessary," Eva said, turning to Worth. "We won't need her anymore, as we have private matters to discuss. Right, son?"

Worth gave his mother a withering look as he opened his mouth to refute her words. He never got the chance to speak.

Molly beat him to the draw. "Fine, Eva. I'm sure they can depend on you to mix and serve their drinks."

With a horrified look on her face, Eva opened her mouth to speak only nothing came out.

That was when Molly smiled her sweetest smile yet and spoke in her syrupiest southern drawl, "Good night y'all. I sure hope you have a pleasant evening."

Sixteen

Man, he was glad that ordeal was over.

Then Worth felt his conscience pinch him. Those were his folks he was thinking ill of, and the woman he'd been squiring around. Even though he had no intention of marrying her, he should still treat her with respect. As for John, there was no problem. He was a good friend and seemed to want only what was best for Worth.

The others—well, Worth wasn't so sure. That was why his feet were heavy as he made his way toward his bedroom. He paused in his thoughts, toying with the idea of grabbing another beer. Since he'd already had more than his share, he kept going.

His parents and Olivia had tried to pin him to the wall the entire evening, but he'd held firm in his convictions. He still hadn't made up his mind about running for office, which was not like him. *Waffling* was another word that normally wasn't in his vocabulary. Again, until he was fully committed and excited himself, he wasn't going to sign on just to please others.

While the political pressure hadn't been comfortable, it hadn't bothered him nearly as much as his mother's put-down of Molly. When Eva had all but dismissed her as nothing more than a servant, Worth had been furious. Yet he'd kept his mouth shut, which made him despise himself. But what could he have said that wouldn't have sent up a smoke signal? And for what purpose?

He wanted Molly, wanted her so badly he could taste it. But his bodily needs and cravings were nobody's business but his. Besides, nothing would ever come of his hot, scorching desires.

He'd already suffered third-degree burns at her expense, and he didn't have that much skin left to spare. Besides that, she was no longer a road he wanted to travel.

He was certain Molly didn't want to relive that pain and heartache, either. Yet if she didn't hurry up and leave, he wasn't sure he could keep his hands to himself. God, he ached to touch her, to taste her, to…

"Stuff it, Cavanaugh," he muttered, upping his pace down the hall. He was one tired mother and the sooner he got to bed, the sooner his mind would find relief.

He almost laughed at that thought. Since Molly had entered the door of the ranch house, sleep had escaped him, except for short catnaps. Thank goodness, he was lucky he didn't need much shut-eye to keep going.

It was when he passed Molly's room that he heard a sound, a sound he couldn't identify. Not at first, anyway. He paused outside her door and listened.

Sobs.

Muffled.

But gut-wrenching sobs, nonetheless.

Worth continued to stand as though cemented to the spot,

not knowing what to do. Then, as if his hand had a mind of its own, he slowly twisted the doorknob.

She hated them all, especially Eva.

Molly had never been vindictive and didn't think of herself as that now. But she'd had enough of those people and could not wait to get out of their sight, determined never to see them again.

When she'd been dismissed like a piece of garbage by that conniving, mean-spirited mother of Worth's, she'd almost packed her bags, put her son in the car and hauled it out of there.

By the time she returned to her room, took a hot shower, slipped on a silk nightgown and crawled into bed, she had calmed down. But not much. Now, as she lay in a fetal position, resentment and anger welled up inside her, so much that she wanted to scream. Instead she cried.

Molly didn't know what she'd expected after the attack in the living room. Yes, she did. She had expected Worth to defend her, to take up for her. Then she realized that was not only crazy, but it wasn't going to happen.

After all, he was the leader of the pack against her. From the get-go, he'd resented the hell out of her—first, for returning to the ranch and second, for staying. The only reason he tolerated her was because of her mother's health problem.

Another sob stuck in her throat as she curled tighter. If only she didn't care what Worth thought or did. If only she didn't care he hadn't come to her rescue verbally.

But she did care, and that was what was killing her.

Trapped.

She felt like a trapped animal, and that didn't sit well with her. The Cavanaugh clan had already wreaked more havoc in her life than anyone or anything ever had. And they were continuing to do so, which made her feel badly about herself.

Especially since she still wanted the one man she could never have. Worth, she had decided, was in her bloodstream, and she would never get rid of him. No matter where she was, if he came around, she would want him. She had decided that would never change. But that didn't mean she had to give in to that desire, that craving of her body.

Once she left the ranch, she would lick her wounds. Time would take care of much of her pain. Too, she had Trent. From the day he was born, he had been the main focus in her life. Once they arrived at the ranch, Worth had cluttered her mind. Once they were back in Houston, Trent would take top priority again.

Her son and her job.

An awesome combination. With both, she could be happy and content once again. She didn't need a man, certainly not one who didn't want her or he wouldn't have let his parents send her away.

She just had to keep Trent and the secret she bore up front in her mind, and she would prevail. Those two things gave her the courage to uncoil her body and try to get some sleep.

Molly had just tossed the blanket back, the gas logs burning low, making cover a bit much, when she heard what sounded like the knob on her door turning. She stilled herself and held her breath.

"Molly?"

Worth!

Oh, God, what should she do?

"Are you all right?"

She could barely hear him as he was as close to whispering as his deep voice would allow.

Pushing the panic button, she remained silent, hoping he'd get the message she didn't want to be disturbed, especially by *him*.

Her ploy failed.

Then the door opened more, and he walked into the shadowy room. Her heart jumped into the back of her throat making speech impossible. Once again her silence backfired, seeming to give him courage to forge forward until he reached the side of her bed.

Molly squeezed her eyes tightly together, praying he would think she'd fallen asleep. She realized, however, that the fresh tears saturating her cheeks said otherwise. When she felt the mattress give beside her, her eyes flew open.

"Worth," she said in an aching tone.

"Shh, it's okay." His voice literally shook with emotion as he stared down at her in the glow of the fire.

"No, it's not," she whimpered, feeling a new set of tears cloud her vision.

"You're right, it's not," he acknowledged in that same emotional voice. "I should've kicked some ass tonight, mine included."

"I want to go home." Her tone was so low, she wasn't sure he had heard her. He had.

"I don't blame you," he said, letting out a shuddering breath.

Another silence.

"You…you should go," Molly whispered, starting to curl into that fetal position again.

"No."

The edge in his voice stopped her cold.

"I want to look at you." His voice now shook. "You're even lovelier than I remembered."

Without thinking, Molly lowered her gaze and saw that her breasts and nipples were swollen and pushing against the silk. When she raised her eyes, fire burned in his, especially when he reached out and removed one strap, exposing one full breast.

His breathing faltered, and he closed his eyes for a moment.

If only she hadn't let Trent spend the night in Maxine's room, she'd have a valid excuse for calling a halt to this madness.

"Molly…please don't send me away."

"Worth, you're not playing fair." She felt desperate not to give in to his pleading, but she felt herself weakening.

"Tell me you don't want me, and I'll go."

"I don't want you."

Worth focused on her with piercing intensity. "Do you really mean that?"

"No…I mean…" She couldn't go on, not when his hand cupped that exposed breast and a moan of despair escaped her.

"God, Molly," he ground out, leaning over and tonguing that bare flesh until the nipple was ripe and pulsating. "I can't leave you now."

In that moment, she was lost. It was beyond her capacity to do anything more than lay there and let him have his way with her. After all, that was what she'd been wanting since the day she'd arrived and had seen him.

Like she'd admitted, he was in her blood and she would never cease to want him. Now was her chance to love him one last time. And she wasn't going to pass it up—right or wrong.

Molly trembled all over when he lifted his face and their eyes clung. Sensing she was his for the taking, Worth cradled her face between his palms and tilted her head toward him. "I need you so much," he said in a low, shaky voice.

She believed him because she felt the same hot need blazing inside her. That summer with him had been the happiest of her life and it had given her the gift of a lifetime— her son. Despite knowing what she knew now, and what she'd been through these past few weeks, she would let him make love to her, even if it put her soul in jeopardy.

He bent to kiss her, and her lips parted to the wet thrust of his tongue as it plunged deeply into her moist cavity. She clutched at him while his hands wandered over her body. It was after she felt a slight chill that she realized he had removed her gown, leaving her naked before him.

Without taking his eyes off her, he stood and removed his clothes, giving her the exquisite luxury of perusing his nakedness. So as to make room for him on the bed, Molly scooted over, and he lay beside her, drawing her to him—flesh against flesh.

His hands circled her back, drawing her close against him, the surge of his manhood waging war against her lower stomach. "You are still the loveliest creature on earth," he told her huskily before his mouth returned to hers with feverish urgency.

She rejoiced in the feel of his lips tangling with hers, especially after he sucked on her tongue, further deepening and lengthening the kiss. Only after they couldn't breathe any longer did he come up for air.

His eyes were glazed with passion, he reached for her leg and swung it over his hip, giving him access to her most sensitive place that he instantly covered with the palm of his hand, then inserted a finger into its warmth.

"Ohh," Molly cried, bouncing her buttocks up. It had been so long since she'd felt this emotion, this high, that only his touch could bring her. Not only did she want his fingers to work their magic, she wanted him inside her, pounding her until she was spent.

And satisfied.

Realizing she was ready for him, she heard his breathing quicken at the same time the burgeoning thickness of his erection tangled in the curls at the entrance to her moist core.

Then it hit her that neither were protected. She drew back.

"Molly?" he asked in a guttural tone. "Please…"

"We…you don't have any protection."

"It's okay," he ground out. "I promise."

"If you say so," she responded in a frantic tone, revealing

how much she wanted him whether he spoke the truth or not. Besides, getting pregnant twice, accidentally, with the same man, was not about to happen, whether it was the right time of the month or not. Fate had to be on her side this time.

She didn't want to think about that now. She only wanted to think about how it would feel to have his hard flesh invade her softness. With only that in mind, Molly reached down, clutched his erection and guided its big, velvet-smooth tip into her aching flesh.

"Oh, my, Molly," he groaned, shoving himself into the heart of her.

She couldn't help but gasp, having forgotten how big he was. Still, her muscles contracted around him; and because she was so ecstatic he was inside her, she framed his face with her hands, bringing his eager lips to hers, where they clung.

She had thought this one last invasion into her flesh would be enough to last her for the rest of her life. She knew better now. When he began to move, and his breathing grew hoarse and labored, she realized she wanted more.

She wanted him forever.

Because that couldn't be, when she felt him empty in her, and she climaxed like never before, she buried her face against his chest so tightly it took her breath.

"Oh, Molly," he cried, shuddering in the aftermath of that awesome coupling. "My Molly."

After it was over, he kissed her all over her face. With him still inside her, he brushed her lips with his, then they both closed their eyes.

And slept.

Seventeen

Molly awoke with a start, especially when she felt her leg entwined with a hard, hairy one. Outwardly, she remained immobile, but inside her was a mass of quivering nerves.

Worth.

Had they made hot, torrid love all night? Surely not. Surely it was only the middle of the night, or earlier. That was why he was still with her. She stole a glance at the clock; it told an entirely different story. It was almost six o'clock. Suddenly she felt like a giant hand was squeezing the life out of her heart.

She could be pregnant. *Again.* Although last night, when they had briefly discussed the fact that no protection was in the offing, he had told her not to worry, and she hadn't. That was because she'd been in the throes of passion and nothing had mattered except feeling Worth inside her.

But with the dawn came reality and with reality came fear.

Yet she didn't want to think about those emotions, especially with Worth's warm body still wrapped around her like a blanket.

Yet she had no choice.

"Worth," she whispered, nudging him awake.

His eyes popped open, and she realized that for a second he, too, was disoriented. Then it apparently hit him where he was; the muted groan against her neck told her that.

"No," she said in a desperate tone.

He paid her no mind, continuing to nuzzle and lick.

Oh, dear Lord, Molly thought, feeling her body weaken then ache for him to make love to her again. But she couldn't allow that, not with Trent having jumped to the forefront of her mind.

"Stop it," she whispered again, this time with more force.

Worth pulled back, confusion mirrored in his eyes. "What's wrong?"

"It's nearly six."

"In the morning?"

"Yes."

"So?" he muttered, still making no effort to dislodge himself.

"You have to go."

"Why? It's my house." Propping himself on his elbow, Worth leaned over and gave her a raw, devouring kiss.

When he pulled his lips off hers, she was as breathless and rattled as she'd ever been. Damn him. He refused to play fair, having stirred her body back to life.

"I loved making love to you," he said in a lazy tone.

Her gaze was intense. "Me, too."

"It was even better than I remembered."

His eyes had turned into banked down coals of fire as she felt him harden against her leg. Somehow she had to get him out of this room, but first she had to know what he'd meant last night when he'd promised she wouldn't get pregnant.

"Worth?"

"Mmm?"

He sounded like his mind was a million miles away, only it wasn't. It was on getting himself inside her again, as he was busy urging her legs apart.

"Why are you so sure I couldn't get pregnant?"

His body went stiff as a plank, and for the longest time he didn't say anything. Then he got back up on his elbow and stared into her face, his features contorted. "Not long after you left I had an accident."

A feeling of dread spread through her. But she didn't say anything. It was up to him to tell her what he wanted her to know, not that it would make any difference, she assured herself. They were destined to live separate lives.

"A horse kicked me in the groin. Kicked the hell out of me, actually."

She winced. "I'm so sorry." And she was. Even though he had hurt her to the core, she didn't wish him any ill will, not when it came to his health.

"Me, too," he said, his tone bleak. "As a result, I probably can't father a child."

Molly almost freaked out, which made speaking, or anything else, impossible.

Only you do have a child, a precious son named Trent.

For the first time since the birth of their son, she yearned to share that news with Worth, to take away the pain she heard in his voice and read in his face.

Only she couldn't.

For her own self-preservation that was impossible, especially with his parents in the picture. However much they might despise her, if they *knew* she had their grandson, they would pull out all the stops to take him away from her. And they had the money and the power to do just that.

As for Worth, she had no idea how that would affect him. She suspected he would follow their lead. Hence, she had no choice but to keep her mouth shut and guard her secret more now than ever.

Which meant she needed to leave ASAP. Today wouldn't be too soon. Knowing that wasn't going to happen, she would be forced to sharpen her acting skills.

She refused to give up Trent or share him with the man who had broken her heart, who was well on his to way to doing it again.

Fool!

"Molly?" he asked in a sandpaper-like tone, placing his lips against her forehead.

"I'm not asleep, if that's what you're thinking."

"Now you know why we can make love all we want to and don't have to worry about it."

She stared at him wide-eyed. "That's where you're wrong."

It was obvious he picked up on the censure in her tone as he pulled his head back, not bothering to mask his confusion.

"This was our swan song, Worth," she said with emphasis.

His jaw went rigid with fury. "So this was our goodbye nookie, huh?"

She knew that crude statement stemmed from the fury that rearranged his features. But she was furious, too, scooting away from him. "Please go," she said in a terse tone.

He reached for her. "Molly, I didn't mean that."

"It doesn't matter," she replied in a dull voice. "This was a mistake and we both know it."

He sighed, but didn't argue, which cut her deeply again. It was then she wondered again how she could have ended up in such a position. But when it came to Worth, she had never used good judgment, and time and years apparently hadn't changed that. But it didn't sit well with her or make her proud of herself. On the contrary, it made her sick to her stomach.

Suddenly thoughts of Trent popped back into her mind.

He was usually a late sleeper. But since he was with her mother, she couldn't make that call. If he were to simply wander back into their suite…

The repercussions of what would happen if he chose to do that this morning didn't bear thinking about. As far as she knew the door was not locked.

Great.

"Worth."

"I'm going, Molly. You've made it quite plain how you feel."

The bitterness was so thick in his voice that for a second she felt sorry for him. Then she mentally kicked her backside for that thought. If it hadn't been for him and his betrayal of her years ago, both their lives would've been different.

Now it was too late.

She would soon go her way and he his.

Jerked back to the moment at hand by him rolling out of bed, Molly found herself gawking at his backside, mainly his buttocks, which were firm and perfect—buttocks she had caressed at will.

When he swung around and stared down at her, she swallowed a labored gasp. Pain was evident in his eyes and face. Only she wasn't looking at his features, God help her. Molly's eyes feasted on the rest of his body, equally as perfect—the muscled arms and chest, the dark hairs—just the right amount—that covered his stomach, down to his fully aroused manhood.

Hot adrenaline rushed through Molly as that turgid flesh made her ache to reach out, and not only caress its big, smooth tip, but surround it with her mouth.

"God, Molly," he whispered in an agonized voice. "If you don't—"

Feeling a flush steal over her face, she quickly averted her gaze and said, "Please leave."

He didn't move immediately; he was too busy uttering harsh obscenities. Then moments passed, and she finally heard the door open and close. Only then did she grab the pillow, hug it close to her chest and let it absorb the tears that freely flowed.

Recriminations?

That soul-searching time had come. Surprisingly, though, she had no regrets. She refused to beat up on herself for letting her body overrule her mind, since she knew it would never happen again.

And for that she was as sad now as she had been the day five years ago she had walked out of his life.

Worth rode the horse until both were tuckered out. Although he hadn't covered anywhere near all of his property, he had achieved his goal.

Riding had definitely tempered the anger that threatened to blow his insides to smithereens. Before Molly had come back to the ranch, he'd been at a crossroads in his life, trying to decide whether he wanted to be a full-time horse breeder or a full-time politician.

Now he was more mixed up and uncertain than ever before. He still wanted to breed horses, but without Olivia's land it wouldn't be on the scale he'd envisioned. And he wanted to run for office, though the fire in his belly still wasn't there.

He was in one big mess.

He blamed Molly. From the moment she had walked in the door of his ranch house, she had screwed with his mind. After yesterday, it was more than his mind. She had screwed with his body. She'd screwed *him*. Not true, he told himself. What they had done had been more than simply screwing. They had made love in the truest sense of the word.

As a result, Worth didn't know how in the hell he was going to keep his hands to himself now that he had gotten another taste of Molly's sweet, succulent flesh.

What awesome, heady stuff. Not only had his body exploded, but his mind, as well. And he wanted more, dammit. But she had made it clear that wasn't going to happen.

Soon she would be gone. That thought made him nudge the horse in the side and send him galloping once again. However, nothing worked to remove the thought, the smell, the feel of Molly from his mind. It was as if she'd been permanently implanted there.

If that were truly the case, then he was in big trouble. This time she would leave and never return. So what could he do about it? Ask her to stay, a little voice whispered, which would be the height of insanity. He couldn't trust her. Hell, she'd run off once. What was to keep her from doing the same thing again?

Nothing.

That was why he couldn't take a chance on exposing his heart and having it broken all over again. Ergo, he had to let her go. And get on with his life.

Some things he could change and some things he could not. Molly happened to fit in the *could not* category.

"Trent," Molly called from the porch, "it's time to wash up for dinner."

Her son didn't answer right off as he was playing with a ball, pretending he was one of the Harlem Globetrotters, and seemed to be having the time of his life. Since it was near dusk, she didn't like him outside alone, and Tammy had already gone home.

"Aw, Mommy, I wanna play a little longer."

"Trent."

"I'll watch him."

As always the sound of Worth's unexpected voice never failed to slam-dunk her nervous system. Dammit, she wished he'd stop appearing out of nowhere.

"Oh, boy, Mommy! Can I stay with Worth?"

She wanted to yell no, but she didn't. Again, why punish her child for her misdeeds? What difference would it make anyway? Their time was on the downhill slide, as her mother was getting better, and stronger, every day.

Their departure couldn't come soon enough because she was beginning to take a trip down Guilt Lane, to beat up on herself, something she had promised she wouldn't do. But Trent needed a father and she knew it.

All boys need a father.

Trent had one he would never know. Suddenly, that thought was overwhelmingly depressing, thinking how much Trent loved this ranch. Not only was she robbing him of his inheritance, she was depriving him of his father.

But if she told the truth, *she* would lose her son.

That couldn't happen.

"Mommy!"

"All right, Trent. You can tag after Worth until supper's ready."

With that she turned and went back into the house, hoping that decision wouldn't come back to haunt her.

Thirty minutes later, Molly returned to the porch and only caught a glimpse of Worth. A frisson of uneasiness ran down her spine. "Worth," she called.

He stopped in his tracks and swung around.

"Where's Trent?"

He made his way closer to her, his features pinched. "I don't know."

"What do you mean you don't know?" Her voice had reached the shrill level.

"Hold on. I'm sure he's okay. I turned my back for a second, and he was gone."

Molly leapt off the porch and ran to Worth. "Where have you looked?" she demanded, trying to keep her panic at bay.

"Everywhere but the barn. That's where I'm headed now."

"Trent!" Molly yelled over and over. No answer.

By the time they reached their destination, Molly was beside herself; her mind had become her own worst enemy. And Worth. She could have gladly strangled him, but since that wasn't possible, she kept her mouth shut, almost choking on her suppressed fury.

"I'm sorry, Molly," he said, entering the shadows of the barn. She merely flung him a go-to-hell look.

He blanched, but didn't say anything back.

"Trent, are you here?"

"Mommy, Worth, look."

Both pair of eyes shot up to the hayloft. Trent was standing near the edge of the loft that overlooked the cement below. Fear, like poison, spread through her as she stared at Worth. He, too, looked green around the gills, though when he spoke his voice was even and cool.

"Stay where you are, Trent. Don't move."

"Wanna watch me walk—"

"No!" Molly and Worth cried in unison.

The boy froze.

"I'm coming up to get you," Worth said. "Meanwhile, stay right where you are, okay?"

"No, I'll come down."

"Trent, no!"

The boy paid no heed. He turned, then slipped, miraculously falling straight into Worth's outstretched arms.

For a moment no one said a word. It was as though they were all paralyzed. Finally, Trent rallied and said, "Are you mad at me, Mommy?"

"Put him down, Worth," she said with a quiver in her voice. Worth did as he was told.

Pointing at her son, Molly added, "You go straight to your room and wash up. I'll be there shortly."

Trent hung his head. "Yes, ma'am."

"Go. I'll be watching until you get inside."

As if glad to be away from his mother's wrath for a few minutes at least, Trent took off in a dead run.

Once he disappeared into the house, a heavy silence fell over the barn.

Worth was the first to break it. "You're pissed, and I don't blame you."

"Pissed is too mild for what I am." Her voice dripped with icicles.

"He's okay, Molly. Besides, he's a kid, a boy. They try daring things like that."

"Don't you dare tell me about kids. Especially mine."

"Well, excuse me." His hands clenched. "I told you I was sorry. What more do you want?"

"I don't want anything. Your behavior just proves that your word is as worthless now as it was when you asked me to marry you five years ago."

"What the hell are you talking about?"

"I think we're past the pretend stage, don't you?"

"If you have something to say, then spit it out, 'cause I still don't know what the hell you're talking about."

"Your parents."

"What about my parents?"

"Are you saying you didn't send them to me to try and buy me off?"

Worth rocked back on his heels as though she'd sucker punched him in the gut. "I didn't send them anywhere, and certainly not to talk to you."

"You told me you loved me and wanted to marry me, only to then back out."

"I did no such thing. You're the one who lost your nerve and ran off like a scalded dog."

"Only because of your parents. After they came to me and expressed your feelings, telling me that you didn't love me, but didn't want to tell me for fear of hurting me worse."

Worth's expression turned dark as a thunder cloud.

"Oh, and to further insult me," Molly drilled, "your parents offered me money, lots of money, to get lost."

"That's a lie. You're making all this up to appease your conscience. My parents wouldn't do such a thing."

"Are you calling me a liar?" Molly retorted hotly.

"For God's sake, Molly—"

"Ask them." Her gaze, filled with disdain, wandered over him. "If you've got the guts, that is."

Eighteen

"Son, what a delight," Ted said, opening the door wide enough for Worth to stride through. "You're just in time. Supper will be ready in a few minutes."

"I don't—" Worth never got the rest of the words out, as his mother came around the corner into the living room, a smile on her face.

"What a nice surprise, darling." Eva gestured toward the plush leather sofa near the gas-burning fireplace. "Have a seat," she added with a wink. "I have a feeling you've come to tell us something that will call for a celebration. What can I get you to drink?"

"Nothing, Mother. Please, just sit down and stop talking."

Eva put a hand to her throat. "Why, that's not a very nice way to talk to your mother."

Worth cut his eyes to his father who no longer had that warm look on his face. In fact, his features appeared rather grim, as if he sensed something was terribly wrong. "You, too, Dad. Sit."

Eva's eyes widened. "What on earth is wrong with you? You're acting so unlike yourself." Her frustration and anger seemed to be gaining speed. "You can't just come in here and order us around. This is our house."

"Mother," Worth hissed, "be quiet."

Eva sounded as though she might strangle trying to get further words out of her mouth. Then Ted glanced at her and shook his head, frowning.

Worth watched his mother toss him a go-to-hell look, but she didn't say anything else, thank God. Though she was his mother, he was as close to choking her as he'd ever been in his life.

That was not good, but his fury factor was off the charts, although he was trying his best to keep his emotions under wraps. After all, Molly could be lying to cover her own skin, but his gut told him that wasn't so. Otherwise, she wouldn't have demanded he face his parents.

Besides, he'd reached the end of his rope, and there was nowhere else to go, or anyone else to rescue him—except himself.

"I guess you're not running for office, son," Ted finally said into the uncomfortable silence.

"The election's not why I'm here."

"Then why are you here," Eva demanded in a cold voice, "especially with that mean attitude?" She grabbed a tissue and dabbed at her eyes.

Worth rolled his. "Spare me, Mother, you're mad not sad."

"Stop talking to me like that, Worth Cavanaugh. I've taught you to have respect for your elders, especially your parents. What on earth have we done to make you look at us like you despise us?"

"Does the word *Molly* give you a clue?"

"What about her, son?" Ted asked in a guarded voice.

"Oh, please," Eva put in with added dramatics. "Do we have to talk about her?"

Worth didn't mince any words. "As a matter of fact we do."

"What then?" Eva demanded in a resigned, but sharp tone.

"Did you two have a conversation with her before she left that summer?"

The room got funeral-home quiet.

"I don't know what you're talking about," Eva finally said in her lofty tone. "We had several conversations with that girl."

Worth's ire rose, but when he spoke he still held onto his cool. "That girl, as you call her, was my fiancée."

"Oh, Worth, for crying out loud." Eva flapped a hand with perfectly manicured nails. "She was just your play toy and we knew it."

Worth clenched his teeth, reminding himself that she was his mother, though at the moment he wished he'd never been born to these two selfish snobs.

He couldn't change that, of course. What he could change was the here and now. *And the future.* No more messing around with his life.

"Did you talk to her?" Worth asked again, his gaze including both of them. "And don't lie to me, either."

Eva whipped her head around to Ted who actually looked like all the blood had drained from his face. Worth watched him nod to his wife.

She in turn, faced Worth, her lips stretched in an unbecoming tight line at the same time her eyes sparked. "Yes, we talked to her."

"What did you tell her?" Worth stood and loomed over them. "The exact words."

"Will you please sit down?" Eva asked, clasping her hands together in her lap. "You look like a panther about to pounce, and frankly, that makes me nervous."

"Mother!"

"All right." She raised her eyes to Worth. "We told her you didn't really love her, and that you didn't want to marry her."

An expletive shot out of Worth's mouth.

Eva's head flared back, and she glared at him. However, she seemed to know better than to reprimand him.

"Go on." Worth could hardly get the words through his lips; they were so stiff and his mouth so dry.

"Well, we told her she wasn't good enough for you, but that you didn't want to tell her yourself, so you asked us to do it."

Another string of expletives followed.

Both Eva and Ted sucked in their breaths and held them, staring at him as though their son had suddenly turned into some kind of monster they didn't recognize.

"We…we thought we were doing what was best for you," Eva said in a tearful voice. "We didn't think she was good enough—"

"Your mother's right," Ted chimed in. "We thought we had your best interest—"

"Shut up! Both of you."

Eva's and Ted's mouths dropped open, but they shut up.

Worth leaned in further and spoke in a low, harsh tone. "I loved Molly and intended to marry her. As a result of what you did, you've cost us five miserable years, and the two of you ought to be horsewhipped."

"My God, Worth," Eva cried. "Listen to what you're saying."

He paid her plaintive cry and words no mind. "But because you're my parents, I hope I can find it in my heart to forgive you. Only not now. I don't want to see either of you, so stay away from me, you hear?"

He turned, strode to the door and slammed it behind him with such force, he figured he shattered the expensive glass.

So what? He'd never felt better in his life. Yet he still had a major task in front of him.

Molly.

Despite the chill in the air, sweat broke out on his forehead and his knees threatened to buckle. He had to find Molly and make things right.

"Mama?"

Maxine smiled and patted Molly's hand. "You haven't called me that in a long time. Usually it means you're upset about something."

Molly pulled at the sheet on her mother's bed and finally looked her in the eye. "It's time I left."

Maxine frowned. "That's fine, honey. I'm so much better. In fact, I was thinking about—"

"No. The deal is this. Only if you let me hire a private nurse will I leave."

"I don't need one. I already have a therapist."

"With me gone, you need both. And Worth needs to hire another temporary housekeeper. You have to tell him that. He'll do it for you."

Maxine blew out a frustrated breath. "I sure reared a stubborn child."

"That you did. Those shots in your back, combined with physical therapy, have done wonders. You've made tremendous progress. It's just a matter of time until you'll be your old self."

"Only I'm not quite there yet, right?" Maxine asked with raised brows.

"Not quite."

"While I can hardly bear the thought of you and Trent leaving, you know I understand. On second thought, maybe I don't."

"I just need to get back to the office."

"I think there's more to it than that," Maxine said, then paused. "It's Worth, isn't it?"

Molly could only nod; her throat was too full to speak.

"If he hurt you again, I'll strangle him myself."

"It's okay. It's just time for Trent and me to leave. You love it here. Worth loves you, and I don't want to mess that up."

"I still say you two should've married."

"Well, it's too late for that now," Molly said bitterly.

"It's never too late for happiness, my dear. If it's pride we're talking about here, then let it go. It can bring down the biggest and strongest."

"Mama."

Maxine held up her hand. "I'll say no more. When you're ready to talk, I'm ready to listen. Nothing you've ever done, or could ever do, is unforgivable in my sight. Remember that. I love you more than life itself."

"Oh, Mama," Molly sobbed, leaning over and holding her mother close. "You're my rock and always have been. Maybe it's time I shared my heart."

Maxine reached up and trapped a tear running down her daughter's cheek. "I'm listening, my sweet."

Holding tightly to her mother's hand, Molly began to talk.

She was all packed and ready to go.

Yet she hadn't called Trent. She hadn't had the heart to do so yet as he and Tammy were somewhere on the grounds, running and playing.

She had just walked out on the porch, searching for fresh air that would hopefully calm her nerves, when she heard a knock on the door. She didn't bother to turn around.

"It's open."

When no one said anything, she made her way back inside.

Worth stood leaning against the door frame. Her stomach did its usual thing, and the saliva in her mouth dried up.

"I know I'm the last person you want to see," Worth exclaimed, his gaze zeroing in on the bags on the floor.

"That's right," she said, feeling goose bumps dance up and down her skin.

"I spoke with my parents."

She merely shrugged.

"You were right."

His face seemed to have sunk so that its bones took on new prominence and his voice had a crack in it. That was when she met his tormented gaze head-on.

It was in that moment that Molly knew she still loved him, that she had never stopped and that she would love him until the day she died.

"I'm so sorry they interfered," Worth said, tilting his head as though to keep it above water. "You've got to believe I had no idea any of that garbage had gone on behind my back."

Suddenly a ray of hope burst through the dead spot in Molly's heart, and she saw the possibility of swallowing her pride, like her mother said, and starting anew. If he were willing, that is.

"But that doesn't excuse what you did, Molly."

In one instant, Worth brutally dashed that ray of hope. "And just what did I do?"

"When you left me, you obviously married the first guy you met and screwed his brains out."

For the longest time Molly couldn't speak. The pain and humiliation were so severe, it put a vise on her throat. Finally, though, she rallied and spat, "How dare you say a thing like that to me? Have you no shame?"

"Tell me it isn't true." Worth's tone remained unrelenting. "And I'll take it back."

"Of course, it's not true."

His features contorted. "Then, dammit, what is the truth?"

Almost choking on her words, Molly lashed back, "I never married. I made up that story for my and Trent's protection."

"Okay, so you never married. You just screwed his brains out!"

"No, I didn't!" Molly cried out in fury.

"Well, you obviously let *someone* have your body," Worth said with a sneer.

Molly felt her fury rise to a new level. How could the man she loved say such awful things to her? She felt her face heat as words came screaming from her mouth. "No man has ever touched me but you!"

God, how could she have said that? She clasped her hands over her mouth to stop a wail from escaping. Molly knew the answer, and it made her sick at heart and sick to her stomach. She had been goaded into revealing the one secret she had sworn to take to her grave. But words, like arrows, once released, could never be recalled. The damage had been done.

Standing stonelike, she watched Worth's face as her words sank in. A myriad of emotions crossed it, none of which she could read. Was he already planning how he was going to rip Trent out of her arms and claim him as his own? With his money and power, Worth certainly had the means and power to do so.

Molly grasped her stomach, giving in to the fear that stampeded through her.

Worth, meanwhile, crossed the room with lighting speed, grabbed her arm and demanded in a raspy voice, "Did you say what I think you said?"

She could only stare at him, searching frantically for the words to right a wrong. She could deny what she'd said, or she could remain mute and let her words speak for themselves.

"God, Molly, please tell me. Is Trent my son?" Worth moaned softly. "But even if he isn't, it doesn't matter. I don't think I can live a moment longer without you."

Without thought, Molly's hands came up, encased his face and delved deeply into his eyes. "We—Trent and I come as a package deal," she murmured around the tears clogging her throat.

"So, he is my son," Worth said, his voice husky with emotion.

"Yes," Molly whispered. "Trent's your son."

He rocked back on his heels, his breath coming in heaves. Molly instinctively reached out a hand. "Worth?"

Worth clasped her hand and said, "Trent's really mine?" This time awe filled his voice and tears filled his eyes.

She pulled back and peered into his contorted features. "Yes, yes, yes."

"Oh, God, Molly, I can't believe that."

"Do you hate me for not telling you?"

He didn't hesitate. "I could never hate you for anything," he said fiercely. "I love you too much. In fact, you're the only woman I've ever loved."

"And you're the only man I've ever loved," she replied breathlessly.

"Molly…" He pulled her into his arms and simply held her for the longest, sweetest time. Then peering down at her, he said, "I want you. I need you. But most of all I love you, and I'll never let you go again."

He kissed her, then, so hard, so long, and so deep and held her so tightly, she couldn't tell whose heartbeat was whose. It didn't matter; in that moment they became one.

One Year Later

"Oh, yes, Molly, don't stop."

"As if I would," she whispered, atop Worth, continuing to ride him, slowly, then faster, until they climaxed simultaneously.

Exhausted, she fell onto his chest, hearing their hearts beat as one.

Moments later, Worth maneuvered so that he could get to her lips, giving her a long, tender kiss. Only he didn't stop there; he lifted her a little more and put those lips to one breast, then the other, and sucked.

"Ohh," Molly whispered. "You're about to get something started again."

Worth chuckled at the same time he rolled her over so that she was now under him. "That's my intention."

"But it's so soon," Molly pointed out with an answering chuckle. "You…we just came."

"I know, but don't you feel him growing, even as I'm speaking?"

Molly merely sighed and placed her arms around him. For the longest time thereafter, the room was quiet except for their moans.

A short time later, they faced each other satisfied, but worn out from their marathon evening of lovemaking.

"So, Mrs. Cavanaugh, how was your day?" Worth asked in a husky tone, his eyes still a bit glazed over with passion.

"Good, Mr. Cavanaugh. How was yours?"

"Busy as hell."

"That's a good thing, right?"

"Right, my precious."

Molly was quiet for a moment, reveling in the glow of happiness that had surrounded them since that day they both learned the truth about their pasts. Although they had yet to tell Trent that Worth was his real father, it didn't matter, at least not now.

When they told him they were in love and were going to get married, Trent had asked if he could call Worth daddy.

Thinking back on that day still tugged at Molly's heart and would be forever imprinted there.

She had cooked a special dinner with all the trimmings—candlelight, flowers, pot roast, Italian cream cake—wine for them, a Shirley Temple for Trent. Once the meal was over, they had gone into the living room where Worth had reached for Trent's hand, drawing the child onto his lap.

"Your mom and I have something to tell you," Worth said in a none-too-steady voice.

"What?" Trent mumbled, eyeing his mother and sounding uncertain.

"It's okay, sweetie," she responded with a smile and a wink.

"How would you like to live here all the time?" Worth asked, also smiling.

"Wow!" Trent cut his gaze back to his mother.

Molly grinned. "That's what I think, too."

"Your mom and I are in love and want to get married."

Trent made a face. "Does that mean you'll be kissing Mommy all the time?"

Both adults laughed without restraint.

"I'm afraid so," Worth finally admitted, having regained his composure.

"I guess that'd be okay." Trent cocked his head to one side as if trying to figure out how best to communicate what was churning in his little mind. "Would you be my daddy?"

"You betcha."

Trent seemed to think on that for a moment during which Molly held her breath. She suspected Worth was doing likewise.

"Can I call you Daddy?"

Worth's mouth worked. "I'd like that a lot."

A smile broke across the child's face. "Man, now I'll be like all my friends. They all have daddies."

Molly looked on as Worth grabbed Trent and hugged him

tightly, all the while seeking her eyes that were filled with tears. Only after blinking them away did she see the ones in Worth's.

Several days later she and Worth exchanged vows. From that moment on, they had become a family.

During the year they had been married, her mother's back had completely mended. And though she had insisted on keeping her job as housekeeper, Worth had said no, that it was time for her to retire and enjoy life—mainly her grandson.

Maxine hadn't argued, and thus was having a ball.

As for Eva and Ted, they were another story altogether. Even though civility became the order of the day, a wedge remained between Worth and his parents. While Molly hated that, and felt responsible to some degree, there was nothing she could do. Worth had to work through his problems with his parents in his own way and in his own time.

Following that fierce altercation with Ted and Eva, Worth had decided not to run for office, vowing, instead, to concentrate on making her and Trent happy, along with building his horse breeding empire. He and Art had figured a way to make it work without Olivia's land.

"You're awfully quiet," Worth said, interrupting her thoughts, dropping a kiss on the tip of her nose.

"I was just thinking about this past year and everything that's happened."

"Such as?"

"Us. Trent. Your estrangement from your family."

Worth grimaced. "I've been thinking about that, too, but right now I still can't get past their mean-spiritedness."

"Maybe one day you can because of Trent. They are, after all, his grandparents, and I want him to know them."

"You're right, of course. I'm sure they're sorry and are suffering, but I can't completely forgive, nor can I forget." His grimace deepened. "They cost me almost five years of my son's life."

"I know how deeply that cuts, but—"

"You think I should try and make amends?"

Molly nodded her head. "I'd like that for the reason I just said, Trent. However, it's your call as to how you handle your folks."

"Well, Christmas is knocking on the door." He paused. "We'll see what that brings."

Molly smiled, then kissed him. "You're a good man, Worth Cavanaugh."

"And you're a liar, Molly Cavanaugh. I'm a son of a bitch and we both know it."

They giggled, then hugged.

"Do you miss your work?" he asked when their laughter subsided.

"A little," she said truthfully. "I miss Dr. Nutting, my old boss, but he certainly understands why I didn't return."

"Have you thought about working here full time? I want you to be happy at home, but if not, that's okay."

She heard the forlorn note in her husband's voice and laughed. "Are you sure about that?"

He grinned. "Well, I might be a tad jealous."

"Actually, I was thinking about doing some volunteer work at the local clinic a couple of days a week. That way I can keep my license current. I just hadn't gotten around to telling you."

"Hey, that's a great idea."

"I thought so, too." Molly stretched, and in doing so, exposed a nipple to his greedy eyes and lips. He latched on to it and sucked.

"You know our life is pretty much perfect," she whispered, "even if I am married to a badass."

He laughed again, then sobered. "I just wish we could have

another child. I'd like to be there for the whole meal deal, so to speak, watching your belly grow and feeling our child move."

"There's no time like the present to get started."

Worth gave her a perplexed look. "You know what the doctor said."

"Doctors don't walk on water. They make mistakes every day. I suggest we begin right now proving yours wrong. And the rest of our tomorrows, if that's what it takes."

"Oh, God, Molly," Worth whispered, tossing a leg over her hip, "I wouldn't want to live life without you."

"Nor I without you." She smiled at him with love. "So how about we get busy and make that baby."

* * * * *

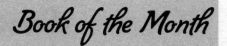

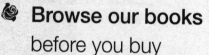

The World of Mills & Boon®

There's a Mills & Boon® series that's perfect for you. We publish ten series and, with new titles every month, you never have to wait long for your favourite to come along.

Blaze®
Scorching hot, sexy reads
4 new stories every month

By Request
Relive the romance with the best of the best
9 new stories every month

Cherish™
Romance to melt the heart every time
12 new stories every month

Desire™
Passionate and dramatic love stories
8 new stories every month

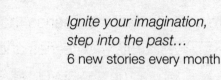